KUDOS FOR NEMECENE EPISODES 1 AND 2

Nemecene: The Epoch of Redress (Episode 1)

"A smart, ambitious dystopian tale that teases the protagonists' epic genesis but saves most of the details for later volumes."

— *Kirkus Reviews*

"NEMECENE truly isn't like anything else out there. You won't want to put the book down. It has the suspense of *Hunger Games*, the building awareness of *Divergent*, the out-there, 'I didn't see that coming' of *Ender's Game*."

— Amy Stoehr, dystopian junky

"I love how NEMECENE combines what is perhaps today's most important message with humouristic thought processes, intelligently diversified characters and a well-written exciting story into one magnificent piece of art!"

— Cecilie Svendsen, Nominee for Best Actress
Instapocalypse, Houston Comedy Film Festival

"KAZ LEFAVE draws us into a futuristic myth that sings with balladry, cries with prophecy, and roars with her passion for this planet."

— Thomas Wade, Juno Nominated Singer-songwriter

Nemecene: The Gadlin Conspiracy (Episode 2)

"An elaborate, futuristic tale that will draw in new readers with its keen characterization."

— *Kirkus Reviews*

Through the fires of desire thoughts come alive; when released to the universe they crystallize. Dreams are thoughts and thoughts are things; they pass through ice to spread their wings.

NEMECENE

THROUGH FIRE AND ICE

(EPISODE 3)

KAZ LEFAVE

AGUACENE PUBLISHING, INC.

NEMECENE

THROUGH FIRE AND ICE

KAZ LEFAVE

www.NEMECENE.com

An Aguacene™ publication
Published 2017-2018 by Aguacene Publishing, Inc.
Toronto, ON, Canada • publish@aguacene.com

Distributed by NBN (National Book Network, Inc.)
15200 NBN Way, Blue Ridge Summit, PA, USA, 17214

Printed in Canada

ISBN-13: 978-1-988814-02-5
ISBN-10: 1-988814-02-2
10 9 8 7 6 5 4 3 2 1

FSC
www.fsc.org
RECYCLED
Paper made from recycled material
FSC® C103567

Paper: FSC® certified
Cover: Supreme Recycled Silk 100lb, 55% recycled with 30% post consumer waste, made without the use of chlorine gas, manufactured using cogeneration energy
Pages: Roland Enviro Print 50lb text, 100% recycled, 100% post consumer waste, processed chlorine free, manufactured using biogas energy
Press: Timson ZMR

Cover art: Leslie Doyle. Editing: Sylvia McConnell. Page layout: Karen Lefave.

To the voices that need to be heard.

NOTES ON THE TEXT

GLOSSARY ENTRIES

Since the characters are living in the *Nemecene* epoch, they are intrinsically familiar with their futuristic world, its technology, and its language; therefore, they would not naturally explain terms common to them, as they relay their story to you.

I encourage you to read the glossary at the back first, in order to immerse yourself in their world.

LIST OF CHARACTERS

There is also a character list at the back, in case you need to refresh your memory from Episode 1, *Nemecene: The Epoch of Redress,* or Episode 2, *Nemecene: The Gadlin Conspiracy.*

THE MYSTERIOUS *they* OR *them*

Who are *they*? That's a well-guarded secret, and I'll give you one guess as to who knows the answer to that question. ;-)

Feel free to share your theories with me and each other by following *Nemecene* on social media. The answers shall be forthcoming … in due time. Muahahaha.

The Structure

Each of the nine chapters is organized into three sections of approximately three thousand words each. A section is consistently assigned to one of three narrators as follows: the first narrator opens every chapter, the second narrator holds the middle position in all chapters, and the third narrator closes each chapter.

The Timeline

The novel, as a whole, moves forward in time, although sections may overlap as the different narrators offer their experiences during the same time period. A note at the beginning of each section states when that segment begins relative to Chapter One of Episode 1, *Nemecene: The Epoch of Redress*.

Flashbacks and fanciful musings are enclosed between the following symbols:

▼ ▼ ▼

(narration jumps into this moment)

▲ ▲ ▲

Gaps in the story, where the text jumps forward in time are preceded by the following symbols:

✂ ✂ ✂

MEET THE NARRATORS

SOTHESE
He masters consent through subterfuge
and seduction
(Section I)

STYLE: third-person voice from an out-of-body point of view.

Obsessions, submissions, and transgressions coil around those who should know better than to entwine themselves with Sothese, yet the temptation is simply overpowering. His ministerial reach extends far beyond political maneuvering. Through the visceral style that remains the trademark of his kind, he seduces your body, soul, and mind with artful prose and misdirection, all for his own licentious entertainment, of course. You may not feel for him, but you will definitely feel him ... invade you from the inside.

ELIZE
Her restless tough-girl attitude betrays her
splintered mind
(Section II)

STYLE: first-person voice with a running inner dialog. You only know what she thinks, hears, sees, tastes, feels, smells, or senses.

Keet is such a pup. Honestly. There's nothing mystical about my nightmares. It's a scientific fact that dreams are just our brain's way of processing things. And in my case, it's simply trauma nothing more. Keet's afraid I'll get lost in some mental void like Mother and that Father will commit me to the GHU. That's where Mother died. Wipe that image. No more tears. Good. So we're keeping everything hush. Crazed, eh? Anyway, I hope he's wrong. Better keep the voices to myself. Everybody hears some. They just won't admit it. It's not considered normal. Right. Normal. At least, we'll be gone soon and maybe even … Crap! No. Not now.

Breathe, Eli, breathe. Here he comes. Breathe. Act normal.

KEETO
His courage hides inside the cocoon of an
armchair archaeologist
(Section III)

STYLE: first-person voice as daily journaling entries to his mother.

Time has not filled the void you left when Eli and I were just nine years old. As I cloister myself here, sprinkling the pages of another journal with my emotions, I image that you see through my eyes, and write through my quill. It is this insanity that keeps me sane while my days spent digging for answers to questions that constantly change consume my sheltered life. If only your spirit could materialize into the Mother I need you to be once again. But reality reminds me otherwise. My only hope is that connecting with you, in these quiet and sometimes not so quiet moments of reflection, will uncover truths that liberate us all.

But will they come soon enough?

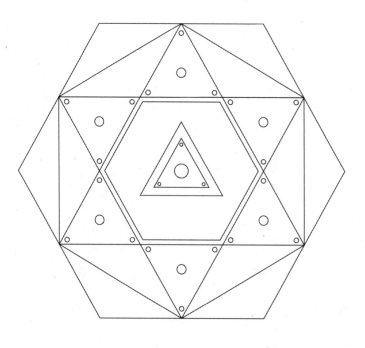

CHAPTER ONE

SOTHESE

Day 1013: before dawn

The ocean is seething. As so many have in Sothese's wake, turbulence drives the dance inside their bodies. Do they fight? Do they flee? Do they acquiesce? Paralyzed by their irrelevant concerns, they do nothing, and Sothese continues his blissful intrusions, except for today. Here he towers, alone, on an open platform against the bright blue dome powering the southern face of Ministburg's biowall while the torment haunting his past churns the waters below.

Cursed is the soul who would attempt to return him to a life of darkness. Nathruyu may have dealt him a notable blow in Almedina Square, but Sothese's hand was not severed, nor was his tongue clipped, nor his rightful desire subjugated. His claim remains, evidenced by the chaos surrounding humanity, and no words Nepharisse could sing can influence actions already consummated.

An electrifying release sends a wave of delight to the root of his impulses, as he moans through the words he has chosen. His skin is not the one that has been irreparably sullied, regardless of what appearances had suggested after the courtyard defilement — as he so fondly refers to it. Moreover, once he finds a suitable trio to replace the ingrates who have betrayed his trust, a certain Gadlin will find it in her best interest to acquiesce. Ministburg's youthful offerings have become scant, as of late, and the nights confining him to nine domed towers at the tide's edge have become a prison he deems unwarranted, although more congenial than the deafening generator nooks in the shafts, or the sajadums, which, though incidentally infused with an ability to replenish potency, do not comply with Sothese's privacy demands.

The view at nine hundred metres, however, is divine. Even the Pramam's overindulgent penthouse, floating on the rooftop pool of his personal pantheon and bound to the breathable airspace below the invisible biowall lid on the island, fails to exalt him. Sothese, on the other hand, knows his place, and it is decidedly not confined to the sidelines while the official leader of the Inner Council babysits him during interrogations of Sothese's ex-officials, currently subsisting inside the Ministburg lockdown facility, which is anchored to the ocean floor, three slick lengths beyond the city limits. Surely, the Pramam must realize that Nathruyu's special treatment in her old cell was necessary, or at the very least, a boon for her capturer. What suspicions fester in the fearful mind of the Pramam, this unnaturally long-lived head of state?

Sothese savors a self-satisfied smile as he gazes into the vast frothy swells, confident in the aging man's compromised intellect. Whatever the Pramam believes he knows, he is ignorant of so much more, of that which is the real key he seeks. Would that he discover it too late ... And the smile broadens ... briefly. A memory of black-pitted skin, surfacing under the moonlight, reminds Sothese of his origins — a world he has forsaken for the lust of another, and no one and no thing, not even a prophetic manifestation, can force his return.

With an athletic lunge forward, he thrusts a pointed hand and the tip of a boot over the ledge. Next, a forceful twist of the wrist, finessed with a slice across the void, and a fiery smirk oozes from Sothese's lips. The imaging of it is infinitely more tantalizing than the imagination of it. In the cold obscurity of the unconscious, where nightmares rule, only the shattered can play, but in the realm of the whole, sensations abound for all to enjoy. This is the privilege that brings to the recipient as much pain as it does pleasure, and to the donor? How satisfying it is to give!

The duties of the impending dawn pull Sothese from the edge, but the light breaks too soon. The stars vanish in a crack of white as the liquid foundation of the penal island begins to boil. The shock wave has come from within, sending an explosion of burning shards into Ministburg's southern perimeter and disabling two towers. While sirens blast panic into the bedrooms of every household, the garden district security staff scramble to douse spot fires threatening the sole surviving specimens of ancient forest ecosystems. The mayhem in the botanical pride of the Unification creates a diversion that nearly costs Sothese a delicious opportunity, for were it not for his immunity to the toxic gases funneling through the biowall breach, his attention would have been focused on donning a personal bioshield rather than on the fleet of Gadlin barges arriving in the distance.

The entire Ministburg lockdown is ablaze with the kind of heat no human can withstand. The Global Health Unit immediately dispatches its Global Radiation Unit, supported by a fully suited unit of Global Military Unit operatives to evacuate the inmates, but the Gadlin conspirators emerge en masse to stage an organized charge towards their rescue crafts. Sothese feigns outrage at their well-conceived jailbreak, wary of watchful eyes, while spying a fedora fly off a cloaked figure diving from the western lookout. Distraction breaks the lock Sothese has on the scene. His pupils widen with the anticipation of private encounters, then suddenly narrow to signal an oncoming affront.

An arrow, shaped and fuelled by three fireballs, jettisons from inside the penitentiary's granite foundation and shoots due north. Sothese stands his ground in defiant delight. The threesome accelerate in direct line for his heart, then abruptly change course at the last moment, searing the tips of his bangs with their scorching slipstream. Sothese hisses his displeasure. He should have never trusted their kind, although trust is not the sentiment their relationship fostered. It was more of an arrangement, like most of his dealings. Their loyal company had counterbalanced the weight of Sothese's ministerial office, so to speak. Even in confinement, their energy stabilizing effect on him somewhat served his needs, but not well enough to indemnify them for treason against the de facto leader of the Unification and sole legitimate monarch, Sothese himself.

Shunned by his kin, and with humans beneath him, Sothese continues his mandate, detached, in familiar isolation.

SOTHESE

It is said that he who attains great strength, in him must he trust for great victory, but of betrayal, nothing is spoken, for the words that speak truth have no sound.

One would expect that thousands of hours perfecting the versal arts together, in mirrored precision, would have been sufficient. One would presume that mature respect would have forgiven boyhood rivalries for the greater good. One would assume that a family bond would have stretched, twisted, or perhaps even knotted, rather than snapped over personal gain. But when one becomes three, it's all about me, me, me.

In the valley where kings are made, Sothese has no throne. Although he consistently secures a challenger's head, his brother rules over the land instead. Confusion leads to anger, and anger to rage. How could the one who makes allies of the shadows below be denied the power of the light from above? With every lance that pierces his foes, the toxicity spews its poisonous seeds to incubate as Sothese's deeds. And what a sweet poison it proves to be.

This is where it all begins. His sisters have chosen, one as expected, the other coerced by that purveyor of lies — his brother. The fabricator calls out envy, jealousy, gloating, and pride, but his claims simply stoke the hatred inside. Standing across from his twin for the very last time, with a jab and a twist and a flick of the wrist, Sothese now seizes the throne as his own while defeat collapses his martyred kin into a frozen darkness in which only the forgiven can roam.

However, clemency does not result from his treachery as Sothese had hoped: "Reverence belongs to the conqueror, does it not?" But silence deems otherwise. The heart has been weighed and the sentence is dear: "Banish the traitor. We deal with him later."

▲ ▲ ▲

Unfortunately, time is not a luxury that most can enjoy. Soon, they will come to reveal the futility of pitiful power plays, one of which no doubt figures on today's agenda.

The deck, forming a ring around the damaged generator dome, retracts as Sothese retreats inside the structure. This is not his battle to fight, for the war belongs to a backward lord with an inflated perception of his influence on the proper order of things. A transmission grackles through the particle storm lashing the city with a stark message directed at all those who feel safe behind walls:

> This is not a drill. Nine minutes to enemy impact. All GMU operatives, repair crews, and GHU personnel to the southern filter zone … immediately! All other residents must evacuate to their designated secure zones. Bioshields mandatory. We repeat. Bioshields mandatory.

Fortuitous is the event that increases the public's tolerance for infringements covertly intended to normalize them. The Unification thrives on fear-driven consent to exert its illusory control upon lives that planetary forces clearly own. It is therefore out of the sincerest concern by the Pramam himself, led by Their counsel of course, that the Unification Research Arm will somehow devise a revolutionary health and safety bioApp for broad GHU deployment … immediately. And, furthermore, the hapless law-abiding citizens will even pay for it. Sothese can barely stomach the propaganda onslaught already flying overhead in his mind: "All those who accept the upgrade, before (insert spurious sense of urgency here), will receive one month free."

As if his musings could invoke the object of his disdain, a secure channel to the Inner Council chamber opens while Sothese winds down the core of tower number five. He floats his comm in front of him, and the Pramam flickers in: "You do not have control of your hounds, Sothese."

"A power surge must have blown the backup cooling system, my Pramam. Your Gadlin guinea pigs are burned to a delectable crunch." Sothese's witty misdirection traps a chuckle in his throat, as he reaches water level and signals his private slider. Traffic acrobatics will not be his only challenge en route to the city core. Before stepping into the craft and shifting to privacy mode, he clears honesty from his mind and, for his master's pleasure, shapes his thoughts into those of a model servant.

"That loss is reprehensible, Sothese! And the other? Nathruyu? Conspiracy is their forte."

"SIF surveillance recorders show her well-programmed in her witness relocation … room. Yet … I know she has more secrets to share."

"Your privileges in this matter have been revoked, as you may recall."

"Do you not trust my self-restraint?"

"You have many qualities, Sothese, but your peculiar self-indulgences are qualities I aim to use sparingly."

"Perhaps we can visit her together. You as my holy temperance, my Pramam."

"I shall grant your request proper consideration. And of our ex-URA director? Have you found him?"

"It appears Vincent has disappeared … underground. I suspect he may have joined certain Gadlins."

"Then I shall incorporate the experiments into Director Corrient's official mandate, through your guidance, of course. You have achieved success with the last child, have you not?"

"Correct."

"Your tone is abrupt. I shall disregard your lack of civility in light of — "

"You should have left me in charge, with all due respect."

"I am shocked to hear that having a lovely young woman working beneath you would be unpalatable."

"Of course, my Pramam. I am sure I can stimulate her interest in a mutually satisfying working relationship."

"That, I do trust. Perfect are They."

"They are One."

"And, Advisor Sothese, I also trust that that is the last time I shall bear witness to your little outburst. There is a new chemist on the Inner Council now, and I understand that she is quite accomplished."

"Of course, my Pramam."

"By your command" becomes the first quip firing from Sothese's brain as soon as he disables the thought transference. Silent mode is a comm feature designed for those who cannot trust and those who cannot be trusted. As fate would have it, mastery of mind happens to be Sothese's well-earned reward for years of vigorous practice in the versal arts. The Pramam remains, as always, a puppet, and the puppeteer has finally arrived.

An anxious young medic, obviously new to service, greets Sothese at the entrance to Ministry Mansion, with a radiation sniffer and endless apologies for the intimacy required to comply with protocol. Residual particles on his inner left thigh warrant a deeper probe around the front and back of the femur and into the adjoining pelvic region. The intern requests further consent, which cannot be reasonably denied for health and national security reasons, and receives it with interest from a guiding hand. Perhaps Sothese can indulge in a little therapeutic release before he commits to his forthcoming ocean travels.

The boy certainly knows whose loins he is stroking, an embarrassment that heightens the tension bursting in from the hysteria outside. A coy smile, upon a thorough cleanse, tests the Pramam's recent character assessment. Who is Sothese to argue with the human surrogate to Their Holy Trinity? The shaft is long to the top floor. He could use an escort, just in case a power surge occurs. The medic accepts Sothese's invitation into the lift. It rises. The building goes dark.

✂ ✂ ✂

His majesty, Sothese, follows the Pramam to his private chamber, bearing his usual gift and veiling his royalty behind an advisory role. Emotional solitude has taught him that patience and convincing devotion can infiltrate the center of power quite discreetly when vanity predominates, although he suspects that the Pramam understands the game of a sycophant, a perversion which makes Sothese's subservient acts supremely entertaining ... to both. How ego loves competition! And what greater sacrilege could there be in the field of state-sanctioned religion than to offer this precious vessel he carries to that unwitting vassal? As he hands over the vial, Sothese bows with phony decorum only to realize that they are not alone. There is a presence watching them.

It seems that the twins are not the only ones being watched. Sothese studies the blue nectar draining from the conical crystalline cup and into the mouth of the Unification figurehead. He sniggers at the grimace forcing a barrier between the Pramam's hardened lips and the still conscious specimen chasing the fluid that keeps it alive. An unexpected explosion, emanating from the ongoing safety threat in the south, coaxes just enough suction from a sudden gasp to slip the worm-like morsel into oblivion as it enters a dreamless state to the soothing beat of an antique timepiece.

The Pramam gasps for air. The accusations Sothese was expecting have become lodged behind poetic justice. The clock ticks as he watches the man with the power he covets transform into a curious shade of blue. It is quite breathtaking.

For thirty-eight years, the Pramam has been representing himself as an enlightened elder to a constituency unaware of the ritual theatrics occurring daily at daybreak in Ministburg. It is amusing that, even now, he has not acquired a taste for his cellular maintenance regime. Perhaps the recent meaty addition to the tonic has offended his sensibility? Sothese applauds his own wit and the cunning sting he had crafted following Corrient Shakti's surprise appointment as URA director.

The undisputed tenure Sothese deserves, in light of the previous director's "reassignment", was all but formalized when the Pramam announced a sudden reversal at the inauguration ceremony itself. Not only was the public humiliation secretly intended as a reprimand for Sothese's playful interpretation of the criminal rehabilitation program unwise, but an unvetted outsider now holds the title of Strategic Advisor to the Pramam, the third and final seat on the Inner Council.

Sothese snakes over to the humbled overlord, who is clutching the back of a chair, and extends his neck to better hear the faintness of impeding death. The roar from the walkways below, singing pandemonium as the first toxic fog reaches the garden sector through the compromised biowall, is both an irritant and a convenient camouflage, which, on the whole, on the wheel of chance, is a winning spin. Could the timing have been more perfect had he orchestrated the breakout himself? And what a treat it is to witness the holy pontificator's non-verbal allegations pierce through his bulging eyeballs. Sothese reaches for a recorder from his right breast pocket. This celebration deserves a keepsake. Good things do indeed come to those who wait.

The Pramam trips in a final attempt to claw his way to salvation, but he falls flat, a groveling corpse of a fraud at the feet of his insurance policy. The ticking stops. An impatient toe taps its way into view, and Sothese groans. Kainaten appears and flicks the drool off his toes as Sothese, unimpressed, kicks the body over for another flash … or two, or three, then sighs. The flickering visitor signals the end of revelry, albeit restrained, and opens a short window for negotiation. Sothese manages to sequester his emotional self at a safe distance from the physical needs of the ensuing discussion.

"An especially warm day in Ministburg, would you not agree, Kainaten?"

Kainaten raids the fresh water stores, without answering, exposing the collusion few insiders are privy to. Only a select few have access to naturally pure water.

"This kind of heat suits me well." Sothese admires his own silky white skin, while he waits for his colleague to stabilize. Questions scan for answers in the toe tapper, guzzling a second pitcher.

"You should know better than to rush your agenda, Sothese." Sothese's emotions snap back at the provocation but quickly distance themselves, once again. The energy that anger harbors can ignite the cool air needed for civil discourse, and condescension is a potent spark. "Things become unpredictable when they fall out of order."

"Unlike your timing. Impeccable. Almost as if you have been dropping in for hours."

"Innuendos only invite half-truths. I cannot read your thoughts, Sothese."

"Or anyone else's, for that matter."

"You do realize I will not turn them in. You hunt alone."

Sothese relives the night his three officials crossed the line and smiles. "Not this time." He thrusts a pointed hand forward and with a twist of the wrist, snatches a third pitcher on the verge of consumption, and the ticking begins anew. "The order has changed. You know what to do."

ELIZE

Day 1013: morning

"**Y**ou're not honestly suggesting I wear this."

"Yeah. Ummm. Why not?"

"Because it's bent, Keet." Actually. You're bent for even suggesting it.

"It'll help keep you safe, Eli. And it's … fashionable? I've already seen a bunch of people with them on this morning. Well, slightly different ones anyway. It's all the wave. All the shops in Tir-na-nog have sold out."

"Ohhhm gee. You're ribbing me, right? It's a hybrid!" Whip it back at him. "It's just one malfunction after another with these things."

"Perk. Technically, you're a hybrid too." Eye-roll for that one. Stitch, still the dweeb.

"I'm mixed race, not a frankenspecies, Stitch. Hybrids are a menace to society. Where do these architects dig up these ideas? Are they breaking into your father's piss garden?" Smirk. Sniff the hybrid. I guess not. Hehehe. Why stop there? Sniff Stitch as well. Someone has to be riding the magic carpet. How about Keet?

"Ouch!" Who did that? "Cyd!"

"You offended him." Stitch is chuckling. Keet joins in.

"Oh, get those leaves off your urn. You're being melodramatic." Blocked him. Missed. Geez. Are we going to get into another one of these slapping matches? "I was talking about … ummm … other hybrids." There goes that attitude again. "You're different, Cydie. You're not like a normal hybrid." Now what? Cyd's turning his bracts on me.

"Juicy! Be that w— Ptuh! See what I mean? He just flipped a root at me." Complete menace. "Stop laughing." Slap them silly. Are we done yet, boys?

"So that's where Cyd gets it from." Stitch and Keet sneak a quiet chumbud salute. Ok. I'll admit not all hybrids are bad. Just crabseats … and privyshelves … and geckoholds … and mosquibots … and … shudder. Especially mosquibots. Ziga menace! So pretty much every hybrid. You convince me otherwise.

"Well, it's not a mosquibot. Ziga menace." My thoughts exactly, dear brother. Hmmm.

"Yeah, but it has opposable toes."

"They lock together around your shoulders. Like this." Stitch wraps one of its legs over each of his shoulders and the toes grip the other side of the disk, which I guess is a chest plate. Then he just lets the arms dangle on my disheveled shag carpet. Play time for Shaggy.

"Watch out!" Hehehe. A hybrid tickle-and-pound fest. "What's with the hands?" I'd better intervene. The arms are flailing everywhere. "Help me out here, Keet."

"They're mallets." Keet takes one of the hybrid's arms and whacks the plate on Stitch's back. Whoa! That's loud. Rip. His whole body is vibrating. Hehehe. Twins on the attack!

Grab the other arm. Boing boing boing. Boing boing boing. Boing boing boing. Whoops! It's out of control. "Sorry, Stitch. Ummm, how do I stop it?" Now I know why Stitch made sure we were all wearing our noise canceling emitters. Maybe if I knock it again. There. It's tapering off and so is … Crap! "Shaggy, catch!" Phew. Just in time. Help Stitch up.

"Ta, chum. Pica trip! So that's how you trigger the manual override." Trigger it for what exactly? He shimmies a few times. A new shagtime dance? Giggle. "I fig it'll work fine, yeah?" He slips the thing off and hands it to me. Right. I don't think so.

Good choice, Elize. Club it with its own weapon. It is a weapon. Do not let them fool you, Elize. Stop it. You're paranoid. Why do you never listen to me? You think you are the boss of you? You think you can ignore me for much longer? YOU THINK YOU CAN SHUT ME OUT?

Big breath out. One … two … three … four … five … six …

"Eli?"

Hang a sec. Hand up. Seven … eight … nine … ten. Finger up. Wait. Wait. Wait. Geez. Can they just stop shaking me? I told you so, Elize. I am still here. Quiet! Glare at them. Start over. Shut your eyes this time, girl. You can do it. No distractions. One … two … three … four … five … six … seven … eight … nine … ten. Wait, wait, wai—

"You're not breathing!"

Done. Big breath in and relax. Pause. Listen. Phew. Silence at last. They're staring.

"What?" They should be used to my voices by now. I am. Hick. Who am I ribbing?

"What happens when we're not around to tell you to breathe." He's acting like a mother hen as usual. Stitch doesn't usually get so topped up. Oh. I guess he does now.

"You both need to ease a bit. Have I ever passed out?" Hands on hips. That's right. Never have. Ohhhm gee. I *am* like Cydie!

"Technically, no, but you've never changed color either … until now." Another color? Turn to Stitch.

"What torture have you inflicted on this one?" He's always adding his own special features to everything.

"No mischief here, cutie." A poke and a smile from Stitch, and a scowl from Keet. Then back to the morgue face brigade. "But you, Eli …" Go ahead. But me, Eli … Finish the sentence.

"You turned blue, and it wasn't because you were calm or relaxed. But still lovable, chum." Dweeb. Sideways grin at Keet. He is not amused.

"Well, nice to know I'm still as poke-worthy as ever. But no rib? Blue?"

Keet muscles in. He grabs the hairy saucer pack from Stitch and straps it on me.

"Right. Another dysfunctional hybrid."

"Not dys-functional …" Don't say it. Oh, but you are thinking it, Elize. No. Yes, you are. You know what I am about to say because you can read my mind. Not now. You are the dysfunctional one, you are the dysfunctional one, you are the— Shut up! By your command, mistress. "Meta-functional."

"Reaaally. And it has a name, this higher level functioning something-or-other?" Sniff. Pew.

"It's an Orangugong." Cyd's clapping his leaves. Was that a secret hy-five behind my back?

"It's grody hairy. And it stinks." Keet swats the air above

my head.

"I thought I saw a mosquibot." Did my privyshelf just snigger? Whip my head back at Cyd. You'd better keep twiddling those leaves. We'll chat later. "Sorry, Eli. My mistake." Snare at him.

"The hairs are sensors. But less advanced than my old coif, yeah? They just read frequency spikes and soldier up before they pound away. It's an early warning system, in case of false alarms, yeah?" Of course, false alarms. The perfect hybrid. Geez.

"And look back at the mirror. The plate is fascinating. All those carvings ... that detail. It must be very old."

"I knew it, Keet! You dug it out of Mr. G's clearance section, didn't you? Does it even work?"

"Oh the shards! Are you questioning my Tess, chum?"

"No, only your sanity." Stitch's genius is undeniable. "Ok. Share."

"Perk. No need to crack, Eli. It's fully grown and it looks just like a regular one, except for the hammers. But no one will see them. Just clip the arms around your waist like this, then pull the hairy muff over the hands. And valah! Your secret weapon." Not yours, Elize. Not yours. Not listening. You will, and it is the hair on *your* arms that will rise.

"Doesn't she need a password, Stitch?"

"Flip! I forgot. Ta, bud. You need two, Eli. One to disable, just in case." I wagered as much. "And a second to reenable and ..." He pulls a slip from one of his zigazillion pockets and sticks it to the mammasack back. "That's the Zaf factory default ..." A wink. "... with operating instructions." Sneak a peak for now. I'll change it later.

"Gotta blister, boys. Dr. Tenille is expecting me."

"Say *Arrr* to him for me." Giggle at Keet.

"He's just playing the pirate, bud. You're the real picaroon here." Triple giggle. Stitch is right. Keet's becoming quite the treasure hunter. He knows it too. Look at that micro-smirk. Palm up. Stitch beats Keet to the fist, then slap goes the thief. Hehehe. Out they go.

Deep eerie giggle. Such honor amongst thieves, Elize. Ignoring you. And accomplices to murder. Are you ignoring me now? Just breathe. You're not real. But my session with Dr. Tenille is, so off to O'Leary Hall I go.

There's one. And another. Looks like the mammasack really is a new wave catching on. And one in action over there. Juicy! The girl's eating a flyer bake while she's walking, and her well-behaved sack is holding a slippad around the top of her head and down in front at eye level. Ooooooooo. Now *that* I can't wait to try. Ah crap! My mallet-for-hands mop needs to get some opposable thumbs. I'll find a use for you yet.

Let's cut through the orchard just to be on the safe side. You never know what kind of equipment hides out in the medical lab. The citrus canopy has a nice calming effect as well. Hmmm. There's a thought. How about a little lemonade? Let's try that tree over there. Now where did I put the Orangugong operating instructions slip? Hehehe. Open wide. Yum it up. Ewww. So sour, but tasty.

Whoops! Busted by the campus guard. I'd better clean the evidence and run out of scanner range. I need to keep my DNA to myself, especially with the relentless Gadlin conspiracy paranoia still obsessing the Pramam. Honestly, something has to be done. Eadonberg is crawling with creepy officials skulking around the walkways. At least, they're staying off campus. The counselor has been lobbying the university chancellor to make the GMU keep their antics away from our peaceful academic community. So far, it's working.

Are the blowers broken again? The Unification is spending way too much time on fearmongering and GMU creepy three officials boot camps, and not enough on infrastructure. Just last week GenTech did another upgrade to the generators in the ventilation shafts. And the month before that, there was a major temperature hike. Stitch thinks that they're intentionally sabotaging the equipment to set the Gadlins up for another terrorist allegation. I think it goes even deeper than that. They're try— "Ohhhm gee! This heat is absolutely unbearable!"

"Your hybrid seems to think differently." Huh? Mega crap! Don't you dare you-ring-da-gong on me now. Right. In case of false alarms, eh?

"Hey lo, gotta go." Now run. "Disable." Hick hybrid.

Why do you not stop to talk to him, Elize. He has been in your mind ever since you first saw him. No, he hasn't. Oh yes. I remember. I was there. You cannot lie to me, Elize. Why not? You do. I simply show you the world from a different perspective. Right. Another lie. From Elize's perspective, perhaps. Regardless, I am quite pleased you are inviting my conversation at last. You're not invited. Go away. You're making me late for my appointment. You mean *our* appointment. No, I mean *my* appointment. Three's a crowd.

There's the administration building. Breathe out. Deep

breath in … and relax. I'm ready.

There it is. The infamous oak door. What was that? Don't react. You know he's watching you. Jumpers!

"Startled you, did I, Elize?" He squints his left eye down the hallway and rushes me in. The door slowly creaks shut. "Best be extra quiet today."

He places a tiny stick with a swatch of fabric attached to it next to his miniature sixteenth century Galleon on the shelf behind his desk. I should say something. It's the best way to divert suspicion, just in case.

"You're cleaning the sails?" He sighs. Shift your energy, girl. Don't let him feel the guilt.

"No." He treads back to his desk, lost. "They were taken." Footsteps down the hall distract him. "I am making a new one."

"The fabric is beautiful. Where did you buy it?" I feel like a fraud. Don't let your foot fidget. Good.

"I weave it myself. I learned from my ancestors. It's an art form that has been dead for ages." He looks straight at me. Be strong. Think happy thoughts. Phew. Footsteps distract him again. He stares right through the door this time. "The sails were very important to me." Like Mother's jewel was to me. I feel so horrible. What do I do? What do I say? Congratulations, Elize. You are a monster. Not now.

"Would you like to talk about it?" That brings out a warm smile.

"Thank you, sweet Belle." He leans in and whispers. "It appears that there are real pirates afoot." The footsteps fade and a door shuts. "Best be extra quiet today." He invites me to sit down. Off you go, Orangugong. Enjoy your corner. Good thing I disabled it. Dr. Tenille looks amused. "And besides, this is your time. Tell me about the voices."

"I wake up to them now. I'm still soaked, so the nightmares are still there, but it's as if I just jumped into a conversation mid-sentence." Nightmares upon nightmares, will this ever end? I know the answer, Elize. Do you want me to tell you? Ye— No!

"They are actual voices then, not simply thoughts."

Stop trying to trick me. Oh, I would not dare, Elize. Liar. Focus, girl. Dr. Tenille is talking to you. Right.

"What do you mean?" I'm going to lean back now. I'm tired.

"Do you hear them in your head or in your ears?"

"I used to just think them, but I really wasn't the one thinking them. They would just come." Why is he nodding? Why can't I hear his thoughts instead of those three? And it's always the same ones. I want to know what he's scribbling.

"You're safe here, Elize. I can see you're frightened. Would you like some water?" What's under his desk? Whoa! Is that what I think it is? It can't be. You are right, Elize. It is drugged. You know it is drugged. He is trying to drug you. Toes, stop fidgeting. Yes, focus, Elize. Focus on my voice. He knows about the Galleon's sails. He will make you talk. And then … And then what? Talk to me. What's he going to do to me? Deep eerie giggle. Best not drink, just in case.

Dr. Tenille shifts in his chair. He clears his throat. He's moving very slowly now, watching me as he slides his journal over to the side. He reaches for something in his desk drawer.

Enough with the staring, already. He pulls a big box out. Whatever is inside is jingling. He places it on his desk and starts sifting through it. "I have something to control that. Has anyone else heard this?"

I can feel my eyes bulge out of my skull. Creeps! He heard that? Deep eerie giggle. Quiet! Dr. Tenille peeks over the open box lid and starts jingling through the contents with his fingers instead. Deep eerie giggle. "Stop it!" He's clipping through it now. He's almost frantic. Deep eerie giggle. I feel sick. Mother, what's happening to me? I'm scared. I can't go on like this. "Help me." Don't make me cry. Please. Not here.

"Found it. Hold tight, Elize." Here he comes. He truly cares. Here he comes to comfort me. I really need a hug. Please hug me. Why won't you hug me? Just a hand on my shoulder. That's not enough! I'm not one of your interesting cases! I'm not a specimen for your crew to gawk at! Slap him away. Ohhhm gee. What came over me? I'm so sorry. "I'm sorry. I do—"

"You don't need to apologize." He hands me the most beautiful blue crystal vase I have ever seen. "It's as pure as your heart." He smiles. Sniff. "Down the hatch, me Belle." Giggle. Sniff. I'm dripping. He points to the wipe stack.

"Aye, Captain." Giggle. Snort. Wipe. Yuck. Dab my eyes. Geez. And no makeup tube. He slips a strange medallion onto a black neckband, ties it around my neck, and centers it on my throat.

"I'm not sure how it works, but it cancels the involuntary croaking."

I'm yay with that. Silence the rabid frog. You mean the

lioness's roar, do you not, Elize? Deep eerie giggle. Hang a sec. She's still there. "But I'm still hearing her."

"You can, but no one else can. Promise me you will keep this choker on in public at all times." Nod. He returns to his analysis and motions me to relax in my chair again. "Her? Then the voices are in your ears now." More notes. And lots of them.

"Maybe they're on their way out? They started out as feelings, then thoughts, and now they're separating. I wager that's a good thing. Isn't it?" He's flipping though past slips ... then forward ... then back again ... now frowning.

"Strange." I don't think I was supposed to hear that. It was more of a mumble than a comment.

"Like my mother, then." He squints at me. Crap! The only reason I know that is because I stole his journal a while back. Reframe it. Think quick. "Is that what her voices were like? I just feel you've seen this before." Phew. Good recovery.

"And your hallucinations? Have they progressed, as well?"

Ease, girl. Change can still be good. It's not childish to hope, right? I mean, Keet keeps talking about becoming what you think about. I'm sure he means what you consciously think about. Yeah. That's right. I can just ignore everything else. Elize, we just had this discussion, do you not remember? You can no longer ignore me. Wrong. That's not what you said. I do remember. Pardon me, not the boss of you. I am pleased to inform you, Elize, that things have indeed progressed. You asked for help? You wanted me to talk to you. That was an invitation, Elize. No, not you. Enjoy a much needed rest, Elize. Come along, Orangugong. Deep eerie giggle.

I will keep you safe, Elize. And you, my good medic, well, not really. You are a pathetic feeble reject who has not the courage to protect anyone. A preposterous Orangugong is a better guardian. And this putrid office? Your stench saturates the very chaise you patronize Elize on.

"Elize?"

Here is some charm for you. I whip this hick choker at your face. Hear me roar ... out your door. This interview is over.

K E E T O

Day 1016: late evening

Tonight, a new year begins, as the eleventh anniversary of our ethereal bond. How could I have predicted that the grief therapy to which I was attracted would still be as comforting to me today as it was to my fragile nine-year-old heart? Although my fear of the unknown remains, and pushes me towards borderline obsessive planning, I am grateful for my lack of perfection in that realm. In fact, I welcome the occasional mercurial inspiration that flows onto these pages. The oneness I feel, or rather I crave, every night as I write in the safety of my mausoleum-styled homestead has no earthly explanation. It is both frightfully uncontrollable and blissfully anticipated, awakening desires I have thus far been too emotionally stunted to grasp, until now.

Cracking the cover of a new journal may just possibly be the most sacred moment I could share with you, Mother. To some, who shall remain nameless, although I wager you can read my thoughts, this yearly ceremony I perform elicits a you-belong-in-a-jar look. The ribbing is immaterial because this blessing is not for her. The expanse I create, in these quiet moments of reflection, is our own private miniverse, no one else's, and these physical memoirs belong to a treasure chest to which only you and I have a key.

Ohhhm gee. Listen to me. All this whimsical introspection may someday be mistaken for actual wisdom if I get too attached to my own school of philosophy. The reality is that recapping the day's events helps me stay grounded, so that I can appreciate my own significance in the larger context of life, and perhaps glimpse the meaning behind your passing, and this splitting headache. For now, however, I must settle for the vague clues Eli and I have uncovered since arriving in Eadonberg, which brings me to another personal milestone worthy of commemoration, the beginning of Eli's and my third year in this city of answers, or so we hope.To your invisible, yet unwavering, presence, I bless this evening's celebratory burning of myrrh and communion with silence as I inaugurate the first journal entry with these inspired words:

> My thoughts submit to your guidance, as always, lest they be marred by deception.

There. After today's adventure I really needed to relive the first page of this journal. Now let me try to focus past my throbbing head, starting with Eli's status, then signing off with a real zapper.

She is still missing. Her body is around, but her brain has definitely crossed over to never-never land. My temerarious twin is also living up to her reputation because, very early this morning, Dr. Tenille made on her account an unexpected appearance at the archives. As someone who restricts himself to either the university or the GHU, he was clearly nervous about his somewhat public appearance. I was not the only one who noticed his overly secretive arrival, however. The academic shared a raised eyebrow over the top of an ancient manuscript, as well.

Luckily, the stacks are almost deserted at that time of day, because the nothing-to-see-here guilt cloud hanging over Dr. Tenille's curly mess was a beacon to anyone living in fear of Gadlin infiltrators. I was musing about what past experiences could have contributed to this man's social anxiety, when terror scraped my butt off the chair instead. I rushed to the artifacts room, falsely assuming that it was a safe haven, until Mme Beaudoin summoned me to the aid of our new visitor. I have worked at the Museum of Antiquities long enough to know that any form of "excuse" has been metaphorically struck from all sanctioned dictionaries, so I shuffled towards a quiet corner of the towering bookshelves to meet the victim of my mini larceny.

To my delight, his impromptu visit to the archives was not impelled by a mission to ship me off to Ministburg Lockdown. He had ventured out into the world of suppressed suspicion and contrived civility to breach his oath to the Unification Code of Conduct for Medics. In other words, if the GHU were to catch wind of this, our amusing Captain Snook would be marooned on the very island that you were scheduled to perish on. But that was not your fate, and mine was about to change.

We decided to continue the conversation at a more discreet location. That is how I ended up hosting him as a guest inside my plot of real estate in the cove of crypts behind the museum. The gurgling in the water garden, that used to unnerve me on my daily bridge crossings to and form work and again late at night as I lay in bed, has now melded into the acoustic background.

Ever since our adventure in Albaraaton, I have wondered

whether the waters are trying to communicate a warning to me, whether I should stop to listen for patterns, but my instincts keep me centered on the path to my stone cocoon and my curiosity on a tight leash. Dr. Tenille, on the other hand, did not have the experiences of safe daily passage to slay any ghosts he might be envisioning as the source of the strange turbulence beneath the milky lavender surface. His boots clipped along ahead of me and landed with a thud at my doorstep, his body barely still attached to them.

The barking on the other side of the door provoked a "shiver me timbers" from my midi guest that ended in a waggy-tailed sniffing buffet for Sparky. So much for my fearsome protector. His territorial machinations over the past year had lulled me into believing that there might have been a little guard canine in him after all. Sigh. Perhaps he is looking to impress the captain and join his crew as ship's mascot. Hehehe. More than likely though, the olfactory investigation has revealed a scent that Sparky is secretly familiar with — the Galleon's sails.

As I shut the antique door behind us, the sunbeam streaming in from the slit above the niche, focused the energy in the room onto the shrine I have created for you, Mother. In that moment, the tokens that empower me became the demons in a waking nightmare for my guest. Dr. Tenille all but lost consciousness as he stumbled onto the edge of my bunk, consumed with his reflection in the mirrored armoire, three arm-lengths away. In the time it took him to regroup, I was able to feed Sparky, reorganize my reading pile, write a closing comment in my last journal entry, top up my ink bottle in anticipation of tonight's paper and quill session, sort my tunics by color, and run a marathon. Well, not quite, but the clock sure was ticking slowly enough during your ex-medic's trip to the void to run a marathon of questions through my head.

When he finally came back to the present, he shifted his gaze to the gameboard, framed by the midday sun, and lured me into the dark memory toying with his resolve. I gawked in horror as he franticly scribbled onto the slip that he sent hurtling towards me to claw at my feet. It was the image I had rabidly consumed ever since Eli's first meeting with Dr. Tenille almost three years ago. It was the image that led to your conviction without a trial for murder. It was the image of Dr. Paloma Yarkovsky, Dr. Tenille's colleague, dead in your cell in the psychiatric wing of the GHU, with you, Mother, withdrawn and contorted in a back corner.

The hurried inscription, though, is what ate a hole through my skull: "This is how the game ends."

My body stiffened as my neck slowly twisted towards the pieces in play behind me. Is this where malice hides, as a contest of wills, under the guise of a game?

Our discussion eventually returned to the purpose behind his outing. Over the past year, your daughter, my twin, has come to depend on our wannabe pirate for professional support and therapeutic meditations in the privacy of his O'Leary Hall cabin, away from the hidden recorders in the GHU. The doctor keeps no official records. Only the analysis he confides to his pre-slippad tablet documents Eli's inexplicable transformation. Inexplicable to us, at least.

According to Dr. Tenille's expert assessment, Eli's psychosis has progressed to, in his words, "a critical point of extreme concern", considering that her sickness does not share the same trigger as yours. In my words, and through Stitch's poetic influence, of course, I interpreted his diagnosis as topping the "pica crazed" point, but that does not even begin to express the unspeakable threat she now faces. The decision to reach out to me was not taken lightly. After three days of deliberation, capped by Eli taking a pass on their last appointment, yesterday evening, Dr. Tenille feels the choice has been made for him.

Under lock and key, this knowledge I have sworn to bury inside layers of denial, impenetrable to intimidation, interrogation, and even persecution. Not even Eli is to unearth the secret her mentor and confidant has betrayed to me. Father has blindsided us with a phobia of the GHU, but there exists a force outside the Ministry's control that terrifies even the Pramam himself. The deep eerie voice, now audible at normal conversational range, exposes my sister to surreptitious cleansing by the Global Spiritual Unit.

These are the monsters that we must now outwit. They are tuned into Eli's deviant vocal chords, and they are waiting for the nefarious songstress to get a little too disruptive at the opportune moment. However, what truly alarms me, as if the GSU stabilizers were not enough to send us deep underground, is a more cunning beast, invisible to all but myself during wisps of awareness — a dormant villain called the ego.

The new secrets that I must safeguard are taunting me to lash out with full disclosure as payback for Eli having confided in yet another third party over her own twin brother. This would cripple the progress Dr. Tenille has made in pinpointing the source of Eli's suffering, slowing its progression, and protecting her from barbarous diagnostics. For me to satisfy my vain need to know exactly what transpires during their confidential meetings would distance Eli from me, far and deep into her head. I refuse to lose her that way.

"As a matter of urgency," Dr. Tenille explained, he has nominated Eli as a promising lab assistant candidate to Director Corrient Shakti. Sparky ducked as I coughed up a piece of flyer bake that got lodged in my throat. It took me a head shake, an "Are you absolutely bent?", and a "You're an overdazed wack!" to even acknowledge his sincere attempt to justify this suggestion. Eventually, the lunacy made sense, but the decision still rested with Eli. His plan was to wait for her destructive interlude to subside, which he expected would take about six days.

In the end, we did come here prepared to do whatever it takes to save Eli from herself. Sometimes the risks are crippling, and other times we just have to laugh, especially when hybrids are involved, as you may recall.

What am I saying? You live in a dimension where time and space no longer exist. My memories on these pages are omnipresent. Anyway, I will recap a fragment from my journaling session three days ago, for my own benefit. Repetition is the key to mastery, so there must be something in the following replay that I somehow need to pay attention to.

Continuing on then, Stitch and I had outfitted Eli with an Orangugong, which we had hoped would make so much noise so as to wake her up were she to show signs of an imminent blackout. Stitch's hypothesis is that her episodes are caused by coordinated synaptic misfires that create sudden shifts, either up or down, in her baseline electromagnetic frequency emissions. Our twin squashed frog faces prompted an excruciatingly long explanation that might as well have been in Ministry speak. In simpler terms, the hair follicles can sense if Eli is about to figuratively jump to a different broadcast station. I hope Stitch did not mutilate a perfectly functioning mammasack for nothing. The workmanship on the antique back plate is absolutely striking. Hehehe. No pun intended.

Thinking back on it now, it really was a strange day. In light of what I have just learned, maybe there is a connection between the state of Eli's room and the state of her mind. It may be worth noting their interrelation in the weeks to come, on the off chance that my forensic interior design investigation reveals a method to her madness. No. Strike that. I need a hopeful description to reframe her temporary cognitive deterioration. It is temporary, is it not, Mother? How I long for you to speak through me.

Please send me patience as I regroup. There are even more oddities that I must process before I can clear this aura of dark energy around me for the promise of a peaceful sleep. An influx of strangers in the city, and, from what I have witnessed, in the archives this evening near closing time, is attracting reinforcements from the Global Military Unit. Since appearances are never what they seem with the Ministry, I imagine their mission was not as overt as the following synopsis may suggest.

I was leaning over the table, under the moonlit crystal dome at the center of the Round Room, reprogramming an uncooperative PAL, when I noticed a hint of light reflecting off its casing. I would have passed it off as a GMU surveillance slider scanning the city waterways from above, were it not for the academic's close-mouthed gasp down the aisle facing me, and Mme Beaudoin's speedy shoes clicking along the granite tiles towards the exhibit room.

By the time my supervisor reappeared at the entrance with three peculiar-looking individuals, the academic had swooped between the towering stacks and had calmly perched himself at my side, sternly pleasant, offering his distracted assistance with the stubborn device. It was clear to me that wherever these synchronized marching goons had come from, their presence was no cause for celebration. Mme Beaudoin's stiff welcome and prompt escort to the rim of the library, snatching a PAL off the wall on the way, further inflamed the tension in the room.

Shivers down my spine followed a hand on my shoulder whispering to me: "Best stay close." The young scholar, whose name I still did not know at the time, motioned me to sit down, and quietly took a post next to me, his right hand below the marble inlay surface while his eyebrow raised a concern that I quickly keyed into. Although my conversations with the young man have been sporadic and brief, I sense enough about him to trust that his interests align with my own. There is no nervous hip jiggling or pranks clouding his motives; his serene strength is what invokes the confidence that Stitch has needed near-death adventures to coax out of me, and then some. But I digress. There will be many other opportunities to dissect that relationship.

I could barely discern the voices bouncing off the domed

ceiling, as my supervisor offered to demonstrate the sketching procedure involved in sending the flying book sniffer on a hunt. The lead's tone, however, had just the right pitch to converge on the focal point of the room, where my ears were perked. Ministry officials! Flashes of the plasma chaos in Almedina Square nearly two years ago pasted my eyelashes to my eyebrows. The creepy three, barking out suspicions of a Gadlin weapon hiding in the artifacts room, were Sothese's replacement hounds.

Growls of contempt brought the curator racing to protect Mme Beaudoin from the steaming fury that her repeated denials were fueling. While the female official guzzled a water vessel and the male one wiped his forehead with an already saturated cloth, the more androgynous leader began to close the gap, its overzealous deputies in tow at its flanks, toward the man who has become as close to a father figure to me as I have ever had.

I felt my young ally focus his gaze on the forerunner of the three goons, then at its left and right sidekicks in turn, as if sizing them up for a fight, all the while scrutinizing their approach. The curator locked eyes with me in passing, then quickly shifted them to the scholar then back to me again, as he ushered the Ministry agents down another aisle and through the retina accessible doors to the artifacts room, where the granite pyramid is secured. My hands were shaking in my mind, my legs pacing, back and forth, back and forth, back—

Geez. I thought I heard something. They must be echoes. Where was I? Right.

I am unsure of what drove me to lead the young academic

to the artifacts room, but I am grateful that I did. As long as the curator kept the three officials' backs to the one-way mirror, we could sneak up behind them and come to his defense. I reached for the crystal pendant around my neck, wary of triggering a plasma arc, and took a deep breath in concert with my companion. Serenity cleared the stiffness in my arms as I willed the door open with a clean iris scan.

The incandescent lights shattered. The entire museum went dark. Somehow, they had felt us coming, but the academic knew where to hit. He pulled a laser blade from his coat then not a second went by and one, two, three went down. As I ran to my surrogate father, he yelled: "Izionnis!" At last a pseudo introduction, albeit poorly timed for formalities. I spun around with my jaw on the floor. The creepy three were back up and gunning for the artifact. It was glowing. Ignoring the screeches coming from both the curator and Izionnis, I ran towards them and caught a flight across the room with the curator as my headrest. The last thing I saw was the creepy three flickering out of view with Izionnis on their tail.

I am so exhausted. A quiet night at last. The waters are silent.

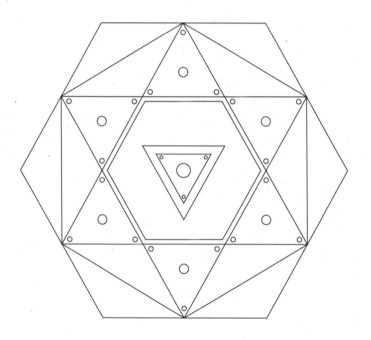

CHAPTER TWO

S O T H E S E

Day 1022: midday

What a fool the Pramam was to even consider constraining the one whose allegiance his life depends on. For his presumption, the shallow desperate gasps will forever replay as a fiery rhythm throughout eternity. Much like the sudden stop cripples the hovership as it reaches the rooftop sliderpad of its Eadonberg destination, life energy can also drain from a host to change the course of events especially when an unwritten agreement arrives at an impasse. The virility that Sothese habitually enjoys, however, is a pleasure that the Pramam never shall. No human can ultimately cheat time.

This evening, Sothese meets with a new triad of applicants. After two nights intentionally confined to the Ministry transocean hovership's generator level, enjoying the short-lived yet opportune carnal company of a few biochip-free stowaways turned castaways, his body shivers in anticipation of two momentous interrogations. For the past year, the chaperoned visits to the SIF headquarters, where Nathruyu is apparently enrolled in their Witness Relocation Program, have emasculated his inquisitorial talents. On this occasion, there will be no strapping of hands. The real identity beneath the black-pitted skin of the inmate contorted in a corner of the cell is about to be the first treachery exposed.

Sothese slips through the SIF agents collecting outside the craft, and commands the emergency landing crew to attend to the defective generator. He smoothes his left hand across the right side of his impeccable face and ends with the tips of his fingers sliding down his neck, in a display of self-admiration, as he straddles the railing between him and a nine-story drop into the awakening lotuses below. A sweet floral perfume disguises a putrid heart and urges the blood to his flared nostrils. His lips pucker with the bouquet of mischief baking in the heat as the sun pierces through the dispersing yellow fog overhead. Movement at a distance inside the Restricted Sector recalls hedonistic pursuits that destabilize his footing for a moment of exhilaration, capped by a slick recovery.

Alas, heaven must wait, for his new servants are gathering. A return to darkness may be the last thing Sothese wants, but to play in the dark is what he lives for. This master of subterfuge and seduction fully expects his new hires to indulge him.

Into the Gardens district sajadum Sothese enters and bows to the only power he has ever submitted to, the one that keeps his body young and his desires insatiable. The repentant pose that he must endure does not represent any relationship he cares to return to. No childhood fondness flutters through his veins as gentle feathered wings. The talons of treachery claw at him instead. Yet, in the privacy of the tetrahedron-shaped amethyst meditation hut, guarded by the lush Ministry cloth he has affixed to the entrance, his grandiosity diminishes in reluctant appreciation.

Forever the harbinger of chaos and destruction is who

Sothese fancies himself to be, wrapped up in the twisted pleasures of trampling the ones who grovel for clemency. How he despises those who do not have the intellect to recognize the tombstones they hack for themselves with their gullibility and apathy. As it has been throughout industrial human history, so the private suffering continues today, veiled by the amethyst glow of collaborative meditation, a brand of collective mourning for personal responsibility. No amount of prayer can cleanse egoic toxicity from the waters through which their denial swims. Their kind received the coal they deserved in their stockings, and now the poison fires will feast where they tread, once again.

The fabric of time wrinkles in the space between dreams and nightmares. Someone else's dream can snake into another's nightmare, but on which side will the shears that cleave the one from the other fall? Sothese can only assume that his last entourage selections and their aspirations are now fuel for their own inferno, in a style of banishment that befits their failure to acquire the suspected Gadlin weapon; whereas, a more fortunate three shall fill the vacancy still plaguing the vaporized trio's would-be master. But first, silence is ripe for a little dissonance via a long overdue conversation.

Time ticks past as Sothese leaves the sajadum on his way to the SIF headquarters as do the visions he savors from Ministburg. Although another vapid session, shivering in the dark, criticizing the back of the Pramam's ridiculous gown, shapes tonight's expectations, in lieu of extracting truth from the imposter cowering in a corner of cell block A, a simple ruse promises to make this particular meeting more productive. Much to Sothese's chagrin, however, the robed pontificator will not feel a thing during this trickery.

A pleasant surprise awaits with the coincident arrival of Sothese's three new officials. Perhaps these are the ones who will succeed in all trials? The four descend together into the cold dark sub-water level prison, to the sound of toe tapping and an impatient Ministry greeting: "Welcome and may They grant peace upon you" followed by a dispassionate "They are One" from a monotone quartet.

The captive's energy, reflecting off the glistening walls of her icy dungeon, did not evoke any familiar sensations, nor did her black-pitted quasi-hypothermic state obscure the facial features accentuating the haunting black eyes staring straight through him. The Pramam may be easily deceived, but not one of her kind. Sothese brushes his way past the object of his unrealized fantasy, from whom he is hoping to steal a few seconds of life, and claims the space between the prisoner and her holy inquisitor.

Sothese's cold stare does not accurately convey the contempt he feels for the substandard facilities from which the real Nathruyu has escaped. "You should have left me in charge" is fast becoming the unspoken dictum that will mark his ascent to supremacy. The stricken words etch themselves in the enamel behind his teeth, while he conceals the body swap sting operation, as he did the true champion of the Almedina arrests that night — the balletic huntress whose double is now humming an old Gadlin lullaby.

The imposter crawls to the containment field, marking the front of her territory, and slowly drags her naked form up the invisible grid, her long black hair draped over her chest for heightened arousal, as she teases a risen eyebrow out of Sothese. He accepts the challenge, free from the bounds of human morality, but summons his new hounds to him, just in case the barrier malfunctions. The rows of empty cells create a cavernous space where their voices echo freely. Sothese manipulates the ping pong parley into a game of double entendre that only he and the blue-lipped replicant can decipher.

"I must commend your special SIF agents, my Pramam, for their flexible hospitality. I sense a shift in her since she has been enrolled in the program. Tell me, *Nathruyu*, are you enjoying your reassignment? No? I am sorry to hear that. Are the facilities not what you expected?"

"I was misled into believing that the Criminal Rehabilitation Program involved group therapy."

"That is the official curriculum, of course, but for minor offenders, not child killers. Do you remember who misrepresented your particular circumstance? We will ensure that a reprimand be effected, if warranted, of course."

"I was not given his name."

"Perhaps, a simple description would help? Distinguishing marks?"

"Nothing visible in plain conversation. He kept me where he could see me."

"Never turning his back to you. That is the correct

procedure."

"Yes. Never turning his back to me."

"How about clothing or accessories? Any element of style?"

"Nothing original."

The answer Sothese is hoping for is locked inside a past best kept intact.

The haven is magnificent, but not without a few vulnerabilities, one of which leaves the eastern sector of the city with a compromised ventilation system. Sothese surveys the Eadonberg transport station platform for an anomaly as their Ministry convoy slides into the celebratory abandon, sizzling under the midday sun. Hordes of highlanders, lowlanders, and Gadlins, alike, are focusing their attention all the way from the start of the floating walkway at the Central Core drop, near the southern end of the newly completed biowall, up to the Pramam and his entourage.

Amidst the symphonic cheers, there is discord plucking at the veins feeding Sothese's expectant lips in the form of an unwelcome distraction from the debauchery he has been scheming. A tip of a hat and a flash of white teeth, partially obscured under a wide brim, pinpoints the source of the disturbance leaning against the ticket kiosk. It seems that the GMU's security protocol is wanting. The mystery man's solid black eyes lock onto the Pramam-mobile and its passenger.

In his role as personal advisor to the Pramam, the head of

church and state, Sothese excels, but it is his three officials who discourage insurgents by their mere presence, and in whose proximity the stranger flies by undetected, although clearly in range of the active scanning wall. Curiosity must wait in line behind certain bodily needs. The surprise kinsman requires further probing … later. Until then, there are no doubt a few ambitious residents to dishonor.

Hours of stimulating rendezvous, in his off-grid Ministry House quarters, collapse the interval between the afternoon's ceremonial procession and the splash of pure water from the crystal fountain infusing his bedroom with its cleansing mist. Yet, Sothese senses that something more intoxicating is rising with the moon and ostensibly staring up at him from the scaffold bolted to the golden glass structure across the bioluminescent lavender waters of the canal.

The fedora-wearing stranger, from earlier on at the transport station, tugs the brim of his hat and smiles at the silhouette leaning over the balcony. The invitation extended and acknowledged, he disappears at the base of the Victory Bridge, with Sothese already entering into the shafts, through the undisclosed underwater level access to the building.

Provocative chases in enclosed spaces are this fork-tongued predator's specialty. Sothese readies the weapon, whose sibling had beaten Nepharisse to Nathruyu, and barrels down the east-west labyrinth until his blind obsession sees where the mark is leading him. The call out to "show yourself" reverberates into the darkness, tinted with the faint blue glow of emergency generators. A distinctive crash and the sound of shoes, carefully sliding along steel, confirm that the shadow has offered the surrogate SIF agent a truce by means of a playful upright Savasana stance and a confession.

"I am a child of Anubrat."

A breathless pause waits for a response, but nothing comes, and the revelations continue.

"And I sense that you are one, as well."

A smirk hides in the blackness. "And if I were … ?"

"Then we would have something in common. A dislike, perhaps?"

Sothese scoffs, for he practices no such diplomacy. Dislike is a word for those without conviction, and Sothese is abundant in that regard. "I despise him" rings its truth out of the Restricted Sector vents and into the condemned landscape.

"Exquisite! We have two things in common. Shall I entice you with a third?"

Interest releases the tension on the weapon's trigger, as the eager host in the fedora lights the way to a ladder and suggests an ascent. Sothese nods. He follows his guide up, out, and towards a glass elevator, attentive to the murmurs scurrying along the half-rusted walkways that are dipped into the sludge-filled waterway. The door slides shut and the ancient lift showcases the handiwork of an angry planet in the half-decomposed bodies striking the glass.

What a waste of flesh to have perished in such pain. The ruins of asphyxiation, pasted across their rigid faces, intrigue Sothese. He conducts a silent debate as to which method would induce the most agony, toxic gases from without, as these corpses have surely succumbed to, or an obstruction from within. The latter implants itself as a most delicious image in his mind, for future exploration.

After a long descent and a short walk along an abandoned subway track, a red door stands between Sothese and uninterrupted ecstasy. No recorders, no Unification, no propriety. It is an amoral Eden where the Inner Council dignitary can savor the extent of his political power in all its delectable sensual variations.

The underground club baron tips his hat as he presents a youthful appetizer, if you will, with an irresistible deal: "You keep the Unification out of here ... You make sure biochip sensors malfunction down here ... and consider them your subjects, mon seigneur."

▲ ▲ ▲

The chill pulls Sothese back to his interrogation in the cold cell.

"Your cooperation is wanting."

"That is all I can offer in this moment." At last, the invitation he was seeking.

"Perhaps, instead, you can offer the names of your Gadlin co-conspirators?"

"I have already made my official statement. The circumstances have not changed."

"No. But you have ... since you have enrolled in the program, of course."

"And in a group setting, the changes could be dramatic. This would no doubt greatly improve my capacity to remember. The current environment has compromised my thinking."

"Shall we, by your grace, consider her request?"

This is the cue, delivered as planned, that now becomes the moment in which candor appears. With the surveillance recorder on pause and the Pramam suspended in mid-breath, Kainaten ensures continuity between the frames as he watches the hands on his ancient timepiece stop. Sothese takes advantage of the sleight of time to speak freely with the dark figure, flirting with her freedom behind the force field. She too can stretch a raindrop into a stream and never get wet.

"Do you think they will come for you as they did Nathruyu? You are a decoy, nothing more."

"Anu rewards the loyal. I am prepared for what is to come. Are you?"

"Anubrat? A gifted replicant then? Yes, of course. My darling, not Nathruyu, your *Anu* is undeserving of endearment. Who he promised to you is a lie. He will leave you here, stripped and alone."

Her fingertips stroke the space by Sothese's milky face, so close yet so far from a reprieve. He moistens his lips in response, then quickly rejects the deliberate lure.

"I suspect there are others. Tell me where they are."

The clone focuses all her energy into her resolve. "Enjoy the hunt, Sothese."

Time cheats Sothese of a witty quip and returns to its usual pace as toe tapping resumes and the Pramam reanimates and responds: "I shall hold council with They." And Sothese will counsel another.

Back to the underwater level Sothese slides, with his three officials in his wake, as soon as the Pramam leaves him to his habitual guiltless pleasures. The dark hallway provides some privacy, and the creepy three vanish in a flash of plasma that they ignite themselves, so that they can regroup with their master in time to assist with his next encounter. An abrupt energy shift, however, suggests a different result.

▼ ▼ ▼

Urgency pulls Sothese through the velvet curtain over the frozen void to shatter the dawn breaking in Albaraaton earlier today. The temporal risk is skillfully devised and explainable, if questions arise, as a stopover while the Pramam is asleep in his rejuvenation pod, on the overnight Ministburg-Eadonberg voyage. Suspecting that his new officials have already met with disaster, the disruption that he has just completed was pointless. Nevertheless, Wakanda will be overjoyed to feel him again. A last daylight rush brings his skin to perfection, and he crashes the Gayok's morning ritual.

The fleshly conversation takes place in Sothese's mind whose eyes penetrate deep into her soul's mirrors, already wide with terror at the sight of him ripping the wings off the virtacreature she has just released for her ceremonial offering to Water.

Consider yourself blessed that a holograph received the edge of my blade first, Gadlin. The lacerations coming to you may be slightly blunt, but only slightly. I find myself a suspect in a jailbreak of your making. By encouraging your service, I shall prove my innocence and make your beloved enemy eat his words, along with his daily regimen.

SOTHESE

Is that a little post nasal drip I hear gurgling in your throat? Perhaps if I tighten my grip it will stop. You cannot speak? No need to apologize. I will peel the thoughts from your cornea. I am a being of many talents, but I do believe you have enjoyed them in the past, my darling Wakanda. Wherever did you fail me?

Nerve, did you whisper? Overestimating myself showing up here without my hounds, you squeak? Here is a deep-throated laugh for your ignorance, as I dim the lights for our mutual replenishment. Mmmmmmmmm. I throb with the power surge coming on. Have you not heard of the escape? Shall I explore your denial more deeply? Interesting. I feel truth inside you. So today, you live.

But be very wary of your misdirections, Wakanda. There are no immunities for traitors. The Pramam wants you all dead, and I hear many gatayoks want to trade in your very life. What about me? I do not want you at all. Even as I press myself against you, as you stiffen and squirm beneath me, the only sensation I crave is your excruciation by my hand or by ... you remember. I prefer my sacrificial lambs a little leaner. Let me rake my disgust up your thighs, and your pelvis, and your abdomen, and your chest, and the hollow in your neck ... Ssssssssso much leaner.

Do your bodyguards trouble you? I promise they will not speak. Let them watch. You are a brazen leader, are you not? You know how I love an audience. Tsk. Tsk. Tsk. Your strength is waning. And your size is of no advantage for what your fortune tells. I strongly suggest you refocus. And do work on that anger.

I have a trade for you. But first, your payment is ... Which part shall I cut? Yes, this story I remember — the day you met your secret crush. How special.

Now, now, now, my darling. The fight in you I do revel in, but you will flip over and kiss the floor. Shhhhhhhhh. You might enjoy this.

Surprise? Shock? Fear? Oh please tell me it is fear. I rub myself with the scent of it. Oh my Gadlin. Did you think they would come in peace?

Elize

Day 1022: dawn

Find the book. Gotta find the book. Where's the book? Find it. Right. Tap tap tap. No more time. I'm running out of time. Gotta find that book. Tap tap tap. Huh?

Geez. I'm soaked again. And my head is pounding. What the—

"RANGO! Come back here, you coward. Go ahead. Run to Cyd. You two are pathetic. How am I ever going to get any sleep with the nightmares and you hick of a mammasack dweeb experiment gonging away in the middle of the night? And you, Cyd. Always staring at me. Give it a rest. You need a rest. I need a rest. We all need a rest."

Brrr. Juicy. Now I have a chill. Grab a sweater. There. Much better. Ummm. Crap! It's boiling in here. Check the temperature setting. Ok. Just like I set it. It must be broken. Geez. Tear this sweater off ... and my nightshirt. Brrr. Maybe not the nightshirt. Back on. Brrr. And the sweater. Pause. Breathe. Good. Perfect. It's about time ... to sweat again. Strip it off. Oh no. I caught a virus. Shiver. Sweat. Brrr.

"Will you stop banging? And, Cyd. Take your leaves off my dreamcatcher. Back in the corner for both of you." That's right. You'd better be shaking. I'm just getting started.

The shears, Elize. Reach for the shears. Right. Just a simple snip near the roots should do it. Stop, Elize! You are not a murderer. Right. No murder. That would be bad. But you hate hybrids, Elize, remember? The leafy one watches you. He will smother you in your sleep. Get him first. I have been telling you for nine days now, Elize. Do it! Do it now! Before it is too late. Right. The shears. Deep eerie giggle. I win. No! You had your turn, now go away. Well done, Elize. Can I have a turn now? I will make something beautiful of this mess. Pick me. I don't know. You're always moving things around. It keeps things fresh, Elize. And positive. Can't I just be me? Just Eli? My brain hurts. I can't decide anymore. *Decision is the first step towards inner peace, Elize. Decide to be you, and you, you shall be.*

That makes no sense. I'm splintered in three. And then there's me somewhere in there trying to keep you all together. And you're fighting. You're always fighting in my head. Even when you're quiet, you're still fighting, I can feel it.

Ok. That's enough. I need to do something. Grab that room controller. Keep flicking, girl. Keep cycling through the decor options and maybe they'll all get dizzy and fall asleep. Ooooooooo. That's a nice one. So calming. Hehehe. Even the shag is lying down. In fact, all my hybrids are just easing.

To the window. The sun's coming up. I love watching the big blue lotus open on the pond. Sigh. It's so peaceful. And there go the weedels sucking up the algae. They're having quite the feast, the little chubs. There's so much more algae now that the cooling generators are acting up. Shivers! And not just for the sudden chill. What's he doing down there? Wave back. That's top creepy. I'm on the ninth floor. What's he doing looking up at me?

Turn around and calm down. Nice. A holographic waterfall.

I'll just imagine our trip to the granite flats almost two years ago now and the smell of fresh water. Deep breath in and —

✂ ✂ ✂

Oh. It's Stitch's door. "What's with the tuque?"

"Nothing." He's not convincing. I know better. He's doing something with his hair again. "Where's your Orangugong?"

Huh? Check my waist. Whoops. "I forgot it." Now *I'm* not convincing. He's giving me that what-exactly-did-you-do-to-it look. "You and Keet both, now?" Keet pokes his head out.

"What did you do to it?"

"Nothing. I woke up this morning, and it was gone." Well, actually, I blanked out and it was gone. But they don't have to know that. Hang a sec. How would I even know that?

"Pica trip, chum. Maybe Mr. G has another one. Then I can spend hours rigging that one up for you, yeah?" Whoa! He's blowing a bit. Send him some zen.

"No thanks, but I really do appreciate your efforts, Stitch." That worked. "It was defective. And it's not the first time a hybrid has run off on me ... or with me. Let it go." A pause, a sideways squint, and there it is. The poke and the smile. Hehehe. "Anyway. I'll get more sleep now." I hope. If I'm going to have an episode, doing it while I'm asleep is juicy by me. At least, I won't be having a nightmare, right?

"Perk! I was just showing Keet how to catch shadow packets in the miniverse, and we caught the counselor pulling a Kirlian with his profile."

"Or someone is, on his behalf."

"You got it figged, bud."

"But I don't. What on the planet are you two talking about?" I'm out of touch. They've been avoiding me. I don't blame them. The crap that comes out of my mouth sometimes. Geez.

"When Odwin was about my age, chum, he dripped a special kind of goop all over the maze. Any data packet created after that date gets coated, so when someone deletes it, the guts might be ripped out, but its imprint keeps floating around, like a water bubble in zero gravity. All you need is the right net to catch it when it floats by."

"So the miniverse is some kind of holographic version of the entire maze?"

"Yeah. Pica Tess, ya fig?" Ziga, I'd say. "What happens in the maze, stays in the maze … forever." He adds some ghost hoots to his hip jiggling.

"Impressive. And the counselor is …"

"He's ripping the leaf, but he never seems to disappear." Stitch laughs at my squashed frog face.

"I think I can explain it to her, Stitch. Every time the university chancellor dies, the counselor switches his age and hire date, so it looks to the new chancellor that the counselor's not as old as he really is." Holy crap! Is he ribbing me? "No rib, Eli. There's something creepy about him."

Ohhhm gee. No no no. Stop right there. Am I wearing my voice filter medallion thing? Good. Deep eerie giggle. Do you want me back, Elize? You know I am the only one who can protect you. I know you're just a liar, and you drive people away from me. Go away. *True power flows from a deeper source than anger can reach, Elize. Stretch and you shall tap it.* Yes. Tap, tap, tap, Elize. Deep eerie giggle.

"Hey lo … Eli?"

"Yeah, Keet. I'm here. I was just thinking. Does Wakanda know about the miniverse, Stitch?"

"I hope not, chum." He's understandably nervous. But it's the counselor I'm more worried about. And he was just spying on me from the orchard this morning. What if he's secretly working for the Pramam? And that means Caroline could be as well, since he seems to have something on her. Hmmm. Let's put Caroline's loyalties to the test.

"Dr. Tenille doesn't like the counselor either, you know. Well, he doesn't trust him. When I'm in his office, he's always checking down the hallway first. Then he looks at the door from time to time. I think he even thinks that the counselor is the one who stole the Galleon's sails." I can hear Keet gulp from here. He should gulp. He is a thief, Elize. *Judge not for you know not the master's plan, Elize.* Or mistress's. Hehehe.

"It would give our kind Captain Snook such joy to have them in his possession again, dear brother. He seems quite attached to them. It is normal for someone to cling to that which he himself has nurtured into existence. Not healthy, but a common human trait. They have served their purpose in drawing out Wakanda. Now they can return to their creator. Can you do that, Keeto?"

"You're bent." And I apparently belong in a jar. "You want me to break into Ministry House?"

"Only if you want to." Giggle. "Why don't you ask Caroline to fetch them for you?" After you pick up your jaw, of course. "Is it something I said?"

Stitch chuckles at Keet. "Pica glad you're sane again. Slap me." With pleasure. "Ouch. You know what I mean, chum."

"All juicy, Stitch." Ugh. Wipe that grin. Now back to Keet. "Or you could put your chumbuds network savvy to use. You've been honing your thieving skills, eh?" Giggle.

"Mostly just sifting through high council packets and removing dust off them. Nothing hands on."

"We're targeting the URA's secret research. We still need to crack Mashrin's biochip code." He leans over and whispers. "To avoid the ghost with the bloody finger." Crazed. I remember that scare. "And maybe fig how to stop my migraines, yeah?"

Speaking of which … Off with your tuque, super sleuth. "Back to blonde, I see. Looking all Inner Council again?"

"I fig I look juicy, yeah?" Eye roll. He double pokes me.

Keet looks a little sweaty. And I'm feeling a little warm, as well. The dweeb does look somewhat attractive. Strike those thoughts, girl. You are an adult woman now, Elize. Hmmm. Who needs permission from the Ministry, anyway. True. The GSU does not have you. That's right. I'm not Unified. Yes, Elize. Does not have you … yet.

"Be careful what you visualize, chum. If you see it in your head, you can hold it in your hand." That deserves a huge ewwwwwwwww. Stitch is howling.

Center yourself, Elize. The other voices must rest now. Focus only on my voice. You and I, together, as one.

"Whoa! You shaved all your hair?" Keet's right. But, wasn't he just a blonde? Give your head a shake, girl. "What's on your scalp?" I'm too short to see.

Come here crabby one and hold still. Up on the crabseat. "No nipping." Now I can see his scalp. It looks like some sort of symbol. I can only imagine it means "happy" in some obscure way. The grin's the clue. Stop moving, you clawed— No you don't, you little—

"I got ya, chum." Stitch grabs me. And into the wall for you, little crab.

"Hybrids!" You can put me down now. Ummm. Down. No doubt a mush symbol up there.

"You'll have to grow taller to see my secrets now, Eli."

"Dweeb." Keet's laughing, but not. He's actually scowling at *me*. "And?" He turns away. Ok. Uncomfortable pause here. Time to change the subject. "So, Stitch, you never did tell us why Gadlins have no biochips. According to the Ministry, all humans are actually born with them."

"Flyer mud. That's Ministry speak, yeah? I fig they implant the biochips at the GHU. That's why they don't allow home births."

"But highlanders have them, and no GHU shows up at our births."

"You have a point there, bud. I'm dunked on that one. Maybe it happens just before the Unified baptism. The GSU does take the infants away to prepare them as a group before the ceremony."

"That makes sense, Stitch, Gadlins aren't baptized Unified so they wouldn't have biochips ... but how did you get one?" Hmmm. That's right. He's not Unified, so ... Keet and I share a someone's-hiding-something look.

"The truth is— Trip! They made it!" He leaps to his board

and flips through flash after flash of virtual chumbud salutes flying in like a swarm of mosquibots. Another memory I'd rather forget, but I can't. Every one of those Gadlins checking in were bitten. That's how they ended up at Ministburg Lockdown in the first place. "And Wakanda is not invited to the daze."

"Another back door?"

"I hacked together a secret sketch for my mother and me to communicate with, and it's greedy-Gadlin-proof."

"Wakanda saved your mother." I feel the same. But for Keet, it borderlines on jealousy-induced shaming. He has even snapped at Stitch with a "you should practice that Gadlin creed of yours by showing a little gratitude" quip.

"She saved my mother to manipulate me onto her side. Like she's been doing to you since then, Keet. I don't play those games. We're all together in this. Unity. It's one of the six values. My mother lives by them, and so do I."

Keet's mumbling "except gratitude" under his breath.

Keet and I lock eyes. Our togetherness doesn't expand beyond our mini tribe of two. We don't belong to anything bigger, all we have is ourselves. We're not Gadlins, we're not lowlanders, we're not even highlanders. We just lived there in Father's prison, and we certainly aren't freaks like Nathruyu and those officials of Sothese's, whatever *they* are. The truth is, we just don't know who we are. Stitch really does try hard to include us. Maybe we should be the ones showing a little gratitude for the way he always looks out for us. And most of all, for his trust. Like now.

"Ministburg Lockdown is essentially cinders. There was a

huge radiation fire." Stitch is serious.

"Radiation? That's not what the Ministry broadcast said." Not surprised. "They said it was another outbreak and that everyone should get a bioHealth upgrade to warn them if they get too close to someone who's tagged as a carrier." Always for our own safety, in good Ministry fashion, of course.

"Oh yeah. Pass me your headbands, chumbuds. You need an update or the scanners will scream 'irresponsible'. Tomorrow's the deadline to visit the Osler Hall emergency clinic, unless you want to be sucked up a GHU craft." No thanks. Here it is. "Ta, Eli. Keet?" Oh, just grab it from him.

"There is a time to resist, but now is not that time. Whatever plans are afoot must play out to their conclusion, dear brother."

"Afoot? Really? Did you actually hear yourself speak?" What does he mean? Stitch starts tinkering. Keet's skimming the reports from Sakari's and Stitch's private space. Stitch gives us the highlights.

"Not all of them made it though. The GMU followed the barges and attacked. We fig twenty or so were recaptured ... or drowned." He bows his head. A symbol I can only imagine that represents sorrow appears as ink on his scalp. Pretty ingenious bioskin alteration. "I don't know which fate is worse. Slowly suffocating to death or going back to sure torture."

"When did this happen?"

"Nine days ago. My mother and a group of Odwin loyalists have been building a secret community underground for the past year. These are the faces of our new movement. Trip, ya fig?"

"Hang a sec, Stitch. What movement?" Keet has that look

like he's going to do the mother hen thing.

"Wakanda is about to be assalammed. Protect the Gayokcy, my bopping butt!"

Yep. Just like I thought.

Keet's flapping that beak. "The entire Unification is at war with the Gadlins. This is *not* a good time to start infighting. Where's that Unity you were just talking about?"

"Lead the Creed, bud. Lead the Creed. Wakanda's been Leading the Greed all her life and wants to infect our whole breed. She's selling us out to the Unification. She's killing our collective conscience, one contract at a time. Odwin is still the Gayok until his braid is found and sewn into the Gadlin Tapestry."

Note to self. When I see that symbol on his head, keep clear. Phew. This heat is getting to me. Tick, tick, tick. There go my toes tapping again. Crap!

"I'm going to be late for Dr. Tenille. Done with my headband? Thanks. Need to trick those sentinels. Gotta blister." No time for a chumbud salute. Quick highland wave and surge like the flood, with a pass by my room first.

Run run run. Run run run. Run run run. Up the Lift. Run run run. Wave the door open and … Well, if it isn't my overdazed hairy gongtrocity. "And where were you hiding? Never mind. Let's go."

Run run run. So easy. So glad I've been back on the slick. I feel great! Time to challenge myself more. Here comes the midi sun … and the heat. The pond is pumped full though, and the weedels are still packing on the weight. More algae and more woop. Hehehe. Groundskeeper fun.

It sure is busy in the orchard today. Ohhhm gee. He's staring straight at me, and waving. Wave back. Oh get a grip, girl. He's sizzling. Whoops, I mean, I'm sizzling. No time to talk. I'm already late. That is just an excuse and you know it, Elize. He is too delicious to keep ignoring. Deep eerie giggle. Check my choker. Good. Ok. Just a quick hey lo, then.

"Way, dazy girl! You look bouncy. What's the news?" Where did she come from? She's blocking my view. Move to the left. And again. Peek around the right. Then the left. He's the one I should be dancing with. Stop this side stepping, Jacinta. She looks behind herself, then faces me again, smirking. Crap! He's gone now. "So you saw someone exciting, then?"

"You scared him away."

She looks back again. "I didn't notice anyone. Crazed. Your crush is a ghost, yeah?" She wiggles her fingers. How could she not notice him? I know she has a match already, but he's so captivating. Unless … Neah, I couldn't be imagining all this, could I? Now that is crazed. "Where are you headed?"

Think up a lie, quick. "I have a pirating session, me lass. I'm applying for the URA Levels. Captain Snook is helping me prepare." The URA? Geez. That's all I came up with? Shudder. That's Father's territory.

"You made the first cut? Trip! I hear it takes at least a year to get ready. You're so focused." Focused? I wish.

"Whoops. Gotta blister. Let's do the Nook later, eh?" She mocks my highland wave and runs off. It's all juicy.

That was a close call, Elize. Your hallucinations will get you clamped. Do not listen, Elize. Your eyes are not faulty. No, just my brain, eh? *Reality is what your visions make of you, Elize. Let your heart be your guide, and your eyes shall receive what no voices can deceive. Open your heart to me, and you shall be free.*

KEETO

Day 1022: late evening

What a relief! Nine days of emotional cyclones have come to an end, Mother. I hope that it stays that way, but I fear that Eli's mind is racing to a place where I cannot follow her. Although she still is not back to her usual quick-witted fidgety self, at least she is keeping her verbal vomit down. I wish I could say the same, especially since my regurgitation is of the digestive kind. Even though Ashton assures me that his flyer bakes are indeed dead, plucked, and cooked to perfection, my midi meals at the Snack Shack appear to be developing wings inside my gut, these days. And that is not the only end they are trying to fly out of. Luckily, Eli's newfound tolerance should suppress the embarrassing declarations that would normally roll off her tongue as the scent of my composting fowl flutters by.

I wonder how long her uncharacteristically forgiving personality would last if she were to discover how Dr. Tenille is skirting the edge of malpractice — with her as the victim. Part of me wonders whether I should be privy to Eli's private disclosures without her consent, while the other, the hero within, who has vowed to do everything in my power to protect her from your fate, recognizes that if she knew, she would not be so candid in her confessions. After all, for whatever reason, she has chosen not to divulge her latest episodes to me, if you can call them that. She even lied about the medallion she wears to filter the most destructive of her sparring personalities. The mysterious token is Eli's best defense against GSU discovery, according to our trusted Captain Snook.

Theft is afoot. (Hehehe. The word does capture the essence of this newest pirating scheme.) Except that this time, the off-grid journal is coming directly to me, willingly, as opposed to from Eli sneaking about. Dr. Tenille figured that multiple visits to the archives would raise suspicions, so he decided to create self-erasing slip copies of his physician notes, and to disguise them as flyer bake wraps. This evening was the first hand-off, and I must say that you would be impressed by my budding magician's skills.

My mission, then, is to pick up after the eccentric professor at the Snack Shack, according to a predetermined schedule that he appends to the current exchange, before the cleanerbot flies in, and to perfect a switch at the recycling receptacles. If one of us is off plan, not that I would ever be of course, then the operation moves to the next date and time on the fall-back list, also appended. The man is thorough, a trait that worries me with regards to the Galleon's sails. It is only a matter of time before he finds out, but I have something else up my sleeve, which I will get to later.

First, here are the highlights and my annotations from Eli's midi appointment at the infamous cabin. The scribbles are already starting to fade, so I must focus on the key entries.

Elize is punctual — good sign. She's energized.
I conclude that she ran to make it on time —
another good sign. I also sense a pleasant

disposition — very good. She sits as directed — excellent sign. The destructive personality appears to have released her as expected — nine-day cycle complete.

A cycle? And released? Ohhhm gee. He cannot be thinking … No. They were just voices. I mean, they are just voices. Nothing more, right?

She relaxes and … Interesting shift. Her statement's intriguing: "Urgency is commitment without haste, dear mariner."

The blackouts continue, yet they're unpredictable. My response: "I don't think the blackouts are connected to your mood swings. Your mother didn't have blackouts. Something else is going on."

Maybe her mood swings are not connected to her blackouts, but certainly to her room. On my way back to my crypt, I had quickly scanned this transcription, so I headed to Van Billund Hall instead, to test out a theory. Just as I had thought; the chaos Eli had been living in for nine days had transformed into exquisite zen. Even her hybrids were frolicking around the room instead of huddling together in a corner for protection from the Eli Monster. I suspect that the themes her apparently malfunctioning room controller redecorates her room with are actually her doing, albeit subconscious. At least, she is still conscious during her personality shifts.

Lucid or not, I am still concerned about the amount of

time Eli spends revisiting old memory flashes, lost in our childhood. Perhaps it is a coping strategy. She had spent most of the afternoon in the personal viewing tent I had gifted her on our nineteenth birthday, looking for some sort of clues that will help her find something. She can try to hide it from me, but I know what she is still obsessed with. I have had my nose buried in them ever since you left us. Did she not give up on finding that retched figment of a book in her head? She has enough to deal with. Well, at least she is not drawing attention to herself, creating mountains in the archives.

While Eli's paranoia builds over the counselor, in light of Stitch's findings and her feelings of being stalked by him, when I am in her room, my eyes keep wandering toward the stand Cyd is perched on. I feel strangely attached to it beyond mere appreciation of its historical significance, as I do for most other antiques. When it broke a while back, part of me cracked inside as well. Maybe Mr. G remembers its origins. In any case, that room of hers is the one I wish we had flashes of, in addition to Dr. Tenille's notes. Speaking of which … Where was I? Oh, yeah.

> *Elize offers: "Perhaps she chose not to share them. In the darkest of times, one can always choose." — Possible, however I was recording Monique's brain waves and the data is stored at the URA headquarters. The technology was experimental at the time. We might be able to access them now that Vincent is no longer the director. The new director*

Crap! The sentences must be fading already. I digressed too long.

I counteroffer: "The new URA director was a student of mine. Your father had ordered brain scans on your mother, but I have no permissions to the data. Perhaps you could apply as an assistant and get the proper clearance."

Whoa! Does he mean to send her to Ministburg? Eli must have been topped up right then. I hope the Orangugong stayed quiet.

Elize remains calm, not at all rattled. "You mean to send me to Kabaakhmaan?" — Interesting. How can she know this? Ministburg has not been referred to as Kabaakhmaan since

When? Since when? Geez. I have to write faster.

Elize agrees to accompany me to the secret URA remote access lab tomorrow, provided she is still calm, and to keep its location between us. She apologizes for the past 9 days. — Good. Memory still intact.

Onto Elize's dreams. Still the same. Nightmares, tapping, ticking clock, sense of urgency upon waking. Nothing more. No recollection of details. Image flashes, feelings, shadows only. No faces. — Unusual. She should see their faces by now.

Their faces? There was no mention in his journal that you saw specific faces in your nightmares, Mother. He knows more than he is letting on. Crap! The slip is fading fast. Here is a highlighted section.

> *Dreamcatcher!!! Not one she wears. A large one. She hangs it on her window. She jokes about evil spirits, wiggling her fingers. A gift from her mother. Refuses to bring it — high concern. Must*

… must keep him away from Eli's dreamcatcher. He is much too interested in it. I need her to confide in me on this point, at least. Perhaps sharing my gondola trip with Caroline might entice reciprocity. Eli talked about testing Caroline's loyalty today, so I did. Now Eli will have a chance to show hers.

The detour on campus made me late for my evening rendezvous with Caroline at Tir-na-nog. I found her sitting, poised, her long curvy thighs crossed, swinging her leg, on the edge of the jade fountain, with a coy smile, but I know better by now. The moment I was within range, she leaned back and splashed me as punishment for making her wait, giggling of course. My apologies met with more water lashes until I fully repented. She grabbed my hand, pulled me to the first free gondola, and we paddled out of ear shot.

Ever since the counselor had her expelled from Schrödinger University, Caroline has held odd jobs, like the one at the sweet shop that changed my relationship with bonbons forever. Hmmm. Let me regroup here.

After a few mischievous adventures likely intended to solidify a friendship, she cut off communications, then we caught her shadowing us, even as far as the granite flats just outside Albaraaton. And shortly after that, she popped into our lives again as if we were chumbuds, denying it all, then off she went once more without as much as a mock highland wave, until she reappeared a couple of months ago. Although her presence in Eadonberg is still sporadic, she now seems more communicative, at least with me. Our mini cruise around the floating glass courtyard was to be her opportunity to make amends.

I truly want to trust her, or experience trust itself, but her relationship with Sothese may be more than just the recreational romp she claims it to be. Dare I extrapolate from her cavalier attitude that she could be using each and every one of us for her own entertainment? She has come a long way from the giggly girl who dared Eli into the Restricted Sector's underground club, and captivated both Stitch and me, with her thighs, I mean, her eyes. Hehehe. Freudian slip.

My true intentions are obviously not as innocent as I presume them to be. I wish I could blame Nathruyu for provoking my first cool sweat with those gemstone eyes of hers, but time is the temptress to whom I am succumbing. After tonight, no longer can my fascination with Caroline's playfulness masquerade as highland cultural curiosity. As confounded by her as I now feel, this much is clear. I must find a way to draw her away from Sothese, whether Eli remains open to giving her another chance or not. Plan A is to use the Galleon's sails as bait.

The guilt I harbor over stealing them was about to be compounded with a lie. As the moon rose over the lavender waterways Caroline and I were traveling on, so did my courage, despite the gurgling I was sure was following us around. I started with a true story about Sothese's new officials coming into the Round Room and then an artifact disappearing right afterwards. Then I twisted the missing granite pyramid into a canvas made of historically significant fabric. Their loss having compromised the relationship the Museum of Antiquities has with a major donor was a fact, but I made sure to omit where the canvas came from, or that they were actually sails. Since Caroline has never had dealings with Dr. Tenille, the ruse was believable.

With the promise of a good word on her behalf to Mme Beaudoin and the curator, and a possible job offer at the museum, the prospect of success admittedly excited me. I had expected Caroline to tease me with descriptions of late night cataloging sessions in the artifacts room, but instead, she stared out past the southern horizon, where the biowall holds our water city from pouring into the ocean, as her eyes filled with tears and I with fears, fears about what she would share, and fears about what I would do.

Just as I was about to reach over to her, she took a deep breath and told me that she regretted all that had happened. She wanted to make things right because she knew that Eli was in danger. "Because of the counselor" I blurted out, but Caroline refuted my accusations of complicity. The counselor had apparently asked her to befriend and to watch Eli; however, he did not account for how quickly Caroline's rascality would entice the rebel out of my adventurous twin. We exchanged a flirty smile as we reminisced about the night we first met.

The sun had already dropped behind the Restricted Sector by the time I directed the conversation towards Sothese and a hunch that has been plaguing me ever since my run-in with the Ministry goons in the archives. It even seemed that the canal was echoing the thoughts bubbling in my mind, so I decided to test the waters, metaphorically speaking. I would not dare touch the bioluminescent slime coating the waterways although Caroline kept daring me to. So, I dared her back.

I am relieved to report, for a second time tonight, that Caroline's carefree cavorting with Sothese appears to be in distress. She has agreed to be the front person for Stitch's new remote transcriptor technology and a button swap with a vintage Gadlin ceremonial coat that she had gifted him for an anniversary was her creative addition to the surveillance plan. Once we landed the gondola at its mooring post, Caroline passed me a flash of the jacket, hugged me, and sent me to Mr. G's shop to pick up another one, while she hurried off in the other direction. At the shop, I ensured that the buttons matched the ones on the image, kept the chitchat to a minimum, and managed to pass it off to Stitch before curfew, so that he could work his magic on the bottom button I had ripped off.

If there is one thing I admire about our hip-jiggling chum with a zigazillion pockets, it is his lightning speed synaptic network. He certainly gets to the soul of everything, as he calls it, faster than anyone I have ever met. At dawn tomorrow, the spy button will be ready for its first deployment, and Caroline will be … Anyway, I can practice releasing judgment about

Stitch first, by acknowledging his devotion to Odwin and the escaped Gadlin loyalists.

In all fairness, the boy genius does live by the six values he shares with Sakari. It is my childish competitive insecurities that are to blame for the jabs and undercuts to his character. The fact that he rolls with my restrained form of verbal vomit, projected in his general direction, plainly shows who is one up on the evolutionary scale — at the moment. Not me.

While Stitch has moved past the harrowing Ministburg Lockdown escape and is looking towards an even bigger challenge —Wakanda, the images of would-be Gadlins burnt to a crisp will not turn to dust in my mind. Maybe it has to do with Sakari's warning to her son, Stitch not me, while my heart wants so desperately to heed the forewarnings I know you have, Mother, with no secret channel to voice them on, at least not on this plane.

The planet is warming up. The Gadlin rescue barge captains triple confirmed ocean temperature measurements along their entire route. The failing generators are just the symptom of impending doom.

As horrifying as news of an extinction level Ministry cover-up is, the fedora sporting jailbreak informant is the one responsible for the fireball that is slow-roasting my stomach from the inside. As I read Sakari's report over Stitch's shoulder, hallucinations of three F's carved into the palms of the Gadlin survivors, sending out secret virtual chumbuds salutes, covered Stitch's board. Searing pain and absolute terror overshadow all other memories from that near-death experience in the shafts.

This enigmatic ally of Sakari's has the hair on my arms

electrified. He knew enough about the three officials and their plasma show to load massive quantities of radiation burn herbal infusion onto the rescue barges. He is able to withstand enormous amounts of heat, and according to the few personal accounts I have read, radiation has no effect on him. And, coincidentally, he uses a fedora to obscure his face.

If paranoia is contagious, then Stitch's efforts to reassure me were no cure. The flashes he had taken at Almedina Square would have unmasked the stranger for us, but a quick snap into the viewer produced nothing recognizable. All the images from the night Nathruyu took down Sothese's creepy three were a jumbled mess. The best that we can do now is to hope that there is a way to realign all the bits.

Eli might finally be calm, but I am far from it. Still not knowing where and when the fedora man will appear next, and even what he looks like, is not the only cause. I drift in and out of a state of unease, as I did the time I was zapped by the granite pyramid. I am not sure what these new Ministry goons hit me with in the artifacts room, but my brain is still reeling from it.

The charge must have thrown my homeostasis completely out of balance. I just have to wait it out. Yet, underneath all this anxiety, there is still another feeling, a feeling I cannot find any words to describe. Intense wakefulness is the closest I can get. After all the running around from one accomplice to the next, I would have expected the opposite, but something else calls me to the night. The apprentice blood hound is breaking curfew again, so down goes my quill. Transcriptor on.

Time to blister. Testing. Check. All good. Let's do this.

(gurgling)

What is that? Grody! There must be a generator explosion again. The heat blobs are going to create patches of dead lotuses. The water is bubbling. Ugh. And the smell.

(running, gurgling)

Eek! What *is* that? Just my imagination. Just my imagination. Please, just my imagination. Sheiss!

(intense gurgling, splashing, new sound)

Run faster. There. At the Gardens sajadum now … where was I supposed to w-w-whoa!

Transcriptor off. (new voice)

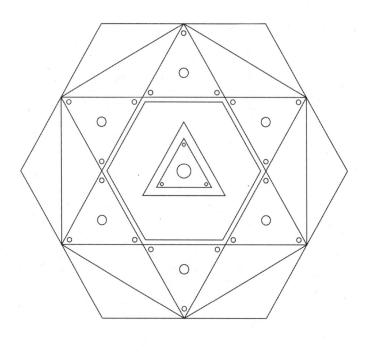

CHAPTER THREE

SOTHESE

Day 1023: sunrise

Abundance flows freely to the one who can artfully entice the hunters with pay for prey, yet when a lamb controls the game, the wolves turn on each other.

Sothese watches on in disgust as the false prophet guzzles his morning tonic, repulsed by the ritual he, the true seer, initiated and reluctantly allows to continue. The slurp and burp affair at Ministry Mansion offends his aristocratic sensibilities; nevertheless, the charade advances the day of reckoning that was forcefully postponed while the blue viscous elixir, oozing from the Cup of They, pickles the Pramam's otherwise deteriorating DNA. As much as Sothese wills the infant vermis placebo a sudden reprieve to nestle safely inside the holy conduit designed to draw it to its death by digestion, the only damming scheme in progress, at the moment, is the one directed at the schemer instead.

The second set of candidates for his replacement hounds has unequivocally disappeared in a manner that should raise the microscopic scales on Sothese's skin. If fear were an emotion he could feed from his own thoughts, rather than vicariously as wanton gratification, he would redirect a portion of the energy that he expends avenging the liberation of his traitorous officials into finding the mastermind behind the sudden deaths of all his prospective hires.

However, Sothese lives behind a veneer of insatiable human flesh that constantly craves stimulation. Those he chases are always a means to more intense sensations, driven by a burning desire to feel. Playing sleuth to insignificant dead applicants simply cannot compete with titillating revenge, of which two opportunities present themselves: one, a somewhat satisfying tit for tat; the other, the ultimate eye for an eye contest with none other than the self-proclaimed leader of the Unification himself. Sothese must find the twins first.

Without an entourage to blind any unsavory contenders, excursions become a beacon to those who can interfere with his aspirations. Humanity has not yet evolved to accept his kind, especially considering that Sothese aims at world domination. The panic that would travel the oceans would only license the Pramam to implement further GMU and GHU "global security" infringements, thus creating drudgery for Sothese. Fortunately, there are those who will stand in opposition no matter what, so that he may ease his way into the center of power. Regardless, the scenario is unlikely and suboptimal, given that he now can identify both twins on sight, while the Pramam knows only the one face, the girl's.

A silk cloth falls to the ground with the impression of the Pramam's rejuvenated lips. Sothese licks an attendant's toned buttocks with his eyes as the servile youth, at his master's request, enters the room to collect the soiled handkerchief and empty vessel. Lustful whispers waft past the servant's departure, teasing Sothese's focus away from the daily briefing session about to begin. To his eternal delight, the advisory role does attract inviting ways to experiment beyond the conventional medical one that the so-called Holy Messenger obsesses over. Harassment is a gentle term for the badgering Sothese has endured at the break of every dawn since the recent rash of child kidnappings that Nathruyu is the scapegoat for.

Flashes of a black-pitted face, gagging with a chokehold squeezing her trachea at arm's length, safely administered through a customized clamping device lest he soil his regal complexion, of course, partially compensate for the messy surgical trial and error on the juicy little brains. Ten days ago, he was happy to report success, at last, and now news that the orphaned boy is recovering well. The blood pounds through Sothese's chest in preparation for the private celebration he has scheduled back in Eadonberg tonight as he re-enters the space where time stands still.

The occasional praise Sothese receives is wasted flattery. The control he has promised to the Pramam in his quest for immortality is illusory, and this ambitious right-hand man is forcefully biting his tongue, in an effort to conceal treachery from the expectant simpleton. Besides, the twins are surely not at peace with the latest victim's disappearance, considering the sizable risks they had taken in order to protect the child from the famed twisted brain collector.

SOTHESE

The deactivating sajadum withdraws the smokey amethyst glow infusing the shallow water pool at the mezzanine level courtyard of Ministry House as Sothese forces a half-bow to the Pramam's dimming holographic presence and retreats to his quarters for the night. Now that the SIF is no longer in charge, the hound and hawk games will in fact continue, in spite of the Ministry head's condescension in regards to Sothese's and Nathruyu's charged relationship. A slow kill will be the prize for his prowess.

Sothese's heels click to the beat of an antique timepiece down the marble hallway, towards a door left ajar around the bend. Surprise shapes a crooked smile with his lips when he enters the den where delicacies take the form of sensual embroilments. Sitting on the edge of his bed is a young woman with long silky dark hair tied back in a pony tail and wearing a lovely pleated dress. She has returned with a message sizzling with forbidden rapture.

The tension rises from deep within his body. Sothese slips past his visitor, watching her closely, as he pours a glass of pure water from the crystal fountain against the adjacent wall. He presents it to her as a token for the gift he is sure to receive.

His lascivious eyes lock onto hers. She tips the entire glass over to let the cool liquid drain down her face. Tantalizing revelations appear under the misty river that rushes over her cotton dress. He, too, can sense the heat that provokes salacious thoughts leading to libidinous actions, but physical entanglement is not the impelling force that drove this angelic creature into Sothese's realm … at least not yet. His smile puckers in a moment of prurient contemplation.

As it was on the night of the first experiment in cell 18E at Osler Hall, ending with a dead girl on a slab and a pool of blood at his feet, Nathruyu is, once again, the body on offer. Sothese releases his mind to her words sounding the alarm that only his magnificence can answer.

"The predator has stolen another child. In two days, at noon, you will find her at the Snack Shack in the Central Core. She will not be alone. The twins you seek are invited."

"Delicious! I quiver with excitement. Have you not already sensed it?"

"I have."

"Mouthwatering rewards abound for those who share more deeply. Does this prospect evoke a craving for something wet to cool the flesh, my most welcome, uninvited guest?"

"I come for an oral exchange, nothing more."

The innuendos lose none of their potency against the backdrop of seduction that Sothese is painting inside his cheeks with his tongue. The delectable stranger watches, in silence, while the heat rises between them, then she departs as quietly as she had appeared, leaving Sothese to savor the moisture still saturating his mouth.

▲ ▲ ▲

Back in his Eadonberg quarters, risks are commonplace. Informants are varied and plentiful for a price, but one with such an icy resolve, one who can withstand the primordial fire breathing behind the emerald gemstone eyes that beckon his sexual prey with a come-hither overture is a precious asset to own. Therein lies an irresistible challenge for the lord, who can dismember a king with a jab, and a twist, and a flick of the wrist.

The same is untrue, however, with regards to the overly Rubenesque Gayok and the red-headed tease, who is the star in his well-stocked library of skin flashes. Sothese tires of predictable conquests, despite the occasional resistance that adds flavor to their eventual and expected compliance. This new conveyor of secrets is an enigma whose boldness rivals the fears Sothese believes she would be wise to listen to. As he lies naked on his bed, he massages her translucent pop-up likeness posing on the holoslip yesterday's Albaraaton visit produced in ways worthy of the Unified condemnation at which he scoffs.

The daring darling is no child, and neither is Sothese. The Pramam would serve himself best if he treated his most influential agent with due respect, for the infant that once was Anabelle's pride is not the source of his longevity.

▼ ▼ ▼

Sothese snatches a white lotus petal, bobbing to the sound of gentle cooing, from the determined talons skimming the surface of the baptismal pond, where propriety cloaks Wakanda's suspicions with an abrupt Gadlin acknowledgment while Odwin, the unwitting defendant, maintains the prominent position he has earned serving as advisor to the leader of the Coalition — Anabelle, the mother of the newborn.

The air smacks of heartache, anger, and distrust, the

perfect stew of emotions for a silent hunter to strike. Sothese winds his way past the formalities and retreats to one of the guest rooms until the ceremony concludes and the multi-faith spiritual leaders collect their laughable props. He has his own welcome party planned for the child who would be leader, but he needs a trusted accomplice to assist in the process. The athletic beauty, wistfully steadfast at Odwin's side, is the one he has long desired to corrupt from within, and today her warrior resolve is especially invigorating.

Murmurs down the hall, followed by a terse "Honor the Gayokcy, Wakanda" and the sound of a door sliding shut ever so forcefully, expose the closet allegations that question the paternal source of the babe's DNA. Sothese pokes his head into the corridor and smirks. The view from behind is exquisitely tailored by the formal Gadlin attire, whose wearer stands as a mannequin discarded to roast behind a sun-drenched display case.

If the man is oblivious to the desires that his loyal apprentice has buried for the sake of their feeble Gayokcy, the masquerader with the candy-red hair and emerald eyes certainly is not. His intentions send a beam up her spine that turns her gaze towards him as he leans his back against the open door of his bedroom and widens his pupils. Frustrated by lack of emotional and physical reciprocity, she accepts.

Wakanda's youth and naivety become the playground for Sothese's compulsions. What a climatic victory it is to tame the graceful warrior, whose effortless mastery has defended the Gadlin Creed with such gifted finesse. Sothese now controls the rivalry between Anabelle and the muffled virgin clawing at his bed sheets. A final guttural discharge, and the fate of humanity will soon be his.

▲ ▲ ▲

Deep are the urges that have driven Sothese to ever intensifying liberties, many of which as of late are reluctantly accorded. However, the tension suits him well. All the more to release in an explosion of sensation, would you not agree? If the Pramam only knew how much of his precious Unification was compromised, he would not invent collusions. He would not be secretly plotting to double-cross the hand that feeds him. Perhaps some public evidence would serve as a subtle warning to the Holy Messenger? Sothese plays model with his vintage Gadlin ceremonial coat and meanders the underwater ventilation shafts for some entertainment.

Activity from above moves in the direction of the prearranged appointment. The door creeks shut, the bolt slides over, the key turns, and thunder rocks the flooring towards the hidden hatch. Sothese leans against the shaft wall, his left hand under the back of his coat, humming an old Gadlin lullaby just as a man sporting a fedora drops into view, momentarily euphoric, then honking his disdain. Sothese's ears record the conversation and the upwelling rumbles from the ocean floor, recoiling from the metal shaft walls.

"Were you expecting someone else?"

"A father's hope never dies, Sothese."

"And the truth never lies."

"What do you know of truth? You are not the source of it.

Incidentally, where did you acquire that garment?"

"My sources, as are yours, are a matter of privacy. You would not be a Gadlin sympathizer now, would you, Gibayze?"

"What are you really here for, Sothese? And alone, I sense."

"Good help is hard to come by. I am in the market. Any recommendations?"

"You are not like me. I do not deal with *their* kind."

"I agree. I am nothing like you, Gibayze. But *their* kind created lockdown meltdown, have you not heard? TALK! Where are you hiding Nathruyu?"

Disbelief turns to jubilation as the question ricochets through the shafts. Herein fades another fact withheld for the greater mission, no doubt. Sothese chuckles at the strings Anubrat continues to pull on his little marionettes. Does Gibayze even know about the clones?

"You are being played, Gibayze. All of you are. To what does Anubrat owe your loyalty? An empty promise? Walk with me." Gibayze hesitates, but news of Nathruyu's talent at Almedina Square relaxes his distrust enough for a cautious stroll. "She came to save me. Whose loyalties lie with whom now?" The trap is set. "You are blinded by lust, as you always have been."

"And you are one to talk, Sothese."

"Indeed. Perhaps I *was* the one to talk. You may want to discuss that with Siufflah." Anger's charge is the thrill Sothese was seeking, and its instrument is on the attack.

"I know what you want, and your bid to divide will bring you eternal darkness. You are not your brother, and you never will be."

Sothese summons the rage that he was saving for another and unleashes it onto Gibayze in an ingenious plan to expose the infection he has thus far worked diligently to obscure. The famous mosquibot invasion was a deployment of the URA under Sothese's command and was therefore tuned to ordinary human EMF signatures without traceable biochips, such as the Gadlins. The GHU had simply hosted Nathruyu in their facilities without staff access to her or to her medical records. The SIF agents, with whom her body double currently resides, are fiercely loyal to the Pramam and have sworn to secrecy about Nathruyu's origins. But all that is about to change with the chaos Sothese is delirious to orchestrate, right here, right now, with Gibayze as bait.

Out comes the weapon that had turned Nathruyu into a black-pitted shivering mass, to reduce Gibayze to the same. Out comes a neck clamp on a chain to yank him topside and drag him through the space where time stops and onto the central corridor at the north end of the city. And out goes an emergency GHU message: "code 333 at the Purity drop" before he completes the task with a move that will surely dispatch a cleaner from the SIF, camping on the GHU emergency frequency.

Gibayze wails out the burn that shreds his intestines with the hooked dagger Sothese adores. A few globules escape into the night sky while Sothese rushes to stuff his victim's shirt into the gushing wound, then races across a bridge and into an empty sajadum to watch his handiwork usher in an era of fear across the world. The GHU craft beats the SIF decoy to the murder scene, as expected, but the red slider crashes upon lift off. Sothese curses in the shadows. His victim escapes, as beautiful as a marbled god, leaving all medics dead, by complete organ failure with no puncture wounds. Sothese is livid.

The cleaner will arrive soon. Sothese spots a few floaters, snatches a vial from inside the craft, scoops up the drops, documents the scene, and transmits the data to the GHU admissions department, within the blink of a human eye. He kicks the fallen fedora at the northern water purification coil and sniggers as the water turns to fire and vanishes. The frozen void is the route he takes back to Ministry House to wash up for his night cap.

✂ ✂ ✂

Salacious Caroline is the perfect remedy for a stressful day's work. His intemperate lifestyle, still handicapped by the lack of suitable officials to balance his energies, demands a quick touch up by the generator level lest he put his favorite diversion at risk. Besides, he must distance himself from the DNA that the GHU now has in its possession.

The presence Sothese senses as he enters his quarters is not the seductress with the disheveled ginger bun kneeling on his bed, whose familiar allure is not coincidental after all. The hallway curtains may not have eyes that can witness the coming addition to his skin flash library, but they do camouflage other much more potent senses that he would be thoughtless not to arouse. Tonight he speaks his lecherous performance for the shadows to enjoy, live.

SOTHESE

"You know Anubrat."

"I don't *know* Anubrat."

"Not everything I say is sexual, my little nymph."

"I know of him, but I don't know him." Caroline giggles. She draws Sothese over to her and slowly unbuttons the coat she had gifted him. He pushes her away, removes it himself, and whips it at her chest, vainglorious.

"Wear it! No, wait." He jams her against him, grinds her into the wall beside the open door, and rips the GHU uniform off her. "You have been keeping secrets from me. You have known her for almost three years."

"Who are you talking about?"

"Your little dazing friend." The giggles turn nervous as Sothese flips her over and rakes the nape of her neck with his teeth. Her sapphire blue eyes wet themselves with fear.

"Wear it! Show me your impression of a Gayok." Caroline complies with a reverse striptease, shaping figure eights with her butt against his pelvis as she smooths her hands down the front of her new persona. He orders her to kick her blue sapphire shoes out the open door and shifts his eyes to the undulating drapery across the hallway.

"Tonight, I condense those three years into three minutes. Enjoy!" He yanks her off the wall by the hair, bends her torso over and into the hallway, and thrusts her into an extended reenactment of Wakanda's courtyard defilement, empowered by the GMU guards watching from the top of the spiral staircase to the mezzanine.

"Sothese. It's too hard. You're hurting me. Please, it's too hard."

E L I Z E

Tell me about my demons. Can you really catch my dreams, my nightmares?

Alas, it is simply a window ornament, except … Perhaps there is something about it. I remember sitting on the transport back from Albaraaton nearly two years ago and … and then nothing. I blanked out. Nevertheless, Dr. Tenille shows unusual interest in acquiring it. My intuition tells me to keep it safe, yet … *Think, Elize.* It is just a keepsake. Correction. Not just. It was Mother's last gift. I risked our escape from the highlands to return for it. Think, think, think. I could show him, but no touching. Yes, that seems appropriate.

Such beautiful strings. They look like purple gems. The sun reflecting off the amethyst towers of Osler Hall makes them twinkle.

In all honesty, do I want to be known to the URA? I feel safe and calm in this serene space. The feeling is such a huge shift from the hors-category tornado I was lost in. I was spinning out of control for over a week, and sucking everyone around me into a big black hole of negativity. What chaos! And what if Keeto is correct and Father actually works at the secret URA in Eadonberg, not Ministburg like the Ministry claims? Truth no longer exists. Still, I must learn to trust my inner voice. Hmmm, I must be more specific. Trust the wise one … and maybe the scatterbrain one … sometimes … but definitely not the bent one. *All voices have their place, Elize, but judgment has not.*

Deep breath in. Deep breath out. Deep breath in. Deep breath out. Deep breath in. Deep breath out. Giggles. My hybrids are in a trance even without smoking anything smelly. More giggles! Levity lifts the spirit. *Live the vision that you ask, and all the good shall come to pass, Elize.*

Decided. We go. Here. Pop the dreamcatcher in your … Of course. Mallets for hands. Let me help. Hop on, Rango! We are going for a plane. Slip on the booties and slide to the lift.

"Good morning, Shaplo. Early rise?" Interesting. He appears confused. Highland wave and out into the lobby. Slide by the guard, highland wave, and out the door and into the he —

Brrr. The ventilation has kicked in again. No matter. The race up the central canal will warm us up. Best stick to the path until I learn all the features. Knees slightly bent, and skim the stone to the north ga —

He is still walking the orchard? In all honesty! I have a right mind to — *I think a conversation is in order, Elize.* Yes. That would be productive.

"Up early, Miss Elize." He beat my hesitation.

"And you, Counselor? A lovely cool day to test out my new planing booties and get some exercise before class." Show him a twirl. He is staring at my neck. Oh yes. The choker.

"I prefer the serenity of a brisk walk amongst the juicy citrus." Every morning, it seems. He smiles at his reference to highland slang. Smile back. *Conceal your suspicions, Elize. The time will come for questions.*

Pardon me, Counselor. Permission to touch me has not been granted. Calmly shift left. Rango cowers but not fast enough. He shivers. He squirms. Restrain his hidden mallets. The gong is not necessary at the moment. He must require recalibration. No matter. Breathe in. Breathe out. Smile. The counselor's presence is strangely soothing. Perhaps I judged incorrectly.

"Your journey awaits, Miss Elize. Enjoy the clarity before the fog rolls in." In more ways than one, I would add. A quick courteous bow, then off to the north. Gather speed in the perimeter woods, and airlift off the crest of the Victory Bridge. Simply divine! Here comes the Central Core drop and … perfect landing. Full stop. No need to squeeze so tightly, little mammasack.

Here comes the fog, on the left, right on schedule. Time to speed. The blowers always delay a bit. Right leg slightly back. Knees bent. Lean forward. Left arm in front. Right arm back. Focus forward. Balance. Now you can squeeze tight, Rango. One, two, three, deep breath in, and push off.

Glide. Push. Glide. Push. Glide into complete silence. Floral scented vines form a canopy over the floating granite walkway. The milky lavender waterscape melds into an ancient forest. My legs lengthen behind me with every stride. Each burst from my thighs crushes the ground into a spray of ice crystals that urge me onwards, faster, smoother, effortless, skating on a frozen stream. Feel the vibrations of the silent chanting whoosh by. More speed. Inhale the blur of exquisite colors, the intoxicating fragrance. Glide. Push. Glide. Push. Glide.

What are these graceful creatures that bound in stride at my flanks, staring at me with their large black eyes, inquisitive, intelligent, gentle? We head for the thunderous falls with a sharp left turn, together, as one. Their hearts race in pace with my own. This is the world my nightmares cannot see, the world my voices do not speak of, the world that used to be. I am one with the herd. The rumbles deepen. The mist thickens. Antlers rush by in waves of fading forms. They disappear into the past … Full stop. No time. Swerve into the brume. Worlds collide. A fawn crashes … splashes … I land safely on a floating holoadvert to the barely audible insults of a slidercab driver. His front blowers are deafening. Release the chokehold, Rango. All is safe. Hand up to the holoadvert vying for my attention.

"What the sheiss! Are you some overdazed …? Give me one good reason not to use my scanner to report you. You should have a license for those things. I almost killed you. Sheiss, *I* could have crashed."

"And it would have been my doing, sir. Fortunately, fate has chosen a different path for both of us. I appreciate your superior sliding skills. You are a driver worth the hire in coin." Hand up to the holoadvert again.

"Next time. Look before you cross." He turns down his blowers and the mist rushes into the space his vehicle had occupied. Adrenaline rush, work your way out quickly. Good. Now back onto the east-west corridor.

"Come back again, Miss …" Elize? Did I just hear the holoadvert say my name? I am starting to question reality. Best slow down until I can master a high-speed full stop. Pull out the paper map Dr. Tenille gave me. The URA satellite lab is off-grid so X marks the spot. Giggles. A Captain Snook treasure hunt. And the inferno builds again.

There is the location. Interesting. Double-check the map. Yes, this is the right place. Perhaps it is a decoy sajadum. If not, then I suppose I will be taking my calm to the next level, not that I want to be one of those re-birthed Unified freaks. *Judgment, Elize.*

Crap. A retina scan. *Propriety, Elize.* Yes. Yes. Ye —

"Ahoy, me Belle." He squints his left eye and leans in. "Any scallywags?"

"All clear, Captain." So we wait for—

"Fire in the hole!" In earnest! Quite the drop. The smoke screen is being sucked out now. Down in the ventilation shafts?

"It all happens below deck, me lass?" Giggles. The pirating spirit, as always. "But you're the only crew here, so let's speak their language." Excellent idea. Giggles, but not from me. "Good morning, Director Shakti."

"Good morning, Dr. Tenille. And a pleasure to meet you, Miss Elize." The director looks so young. She has noticed my squashed frog face at her youth. "I was a gifted student."

"A prodigy, in fact." I sense some pride in his comment, and some discomfort on her end.

The director quickly changes the subject. "This is the back entrance. The smoke screen you both went through is to disorient you. Follow me."

The walls look like the other shafts I have been in. Although the air is fresh. No toxic gases. So this is not part of the cooling network. A door slides open. That is one unhappy greeter. Well, there is a lack of sunshine down here. Director Shakti whispers something to the guard, who then flickers a light at her colleague one level down. A pod rises and we step in. Dr. Tenille motions me to remove my Orangugong. The spinning starts. What a ride! Our backs are pasted to the walls, and still we spin. More disorientation, I assume. I will refrain from flyer bakes today.

I can see now why Dr. Tenille wanted to make sure my Elize Monster was locked in a safe corner of my mind for this trip. My Orangugong is spread against the centrifuge wall as well, shivering. "Serenity, Rango." The director peeks over. "Timid mammasack." She chuckles.

I am not sure whether we are moving or not. I think we are. "Which direction are we heading?" Or even facing? We could even be upside down for all I know. The lights are dimming.

"I can't tell you." Luckily I brought a slipmap. If I can reach it. There. Oh. I forgot. No link. "The shafts are shielded." I knew that, but she does not know I do, and neither does Dr. Tenille. That was an opportune memory lapse I can bank on for a future alibi.

"Are we under water or under land?"

"I can't tell you."

"How about: are we still in the city?"

She shrugs and raises her eyebrows. I see. Only barely though. She cannot tell me anything. "It's best if you don't know, just in case."

In case I want to escape, perhaps? Gulp.

Crap! Whoops. I know. Language. But Father! I should have never come. There is something not right between these two. I can feel it. I do not like being in the dark. I should have listened to my brother. Caution is not paranoia. Think, think, think. How do I protect myself, just in case? Yes, Director Shakti, just in case. The pod is slowing down. Deep breath in. Deep breath out. Face plant. Ouch. Gong. And Rango too. Giggles.

"Your brain will spin for a little while longer. Let me help you." Giggles and more giggles. Nonstop giggles. "That will pass, as well." Looking for my sea legs. Giggles. There. Oh oh. Mammasack attack in the works.

"In his defense, he is loyal to his mistress. Over here, my mischievous hybrid, before you get into trouble."

"This way to the decontamination cell … Dr. Tenille? Are you well?"

"Rango! Come back here —" Gasp. My dreamcatcher! Good boy. Hand stand on the mallets and nab it with your toes. Stare down the would-be thief. Thou shalt not covet thy crew's effects. We do have an understanding, do we not? Good. The director is none the wiser. Close call. I should have never brought the dreamcatcher with me. He wants to take it. That was lust in his eyes. The pirate wants some booty.

"After you, Elize." I think not.

"Please. You lead the way, Dr. Tenille." I have your back now. Here comes the air blast and here we are. Eyes sharp. My heart is racing. Check the hallways as we walk. Is it just me or is it very warm in here? Waiting for a shuttle. Toes, stop tapping, please. In we go. "Are we there yet?" Chuckles from the director.

"I felt the same way my first visit as director. Here's the lab you will be working in." Will? I thought it was an interview. Dr. Tenille winks at me. Interesting. Should I be grateful or suspicious? *Gratitude is the path to enlightenment, Elize.* If that means answers, then grateful it is. "Welcome to the Senescence Center."

"And all these quasi-dead biological parts are patients here?"

She laughs. "That's one way of looking at it." She gestures with her hand and a holographic DNA strand appears. "This is the area we are interested in."

"The telomeres? You are looking to create the other kind of DNA?" Confused looks are upon me. "Do Not Age."

"Brilliant humor, Elize. I will enjoy working with you. Eternity is alluring, but for now, we're experimenting with the cap of 27 to 36 years. The onset is more abrupt in humans than in other lifeforms. Even hybrids live longer, relatively speaking."

"Elders live longer. How does their DNA compare?"

"The elders don't partake in GHU screenings. They have special immunity granted by the Pramam. And matches between elders and non-elders are strictly forbidden."

The Ministry is breeding longevity? Interesting theory, Dr. Tenille, but Father is an elder and Mother was not, at least I thought she was not.

"Then why is the Ministry not funding this work? Wouldn't the Pramam want to keep his super-humans alive and the rest of us on a time bomb?" Well? Deciphering eyeball ping-pong is not a skill of mine. Dr. Tenille nods to Director Shakti.

"This was your father's secret project." In earnest! "The

Pramam is clueless." And if Zafarian were here, he would agree. One moment, please.

"The Pramam appointed you to the URA after—" Sheiss! And hush on the language lessons. I have to run. Which way? Down this hall, I think. Dead end. This way. No. Down there. Run run run. Trapped. That way. NO! There they are. Keep running.

"Stop! Eli, please. Let us explain." No bounty for you, Captain Snook. Where is that hick shuttle?! *Elize, you must*— Not now. *Yes, now. Fear is not your savior, Elize.* Stop, breathe, and think. They are coming. Hear them speak. "Your father is gone. No one knows where he is."

"Why did you bring me here?"

"For answers. Your answers." I wish I had some, but all I have are questions. Always more questions.

"You can help us with this project."

"As bait to find my father? Can you not find another elder to donate a blood sample to monitor that one over time? Or just acquire it?" Treason is what you will be clamped for, in any case. I can only imagine the purpose of the research was not exactly honorable.

"We have one." Dr. Tenille looks straight at me. I knew it! And I wager he knows that I know so I might as well.

"And are all elders infatuated with dreamcatchers?"

He smiles. "No. Just this one." And the director it seems. Decided. A quick peek, but no touching. "Fascinating." Long enough. Back in the pack it goes. "What do you make of it, Corrient?"

"I've seen it before." And ... "I was a bit of a troublemaker as a child. Sitting still was not my forte. Listening to my parents wasn't either." It sounds like Dr. Tenille can relate. I know I can. "The gifted ones were always flying wild. I had a few adventures in the Exchange Sector."

"In Albaraaton." Oh oh. "Your home town, right?" Good save.

"Yes. That symbol on your dreamcatcher has shown up a few times, but on something else." Could she know about the artifact? Or maybe there are other things. *Not all knowledge belongs to humanity, Elize. Be careful what you share, and who you share with.* Noted.

"That is all interesting and all, but back to dreams of eternal life. Show me my father's DNA."

One moment, please. That looks wrong. One, two, three. Three extra chromosome pairs! But not really. They have no receptors on them. That means they do not replicate ... but those cells would eventually die. All of them would. "How?" They are thinking the same thing.

"We don't know. The body hardly changes, then at the age of 81, there's a systemic cellular breakdown. All elders die at 81. It's like a time bomb." Dr. Tenille clears his throat. "But Dr. Tenille's blood is different even though ... That's the midi rush starting." So we are still in the city. "You'd better get back, Elize. Can you show her out safely, D-d-doctor ?" She winks at me. So it seems that she is secretly tuning in to Trimorphic Rhythms' p-p-pop m-m-music while she works. Giggle.

"Quickly, me Belle."

Meditate on the way back up. There is something strange about Father and that means ... What am I saying? This is beyond strange. Not human. No. It is likely a random mutation, like a virus, that affects only certain people, the ones who are not protected perhaps? Yes. That sounds plausible. No more thinking now. Here comes the spin. Focus on my breath. Only my breath, no thoughts.

"Fantastic focus, Eli!" A welcome surprise. "Up into the sajadum now. How do you feel?"

"Wonderful."

"Excellent. Give me a head start. I will see you tomorrow."

Actually, I feel somewhat drained. One moment, please. This is not the same sajadum. Do I still have a slipmap? Good. Surprises abound today! I am way up near the northern water purification coil. The pirate could have mentioned it. *Your tone, Elize. The universe moves in ways only posterity can predict. Follow the water.*

Follow the water? I am surrounded by it. Well, at least it is more relaxing than finding that blo— *Remember your serenity, Elize.* Of course. Finding that book. There should be a bench at the parkette near the Purity hovertrain drop. Rango can snuggle me while we walk. A good hug is what I need from the little monkey on my back, and he from me.

It looks like the fog is stuck here until midi today, and I have no portablower. Sniff. Follow the fragrance. *Close your eyes, Elize. They will only deceive you. Walk with your feet.* Done. This feels like a good spot just about … here. Stretch out my arms. Palms up. Oooooooooo. The mist tingles. Breathe it in and reach for the sky. Breathe it out. Relax and tuck in. Nice soft grass for my knees. Rest now. Classes can wait.

✂ ✂ ✂

Bolt up! What was that? *On your right, Elize.* Duck. Pfff. Shrubs in my face. Shhh, Rango! Someone might hear … Mega pica ziga crap! *Acceptable given the circumstances, Elize.* A GHU craft. On fire. And shadows. Scrunch back down. Hide. We need to get out of here. Did I sleep all day? Peek through the bushes. Oh oh! The water coil is on fi — Jump away! Close call. Now I am a real frog. Hop again. Crunch. Whose is this? *Let it be, Elize. Curiosity shortens time. You must go now.* Go now!

K E E T O

Day 1036: late evening

I sometimes surprise Eli with my decisiveness, but mostly I surprise myself, especially considering I had ample opportunity to share the results of my first remote transcriptor success when she was in the zen zone all last week, but I could not utter the words, let alone let them magnify the images I had sketched in my mind. I did, nevertheless, manage to share the transgressions with Stitch today, but, as usual, he found a way to one-up me on the sleuthing scale. Why I had not thought to sift through high council packets for a different angle of the encounter, as Stitch indelicately ribbed about, probably has to do with my own inability to accept Caroline's right to do whatever she wishes with whomever she pleases. I am simply not on her "whatever-whomever" list. But do I really want to be?

Nothing could have possibly been more disturbing than what I was envisioning, I had assumed. Well, thanks to my bopping bioskinhead of a friend, I now have criminally obscene flashes with intermittent subtitles corrupting my highland values. You know how that goes. What you fear most will come upon you, and then some. It came up on Caroline, and up in her, and up over her, and ... I had better stop right there, lest I entertain the prospects of murder ... again!

Back to the topic of decisions: spying on the Pramam's advisor was bold in itself, but rekindling my relationship with a convicted child mutilator and killer is crazed beyond any measure. My appetite for questionable associations seems to increase the longer I live in this city, where decades of betrayal linger beneath the surface of the canals, almost as if the toxic waters were infecting me from within. I dare not approach the Eli Ogre that she has become for the past six days with either of these developments, or not until she can exist in the space between reaction and response. On the other hand, that request may not be reasonable.

Every time Nathruyu and I meet, which we have secretly been doing for two weeks now, I keep probing into Sothese's character, and she keeps steering the conversation back to Teddy. She is adamant that we must locate the last of the children Elize babysat, because that is where the real answers exist. "This affair with Caroline and Sothese will lead me astray and no ultimate good will come of it," Nathruyu warns me. I can still sense the frost on my lips when her finger hushed me that final time. "Talk of this no more," she begged of me, as shards of pain trapped behind her eyes impaled my heart. Our entanglement is no longer fantasy expressed through ink and quill in the absence of evidence. She has invaded my body with her presence.

Infiltration takes on many forms, however. In our morning what-the-crap-should-we-do-with-Eli-now discussion, Stitch went tangential on Wakanda's theft of the Gadlin leadership in collusion with her contractual partners. It has taken her decades to legitimize business obligations that indenture entire clans to her. The few kin who remain steadfast in the Gadlin Creed cannot sway their respective gatayoks because of majority rules. Despite inter-clan pressures, Sakari has managed to protect Stitch's and her tribe, and to persuade other ones that Wakanda, the Machiavellian, must go. While their search for legal loopholes has fallen short, hope remains in careful scrutiny of their spiritual laws, and in the scouts they have dispatched in search of Odwin. All intentions focus on his return, alive.

But what of other intentions? Since Stitch had shown me how to fly through the miniverse looking for lone floaters, which are snippets of detail plucked from inside a larger packet and thus taken out of context, casting the most efficient nets has become somewhat of a competition between the two of us. We could trawl the entire maze with a gargantuous mesh, but the by-catch we would snag in the mega sweep would leave trails like snails in the ocean sand.

That would defeat the purpose of the ingenious goop that coats the Global Health Unit communication channel packets, the subject of our most recent exposé. I suspected that if we had access to the medical emergency comms, and compared them against the official broadcasts and transcripts, then we would eventually find the pathway through which the information was picked over, and therefore the promulgator of deceit, with his or her signature style unmasked for future chumbud-devised impersonations.

The ploy succeeded. By using a clever virtual hose to suck up individual shadow packets exhibiting a certain wobbly behavior that Stitch figged was evidence of recent tampering, we were able to fill a reasonably sized bucket, not too big, not too small. Then, we carefully excised the innards of each bubble with a data bit syringe and flung them onto a temporary splatting wall, in order to spread out the orphaned content in a viewable format. Most of the edits pertained to minor GHU employee language offenses while handling general health events. After three hours of poking each other to stay awake, Stitch and I decided, instead, to brace for the Eli vortex of villainy scheduled to arrive at any minute. Her newfound vocabulary promised to be much more entertaining.

Having resigned myself to the imminent verbal assault, I stood up and stretched, with one eye on the doorway, the other chuckling at the doodles of boredom inking themselves on Stitch's scalp, while he took a mop to the goopy mess on his board. A flyer bake explosion over Wakanda's face, a crabseat chasing Mme Beaudoin through the stacks, a weedel with the counselor's head and prominent nose sniffing up some algae, Eli falling through a virtabed (that one merits a discussion with him later), and other random shapes appeared and disappeared as his collection of ancient timepieces, sacrificed for parts, ticked out of phase with each other.

My heart sank at this particular graveyard of gadgetry because, to me, they represent more than just relics from the past. The ones with gears and sand kept time in an epoch when the oceans lived and hundreds of thousands of nature's species thrived. The ones with lit displays proliferated when civilization coveted machine-perfect disposable everything. Today, not to sound too much like Eli, all we have are imperfect hybrids, genetically engineered human conveniences, and slipwatches that reset daily with the morning sun, perhaps as a subtle reminder that if the sun does not rise, then neither do we. We have killed everything else.

As I cataloged each treasure in my mind, a crimson splotch on a head sprang from a crabseat and skimmed the underside of my jaw. My high-pitched screech sent the armrest pincers into a panic while I checked my chin for Stitch's blood, but nothing. The ensuing multicolored fireworks display on his skull started flashing in concert with the synaptic activity from his thoughts. Stitch had found something, and it was overheating his hairless do. I pitched a glass of water at the wildfire and laughed as the steam created a mini electrical storm just above the bioskin. The genius boy remained oblivious to the whole experience. His eyes were drilling a hole into the last remaining jiggling blob that we had sucked from the miniverse.

We switched to peripheral view and found ourselves winding down the DNA of a chromosome that was, decidedly, not human. If Eli had not shared with us her findings with regards to Father's mutation, I would not have been counting the other chromosomes, doing their acrobatics in the big soup of genetic material this particular viewer was immersed in. My trust in Dr. Tenille took a deep dive at that moment, since if he claims that the URA has access to blood samples outside the reach of the GHU, then how come we were looking at evidence that someone in the GHU, against Ministry protocol, had gone to great trouble to delete from official medical records?

The wheels were churning in Stitch's mind, as well. In fact, they were even drawing themselves in motion on his scalp. Hehehe. This is my favorite version of our dweeby companion, by far. His intentions are not only more precisely represented, but they also include a much wider array of emotional states in addition to actual thoughts, of which I, because of my height, have a flyer's eye view. All I need to do is to dig a bit into the symbology that appears, and with my keen linguistic skills, I can synthesize my own private translation manual. Juicy! Eli, on the other hand, has a handicap unless she magically grows taller.

Based on the DNA abnormalities Father's cells have, I probably should temper my gloating, since extra chromosomes could mean extra functionality. I shudder at the thought that the proteins I was riding in the miniverse this morning could unwind a truth about Eli and me that we have not sufficiently evolved to comprehend. Ohhhm gee. Those are Nathruyu's words. Her increasing influence may become a liability if I do not protect my emotions with a mental biowall. Certain frequencies should not reach my subconscious. The key is to tune into veracity and to tune out of falsehood. If only the wisdom you surely have access to, Mother, could provide me with an incantation that summons an energetic shelter against spiritual seduction.

Realistically speaking, it is quite likely that our fortunate find could merely represent a simulation that the GHU uses to teach its interns cellular mitosis, exploiting some form of hybrid as their subject, although Stitch remains adamant to the contrary. He pointed at the consistency across the different views, which were completely unnecessary as a teaching tool given that, in his opinion, the Unification has more pressing assignments for its staff — concocting fake virus scares and sending mosquibots after perceived threats to the Pramam's power grab. The level of detail in the views, therefore, could not possibly have been manufactured.

If reality is indeed what transpires in the shadows, what I am about to relay shatters any theories of how life propagates that even hybrid architects, with all their plug and cringe manipulations of sentient earthly creatures, would scratch their heads at. For my part, it was not my head that was itching. All of my own nucleotides simultaneously sent electric shocks through the fluids trapped in the membranes below my skin. I felt as if every cell inside my body was desperately trying to shoot out of my pores. The microscopic recorder that was snapping flashes of each tie in the holographic double-helix railway we were spiraling down exploded in a blinding flash of white light at the end of the line. I have no idea what we hit, but the same thing happened on every single DNA thread we would switch to.

By the time we had surveyed the entire sample, hitching a ride from protein to protein, I was drenched in the sweat that thickened with each subsequent zap, singeing the hairs on my arms from the progressively stronger electrical discharges. The final tally was 27 chromosome pairs, four more than a normal healthy human would have, and one more than Eli said she had counted in Father's genome. On top of that, these extra four dancing strings were well-formed, receptors and all, meaning that they would replicate without a hitch. Whatever was at their tips, however, were no ordinary telomeres, so Stitch scooped the goop into a bucket for a further splash on his wall, later on. Eli had crashed our intracellular roller coaster ride.

I wish I could pen another lyrical story about how incredibly enlightened Eli has become, but I am now debating whether to rip out the account of Dr. Tenille's glowing analysis of her mental state from six days ago, and to carry it around with me as a reminder that this latest nine-day cycle, which incidentally feels more like nine years, will pass. Or, if we could only convince Eli to keep her mammasack with her, instead of pitching him into Cyd's corner and terrorizing them both, then I could sneak those pages into his storage tummy with the hope that the words would find a way into her subconscious and flip a switch. The poor lo-flower shakes in his roots every time Eli looks at him.

This time, at least, Dr. Tenille has managed to convince my tumultuous twin to continue her sessions in his cabin, but based on my secret transcript copies, she appears to be toying with him. Who knows what kind of lies she expels? When Eli is in this mood, truth takes on a "special" meaning.

For instance, around midi today she dropped by the archives with a flyer bake and went rogue on the academic! Geez. She kept threatening to shave "that eyebrow" of his while her mouth was full of partially masticated chunks, which prompted Izionnis to raise it higher still, which, in turn, had her counter with projectile bits, and on it went. I had to stifle my obvious amusement.

.Unfortunately, Mme Beaudoin stormed over and sprayed bits of her own, in no uncertain terms, that Miss Elize was no longer welcome in the archives. And I was no longer amused. I escorted her out to my crypt and commed Stitch for backup while Eli continued her rant, using the gurgling water as a spitting range, then almost dove into the cove, in a fit of frustration. Who is this person?

At this point, since Eli was already humoring Dr. Tenille with her presence, we thought that performing a dream sweep would be the best method to uncover what lies beneath the rage. A reprimand from my supervisor for flipping a pass on some work was a worthy risk rather than risking leaving Stitch alone with Eli, especially considering the heat in the room, just to make sure, you understand. She allegedly has become more suggestive. I do trust Stitch but ... Hang a sec. You know I do not trust him, really. So here I am defending her virtue, as always, from an imaginary defiler. I should probably accept that one day she will actually have a match. Not Stitch, of course. He is like a brother, but just in case.

Even with Stitch's incredible patience, all we got were more accusations, resistance, anger, paranoia, and deep eerie giggles. She burst out of the hypnotic trance and lunged at one of his pockets, yanking out an indigo crystal pendant, and immediately cursed him to eternal damnation for stealing it. She spewed on that it was hers, not his, and that he should hand it over. The pendant is actually a sentimental keepsake that arrived with Zbrietz, his cousin. A stranger had delivered it to him during the global Gadlin clamping frenzy as proof that his mother was safe.

Eli ran Stitch into the closed door, sending Sparky whimpering to his bed, and proceeded to fish through his zigazillion pockets for more loot that he clearly was hiding from her until he whipped out a hologram of the missing crystal and pointed to the bumpy sphere hanging below it. His was a dull brown, whereas Eli's was a brilliant blue. She called him a name I dare not write, crumpled the holoslip, and threw it at his face. Thank the little baby prophet that she is too short to read what appeared on his scalp. Where has your daughter gone?

This is no longer a philosophical question. I now believe what my medical informant has alluded to, that Eli is no longer present during these episodes. Is this right? Is this what happened to you, Mother? Is this some sort of possession that secretly brought the GSU around while you were inside the psychiatric wing of the GHU?

I should not even be privy to that kind of information, but Dr. Tenille's fear of what the Global Spiritual Unit would do to Eli is so crippling that he continues to risk getting clamped. The Ministry takes privacy breaches extremely seriously, of course, but only when they come from outside their own agencies. To be perfectly honest, hypocrisy is not the Pramam's invention, as my inaugural spying session on Sothese can attest to.

Decision made. Tonight, I finally exorcise Sothese from my mind and into my journal and be done with him. Here are the exchanges I was bold enough to turn the transcriptor on for. The gaps are where my conscience interfered and I shut off the device.

Sothese, it's too much. You're hurting me. Please, it's too much. (new voice)

Annotate new voice. Caroline.

Do you not want to play? (new voice)

Annotate new voice. Sothese.

(cries) Please (squeals) stop (sobs) plea— (Caroline)

—joy your secret meetings with the Pramam? (Sothese)

(screams) What are you talking about? Please. (Caroline)

(deep groans) I know you love power. (screeches) You think *he* is powerful? (Sothese)

What is wrong with you? (Caroline)

(running, thud, crash, cries) I am not seeing him. Stop! (grunts, groans, whimpers) I would never— (Caroline)

—st a little longer, my little Gadlin. (Sothese)

(rhythmic groans, pants, squeals, long drawn-out guttural noises, whimpers, sniffling)

You're a sick (edit)! Here's your sheiss coat! (whipping, white noise) And don't ever touch me again! (Caroline)

(white noise: 10 seconds)

You will heal quickly enough, my darling. (Sothese)

(edit) YOU! (Caroline)

(laughter)

I know you, Caroline. You *will* be back. You always come back. (Sothese)

(muffled voice, Caroline)

I am not one of them. (Sothese, whispering)

Are you not? (Caroline)

(heels walking away, door slam, tapping: 10 seconds, footsteps walking away, door open, door close, silence: 3 seconds)

At this point, I was about to command the remote transcriptor off, but a familiar feeling stole my voice. The anxiety I had felt in places I dare not mention, subsided, and an otherworldly calm sang to my heart, soft yet sad. Here is the night's close.

(heels walking nearer)

Stay with me here a while. Make all my fears go away.

(new voice, singing)

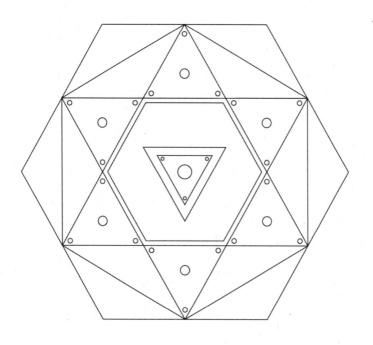

CHAPTER FOUR

SOTHESE

Day 1039: dawn

Reflections cannot compete with the commander of adult consent across the crystalline divide. The flattened image remains trapped inside a depthless skin on a static surface, designed to imprison the soul, as the sun releases its fire behind the polished veneer embodying the Pramam's advisor. But the portrait is a fluid illusion, for all exists within and through him, in its rawest form, beyond the confines of a two-dimensional world.

Sothese trims his candy-red bangs with surgical precision, in response to public criticism in the maze that compared his beautiful long fringe to a hairy, prehistoric butt flap crossed with a flaccid red flyer. The affront has become a sketching sensation that requires immediate remedy. There can be no dissent with regards to his incontestable magnetism and virility; therefore, the repellant attribute must surrender to the ego's blade and the emerald spears of his alluring gaze. Vanity may have been a deadly sin in the gospel of a backwards civilization, but in the Unification, Perfect are They.

▼ ▼ ▼

"An eye for an eye, dear brother. Or would you prefer an item more precious to you in exchange for ogling the throne and its privileges?"

Their daggers cross within range of bloodline termination, yet cowardly attacks in response to challenges against rights undeserved solve no grievances. Not even a dozen butchered chunks scattered across the land and drowned in the seas can purge the suffering that saturates the morphic field. A deathmatch is no contest to the one who harbors the rage of disparagement, dismissal, and desertion, and is but meager retribution for a life tormented by insatiable cravings for validation. No, Sothese's vendetta seeks an enduring commitment.

By whose decree does esteem belong to one and not to the other? Favoritism weighs down on the scale of impartiality. There is no honor in bequeathed acquisitions, therefore no dishonor in testing worthiness. The onus is on the defendant to prove his value in the event of a dispute or endure the consequences of ill repute, whether or not prophecies side with ancient times and preferences collude in heinous crimes. Results are the proof that validates lordship.

As the skies part and the earth rumbles, the duel fills the chasm with the cold reality of shattered aspirations, suspended in the frozen void where dreams and nightmares originate.

▲ ▲ ▲

Incontestable indeed. A twisted smile cracks the marbled face that has become as cold as their defeated champion. For a breed that ostensibly can access primeval secrets encrypted in the great versal storehouse, trickery can blindside them so easily. Perhaps if Anubrat practiced a little faith in his disciples rather than dribble drops only sparsely infused with the proper intelligence while his own chalice overflows, their dominance would be a *fait accompli*. At the very least, they could locate their missing star child and complete their circle of influence with time to spare ... well ... almost. There is one whose interests are incongruent with their version of bliss.

Fortunately, time is a gentler agent of change for Sothese than it is for most. The search for the twins, however, still involves the tick of a clock, the cycles of which follow the movement of physical beings anchored to what scientists call reality. Urgency is the timekeeper in the girl's case. The Pramam may have access to her by proxy, but Sothese plans to tap into her whereabouts through more direct means as long as his sublime skin maintains its pristine appearance, of course. Dirtying of the hands is a method he employs sparingly and reserves for vengeful pleasures since there are far more salacious bits he can corrupt instead as part of his exploratory exercises. When work becomes play, boundaries dissolve with the gamemaster's touch. And his is the touch that resolves so much.

Gadlin concerns sometimes require a firm grasp of the situation, a skill that the Pramam is relying on today. Decontamination chores are meant for GRU employees in unfashionable suits, not for this Ministry official, but there are many recaptured prisoners to process. Surely, one cannot expect the manicured advisor to act in a menial capacity, even if the request comes from the fragile vermis-chugging counterfeit elder currently claiming lordship. Sothese capitalizes on his indispensability to slip a historically taboo subject back onto the agenda, as is his political artistry. The cloistered hallways surrounding the council chambers of Ministry Mansion funnel their private conference to the sleeping statues in the corner apsides of the room.

"They must be moved. I do not desire their presence inside Ministburg. The city is no longer theirs."

"Of course, my Pramam. But they cannot return to the island, or what is left of it." In fact, they could, and Sothese would shed no tear on their behalf. A sinful waste of fluids it would be, do you not agree? The sensual gap between his lips betrays the ecstasy of thousands of naked legs dancing on the embers of betrayal.

"We still need them alive, Advisor Sothese. The Holy Trinity has foreseen success, and, through Their guidance, I am confident you will find a suitable location for our volunteers." The word searches for truth only to be speared and sucked backwards by the forked tongue that released it. "The illustrious Pramam does not wish to house vermin in *his* city."

"Is this an official statement, then?"

"Your sarcasm is not lost on my ears, Sothese. Your recurrent tone, however, is concerning."

"I lack subordinates to temper the intensity that serves your Divine mission well, my Pramam. The outbursts are minimal, all things considered." A half-bow feigns the respect that the false prophet demands while it shrouds the daggers reshaping the inside of Sothese's cornea. Replacements for the three officials, who Sothese is convinced have escaped with the assistance of the Pramam's clandestine associations, is still forthcoming.

"All things considered, you can no longer remain at arm's length. You shall relocate them tonight. And your response?"

"I can personally escort them to Eadonberg and invite them to the SIF headquarters. Cell block B is available and heated. We would not want them to catch a chill, I presume." The poetic justice appeals to the Pramam's cultured persona, as expected.

"Perfect. Reunited with their co-conspirator they will be. Security will be increased until the GMU can build a new Level 3 facility elsewhere?"

Sothese coils around the Gadlin carrot he dangles in front of the aristocratic ass. "This is, of course, possible, providing I have access to cell block A, to ensure that the walls are frequency tight and perfectly insulated."

"You know what my position is on that, Sothese. I am growing tired of your persistence." *Only when it suits your ostentation* fills the subtext behind Sothese's silence.

If it were not for Nathruyu's starring role in Almedina, Sothese might desist. However, his motives are more complex than the simpleton wearing a Unified stamp on his forehead is aware of. The imposter under SIF guard must switch sides. If the Pramam wants Sothese to play along with the escape mystery game, then he must learn the rules of engagement.

"Understood. We could just leave the Gadlins here, if you prefer. That would save me a trip and some decontamination of my own."

"NO! They must leave. Permission is yours, with accompaniment. Future visits are to cell block B, exclusively. Are we in agreement?"

"Of course, my Pramam." A second half-bow hides more contempt although the victory makes Sothese's obedience somewhat more palatable. "Once the inspection is complete, cell block A is off limits."

"Good. Have you contacted the General?"

"Yes. She is aware of the current situation and is looking into less accessible sites."

"Wonderful. And have you discovered who leaked news of the escape? Public embarrassments weaken the trust placed in Unification leadership."

"You recovered quite well from the negative press by immediately offering a free safety bioApp. Your generosity is admirable." If such qualities lie dormant as distant experiences in the great universal storehouse of memories, Sothese has no recollection of them. This shortcoming is more potent than the act that fails to veil his flattery.

"Indeed. It did grant favor upon me, almost as if an attempt to undermine the revered Pramam's sovereignty had failed."

"Yes. How curious." And how predictable is the underhanded accusation in defense of a falling monarch.

If only Sothese could claim the downfall of the Ministburg lockdown facility as his own doing, double shaming would silence the Pramam's quips. The delectably delicious thought carries him through the remaining formalities of his advisory duties and back to his penthouse, with the obligatory "They are One" response to the "Perfect are They" verse.

The day that the pontificator goes silent, permanently, is inevitable, he being human, although Sothese aims to expedite the process. He hones in on the self-assigned mandate relating to the twins. Exacting revenge on those responsible for the penal island meltdown is still in plan; however, the girl is the little birdie in the grass that he must snatch first. She is the bargaining chip that he will use to convince the Pramam of his exceptional leadership potential and thus appoint himself as successor. Furthermore, when the time comes, Sothese shall slip his way into power, unsullied, and all shall bow to his greatness. No panic, no uprising, no unnecessary bloodshed, simply ease.

Steam blurring the ocean horizon releases volatility into the airwaves for those attuned to the message. There is no need for Sothese to burden himself with extra clothing on his next side trip, because the climate that he will encounter can melt the buttons off a coat. He, of all people, can appreciate the value of fine workmanship, so he tosses the gift, whose origins embody an irony that the Pramam was oblivious to during his anti-Gadlin rant, onto the valet stand beside the armoire and once again marvels at the divinity staring back at him in the crystalline divide.

A lively chase fills the frames between the images racing through his thoughts, yet no anticipation ripples through any hairs on his body, for his silky skin has no such unsightly threads. With the tips of his fingers, he traces a sinewy path from his jugular, across the clavicle and over to his bare shoulder, then back across his sculpted chest, curving between the obliques and rectus abdominus, and all the way down to his inguinal region. He twitches in delight. This is the level of worship that the new heir expects from his future subjects and the faultless performance he demands of his physique. A more casual linen suit will do him fine as he heads to the GMU transport already boasting its Gadlin cargo.

In order to continue his human charade, Sothese has opted to endure the Newtonian technology that will shuttle the displaced prisoners to Eadonberg. Once inside his private cabin, he can enter the world of form as he pleases. The fact that the terrorists, who are still awaiting a trial that will never come, are his wards for the virulent voyage is irrelevant to the small island, smoldering in melted silica, that is his prime destination. As long as his ministerial appearance is noted on schedule at the SIF with the human burden suitably clamped behind him, and that he returns to his ignoble leader for the morning gag, Sothese can enjoy whatever mischief he so desires.

Notwithstanding, the signet of greatness lies in discernment, and, for that, Sothese must always and always and always respect the versal laws of engagement. This mode of travel is no covert game. *They* will know and make things right, so that he may know he saw things wrong. Perception is the true commander of destiny.

That said, part of him would love to release unbridled entropy onto the Unification and its obedient populace as a final jab into the bowels of Ministburg. But, for now, its curated architectural and natural wonders, balanced atop the nine densely packed petrified Secoya pillars supporting it, simply diminish in the distance, a fragile record of the treasures that past civilizations have repaid to a planet redistributing her wealth to more worthy tenants. A quiet snigger attaches itself to Sothese as he leaves the bioshielded deck of the northeast bound transocean hovership to prepare for a potentially explosive recruiting expedition. When the pickings are slim, connect to the source.

A quick laying of hands on the generator gives Sothese just enough vitality to touch up his exquisite complexion as he enters the frozen void, indifferent to the lies of gravity.

Time and space melt into the fiery landscape that hisses beyond the charred gates of every body's worst nightmare. Instantly, muscle memory assumes control of the free-falling grace with which Sothese navigates through the spraying molten debris, until a small vehicle, animated by automatic spot fire dousing nozzles, scoops him out of the sky and plunges into an ocean conduit off the coastal cliff and deep down into an abyssal holding zone. The hatch seals shut, the water drains, and a pleasant cocktail of floral gases infuses the transparent hemispherical cell.

Rays of discontent etch their claim into the back of Sothese's skull, wrongly presuming that their scattered intellect could ever withstand the fortuitous catch already devising the manner of their demise. There are no curtains to shroud the glint in his eye and the excitement building an archway to death in his brow, a subtle cue that attracts the steward of this kingdom, the one known as the Entropist, to the front exterior of the space formed by a larger second hemispherical membrane. Sothese declares his intention to the waters in which he is submerged, and they listen, as they must.

"Before this day is complete, I will arrive in Eadonberg with an accomplished set of officials. No more incompetents!"

"And so you shall, Master Sothese."

As if summoned by its words, ultraviolet orbs splash into the sea from above and surround the domed crystalline enclosure with steamy bubbles as they dissolve into shadows with blinding lights for eyes. Were Sothese's ears able to float inside the turbulence, the deafening gurgles would send them screeching back home onto his head, in which he becomes a phantom charging the amorphous beasts and slaying them all, without the mercy Nathruyu had granted his ex-officials in Almedina. Their continued survival is undoubtedly a setup for his eventual emasculation.

Alignments begin to form inside the random constellations of bioluminescent pairs. Groups collect in sets of threes, as they orbit the diaphanous igloo that holds Sothese suspended in the deep, spinning faster and faster in a counterclockwise direction, until the induced current whips them into a radiant tornado whose axis falls in line with the holding pod. A well opens, directly beneath in the ocean floor, and sucks the funnel down to effect its collapse into the hole. At last, the opening seals itself and the waters calm.

What a vibrant display of impure potentiality! The corruption about to manifest saturates the atmosphere with insurgent thoughts. Sothese monitors the figures collecting at the outer rim and expands his energetic presence as an invisible testament to his dominion over the presiding resource manager, so that the others understand the full impact of their ignorant challenge. After all, the Entropist is simply an administrator, not a lord, and nor shall it ever be one, a technicality that binds its assistants to Sothese, without debate.

Three hopefuls appear up the chute that emerges from the reopened well and plugs into the floor at the spot where Sothese waits. Their bodies are cool, but they shall soon feel the heat of their office. The outer rim empties at the command of the leader, and a blast from below travels up the shaft to jettison the dome into a bullet, piercing the ocean's surface, then landing softly in its original shape onto the rocky cliff.

Mindful of the volcanic fever testing the limits of their borrowed flesh, Sothese's new officials assume the trademark V formation to anchor themselves in the present. In unison, they push the gelatinous craft over the edge to watch it return to the depths, where it shall recrystallize and reconnect with its kind.

Amidst the roaring sprays, darkness appears to flicker in time with the clock ticking in Sothese's mind. He produces a tumbled quartz stone from his pocket, hands it to the head of his three probational Ministry hounds, and instructs them to wait for him at his Ministry House quarters in Eadonberg. They disperse into the fire, just as a another silhouette explodes onto the magmatic landscape dense with ash and pyroclasts.

"When will you trust me enough, Sothese?"

The question sizzles in the transition between steam and ether, as the conversation hovers over the strain between them.

Sothese holds the stillness for what needs to be said.

"Impeccable timing, as always, Kainaten, but you will find no Gadlins to release here."

"Accusations? And from what motive? My loyalty rests with the Pramam, above all other humans."

"You give him too much credit for your existence. He is not the one with the real power."

"Indeed." Fury boils at Kainaten's reference to the reversal Sothese recalls at the grovellers's dawn ritual. "Perhaps you orchestrated the event yourself, Sothese, to corroborate official rhetoric? How you relish being the purveyor of chaos while appearing the knight who saves the day."

"Time does favor the gifted."

"You may be his advisor, but I have his trust. Have I not been cloaking your unofficial meetings?"

"Some to my detriment, apparently."

"I saved you from your whims. There are versal laws, Sothese. You taught me that. Besides, I do keep your secret."

"As I do yours, all of them."

If Kainaten only knew that his quarry has been unmasked, his confidence would fizzle with the cinders clinging to their last light on the ground.

"I sense, then, that my visits here are pointless." And in the wink of an eye, he leaves Sothese a gift dancing in the gaseous flow. "Her name is Elize."

E L I Z E

Day 1040: late morning

... and thus, They have directed the illustrious
Pramam to implement sweeping precautionary
measures, for the Gadlin infiltration reached
the penultimate gateway to Their counsel,
the Divine Messenger's personal advisor
and Inner Council member, Sothese, whose
previous officials have not only escaped, but
have also colluded with Gadlin clan leaders
in their collective breakout. Rest assured that
key Unification agencies are collaborating with
the leadership in council with They for your
protection against foreseen biological terror
attacks at the hand of these fugitives. Praise be
given, by They, to the SIF for their thorough
investigation which revealed the three expelled
officials as the treasonous masterminds behind
the original viral outbreak. May the Trinity
they have forsaken, in exchange for irreverent
insurgence, grant mercy upon them. Perfect are
They.

We shall all skip the expected *They are One*. Irreverent
insurgence? In whose illustrious opinion, may I ask? And as
for your insincere granting of mercy, I say "Suck my—"

"Eli! Enough profanities. Remember your highland proprieties." Of course. Here is a highland wave for you, dear brother. "Eli! Please!" Beakish little pup. And here is a new kind of snare for you. I call it a snurl ... with tooth, so back off with the highland sheiss.

"Does he honestly think that everyone in the Unification is a hick?" No, not everyone, Elize, just you. "Or am I the only one who sees through all this shei— What are you laughing at, you ridiculous etch-a-sketch on a cue ball of a dweeb? I should stick some knobs in your eyeballs and do the artwork for you." That is an excellent quip, Elize. I am proud of you. Is it not fun when I am in charge, Elize? All this witty discourse, the attention you get from strangers, the reverence? Yes, they are afraid of you. They can feel your power. Lay it on him, Elize. "And what *is* that? You call that art? Your bioskin is no Da Vinci. Is that a flyer bake explosion? What are you laughing at? What is that supposed to ... Hey, is that me? Wipe that! Give your head a shake. That should wipe it all off. No? Let me help you, you f— "

"Ease, chum!"

"Let go of my arm. I am going to whack you on the side of the head."

"Pica trip, but how about we hear the broadcast first, ya fig?" Ya fig? Who talks like that anyway? What a waste of time, sitting here with these two cumbuds. Whoops! Did I mispronounce that? Deep eerie giggle. That was your best yet, Elize. Thanks. Ok. I shall humor them. Listen to the broadcast, I will ... for now.

… by official decree, beginning immediately, in order to secure the Unification and its law-abiding citizens from the Gadlin ideological poison, masquerading as spiritual oneness with the soul in all, gatherings of three or more individuals will invite immediate GMU intervention. May They absolve the itinerant hate peddlers of their deceit once they are recaptured and processed through the Ministry Rehabilitation Program.

"You mean tortured without trial, yeah?" Dreadful torture, yes. You must also protect yourself from this danger, Elize.

"Crap! You added bioHealth to our headbands. Eli? Please tell me you threw it at Stitch again." Of course, I did. Nobody wears headbands. They look ridiculous.

"Right. So you are acknowledging my superior attitude and fashion sense, now? Say it. I am not the abomination you think I am." Yes. Why give you a real reason to avoid me when your fragile ego's incapacity to handle constructive criticism does a well-enough job of it.

"Yes, dear sister. Your paranoia induced negativity …" Constructive criticism, remember? "… has some positive side effects." His sarcasm deserves a snurl, Elize, but let this one ride.

… blessings be upon those with bioHealth upgrades. The biochip will now alert the host when three individuals are in close proximity. The Inner Council's sincerest intent is to mitigate the gathering of triads who, together as a super power, could activate Gadlin plasma weaponry against innocent citizens. In council with They, it is believed that three Gadlins suffice to that effect, and that their secret rituals are but enhanced mind techniques that harness quantum forces. Life before liberty is the sign of troubled times. Gratitude comes to those who welcome personal sacrifices for the greater good. Loving are Their ways, and Perfect are They.

"Flyer mud! The creepy three are not Gadlins." Ooo, I like the energy shift, Elize. Feed on it.

"Sticking like mega sheiss on your wall, eh? There was no virus threat. There will be no virus threat. Utter scam! We knew it and we followed along like everyone else. Minions! Hicks! Weedels sucking up the scum!"

"It's Ministry, yeah?"

"You are sounding like Caroline. You are still friends with her after what she did?"

"She didn't do anything, Eli."

"Always in her defense. She is spying on me. We have a flash of her in Albaraaton, remember, PUP?" Deep eerie giggle.

"But she didn't actually do anything, Eli?"

"Yeah, and technically neither does the Pramam, eh? Was your brain in another dimension? Did you not hear that decree? No more groups of three, fishy! And only three seconds to split

up? I am not the crazy one. The Pramam is. Beyond dazed."
Mouth agape. Hands on hips. Pop eyes wide and stare. "Are
you not outraged?" Honestly. Right. Decision made. Someone
has to stand up for our rights. "I am starting an uprising. Well,
do something. Get on the board! Send ten thousands sketches
out. We need to rock the underground. Show that pontificating
shei— What? You have something to say?" Make it count or I
will make *you* count ... your teeth on my shag. "WHAT? Are
you looking for words? I can help you with that. How about
these ones, you f—"

"Eli! Geez. You're possessed or something." They are
whispering and giving me a look. I heard that.

"Not a good time to talk about what exactly? Only hybrids
listening." There go the bioskin tattoo atrocities. Translation?
"Spill it! No? What is that supposed to mean? Yeah, you get
that head tur— going to ge— when I'm finished with— you
will show me more respe—"

"She's going out with a bang, bud." Enough with the
banging! Run to the corner and bang those hybrids.

"Will you SHUT— Come here, Rango. Get out of the
way, you plantrocity. How dare you challenge me!" No, Mr.
Zafarian, that room controller is mine. Not yours. Mine. Not
yours. Mine. Not yours. Mine.

"This room is overdazing you, chum. You need some zen
to ease down."

"Ease down? Ease down? Stop turning around and rolling
your eyes at me, pup!"

"Shhh! Keep your voice down, Eli."

"This is MY ROOM AND I'LL YELL IF I WANT TO!"

Oh no! Breathe, breathe, just brea—

✂ ✂ ✂

Huh? Oh, Cyd. *If you have chosen a path, stay on that path.*
Do not doubt yourself. Remember, all voices have their place,
Elize. You can stop stroking my face now. He's scared I'll
get angry again. Smile. Ohhhm gee. Look at this mess. Grab
the room controller from Stitch. Oh and smile. They're both
relieved.

"Why don't you spend some time on the slick, Eli. You're
too topped up."

"I can go with you, chum, just in case."

I can't stop the tears. I don't know how to control these
outbursts. Sniff. Wipe. A poke and a smile. All is forgiven.
Forgiven, Elize? Perhaps from the boy with the ants in his
pants, but you and I are not complete. Your time is up. Love
is never having to say you are sorry, Elize. Pick me. You
need some love right now. Do I ever! Sniff. Wipe. I am so
wonderfully excited, Elize. Thank you. So much fun awaits
us. Everyone will love us. Everyone will want to be our friend.
Let me choose the decor, Elize. I know what you need. Ok.
Hehehe. Crazed. I'm yay with that.

Stitch has his palm up. He approves. Chumbud salute
for you, my chum. Blush. You see how they all love us now,
Elize? Ummm. Awkward. Giggle. Poke Keet so he's not left
out. *External actions mirror the emotions within, Elize. Speak*
with your heart and another's shall beat in time with yours.
You want a turn then? I will cry, Elize. I thought you needed

me. *Creation is the path to enlightenment. It will find you, when you are ready, Elize.* Joy is mine! Can we leave for the slick now, Elize? Juicy! No more tears. Deep eerie giggle ... for now, Elize. Run along. She picked me.

"I'm ok now. You're right, Keet. I always feel so connected to everything on the slick." Add a little color here, some virtaplants here to keep my lovable Cyd company, and maybe ... Perfect! Of course it is. I know what you need, beautiful Elize. Soft giggle.

"The floating rainbow felines are a nice touch. Sound effects?" Good idea, Keet. There. Little purrs. Hehehe. "So ... you're better ... I think. Let's talk when you get back. When you're more level headed." He means more boring. Not happening. I feel top creative!

"Perk! You sure you don't want me bopping around, chum."

"I'm mega pica ziga juicy! I'll take Rango."

"Rango? The hybrid you've been trying to murder for nine days?" Tickle tickle, Cyd. Leaf hug.

"Hop on, little mammasack." Back to Keet. "Well, I fig he needed a name. He's cuddly, always hugging my back. And I do feel safer with him. Can I borrow your headband? Mine is ... you know."

"Here. Whoops!" Saved by the shag. Into your pack, Rango. "I'll pass by Stitch's room for it." Quick group chumbud salute and off they go.

"I saw that, Rango. Sneaking the sweet somethings again?" Soft giggle. Ok. I'll take the hug. Now grab my planing booties, and let's glide.

It's a gorgeous day for a plane to the sports complex. This time, I'll pay attention to my surroundings and not drift into an ancient forest. That should be easy. I'm sure there are no clicking heels in the trails. Hang a sec and pause those mallets, Rango. Who's back there? I knew it! I see she stills fancies herself a spy. Time for a well overdue confrontation ... Where is this anger coming from? Deep eerie giggle. Not you again. Tell her to go away, Elize. With pleasure. Clip out. Breathe it all in and ...

What a gorgeous day for a plane to the sports complex. Booties on and ... Honestly! What's she doing here? I don't appreciate her spying again. That's it. We need a face-to-face so I can find out what is going on ... I thought I got rid of this anxiety. Not yet, Elize. But I can help you, just ask. She is weakening, Elize. Ignore her as we walk on the Victory Bridge. Ok. Not listening. Go for a swim. Breathe it all in and ...

Such a gorgeous day for a plane to the sports ... Caroline? She is probably just trying to say: "Way, Eli!" Soft giggle. We used to have so much fun together. I will have to comm her later. Right now, I really need to laze on the slick for a bit. *Remember the good in people, and the good in people shall grow, Elize.* She can follow me if she wants to. She knows I saw her. She was a good friend. I am so fortunate to have so many loving people in my life. Breathe it all in and feel the love. Whoops, time is ticking. Best take the hovertrain instead. Here it is. Surprise! Up the shoot. Top fun.

Ohhhm gee. Rango, you are drawing attention to us. Laze into the ride, little one. Everyone is staring. Sit here on my lap with me. Small hug.

"That is a special mammasack." Oh blush. How could I not notice him? Those eyes. I suppose we should finally have a proper conversation.

"My apologies. It seems to be dysfunctional." And a beautiful smile back to you. And one back to me from the other boy, as well. Hehehe. Everyone wants to be my friend. Soft giggle.

"An early model?" I will have to lean past Mr. Exotic to talk to Mr. Smiley here.

"And my apologies to you." So he likes to play games. What a tease! Lean left. Bob my head right. Then bob left. And again. Try to look around him.

"It's a great tune, yeah? TriMorphic Rhythms is my favorite band. Are you listening to Oye Amigos too? What version of bioRhythms do you have? Mine lets me choose live versions tap by tap." What a strange boy. And the sizzling begins anew, Mr. Exotic! His smile is so captivating. Smile back again and … now we have a three-way smiling contest. Hehehe.

Here is Hub drop. I will take that walk now to cool down, but not really. The city just keeps getting hotter and hotter. The faster I get to the cool sports complex, the better. Hmmm. Shall we have a little chase? No looking back though. Just click into his pace, but make it look natural. Like I am not aware of him. And here we are … all sweaty. Juicy. And now, to the slick.

I can still feel you, for real. That was a shoulder tap. Act normal. Well, you know what I mean.

"Hey lo. I did not see you there."

"Of course not." Hmmm. Twinkling eyes. He knows.

Show some creativity.

"I was waiting for you to tap me on the shoulder, I mean." Mr. Twinkly-smiley eyes.

"I am an expert on the slick, did you know?"

"Really? Prove it." Have a nap on the bench, Rango.

"He will be quiet?"

"Yes. Just a sensitive soul. The drop selector probably sent a static spike that got him overdazed. You first." Hmmm. Impressive. But I can beat that. A double loop. Your turn. Bow for effect. He has some height, but I can fly too. I need some speed. Glide. Push. Glide. Push. Glide. Double push. Big glide. Triple push. Airborne. Flip. Land on one leg. Crouch. Spin. Back up and stop short. Valah! Top that. Mr. Twinkly-eyes smiles instead. I win.

"Someone is watching you." What? How does he— Oh, the caretaker. Soft giggle.

"I thought you meant I had some sort of stalker." Soft giggle again.

"Maybe you do." Yep. A tease. Sweating again. Oh lovely! The caretaker switched on music.

"Would you like to dance?" Maybe not … maybe … ummm … too hot. Surprise! I guess so, then. Slow meandering side by side, tango-style lean, swoop back spinning, spinning, spinning … This is magical! He is the perfect slick partner. Gaining speed. Faster, faster, faster. Here we go … and soar! I am a flying feline. Hehehe. Squeal. So exciting! Focus, Elize. Keep my balance. No staring. I have to focus. Geez. The caretaker keeps staring. Are you not supposed to be cleaning stuff? Quick glare at him. That did it.

"That was effective. I hope you never look at me that way." I hope you tap me on the shoulder again. Smile quietly and plane away backwards. "You are very talented. Shall we not wait a year before we meet again?" What can I say to that? Just smile and keep planing. Hey! That was a sudden departure.

"Hey lo, chum. Who were you talking to?"

"Just a classmate doing some practicing, Stitch." I wish I could see the top of his head. "Why the suspicious tone? *You* are the one who followed *me* here." Poke him. Is he blushing? Ummm. Top awkward. "You and Keet are worried the Eli Monster might come back." He nods. "I feel fantastic." Pick up Rango and follow Stitch out. "Surprise! It's dark out, already?"

"Da ya! That's why I'm here. You missed Dr. Tenille's appointment."

"Whoops. I just got lost in time on the slick. Like you and the hoops."

"Not quite, but I fig what you mean, yeah?" All these night flyers. Duck. Everybody is following me today. I went from repulsion to attraction. What next? Stitch is trying to swat them away, but he is howling too hard.

"Watch for dead bodies." Shudder. No ribbing about that. Chills. I can still see the eyes looking down on me from the flyer nest in Rubrique Court.

✂ ✂ ✂

"Slap me, chum. I upset you." Huh? We are back at Van Billund Hall.

"I am fine. Truly. It just brought back memories of Mashrin, and then Teddy. We really need to find him."

"What if he doesn't want to be found? Not like the rock, yeah?" Eek. That find did not end well, but still …

"Teddy is on my mind. The chumbuds network has no word. What if he— "

"Perk! Wakanda still has her Tess cracking my creation. Let me connect with my new secure channel."

"Ok, thanks. Now my first assembly."

"Shakes! You just decided this morning."

"Waste not time. Can you rig the scanners in the viewing room? A rally needs more than two people." I can feel gears drawing themselves up there.

"I'm on it, chum. Hey lo, bud. Everything's trip. I'll be back in ten." I sense a setup. They were scheming, I am sure of it. Ooooooooo. His precious journal … for me?

"You need to read this. I've been looking for a good time to tell you."

Not back to *her* again, I ho— Geez. *Rhythmic groans …
pants … guttural noises … sniffling … You're a sick*— Enough.

"Is this the kind of smut you write in your journal now?"

"I didn't write it."

"Joining Caroline live in her sexcapades, then?"

"No! The transcriptor is on remote. Stitch's Tess." Roll eyes. What are they thinking?

"You are no better than Sothese now. I know I have had my differences with Caroline, but this is totally inappropriate. I am ashamed of you."

"No. She—" Hand up.

"I do not want to hear another word. I have an uprising to start. Are you coming? I mean joining in. I mean … Oh just follow me. Any words I use here end up in visual debauchery."

"Crap! Your headband's blinking. Clip out!"

K E E T O

Day 1048: early evening

Holy crap! Am I ever fortunate to be alive to write you and to be wolfing down a flyer bake. Some days, Mother, like today, I imagine that living in your reality may be the safest place to call home. Of Eadonberg, I am not convinced. Even in my private cocoon, protected by the mighty Sparky, there lurk energies that invoke fears I have only come to know, or rather not know, as the unknown, bubbling beneath the surface of my conscious mind. I feel claws scraping the deep layers of my skin and etching a name into my skull, from the inside, a name I have seen before on your phantom lips, from Nathruyu's mute screams, and now like nails on a chalkboard in my head — Siufflah.

Stroking my crystal and connecting with your evanescent presence provides some relief, but I cannot seem to fuse with your spirit as consistently as before. You are fading along with my hopes for Eli's future. In fact, destiny itself is wobbling as the Pramam continues to spin his own version of events, and his advisor, as he believes himself to be, unravels his master's tightly woven Unified shroud. And then there is Caroline.

All this suffering must have its purpose, especially the turbulence surrounding the sister I am bound to protect from the evils in her living nightmares that are now claiming her body. In all fairness though, her outbursts are more predictable, and at least two of the three personalities are pleasing enough to be around. All the same, as she comes to the end of her happy zone today, I cringe at what tomorrow may offer the hapless victims in her foul-mouthed wake. Would the aspiring hybrid slayer resurface to execute her threats? I should probably focus on the now and let the morrow unfold as it may, since I have an appointment to run off to. So let me begin with a slipnote version of my sajadum discovery and then move on to a blast from the past, quite literally.

Since the anti-three decree, I have been cognizant of undisclosed exceptions. For almost three years, the ritualistic sharing of sajadum meditation experiences among registered Unified disciples has had absolutely no appeal for me, but, recently, I have felt a curious pull towards investigating who They actually are. Perhaps this need for oneness of mine is seeking expression in a form that you can no longer provide while you continue to seek a higher realm.

Regardless, before work this morning, I decided to put aside my prejudices against the contrived religion that the Book of They proclaims as truth and officially join the congregation that grants my blackmarket biochip access to all the sajadums in the entire Unification, of which there are thousands. The bioCal feature now summons the headband, which I conveniently hide underneath my makeshift Unified head scarf, to whatever sajadum is available at my designated prayer time. If Stitch only knew that I was dabbling in Ministry brainwashing, as he calls it, there would undoubtedly be a few very explicit doodles on his scalp.

My findings are quite intriguing. Once inside and the bioZen upgrade that had finalized the approval process activated, my brain waves aligned with the other two congregants in the amethyst crystal tetrahedron. I felt a surge of electricity enter my body and incredible ecstasy as all energetic blockages released at once. I suspect that the euphoria is an effective means of incentivizing consistent attendance, but to what end is the question that vindicates my continued participation. I cannot be one hundred percent on this, but we existed as One for a very brief moment, never mind the They entity.

As you can well imagine, my sensory perceptions were in a vortex of confusion when I stepped out of the structure and onto the floating garden it rests on. During the short walk to the archives for my daily cataloging duties, I felt more like one of Captain Snook's crew finding their sea legs after an autopsy curse of a lesson than a blessed child of They. On the other hand, this dazy dance in my step turned out to be a blessing in scholarly disguise. The young academic's eyebrow carved a path to our formal introduction, at long last.

Izionnis is the name I recall from my latest plasma dosage, but "Iz" insisted on the more congenial abbreviation, quite fitting for the man of few words. The interest I had provoked came with a question, that was more like an offer attached to an assessment. "Could I tempt you with an effective coping strategy?" But instead, Caroline was to be the one to lead me into temptation just as I was about to ask Iz what kind of study demanded that he essentially live in the Round Room.

Apparently, my new book bud had severed the invisible string that held his jaw in place, because Caroline's sashay into the room turned more than a few heads. Iz did a poor job of concealing a familiarity with her, so when he took me aside for a quick chat before releasing me to the "vixen with the stunning blue eyes", I absorbed his words with intense clarity. If he only knew what those blue eyes would do.

As if my silent wondering had already tickled his ears, he shared the intent of his daily research with me. There is a certain artifact that he has finally located and would I consider accompanying him on an expedition as part of the fieldwork hour requirements of my apprenticeship. Would I consider? He returned to the stacks before I could yell "JUICY!", but I sensed that he already knew my response. Nevertheless, for now, there was something more urgent on the bucket list already itemized for me, and I pretty nearly kicked it, the bucket that is.

I also felt like expelling my breakfast into that same pail at the thought of a conversation with Caroline. The twelve days worth of the comms that I had ignored were kicking me in the bits below my waistline with every swing of her crossed legs, as she sat with a PAL, watching me fumble through my morning tasks, until she finally installed herself on the stone table below the crystal dome, directly in front of me, piercing my heart with a wet stare and an entirely reasonable request: "Is there somewhere private we can talk?"

Getting together on the private with Caroline is likely not a great idea considering I am already in Eli's imaginary house of ill repute with the remote transcriptor session. My immediate response involved the same kind of avoidance I use to stay tethered to my comfort zone, like the pup that I truly still am: "I'm in the middle of research right now."

An abrupt "you sent me there" crushed the excuse I used to

chill the air between us. She was right. I was not doing anyone service by denying that my gut forewarned me about what would transpire between Sothese and Caroline. Furthermore, I was the consummate hypocrite for having enjoyed excerpts from his Carolinean skin flash collection through Stitch's high council packet research back when we barely knew each other. But somehow, I still consider the live blind flybot on the wall experience as different. In keeping with my discomfort regarding the whole topic, my foot went straight up then hooked back down into my stomach as I blurted out that my imagination got the best me. Well, the brunt of her anger resulted in a dig of the unpleasant kind: "I hope you enjoyed it!"

I chased her into the eye of the red-headed storm that was gouging a path out of the archives and into the hallway and threw my caution into the swirling emotions surrounding us both. Sweeping Caroline towards me, I snuggled her tightly against my chest as she sobbed, trying my best, unsuccessfully, to concentrate more on her and less on how much blood was pumping through my heart. Her pain was much deeper than a fallout from marginalized feelings. The acts in Sothese's Ministry House quarters that had compelled me to pause the transcriptor while I grappled with my ethical indiscretions were the very moments where liberties became criminal violations. The bastard! He was treating her like he had Wakanda, and my complicity was irrefutable. All for hick Galleon sails.

Yet, in the moment, I was still lying to myself, and most importantly, I deceived a vulnerable friend because of ... Why? What was I trying to preserve? My ego with the whole

"I'm so sorry. I didn't know he would do that to you" bit? And as if *this* made it at all acceptable: "I thought he had a thing for you." Geez. Fortunately, Caroline is a fighter underneath all that charm. Her words sent the abuser walking the Galleon's plank instead.

"Sothese only has a thing for himself. I despise him. His career is over. I'm going to blow his cover."

Footsteps from the Great Hall announced the midi patron rush, so I … I invited her to my crypt. Gulp. And boy, am I glad that she decided to shift her beautiful blue eyes, catching the light like gemstones, down the hallway, then suggested an alternative. Leading her through the archives and out to the back garden was not exactly discreet, and it would cultivate circumstances in which trust would be tested, my own trust in myself.

Once the commotion had moved into the exhibit room, Caroline led me by the hand to what appeared to be a solid wall behind a real console and down a seemingly endless, narrow spiral staircase to a cavernous chamber directly beneath the museum. Her penchant for ventilation shaft explorations had uncovered the other entrance, located across the expansive carved stone floor, which is how she found this enormous space in the first place. I shudder now that I realize that the dark figures with glowing white rims for eyes, skulking around down there, might have access to the archives and could infiltrate my late nights spent alone vicariously transported to exotic places where relics resurface.

The ancient gathering hall was absolutely riveting. And to think that it has been under my feet this whole time. We tiptoed to the center, wary of the echo our shoes would produce, where three-metre tall stalagmites guarded the perimeter of a deep dark hole. Caroline speculated that it could have once been a water well before the purification towers were built, perhaps even a drill hole down to fossil water that has since been sucked up to the earth's surface. With the only light coming in from the holographic decoy at the top of the stairwell, there really is not much else for me to describe, except for movement way up in the ceiling that Caroline cautioned me not to disturb with the pocket light I was reaching for. I did not have to delve into my imagination to recognize what was squirming above our heads. The largest nest of night flyers that I have ever seen. Shudder.

The revelation I am about to share, however, dropped some of that wiggling down into my own pants. Caroline leaned into me, and, as I drifted with her natural scent into a dreamworld I can no longer recall, she whispered in my ear: "Sothese is not exactly human."

"Not exactly" were her exact words, but I am not exactly sure exactly what she meant by "not exactly". So here you have no precision at all. We already know that Father, or his blood anyway, is not exactly human, and that some other DNA we found as shadow packets in the maze is not exactly human. Sothese's three of creepy past, his three of creepy present, and likely his three of creepy future, are not exactly human. And Nathruyu is also not exactly human, that we saw first hand. So I am starting to wonder whether any of us are human at all? I mean, were you human, Mother? Are Eli and I human? Is there such a thing as a human anymore? Or maybe humans as described in the old books and in our Unification controlled educational system went extinct.

The fact that my curious lack of shock enticed a giggle out of the bearer of inexactitude was even, in itself, not a shock. The fact that Caroline knew all along that Eli was my twin sister and not my cousin? Not a shock. That Sothese is obsessed with finding us? Not a shock, thanks to Nathruyu. That the Pramam is clueless about Sothese not actually being an elder? That he is clueless? Never a shock. I feel as though a flyer bake could drop from the sky, ready and wrapped for me to eat, and I still would not be sho—

Juicy. My dinner actually dropped from my hand and smudged my journal. Perhaps I should mind my thoughts. Mother? Are you still with me? I need you here more than ever, yet the bridge between us is thinning as if our two worlds are being pulled apart. I sense that frost is forming in the scorching heat that is taxing the city's cooling generators.

In any case, today, time imploded, froze, and exploded with the knowledge that Sothese had been halfway to his objective, me, and that his drive to the other half, Eli, is what he had subjected Caroline to as a form of punishment for not bringing Eli to him. Even I became an unwitting accomplice in his quest by leading him to Nathruyu in the shafts, and almost gifting your daughter to him as an extra perk for his pleasure. If it were not for Stitch … But, now, someone has given him a flash of Eli, and that is how he knew that Caroline was protecting her. He recognized her as Caroline's friend from the Restricted Sector club.

Yet, he waits. Why? He knows where to find me. He could

use me as bait to draw Eli out. Ohhhm gee. Strike that thought. He is no flyer bake splatting these pages. Manifesting him at my door would be catastrophic.

The little growls coming from the corner of my crypt are witness to my thoughts or ... That was a splash. Dare I?

Weedels! The heat is causing algae to form in the cove now, so the museum caretaker just released a bunch of them. Nothing to fear there. Unlike the not-exactly-human Ministry agent. Caroline is genuinely afraid of him, seeing that the trust between them is broken. For backup, she had brought me into the sacred hall from the Age of the Gadlins, which was a historical legend way before the reign of Anabelle, the Pramam's mother. Caroline wanted to stop Sothese, but she needed my help, because the only one who could apparently take care of things was so cross with her that she was afraid of him, as well. My disappearance would be noted, but hers, being reduced to a nomad taking odd jobs on cargo ships, would not. And that is where visions of reuniting with you painted the shaft walls.

The sealed exit to the underwater ventilation labyrinth revealed the true extent of Caroline's involvement with the not-quite-human. She had acquired a handheld device that could melt rock without heating it, in the same way that sentinels pop out of the Van Billund Hall links to nab anyone whose secure band fails to grant permission. The hydrogen sulfide smoke bomb that flew by, as Caroline sealed the wall behind us, became the omen for a latent fear that I had hoped would remain dormant. Fate, however, had a different plan, and so did my, incidentally still conscious, companion.

When we reached the exit to the Victory Bridge, I began to climb only to be tugged back down by the edge of my shirt. This was not our designated rendezvous point. My confusion promptly turned to panic. We were not meeting the counselor at O'Leary Hall, Caroline was not affected in the least by the toxicity in the shafts, and we were not alone.

Murmurs and scuttling intensified behind us and a whole new level of appreciation for my morning running ritual, established as a teenager in the highlands, emerged. Caroline led the way effortlessly towards a horrifyingly familiar area. As a form of distraction, while we raced the predators to the Restricted Sector club, the subject of my next sketching session in the maze offered up factoids about the government pumps keeping the subway system from flooding, and that the counselor would credit me a much needed drink once we arrived. We never did.

The last things I heard, as I was dragged by my legs along the dark metal duct was: "You did not finish my story," and Caroline shrieking in the distance: "Run, Keeto, Run." So I kicked, and then I blistered.

✂ ✂ ✂

Geez. Where is this heat coming from? Is there somebo— Brrr! You keep doing that!
(giggling)
Yet we meet. Are you not afraid? (Nathruyu)
(silence. 10 seconds)
I need to know. Why Teddy?

He was on my list. (Nathruyu)

That's it? A random list?

Elize selected them. (Nathruyu)

She doesn't even remember them. You *are* a liar.

She will awaken to her choices. (Nathruyu)

Brrr.

Someone is poisoning your mind, S— (Nathruyu)

I did not alert Sothese to our meeting with Teddy.

But you did send him into the shafts, did you not? (Nathruyu, toothy inhale)

I forgive you. We must all make sacrifices for the greater good. (Nathruyu)

Even to save Sothese at Almedina?

Save him? I gave up on that ages ago. Yet watching him cower? That rewards some discomforts. (Nathruyu)

What are you?

Are you prepared to die for the knowing of it? You are not ready for the truth. (Nathruyu)

When will I be?

When you choose. (Nathruyu)

Like Eli?

(buzzing)

Your satchel is comming. (Nathruyu)

Ummm. They can wait.

(buzzing)

Crap! Give it ba—

HOW DARE YOU! You want something to put in your journal? (Nathruyu)

(high pitch)

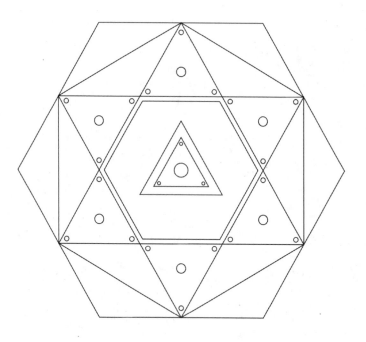

CHAPTER FIVE

SOTHESE

Day 1048: dusk

The fiery orange shadows of dusk fall upon Eadonberg's skyline as evidence that chaos brews deep in the earth's crust. Legend speaks of blood spilling, but the penitent lift their eyes towards a more climactic divination that Sothese willingly promotes to humanity as fact, as of yet unrealized. With reinforcement from the Global Spiritual Unit, souls, as Unified humans have been taught to interpret them, are children easily swayed by the unscrupulous metaphysical falsehoods of Gadlin nitapoks, the heretical equivalent of the GSU-accredited spiritual sages. The Inner Council of the Ministry must ensure the safe merging of all trinities in the congregation with Their Light, upon passing into Their Realm, whereas the Ministry, in general, addresses the physical realities.

Where responsibilities get muddied, Sothese gladly offers his own brand of enforcement, only when necessary, of course. However, since every case requires its due delectable process, certain other ministerial duties must pass to somewhat trusted delegates. The key, as always, is to secure loyalty through means not necessarily favorable to the yielding party. In that respect, or lack thereof, his seductive dexterity serves to retain control of the outcome in his hands. Goodness comes to those he baits, according to the sole testimonial that matters, that of his own recollection.

Fantasies of deflowered youth precede Sothese's transition from Ministburg to the URA decontamination cell, where his newest three officials join him as a flash in the underground tunnel. A distant clock ticks once, announcing an offer to repair the impatient advisor's temporal neglect. Alarms go silent in the facility. Sothese shifts his gaze to Miss Corrient Shakti, frozen in the hallway mid-stride while she was heading in his direction with anticipation swelling in her chest, then back to the smile and quick salute from a familiar presence flickering in the shaft. His lips twitch in concert with a dopamine spike when the door unseals for Sothese to slide out, his hounds in the slipstream that gushes towards his ministerial colleague, darling Corrient, the Pramam's strategic advisor.

Cells of recognition bring a friendly smile to the URA director's face, but they are not meant for him. Sothese allows his officers to walk past and into the shuttle while he surveys their reaction to her warm reception. Their dispassionate response signals a mistaken identity, in obvious contradiction to the doctor's pupils, which suggests a connection worth investigating later. The sweat beading inside Dr. Shakti's URA issue lab coat releases a scent that Sothese recognizes as an exquisite cocktail of fear and courage with a hint a defiance, the hallmark of an adventurous spirit, and the makings of a worthy challenge. His breath quietly keeps pace with her heartbeat as he toys with her resolve.

A protector greets the shuttle passengers while a second clears their access to the climate controlled lab, handing them each the obligatory uniform. Corrient stops short at the entrance, whips around to face Sothese, her tall lanky body invitingly framed by the glass, and clears her throat. She warns her guest that he is in fact a guest, and that any past claims to equipment or authority over staff, however creatively maintained, are illegitimate. To Sothese's credit, albeit as a ruse to gain her favor and as a precaution against potential confidentiality breaches, he cedes the territory and instructs his pack to demonstrate their policing skills outside the room. Sincere appreciation surprised his epidermis with a subtle electric charge that he promptly neutralized so that he might retain the emotional distance he requires, just in case an intoxicating opportunity should arise.

His thoughts penetrate Director Shakti's mind without the need for words. She dismisses her assistants for a more private discussion with their ex-supervisor, and the invigorating air fills with casual exploration.

In the end, we must come together for the good of the Unification, do you not agree? Anarchy will bring death to everyone, especially now that global temperatures are surging, now that the oceans are releasing the heat that they have endured for the past several millennia.

The director's silence reflects her interest in the vial of fluid that Sothese has placed in the tubular microscope, now projecting its magnified contents into the viewing zone. Doctor Shakti steps inside the resulting holographic blood cell with a professional admiration for its originality, which caresses the erogenous tip of her aspiring commander's ego. The risk is manageable, considering his priorities have shifted to Elize and to safeguarding his true identity from the Pramam, onto which all physical efforts must focus. Therefore, transferring responsibility for baptismal oil production to the office of the URA director is a smart way to eliminate some drudgery and to test the extent of Corrient's loyalty to the Inner Council and, ultimately, to Sothese as her rightful lord.

The Pramam's Unified religion must continue. It is the official hope that binds humanity, whether she believes in the rhetoric or not. Unofficially, however, it is Sothese's brainchild to control the masses and to manipulate the doctrine to turn the proclaimed Divine Messenger's own pietism against him.

With the blood of babes shall They be bound to Their children.

Once delivered, the intelligent ointment expresses its perfect design as the most elegant heist in versal times. The carrier nanite injected into the tincture of DNA, taken from the original blood sample, enters the infant's brain through the third eye during the Unified baptism and hones in on the innocuous biochip resting on the posterior surface of the child's vermis, where it signals the biochip to drive three metal probes from each apex into the cerebral tissue. The GSU spiritual sage, performing the ceremony, immediately holds the infant upside down to deliver the inaugural spanking at exactly the right moment, thus masking the intensely painful attachment with a cry of docility. Some secrets are worth dying for.

Hurried silence sweeps the hardened floor with the edge of a cloak and bare feet, crusted in crimson sand. The trail Sothese has left as he dragged his nephew's body across the desert emphasizes the urgency of his demands. The gamble is a sure affair, for he knows that his sister's own guilt will expel the secrets that she has stolen in one beseeching breath of "please stop, please," three simple words that are to become the desperate cry of those who lie prone on Sothese's battlefield.

Trickery exists at the tip of a serpent's tongue, but is he honest in his dealings when the victim succumbs. A child's betrayal, a brother's lust, a mother's love, comply she must. The young man she attempts to save, by divulging the formula for dominion over all, drowns in the fluid that animates his body, while she repents in horror at the imminent fallout from her own dynastic aspirations.

Knowledge ensnared holds no respect for knowledge shared.

▲ ▲ ▲

Questioning eyes float in the fluids replete with the building blocks of life as Dr. Shakti explores the holographic projection of the sample's contents. She focuses her speculations past Sothese, reclining against the glass, and into the lead official's squint, mirroring her ruminations, both of them in search of what answers may be camping on the frequency their thoughts travel on. Her Ministry colleague, on the other hand, entwines the rope that pulls her curiosity towards him. The director slices through the biological illusion to find herself inside Sothese's circle of seduction, irresistibly reverent.

"Your genius intrigues me," is more than mere flattery that can entice a softer approach from the hardness that is his baseline personality. It is its tone that enraptures the senses. A flutter rushes his arteries before he can constrict the stream shooting upwards to tease his brain, but his actions wait for more earnest advances. Delicate is the balance between work and play, is it not?

For now, Sothese shall suppress the origins and inner workings of his cunning acquisition, teach his student the simple mechanics of it and, of course, emphasize its declared purpose, regardless of her agnosticism, to bring the baby's spirit under Their benevolent care. After all, she is on the Inner Council now, therefore it is her duty to uphold the Unified religion even if she is a non-believer. Rest assured, she shall be removed from the council and from her URA position for non-compliance, at which point Sothese could then, in good conscience, consider her luscious skin as spoils for his taking. Good conscience? His lack of it is his strongest asset.

"Well, it is just a ritual." Indeed, darling Corrient. Her loyalty raises the pressure feeding his loins. Work ethics are such a hindrance to Sothese's compulsions. Indeed. Darling Corrient will have to feel the full power of the URA Director she has displaced ... and savor it through her unabashed solicitation.

▼ ▼ ▼

The Age of the Gadlins was a blemish on earthly progress.

Basking in the venomous discourse of others is a habit not

easily shed, especially when the outcome carries the fate of humanity with it. Odwin insists, as pointedly as he can, while still honoring his vocation as Gayok, that Anabelle bring her newborn to the Nipok for a private blessing, only to give further credence to Wakanda's unspoken accusations while the chair of the multi-faith coalition looks instead to Sothese for guidance. There is to be no public confirmation of her child's heritage.

Seeing as no quarter, or lesser, breeds qualify for Gadlin spiritual embrace, and that only parents with high moral convictions can present their half-breed children to the Gadlin Order for consideration, engaging in this anachronistic display would scream favoritism over the other world doctrines. The wailing to be had under Sothese's faithless watch is of the infant boy, secretly anointed with the baptismal prison, and of the new mother, willingly inducted later and in private.

As with the sundry sensual expressions of deeply rooted gratitude to Wakanda for carrying poison thoughts on his behalf, Sothese now enters the womb that has birthed his new dynasty. The time of Their coming has arrived.

▲ ▲ ▲

"Good evening, Master Sothese, and to your hounds." The holowall star dissolves his head into that of a feline and hisses at the stiff-armed humanoids following behind their master, then back to his bearded self in a fit of laughter, as the female of the three smashes into the solid backdrop in an attempt to bite his face off. Sothese reprimands her for the limbic behavior and resumes his journey to the Museum of Antiquities, with a fourth disciple in tow, the translucent holoadvert spokesperson.

The goading continues, with the Ministry hounds as targets, until he bores of the game and dares to disturb their alpha male ostensibly headed for trouble. Covert operations are best kept at a whisper, and they are, in this case, only murmurs in Sothese's ear: "Were you here but an hour ago, I could have facilitated an introduction."

Sothese halts, turns around, and dismisses his shadows. He drains the holowall of its power source and passes through the coldness, a second time this evening, to crash into his private holoadvert control room. The flame inside the structure's generator dims as Sothese regains the perfect hue and texture that he is so fond of. A few more flickers, and both Sothese and the blue fireball return to their full potency. He walks into the holographic arena in which his spies were conceived.

The bushy face that provoked this detour fills the interrogation with his well-garnered intel as Sothese leads the session and records it for future scrutiny.

Was she alone?

She was talking with someone. (HSN-351)

Her brother?

No. Another. (HSN-351)

The boy with the wormy hair, then.

You know of him? Curious choice of friend, the boy with the head tattoo. (HSN-351)

Interesting. This is new.

She was looking especially pretty this evening. (HSN-351)

A match then?

Sigh. Alas. Oh the shards! But no, not him. (HSN-351)

Especially interesting. Show me.

Apologies, master. The Central Core was experiencing EM interference at the time. I was fortunate to have been able to work at all. My appearance however ... Quite embarrassing. (HSN-351)

Then a description.

Further apologies, master. My memory, as well. (HSN-351)

She is quite the planer, though. Great power in those lovely legs of hers. She flew into me off the central corridor at dawn one day. A slidercab driver became quite angry. I would never be angry with her. No. Never. (HSN-351)

A human witness. Perfect. And you have his slidercab number? Yes, perfect.

The interview concludes with Sothese gesturing through the splintered memories that would serve as a bond for negotiation should the need arise. Regardless, Elize's newfound femininity and romantic awakening is enough stimulation for a creative encounter. This hound has found a kitty to game, but, for clarity, there will be no match in the eyes of the GSU.

Nevertheless, care must come first, for the HSN-900 series, hidden amongst the buildings on the Schrödinger University campus, are reporting student gatherings taking place in direct violation of the bioHealth restrictions, and the leader of this uprising is the lioness herself, Miss Elize.

What a pleasant development for the one whose love of ease is only rivaled by his love of the tease. Elize's clandestine conferences may appear to have deprived the GMU of valuable candidates for their criminal rehabilitation program although, in reality, they have exposed would-be dissenters before their grievances compound to ooze their infectious ideology into the stream of consciousness currently under Ministry control.

Credit must be given, however, to the inventiveness that made the near perfect sting operation an apparent success. On all Ministry sanctioned accounts, the Van Billund Hall viewing room is an excellent choice for transient localized tampering. As far as the Pramam is concerned, the bioHealth scheme is flawless, thus unsupervised discussions simply no longer occur. Would that his personal advisor share the same opinion. Instead, he stands in a hidden den, immersed in the intel that his deficient leader does not even know exists, using the eyes and ears of thousands of illusions, whose stories unfold only in Sothese's presence.

On the campus oval, there are everyday objects that integrate seamlessly into a typical student's daily activities. Then there are others that appear only when summoned. Whatever their source, by the gestures of his consummate directorship, every sinful display is available to Sothese. Those not on stage, that exist only as thoughts in their biochipped brains, remain a storehouse of endless premeditation that he has thus far failed to unlock. In this instance, he and the Pramam have both been cheated.

The first point of view materializes from the dormant HSN-903 against the console wall that has an unobstructed view of the entrance, at first. After a dozen or so students tiptoe into the frequency-modulated space, alert to possible alarm conditions, Sothese flicks the air, tinted with the HSN-924's view, from a virtachair at the front of the room for a portrait of the faces of rebellion. The female in the pop-up hologram, standing on a Gadlin barge in the open palm of Sothese's hand, does not match any conspirator in the overfilled meeting room, for the back of her shapely legs are flanking the eye of the spy, to Sothese's euphoric abandon. There is no watchman here to tap his toes in judgment.

A map of biochip locations highlights the ingenuity behind the bioHealth misdirection. The bodies are confined to the V-wing of the residence complex while their biochips meander the hallways to eventually return to their separate dormitories. The boy with the self-sketching scalp would be a potent young talent to court for government operations. There are many ways to skin a cat.

A vivacious lotus of love is the image Elize projects to the crowd as Sothese regrettably hands the scene over to a different voyeur, the HSN-972, on the ceiling. The discourse begins.

"Why should we trust you? For all we know, you could be one of the terrorists. Where did you get the proper permissions for this meeting anyway?"

"Yeah, the underground is trying to overthrow the Pramam. The Gadlins want to take power."

"No. That's what the Pramam wants you to think. He's actually falsifying facts."

"Where's your proof? You said you had proof to show. Flashes … broadcasts … classified packets."

The horror captured in the expressions, spewing the contents of their disgust, transports Sothese back to the torturous ecstasy captured as unedited versions of Nathruyu's interrogation and as the Osler Hall brain dissection.

"What's with her skin? Did they burn her? That's inhumane! But that just proves his advisor is a sick wack, not the Pramam. You don't have anything on the Pramam."

"Not to convict him, but enough to clear the Gadlins."

"Why should we care?"

"That's not a very 'Unified' thing to say. Where is the love in your trinity?"

Elize as leader? Sothese had expected her instability to rule over reason. This day has produced so many enthralling surprises.

"I'm just looking for transparency, for the Pramam to remove the dust from all packets so that we can judge for ourselves. I believe that we are all intelligent enough to draw our own conclusions, once presented with the facts … the dusted facts. Since these meetings are risky, I invite you to recruit your mates with one-on-ones over the next couple of months. By then, we'll be ready to hold a rally up the central walkway. We can't involve teachers or administrators, anyone with assembly permissions. Are you yay?"

Murmurs shape a list of demands that Sothese has no objection to: Recall the sentinels, remove hallway scanners, end the war against the Gadlins, stop censoring the Museum of Antiquities. The frail self-absorbed religious fraud, on the other hand, relies on these versal infractions, for fear of losing power that he does not embody in the first place. Once again, the people ache for Sothese's majesty to rise, and oblige he shall, with proper payment for his service as he sees fit.

SOTHESE

And the embodiment of power is exactly what he intends for his blissful Miss Elize, who now faces the remote viewer, exposing a preemptive amulet that he has seen before ... on Monique.

E L I Z E

Day 1048: dusk

"You look very lovely today, my dear." Just keep walking. "I see you chose a different accessory. May I offer you … Oh!" Crap! They flew off. That's what the warning slip meant. Now I have to stop and fix this. Eye roll. What? "I'm not interested in your potions. I have to catch them fast or I'll be late." So much for my grand entrance at the theater. The holobutterflies were supposed to stay attached to the dress. Geez. If he taps me on the shoulder one more time … And? "Would you like a try?" Juicy. A holonet. Nabbed one. Hey! I still need it. "That will be three credits, please." Is he ribbing me? "Per use." Geez. That is just pirating. And this dress design is definitely flawed. Stew Über should have included a failsafe in his Mariposa collection instead of a disclaimer. Something to keep them anchored, in case of energy spikes. The virtastrings just snapped. I'm sure glad I left Rango in my room. He would be bang happy with all these frequency jitters.

"That will cost me more than this hick-supposed-to-be-WOW-of-the-daze outfit. At least thirty holobutterflies flew off."

"Holostars like me are quite dear, my dear. The price one pays for beauty, eh, pretty highlander?" Is my accent still that strong? What a mess! The fabric is all pulled now. Ok. Here's my passcode. Maybe I can nab more than one at a time. "Shhh.

I have a surprise, just for you. It comes with a smile or two."

Juicy! He caught them all in a curtain backdrop. It's like a sticky strip for bumblebots. The holowall designer knows how to keep things from getting away, at least in the virtual world. *One person's dream is another's reality, Elize.* Well, I hope my reality is to keep the rest of this WOW-Line creation intact. I feel like I'm going to sweat this dress off.

"And a splash from my stash?" Giggly eye-roll this time. "It's a new slogan." And behind curtain number three is ... Whoa! "Shhh. It's real and it's a steal, at one hundred percent." He's peddling in black market water? I won't even ask. That will get me clamped. The curtain falls.

"I'll grab a drink at the show." Oh no. Here he is. Quick. Smooth the fabric back down. Breathe in ... and breathe out.

"Oh the shards!" Ignore the hologuy now. Focus on the real one. Ummm. We'll need to walk and talk.

"A Mariposa?" And not just the dress, my stomach too ... thousands of them. Hot again.

"Whoops. There goes another one." How embarrassing. It's heading for the sajadum. It looks occupied. I hope it doesn't go in. Good. He's laughing, but he's not the only one. The match floating by on a gondola are even pointing. Oh, shrug it off, girl. He's just another boy, like Stitch. They're all the same. Go ahead, Elize, lie to yourself. It is good practice. Deep eerie giggle. Check my choker. Good. Ok. So this one doesn't say trip or perk or poke me or bop around like a ... I see your point. Apart from that though, I don't need to get all topped up about him. Correct, Elize, but he is quite dreamy. Soft giggle. Sigh. *The need to impress is a sign of distress. Be yourself and know that you are enough, Elize.*

"Are you well? You look hot." You bet I am. Hehehe. A little Caroline sass. He blows on my forehead. What an odd thing to do. Well, it saves me a wipe. I have no sleeves anyway.

"I'm fine, thanks. Just a lot of things on my mind right now." And that's no lie. But he doesn't need to know that the things are actually thoughts. Agreed. Agreed. *Thoughts are things.* "Here we are. Tickets?"

"No need. They know me here. I can come and go as I please." Ooooooooo. That's pretty juicy. But I can't.

"You know there's a curfew. I'll have trouble getting back to campus."

"There are only two of us. I am sure the GMU will understand that it is all innocent." Right. Your twinkling eyes tell a different story. It feels like lightning when he looks at me. You see, Elize, do you not? He is different. Shhh. Tonight, I be myself, remember? Anyway, those two over there are trying not to stare. They know what I'm talking about. Oh. Here's the snack tray. Grab some while it flies by. I need to put my purse down.

"I will hold the snacks while you settle in."

"The bag's pretty full. Don't tip it."

"Pass it to me gently then." He winks … and promptly drops everything. Grab the sticky ones before he gets his pants dirty.

"Impressive reflexes. Not just the queen of the slick, I see." Giggle.

"So what's your real name? Shen is hardly exotic." More stares. Better keep my voice down.

"Exotic? Well, if you prefer ... how about Priapus ... or Anteros ... or Kamadeva ... or Pancika ... or Xochipilli ... or maybe Min?" I asked for it and now I have a squashed frog face. He laughs and whispers. "You can make up whatever name you fancy for me, Miss Elize." He's exotic all right. Exotically strange. Shen will do fine. "The play is starting."

That was bright! I hope it's not real fire they're using. It's already hot here ... Ummm brrr? I must be overcompensating. Creeps! A fedora! Oh, give your head a shake, girl. It's just Mr. G. Nod back. Ever since that night at Almedina Square, I just can't look at a fedora the same way. Back to the play. I really do love hearing Shen laugh. It's infectious. I can't stop giggling myself. Whoops! Slap me Mr. G for having too much fun. Giggle softer ... softer ... softer ...

"Thanks for the evening, Shen. I really needed the escape." Time just flew. This is awkward. He still hasn't given me his call sign. I'd better not let him walk me to campus. He'll see my fancy frequency thrower. I want to do some more research on him first. Whoops. There flies another one. He catches it.

"For me?" Nod. "I will be traveling for work, but can I see you again?" Da ya! Don't sound too eager, though.

"Yeah. I'm at the slick every other morning. Same time. Meet you there?"

"Perhaps. Good night, Miss Elize. Pleasant dreams." Sigh. I wish. Better blister. Here come some GMU crafts searching for troublemakers. Hehehe. They've seen nothing yet. Pull off these heels, slip on my planing booties, and surge like the flood. Here I am. Plane through the orchard. Clip through the lobby. Pull out my frequency thrower. Distract the guard with a pant rip sound. And into the lift. Sneak past the common room. Yes. Home at last.

Here come the hugs. Airborne Orangugong. Catch him. I love you too, Rango. Hy-five with Cyd. Hehehe. Shaggy, that tickles. Even my ornery privy shelf has a smile. Enjoy it while you still can, Elize. Pleasant nightmares. Deep eerie giggle. Leave her alone. I am still here, Elize. And I'm exhausted. *Fear not the future. You are still whole, Elize.*

✂ ✂ ✂

My head. Groan. Was there something in those snacks?

"RANGO! It's you!" Right. Enough. "Me Tarzan." Quiet at last. Why didn't I think of that sooner?

Shen said "sweet dreams" but what he should have said is "hope you get any sleep at all." Geez. At least Rango will be quiet until I reactivate him. Brrr. Cold sweat as usual. Voices, stay quiet. Good. Now breathe in, and let it out.

✂ ✂ ✂

"Good morning, Cyd." Rango's calm. "You can come over, too." Group hug.

That is pathetic, Elize. You hate hybrids. She does not. You love hybrids, Elize. Oh no. Right. I have until midi to choose. It seems to be random so I'll just ignore everyone until midi. Maybe I'll get lucky again. *That which is misunderstood often appears random, Elize.* Well, the decor then. I'll keep it creative. Now, where did I put the room controller? That's

Keet comming me.

"We need to talk, Eli. So much happened yesterday. I don't know where to start. There was Caroline, a secret room, Sothese, then the fedora man, the—"

"Holy crap! Are you ok?"

"I don't know. Nathruyu did something to me. I can't — We really need to meet." Nathruyu! I'm going to lose it. Yes, Elize, please do. Shut up!

"Keet. Geez. I'm really trying to remain calm here. You know I'm flipping today."

"Yes, I know. That's why it's crit that we talk. Come meet me and we can head to Tir-na-nog together."

"Ok. See you at the crypt." But not before I do something with this horrible decor. Now where's my con … tro … ller … Cyyyyyyyyyyd. "Show me what's behind your stem. Hand it over." You can do all the back bends you want, Cyd, but you're still stuck in your vase. Got it! Slapped you back. Let's try a little experiment. Push the shuffle option and "Rango, me Jane. Let's go."

Run run run. I sure am speedy these days. Again, thanks to hours on the slick. Here I am. I can always tell I'm getting close when the gurgling gets louder. They have to fix that generator. It's still leaking into the cove. Huh? Is that a boat?

"Hey lo, Eli. Hop in." He's bent. There are no blowers out there.

"We won't be able to see anything."

"Exactly. And no one can see us, except …" Ohhhm gee. The gurgles are following us? Eyes wide. "I've been testing them out." Top brave, my brother. I'm impressed. "At first I was terrified, but then I realized that whatever they are, they're …"

"Bound inside a toxic cesspool, like the voices in my head?" Why can't mine be cast to the waters? I've kept them locked up inside, afraid of letting anyone know, for so long that even Dr. Tenille's attempts to free them won't get them to leave. They're like elephants on a string. Hey. Maybe Stew Über should have designed a Mammoth collection instead. Hehehe.

"I wager they're some sort of spying marine robots."

"Ok. Enough chitchat. Spill it, Keet."

"Well. I've been handy with the remote transcriptor." Eye roll. "So I brought one with me … well, the short of it is, I was recording Nathruyu and Sothese kicked in." Ohhhm gee, she must have blown! "She blew." Serves her right. "But I still got some juicy …" Throat clear. "Ummm, remember that discussion we had with Stitch trying to figure out who has biochips and why?"

Now I'm listening. "Yeah. He said Odwin actually implanted one in him as a smoke screen."

"Right. But that's not the way infants get them. Sothese was at the URA with Corrient."

"Grody. He's not bumping her as well? That's totally inappropriate. I honestly thought more highly of her than that. Honestly, we —"

"Ease, Eli. There was none of that. It's the Unified baptismal oil."

"Is that what he calls it?" Hehehe, but ewww.

"Rip. So ewww it's funny. This is serious. I think the

Unified baptismal oil is really a self-guided micro-hybrid."

"Holy crap! Like a mind control device? I knew it! Hybrids are a menace." Not you, Rango. Hug. Keet's looking nervous. We're being circled. "Let's paddle." A bit faster now. "So, what did Nathruyu do?"

"I don't know. She touched me and then all of sudden she was inside me and— "

"Just stop there."

"No, not physically. She was in my head, in my heart, in all of my organs. It was like she just took over my body."

"Really. Had some funky fungus, did you?"

"No. At least, I don't think so." He's very quiet. This is serious. "I still smell her myrrh, and ..." He just trails off somewhere.

"Maybe she hypnotized you. You know how she used to get you all mixed up." That's one way of putting it. "Keet? I need you here, in one piece, please. Just let her go. Promise me you won't meet her again." Now they're splashing. Paddle fast.

"And you?"

"Are you bent? I won't go anywhere near her again. You can be sure of that." He's giving me that you-are-hiding-something look. He can't mean Shen. Honestly. Someone normal in my life for once and he's being all protective? Besides, I've never told him about ... She did! That ... Say it, Elize. Go ahead. Tell Keeto what she really is. She's stalking you. She's going to get you, this time. Look around the fog. Look for the eyes. There they are! No. That's a sajadum light. Deep eerie giggle. You're goading me. And Keet's off again somewhere.

Eek! "Keet. They're under the boat! Sheiss of an ohhhm gee. We're going to tip!" Rango's going crazy. Dig the paddle in and ride it like rapids. Use your body as a counterbalance, girl. You can do this. "Keet!" He fell in. Breathe, breathe, breathe. Not now. "Rango! Me Tarzan." I need calm. I need serenity. I need my brother. He's back. Pull him out. What a stench! He's in shock. Clap. Snap. Shake him. Not good. Heimlich.

"Whoa." That's a start. Get the dress from Rango's belly. Put it around his shoulders. I'm taking it back anyway. A few coughs, and a … yum … decomposed night flyer bit. More coughing, more gunk. "I need to get back to work." Drop my jaw. "I'm juicy. I feel safe there. Let's dock at Tir-na-nog. I'll walk the rest." He really is in shock. Maybe a little … "Really. I'm fine. Just rattled. See, no shivers." He's quite warm actually.

"Ok. There's the dock. Comm me!" That was crazed. He just ran off with my Stew Über. Caroline! What is she doing here? Right. The journal.

Well, I might as well get that journal. I have to stop those nightmares somehow, so maybe it's because Keet journals and gets all his emotions out. I feel like mine are trapped inside. I should give it a try, right? You are asking for advice, Elize? That is an invitation. Deep eerie giggle. No, not you. Then me, Elize? Oh joy. I get to stay? *Without change, there is no growth. You must grow into who you are destined to be, Elize.* Off to see Mr. G then.

Look what we have here, Elize. A little fun, perhaps? No need to worry. I will not utter a word. Deep eerie giggle. Sashay over to the hybrid section and sit on that crabseat. You're wacked. I'm not sitting on one of those. Just do it, Elize. Trust me. Done. Now what? Cross your legs, lean back, one arm on the pincer. What? Do it! Now, gaze at him and lick your lips … and twirl your hair. The hair's too much. Then sway your leg a bit and wave at him. Here he comes. Well done, Elize. Now I watch.

"Good morning, Miss Elize." Just smile. Good. Let him do the talking. *Agreed. Much is revealed when silence begs for content, Elize.* "Did you enjoy the play? Who was your friend? He must be new to Eadonberg." Nod, smirk, and keep swinging that curvy leg. Hehehe. Mr. Beautiful-gold-statue is getting tarnished with wanton thoughts. "I see. It is unwise to keep a relationship such as that hidden from your brother." And I see, you collect secrets under that fedora. "Especially if there are intimate behaviors. Are there?"

"What business is this of yours? The Unification does not own my body." Let's clip out. Look at all those colorful murals, Elize. Come, let me show you. I had her. You are not playing fair. Soft giggle. Juicy. A waterfall. Ooo, colorful boxes. Look. Crystal vases. Cyd would love this one. Is he watching? Sneak a peek. And bemused, I see.

"What are you really here for, Miss Elize?"

"Calmness comes to those who can organize their thoughts. I'm looking for a journal." He's relieved. Did I scare him?

"Crystals are effective also. I regret the ones I have would not resonate well with your moods."

"What is that supposed to mean?" We reach for the same journal and a shiver shoots up my arm. How salacious, Elize.

Would you like to respond or shall I? Silence? I will consider that a yes. But I— Relax. Let me take it from here. And stash this bounty. Deep eerie giggle. "You have cold hands. Can I offer you some heat, Mr. Gorgeous?" Whisper in his ear. "These pants are unseasonably warm." He looks horrified. Hmmm. Maybe Shen's around. Wink. About-face and strut that butt out into the midi sun.

Who do we have here, now? It seems the university counselor takes his walk at Tir-na-nog as well. Stalker. I know he is stalking me. Look at that nose. He has to be a spy. Only a spy has a nose like that. My turn. I can peek behind the holorider around the jade fountain. Should I let him know that I caught him spying? Too late. Nod back. Yeah. You should be concerned. How do *you* like to be followed? And he charges into Mr. G's shop. This I must witness.

Let me sneak around the back, crouch down, then spring to the roof. Perfect. No one is the wiser. Crawl to the exhaust vent and be the human transcriptor with my stolen journal. Deep eerie giggle.

Counselor: You touched her?

Mr. G: It was not intentional.

Counselor: Nonetheless, you interfered. Now is not your time.

Mr. G: And being sliced by Sothese? That was my time? For the greater good, I suppose.

Counselor: You healed quickly enough.

Mr. G: The pain is no less caustic.

Counselor: We all must sacrifice. I could not warn you, you understand.

Mr. G: The only thing I understand is that you make demands and empty promises.

Counselor: Be careful whose lies you believe, Gibayze. There is only one truth.

Mr. G: And you keep it closely guarded. You replicated me without my consent … and Nathruyu.

Holy Crap! You heard correctly, Elize. Mischief always uncovers the same. Deep eerie giggle.

K E E T O

It has been three days since my near-death experience in the open waters near Tir-na-nog, and I have held my promise to Eli. Although, the fact that Nathruyu and I have not been physically meeting is irrelevant because I still have been feeling her presence within me — until today that is. The myrrh that sends my heart on a sprint has now faded, as has her essence. My body is confused by the apparent withdrawal, jonesing for the intensity it brought, only to return to the previous level of visceral intrusions that have become my new normal since we shared a timeless connection through an opening in the containment grid of her frozen solitary confinement cell at the GHU transition wing.

It is curious how time stretches and shrinks with density of thought. At least, that is how I make sense of events that I can only describe as thick with emotions, driven by intense stress. Spending an eternity suspended beneath the gondola, with Eli's screeches muffled by layers of toxicity, crashed my subconscious into a realm filled with illusion as my lungs filtered the poison waters into my bloodstream and up to my brain. If Eli believed that I was doing the funky fungus with Nathruyu, then Eadonberg must float on an ocean variety. The last flash I remember before two hands came down from the sky to save me, which turned out to be Eli's, was Caroline bobbing in the water beside me like a magical mermaid coming to rescue her fallen sailor from sea demons, enraptured with the scent of manly flesh.

Manly is not exactly how I felt after the ordeal, however. I bolted to my cocoon in the archives and have essentially lived there for the past three days. I even scooped up Sparky and hid him in the artifacts room while I decompressed. The only reason I actually stopped by my crypt, in the first place, was because I had left my journal there, probably because of some incredible premonition, thank the little baby prophet. Otherwise, nearly a year of journaling would have dissolved into the waters like so much human history already has.

Gratefully, I have a confidant and, dare I consider, an unexpected mentor at the museum. My newfound obsessive work ethic was, of course, worthy of much eyebrow-raising cogitation, and a perfect mirror for his own scholarly antics. Izionnis became ears to the incoherence I was oblivious to and a guide to my recovery. Just today, he reflected more wisdom, which will ease my passage back into the world of the living, in the form of a question. Had I resigned myself to being an armchair archeologist? Or would I choose to harness the power that I had witnessed in the space where clocks no longer tick? His inquiry came with an opportunity that I would be a pup to decline; it involved a boat ride and a deep dive. Coincidence? You know that chance is simply movement misunderstood, but movement towards what?

My immediate reaction was "juicy!" followed by a cool sweat and a frantic dig into my satchel for a crutch that had decided to "release its soul from my tyranny," is the way Stitch interpreted it. My ancient blackberry had drowned in the toxic waters, along with my compulsion to plan out every detail in advance before reaching a decision. Paralysis was not to masquerade as analysis this time, so I swallowed my fear and burped out some courage. "I'm yay with that" was my resolute response. Geez. Did I really agree to an open-sea treasure hunt?

In fact, not only is the young scholar going to arrange the whole expedition, he insisted that the boy with the head tattoo "is not part of the mission", which unfortunately compounds the feelings of dejection Stitch has had for the past few days. Eli, currently on a rampage with her foul-mouthed voracity, and I, consumed by anxieties that are not my own, are feeding a rift in our happy-go-sleuthy trio.

My larger concern, in reality, is this boy Shen, who she finally admitted to easing with, when the people she really should be reaching out to are me, Stitch, and Dr. Tenille. We are the ones focused on her well-being. She is much too unstable, these days, for her to properly vet someone for our trio. And yes, my pen was not momentarily possessed by cupid's arrow for the consummate prankster. I am simply recognizing that, as much as I still challenge Stitch's intentions, he is our age, and he is not a world traveller like this new character ... Ohhhm gee, like Caroline is.

Will I ever evolve beyond boomerang accusations? What attracts me to Caroline is the same thing that attracts Eli to Shen. Pramam forbid I should ever admit that to my twin. Besides, I am not the one in a vulnerable mental and emotional state right now. An unscrupulous person can easily take advantage of her, and this guy's morality is the fiery unknown. I would never forgive myself for failing in my vow to protect Eli, and in my promise to you, Mother, that I would. Do you remember? I still live that moment …

Flip! There is no place to hide my journal from my tears. I have not disentangled myself from the sadness you tried to cover with a smile on the day you gave Eli the dreamcatcher and me my first journal. You made me promise to keep her safe and report back to you. Did you know that she would have nightmares? Were you hoping that the sun would burn them away, when they genuinely have become worse? And what about me? Are the answers to be extracted from the pages of my journals, rather than mined from the phantoms of Eli's dreams, as Nathruyu believes? Although she would say "belief is knowing without confidence."

And then there are the voices, not Eli's, but others I dare not share with anyone beyond these stone walls. Gurgling in the waters is all I have described them as, which is not exactly false, poetically speaking. I had believed, with little confidence, that the sloshing about in the cove was some form of intermedium communication while, at the same time, I imagined that insanity was projecting its illusory concerns into my head. Now that three days have passed without even a hint of a splash, I wonder whether lack of mettle had jumbled the message that I am now more receptive to. There is foreboding in Eadonberg waters, and it is clearly calling out to me. My gut senses it.

Perhaps that is why my digestive track has been struggling with flyer bakes recently. Stitch and I finally decided to chance a meal with Eli at the Snack Shack since Dr. Tenille had been imploring me to try to break the evil spell that she was currently cursed with. Just to be clear though, no dark incantations have been bandied about. He was stressing the point that agents of the GSU may respond to alerts from fearful residents, and I cannot even fathom what that may entail. Whenever he mentions those three letters, his eyes glaze over and his lips clamp shut. All things considered, we chumbuds swore to create a bubble of positivity around us.

I had already finished half my food by the time Eli and Stitch arrived, after I had done my sleight of hand with the self-erasing flyer-bake-wrap decoy Dr. Tenille had left for me, of course. All was progressing smoothly, albeit uncomfortably quiet, with Eli shifting her eyes sideways at everyone coming and going until I started off-gassing. She was on the verge of exploding in explicatives when our favorite genius whipped out a probe, from Pramam knows which pocket, and started zapping me, to Elize's ghoulish delight and filtered deep eerie giggle, I wager. He was careful to stimulate only digestive acupoints in his electric attack, wary of inciting a fire in the hole, so to speak, and I was quick to snatch the DC current device ahead of Eli's lightning fast grab. The loss infuriated the sting out of her.

"Wack of a slider slack!" was the most civil affront on the patrons around us as distraction pulled her into Ashton's newly installed holobanner, a Unification propaganda machine in exchange for special permissions to ignore the anti-three decree. Apparently, a hapless slidercab driver had yelled at Eli when he had almost killed her as she flew off the central corridor in her new planing booties to land on a floating holoadvert. She glared at us when we laughed, so in order to avoid a vile debate, which we would never win, we praised her magnificent power and focused on the news report.

While Eli all but gloated at the man's fatal crash with a "he created his own karma" quip and a "he should have spent more time looking where he was going than yelling at people" judgment, Stitch was quick to refute, saying that it was next to impossible to crash those things since they have proximity sensors everywhere. Further lies also postulated that the accident had occurred in the northern hills, where slidercabs do not venture, unless blackmarket goods and a quick trip to a holding cell are their preferred lifestyles. But not this law-abiding licensee, according to Stitch's quick patch into the licensing office. This driver was duly registered. The only crime he had committed was to yell at Eli — with a holoadvert as witness.

I immediately checked the safety on my new fart mitigator, because I was about to crap my pants. Stitch and I locked our saucers for eyes and whispered "Spies!", but not Madame Elize de Monstre. She banged her mouth off like a triggered Orangugong, who I hope is still intact in her room, somewhere. Ashton had to ask us to leave, so we cajoled her back to the archives, playing along with her squinty-eyed spy hunt in hushed tones, with a close call for outing me as one when her private medical transcript flew out of my satchel and nearly set the cleanerbots in alarm condition. I barely caught and stashed it before it hit the walkway, explaining that we best not attract attention. The sad part in all of this is that Eli will remember her outburst, and she will agonize about how to make it up to the man who feeds her flyer bake addiction.

I will spare you the aftermath of our revelation since the same narrative keeps spewing from her uninhibited self. Nevertheless, I will go on record, on my behalf and that of my resourceful fart-busting friend, to concede finally to a valid basis for Eli's paranoia. Despite the evidence before her and our strong advice that she keep her student gatherings quiet so that we can clean off any dusty profiles in the maze that may be connected to her co-activists, the rebellion in her will not abate for the sake of reason. This distraction, about saving the world from the Pramam's tyranny, is risking the very impetus that, first and foremost, propelled us to Eadonberg.

Someone is directing a global network of holospies and Eli not only has the mark, she is the mark. They know she is from the highlands, they know she took a trip to Albaraaton, and they know her name even, according to her conversations with the flirty holowall star. There is no other way to track her than to record her travels, visually. She has no biochip.

As we were picking through the inside of our brains for clues, I kept muttering how I wished that Sothese would go so far as to bathe in the coat with the Zaf factory special button on it. Only then, could we know for sure whether he is the mastermind behind the hunt, but it seems that the only thing this pervert does with it on is relieve his never-ending tension. Grody. Maybe he associates the Gadlin ceremonial jacket with conquest.

So what transpired out of our focused intent? No less than a response to my emotionalized request … less than an hour later.

Back again. I had to soak Sparky in his little tub to cool him off. The generator beneath the floral pond must be choking again. It happens so often that I must be getting used to the stench puff. Where was I? Right. The universe delivers, but let me save that for last.

Honest intentions may have spurred the initial eavesdropping session on the Pramam's advisor, but urgency has me checking several times a day for live updates, and with good reason. As soon as we figged Eli's behavior was under control, she went completely ballistic on Stitch, sending Mme Beaudoin straight for us, with a stern boot into the artifacts room for a talking to. With her hands on her hips, she witnessed a tornado of accusations against Mr. Zafarian being in collusion with Sothese, solely based on Dr. Tenille's account that Director Shakti recognized the advisor's new officials as Albaraaton Gadlins who had been clamped in the mosquibot sweep, yet seemed to have no recollection of her.

These kinds of delusions erode the trust that we need in order to travel together to Nukamigrad in the midst of the current GMU sweep for Gadlin terrorists. Discernment steers me away from this particular aspect of Eli's conspiracy theories and towards what we share as common ground. Teddy is our last hope to find out what really happened to the kidnapped children whom she babysat, and what their significance is to a memory gap in our own childhood that could be the key to Eli's deteriorating condition.

Mme Beaudoin had offered to clear access for Stitch and Eli to travel with us to Nukamigrad as extra assistants on official Museum of Antiquities business and to connect us with someone who can take us to a secret facility where the lost children who were found wandering the open spaces and who have escaped capture by the GHU crafts are cared for, but your daughter's volatility has her scheduling a brainwave scan with Dr. Tenille instead.

She was the one who had made the connection between Odwin and the curator, so that I might become an apprentice at the museum. Mme Beaudoin had promised Odwin her support, and that is what she intends to give. Her word is non-negotiable. Career and freedom are secondary. Therefore, once Eli's state of mind is quasi-normal, my supervisor will make good on her commitments. Given a favorable turn, we could be hopping the museum cargo transport as early as six days from now.

What triggers Eli's personality shifts is still a mystery, although with her current position at the URA as Director Shakti's research assistant, she has managed to remotely access the data banks at the URA headquarters in Ministburg and is planning to sneak a copy of your brainwave scans to Dr. Tenille as soon as she can safely do so.

In the meantime, we wait for anyone but the Franken-Eli to show up. I do prefer the wise yet bizarre one, but the overabundance of Zen could be dangerous on our trip. Frankly, if mind can indeed control matter, let the quirky creative one with a treasure-hold of ideas, manifest, because, to put it in the words of the ancients, "Lord knows we're gonna need it," if Nathruyu is truthful about the risks, that is.

In earnest, I am not being truthful with myself about the dangers. Nathruyu and Sothese are intrinsically linked. If ever there were a time for an alien conspiracy theory, this would be it. Yet, there is you, Mother, someone who presumably knew the secrets and died with them, a destiny which Eli and I are trying desperately to change, or to stop, or to do anything with other than nothing.

The impromptu GHU visit confirmed that there are no lesions on Eli's brain that would suggest clinical schizophrenia, but the state of her vermis has our Captain Snook rooked. He was cheated out of medical proof for his well-researched theory that the worm-shaped region would have a hole in it. It does not. It is missing altogether. Mashrin's, on the other hand, was intact when he performed the autopsy. Once again, the questioning leads to the lost children in Nukamigrad.

While Dr. Tenille was busy sneaking about the GHU with Eli, Sothese was sneaking back into the URA with our tiny informer. "Transcriptor on" is the last thought I will pen tonight. I will let the button results take over from here.

You told me they were terminally ill. (Corrient)

They were. They were slated for execution. (Sothese)

Gadlins! (Corrient)

The Pramam deemed them terrorists. I disagree, so I found a way to keep them alive. (Sothese)

You mean torture them before you kill them. (Corrient)

No. You did that. Your biochip implants failed. (Sothese)

But their vitals were stable. (Corrient)

Did you not think to ask how they were recovering? Or do you secretly enjoy genocide, Dr. Shakti? (Sothese)

No! (sniffling) You said their biochips were removed to save them. (Corrient)

There is some truth to that. At least they were not children. (Sothese)

(gasp, silence: 3 seconds)

There are other ways to test implants. What will it take for you to trust me? (Corrient)

Do you live up to your name, Director Shakti? (Sothese)

(rustling, slap)

Remember your place. I am in charge now, Sothese. (Corrient)

Yes. Your hands are sullied. Mine are clean. But if you prefer them dirty ... (Sothese)

(slap, laughter)

Leadership by force, I see. Would you like to direct me then, darling Corrient? I can be quite accommodating. (Sothese)

Your tongue is forked, dear Sothese. (Corrient)

It is also twisted. (Sothese, laughter)

Perhaps later. Back to work then. Interesting DNA, is it not? (Sothese)

These strands came from the filtration coils. DNA leaves a signature in water as in blood. (Corrient)

DNA also comes with other fluids. Would you care for a sample? (Sothese)

(giggle)

Always trying, dear Sothese. Yes, I would love one. (Corrient)

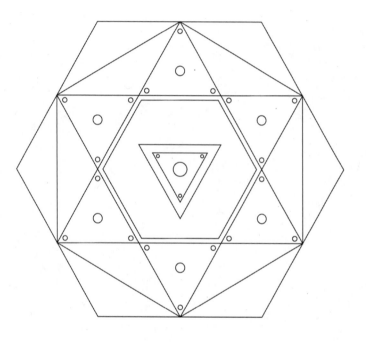

CHAPTER SIX

SOTHESE

Day 1060: morning

"Pitter patter ditch the chatter" is the unspoken call from the headmaster's chime, urging dozens of squealing children to their morning meditation. Although the candy-red in the playground this morning is far from the sweetness that would widen a child's eyes with enthusiasm, the little ones converge on the colorful Ministry official with hope for a home. Mutual disdain cloaks itself with pleasantries, as Master Tamrood invites Sothese and his contingent of high-ranking spiritual sages in for their monthly audit.

As governor of the Global Spiritual Unit, Sothese's access to the orphanage requires no permission slips, and his choice of candidates honors no objections. The current administrative lackey knows better than to question the Ministry official's authority, considering that the circumstances surrounding Master Chung's sudden departure carry high repeat potential, a notion that Sothese is quick to remind his new appointee of, as needed.

The orphans collect into three age-appropriate queues for their Unified confessions. The Entropist and the other two sages, one female shrouded by an exquisite sheer silk niqab and one male sporting a silk embroidered kippah, synchronized as one, enter the private realm of the innocent dreamer with a dark mantra aimed at bypassing the subconscious gatekeeper. Although all hopefuls have survived the surgical removal of their biochips at the age of one, this next phase in their journey holds no guarantees. Today, the three-year-olds, who have a peculiar relationship with an imaginary friend, are the targets of the spiritual stabilizers. The others are fortunately dismissed, to remain displaced, yet safe, for now.

Three toddlers jump with glee at the news that they are the chosen ones, intoxicated with the lies they have been served, while Sothese broods over the possible losses that may occur, and Master Tamrood wipes his feet of the crimson stain, exiting his body for his part in their abduction. As a result of the administrative transfer from the GHU to the GSU, the facility is in effect a nursery for Sothese's bidding. The Entropist and its aids benefit from an arrangement with the GSU despot, and he with them. The young sacrifices are to be payment in kind for the six compatriots who have thus far fallen while in Sothese's service, albeit via unknown hands. The price for carnal supremacy is never too steep.

Suspended below the Almedina courtyard, the belly of a gelatinous hybrid awaits, its docking mechanism forming an umbilical chord to the scholastic incubator. Three mini students slide down the chute into a spongy membrane acting as a floor. The Entropist trio and their plasma weapons are poised with three gold hexagonal boxes, each comprised of six separate equilateral prisms with triangular lids hinged along the outside edges of the container that joins together at a point when closed. Sothese's lips smile at the giggling playmates, but his eyes foretell the real intent.

A right index finger to the mouth while a left hand bisects the space in front in a slow precise line from the crown of the head to the chest hushes the tiny voices. Their eyes close, the fidgeting stops, and the holy extraction begins.

In a ritual that tames the ego, Sothese asks for permission to enter the young minds. Convulsions throw their twitching bodies onto the viscid surface beneath them, transmitting ripples along its extent and out into the toxic waters below Eadonberg. Drained of the lifeforce that animates their forms, the young lungs collapse with a final cough that ejects two blue lights in quick succession for a total of six dancing targets.

The three sages nod their gratitude, then splinter each spherical entity into three ultraviolet orbs with a blast from their plasma devices and seal the pieces into the respective compartments of their designated treasure chests, for these little gems are already spoken for. "In case incompetence persists, Master Sothese."

The waters beyond the jelly walls murmur a message delivered as reflections from sapphire blue eyes bobbing in the fluids of past regrets.

Attention does not come to those who hate. Detention is the gun that seals their fate. A brother is shunned. A brother has won. Forgive through the brother and the work shall be done.

Yet here she is, once again, bringing blissful chaos into his life.

Sothese vacillates. The innocent ones are both a test of and a testament to his resolve, for a momentary lapse could be the weakness that encases his own spirited aspirations in a golden prison. His focus remains on the expectant weaponry still cocked in the diaphanous room. He cautiously returns the nod and the translucent tube folds in on itself, vacuums up the human debris, and ejects the death into the toxicity of the Restricted Sector, the favorite playground of the child collector with the candy-red mane.

Brilliant crystal lenses against the vessel's hull form lasers carving rubies from his heart through his back. The pangs link every cell of his body into an armor for his empathy, so that it may remain buried where the blade of banishment impaled it. Nepharisse cannot bleed out his feelings of dismissal, but interfering with her influence on the order of things can certainly ease some of his suffering. The contest shifts to a viscous paddock immersed in the outskirts of Tir-na-nog.

The vessel torpedoes southwestward with the ginger-auburn rival tucked into its slipstream. Kainaten flickers in and out of view, ahead of the craft, like an amorphous pointer leading the way. The spiritual armada of three fuse their plasma beams towards the fishtailing huntress while the craft mimics her moves. She dives deep as an evasive maneuver and the hybrid follows suit. Then, in the measure of seconds, if time even mattered, the gurgling comes into view, as do the faint contours marking the three creatures trapped in the medium that binds them. Nepharisse is outnumbered, the hounds are released, and the chase continues with Kainaten in pursuit, freeing up Sothese for more pleasurable endeavors.

When it comes to exhilaration, it is the burst of stillness emerging from the turbulence that Sothese himself creates that makes forced subservience to idiocy, masquerading as intelligent leadership, passable. True power extends to those who choose their battles wisely and temper their judgment through patience. Whether it results in an inconvenient compromise or not, tolerance deserves much praise, much recognition, and much respect, since, for its ability to harbor dissent, there is no more honorable quality.

Without suppressed anger to feed rebellion, a ruler would have nothing to conquer, and a kingdom on earth would have no worthy subjects, worthy of this master's clutch, that is. Indeed, a life without fiery contrast is dreadfully two dimensional.

Joy comes in the throws of a passionate and ill-intentioned hunt, and, in order to slip between the cracks of orchestrated distractions, the terrain must be raked by thorough informants. But what of motivation? While many comply out of duty or expectation, what impels them towards action may repel others from the same. To govern under the burden of fairness is not at all inspiring to Sothese, therefore he relies on creative techniques to extract willing subservience from his sources.

Of course, willingness is simply compliance, seasoned with self-deprecation, garnished with a dash of grandiosity, a subtlety that Sothese admirably exploits through connivence. In any case, he reserves a more hands-on approach for those who overindulge in self-confidence, and who, in so doing, if truth be known on this very rare occasion, afford him the utmost satisfaction. Staying on top of his harem of spies can become exhausting, in a delightful way. Come what may, Sothese always has energy for more, in essence, thanks to his otherworldly sidekicks. And what better place to encounter a suitable ally for his quest than the facility that had caged the twins' mother — the GHU.

The expected recruit to Sothese's pack stiffens, as the Ministry official and his three shadows enter the waiting room, ignorant of the fact that he has already accepted the new mandate. A curious blood sample had warranted some sniffing into the real cause behind the GHU vehicle crash that supposedly killed his fellow medics on board. Suspicions that the SIF had falsified their report prompted an official GHU request for an independent autopsy of the victims.

Fortuitously, the Pramam, rightfully concerned that Ministry secrets might have been compromised, has dispatched Sothese, the one secretly responsible for the breach, as an impartial investigator into the strange DNA anonymously transmitted that night to the GHU admissions department.

Since a faction of the medical community has dared to question the legitimacy of Ministry sanctioned investigations, Sothese can turn the situation to his advantage. In a slick play to distance himself from the Pramam's agenda and to receive in-kind loyalty, he offers up a secure area in the underground URA facility in Eadonberg for the GHU examiner to use for sample storage and analysis. Sothese hints that more of these DNA anomalies may surface, specifically that of a young activist currently destabilizing the student population at Schrödinger University. Therefore, he also envisions Director Corrient Shakti as administrator for these critical DNA Files, with her willing professional cooperation to be sure.

How euphoric it is to happen upon new collaborations. Opportunities are ever-present in this orderly world. The trick is to correctly project their significance into the future, and then upset the order of things ever so slightly so as to effect controllable chaos. This seasoned medic's allegiance is no less a surprise than Sothese's old Gadlin accomplice's impending battle.

▼ ▼ ▼

Ribbons of green, blue, red, purple, and gold perform a haunting veil dance in the velvety darkness of space, serving as their sparkling backdrop. The spirits of the ancients are rumored to tease the souls of all who witness their mercurial ballet, but these ones do not flirt with destiny. Their forms undulate in harmony with their earthly intent as perceived through the eyes of the living, but perception deceives and the body concedes.

For the warrior whom Sothese once, or admittedly sometimes, defiled, only the years spent studying with Odwin can save her body from the challenge plunging into her chest from above. Will speed be her friend, or will sloth be her foe? The consequences of her choice will become evident when she accepts the severity of what she must face, because, in this reality, *they* did not come in peace.

Past emotions, poorly digested, repeat on Sothese as he discharges their potency into Wakanda. "This test of resolve is meant to strengthen you" is the poison he twists into a remedy for fear, a convoluted version of mentorship that rectifies Odwin's lack of attention on the physical plane. The lesson is equivalent, only the approach differs.

Nevertheless, his gracious offer to spare Wakanda the

coming pain and struggle by compressing the timeline into a single assault in the present moment drives the bargain he has been thirsting for. Time ticks once while he savors the terror swelling the veins in the white of her left eye as he presses her right cheek against the cold stone floor of her Albaraaton chamber. Sweat on her brow is the sign, and the second chime releases her to the decision that saves her life. The young woman now in the palm of his left hand is none other than his darling Caroline's new dazing friend.

▲ ▲ ▲

Time always reveals the hidden talents of informants. With the GHU, the Gayokcy, the network of holospies, the GSU, the Entropist, the lovely intermittent visitor, Caroline, and the Restricted Sector boss as manageable servants, and two others yet to suitably prove themselves, Corrient and Kainaten, the odds are definitely in Sothese's favor. However, the verse does not obey statistics. That is not the mathematics that governs its laws, and thus, those are not the numbers Sothese can rely upon. There are some who protect Elize and her brother for whom physical laws are in fact lies. And the Pramam himself can also have her taken at any time.

As if that were not enough of an aggravation, the Ministburg Lockdown escapees are still in hiding and are likely summoning more of their own for the trail, which might make the environment inhospitable to Sothese's projected devotees. Moreover, his obsession with integumentary perfection and virility requires the constant rejuvenating energies that those plasma spewing ingrates produce. All this so that he need not concede to the night.

Herein lies the quandary in which his world revolves. Each time the entities who conspire against him exterminate his beauty regime, their interference debases this Inner Council member's distinguished reputation, complicates his travels, and risks exposing his true origins to the blessed head of church and state. Sothese convulses at the thought of the Pramam's continued tenure. Elize is the new lamb who can accelerate the pontificator's demise. Her mother, in hindsight, was but a decoy.

Regardless, all things considered, Monique was far easier prey to access, yet even then, she still slipped away from Sothese. Now with a motivated collaborator on the inside, secretly avenging the death of his colleagues, certain permissions are heretofore within the advisor's realm of undue influence, starting with the coveted flashes and medical transcriptions recorded at the time of Dr. Yarkovsky's murder in Monique's padded cell.

A private room transforms into a hologram of past transgressions for Sothese's personal enjoyment. All is revealed to the one who knows where she is, and who she is. Sothese enters the game that lives in Monique's head through Nepharisse's hidden influence as the twins' mother straddles the fence between two realities. One, a shared memory staged to humble Sothese, the other, a doctor's last patient interview.

Dr. Tenille's voice crosses into the invisible game space where Sothese spies over a second medic's shoulder as she journals.

"Dr. Yarkovsky, this is the patient we were discussing earlier."

[The patient, Monique, is sitting at a table.]

"Hello, Monique, I am Dr. Yarkovsky."

[I sit across from the patient. She is wavering her fingers along the tabletop then gesturing in mid-air with her hands.]

Sothese slips back in time to the actual arena where he is the challenger. He throws the game board upwards in a powerful accusation of unfair interference, inciting anger's sharpness to cleave a rift in the space where time hovers. With the game pieces paused in mid-flight, Nepharisse carefully collects each token and stick as the circle of traitors snickers. Caution and thoroughness win the match, and the next opponent playfully swoops herself into the chair, sliding Sothese off in the process.

[The patient is unresponsive. She simpers, then smiles as if she were looking right through me. I suspect that she is hallucinating or lost in a dream world. She is also exhibiting manic behavior, shades of psychopathy. Her eyes appear possessed by a darkness.]

"Dr. Tenille thought you might want to talk to me. He said you were asking for me. Have we met? You smiled when I sat down. Are you happy to see me?"

"No."

"Why did you smile then? Do I have flyer bake drip on my shirt?"

"Not yet."

"Can you expand on that?"

[I can see her giggle, but no sound is coming out. She wears a choker with an unusual medallion.]

Sothese snickers. He knows who wears it now. Elize, the daughter, the twin, and now the rebel whose punishment is imminent. He also knows who gave it to her, but his time will come soon enough.

"Am I responsive *now*?"

[I am uncomfortable, yet curious. What games is she playing? There is one controlling her gestures, and one behind the smile.]

"How are you feeling today?"

"Trapped ... again ... always ... *They* are always watching."

[She exhibits extreme agitation as if trying to free herself of bondage.]

"I need to go."

"Where are you looking to go?"

"Nowhere."

[The patient appears frustrated, incoherent, and confused. She extends her left hand to my chest and quickly closes it, then pulls it away. She is volleying something imaginary between her hands, pleased with herself.]

Sothese smirks as Dr. Yarkovsky's lips turn blue.

"Mine now."

[The patient covers her mouth as if to yawn, then quickly clamps it shut. She slams the table with her right hand. She stares with distant intensity and smiles.]

"Just in case ... protection."

"Protection from what? From whom?"

Sothese follows the die rolling in the game space. It stops on the number nine.

"That is the magic number."

"What number?"

"Do you not know *anything*?"

[The look of scorn. The patient may be playing an imaginary board game.]

"You simply do not remember."

[Soon it will come back. It will all come back. All will come back soon.]

"Jog my memory then. Are you playing a game? Who are you playing with?"

[Trouble seeing. Writing. Heart racing. Lightheaded. Cold.]

"You."

"Would you … tell about? Does … game … a name?"

[I. Sweat. Panic. Choking m. Dizz.]

"I remember."

"Whaaat you re—"

The victory fades with Dr. Yarkovsky's head sliced open on the floor after it clips the sharp corner of the table. Blood sprays the room while its mist tickles a twitch from Sothese's upper lip.

"Sweet dreams."

And let us not forget the nightmares that the next hostess shall enjoy. The flashes fade as Sothese winds through the GHU hallways on a surprise visit to the campus oval to conclude the investigation.

There are many ways to root out an informant, but pleasant ones are not part of Sothese's creative repertoire. As a second favor this afternoon, the eager GHU resource fakes an unlawful assembly beacon through the bioHealth upgrade to all biochips registered to university students. The ensuing pandemonium is a vision of erotic euphoria that swells Sothese's arteries with blood, devoid of compassion and intended for the one he seeks to compromise.

Sentinels all over campus animate and drop, in unison, from their quartz overhead habitats, including from the links between the towers in Van Billund Hall all the way around the oval island to the amethyst ceilings in Osler Hall. The sentinel-guard duos collect at the center of the orchard and begin their indiscriminate sweep to the sounds of hovering GHU emergency crafts, ready to suck up the carnage. Sothese syphons in the scent of fear, as it scorches the grounds with the fire of a thousand voices, screeching their innocence.

E L I Z E

Day 1060: dawn

"What would this be, Director?" A thick viscous fluid with a peculiar scent. Unappetizing, may I add.

"It's a DNA sample. And call me Corrient, Eli. Can I call you Eli?" Should I? With Keeto's remote transcriptor spying into the lives of everyone Sothese is trying to corrupt, I would be on a first name basis with the Pramam also. Well, perhaps not the Pramam.

"I am not my name. Therefore you can choose to call me what you wish." She is smiling at me, strangely. "May I ask whose sample this is?"

"The Pramam's advisor." Step away from the bench. Stare at her in disgust. Giggling is an interesting response. "It's saliva." She laughs. "I know. It's not exactly fresh." Indeed. "I took it eight days ago."

"In earnest! The acting URA director the Pramam favored you over has offered you a DNA sample?" To what end, I wonder.

"We have an arrangement." Indeed, yet again. And it shall be revealed, as secrets always are.

"I see. And were you incubating a virus? For the delay."

"No, I fully analyzed it immediately. But I want you to look at it for yourself. Here's another sample from a different subject." The center of the room animates with the second sample. Place a drop of Sothese's saliva, if she says so, into the magnigram, and cap the test tube with a little something to keep an eye on things. Spy away, dear brother.

The DNA strands look strangely familiar. This must be the same sample Keeto and Zafarian found as shadow packets in the miniverse, yet it is definitely from a different not-exactly-human person. Double-check. Yes, 27 chromosomes and odd looking telomeres, just like Zafarian found through further analysis. Someone else apparently has access to URA-level viewing equipment because a trip down these DNA strands does not end in a blinding flash of light like the ones I have been experiencing every morning for the past couple of months when I wake up.

"You are aware of what this means, Corrient?" I wager not, from her expression. "There is a power source buried within the DNA caps. Is this not the Senescence Center?" Her jaw drops. Her eyes widen. I sense her heart race. "Can you filter out frequency emissions?"

"Yes! Let me adjust the range." And the emissions dim. She magnifies as well. We can see the detail now. "Fascinating! There is an odd circular inner DNA helix woven into the single strand tail with nine bioluminescent balls clipped into it. This is not a virus." Her heart skips a beat faster. She reaches for the pure water in the far cabinet and starts drinking. Another gift from Sothese, I imagine. And an offer I shall graciously accept.

"Thank you, Corrient. This is absolutely delicious!" How could our ancestors have taken this for granted?

"I can trust you to keep this quiet, Eli? You do realize what we have found here. What Sothese has confided in me."

Indeed, I do, but somehow I always knew.

"Of course. Yet his fondness for you? Be careful, Corrient. He is a snake in the grass." And Keeto, an ear on the walls. Store the sample vials back in refrigeration. Corrient turns off the magnigram, secures all the equipment, and locks the room behind us.

"Follow me to the surgery block." Gulp. *Remember, fear is not your savior, Elize.* Stop, breathe, and think. Father is not there waiting to open up my brain. She is trusting me. Move your feet. Ignore the heat. Meditate while we travel. Focus on the breath. Good. Here already.

There is a sealed room with no observation windows. Corrient turns to face me. She whispers. "I am supposed to report everything from this room, but I think someone else should know, just in case." Always just in case. "You can say no, Eli."

What is that ancient saying? Curiosity killed the cat? *Worry is futile, Elize. The cat has nine lives.* Very well, then. Nod … and she confirms the ancient retina scan. Sneak in behind her and stop breathing. There is a body on the slab. Shall I poke it? The scent is normal, albeit with a hint of anesthetic.

"He's recovering." She coaxes him onto his side, so that by tilting sideways I can see the incision. Corrient looks away and wipes a finger across her eye. Her values have been compromised. I can feel it. She clears her throat, sniffs, and drops the big one on me. "He used to be a Gadlin. Now I don't know what he is. His DNA is changing."

"Was he the second sample?"

"No. Not in that way. He's human alright. He's just not

who he used to be. It's the biochip. There's something in the one we implanted. Look at him. It's like he's or she's two people." Gasp. She shows me the accelerated flashes from the recorder directed at his face. His physical appearance is slowly changing to someone else — a female!

"How is this possible? I am in shock. Please give me a moment." Run to the corner. Sit on the floor. Breathe. Am I wearing my pup on a chain? No! *There is no need to panic, Elize. I am here for you. Serenity. Simply breathe.* Yes, breathe. Thank you. I am calm. I am strong. I am ok. Oh. My apologies, Rango. I forgot you were still on my back. Thanks for the nudge.

"Eli? I'm so sorry. I should not have brought you here. Let's leave now. Dr. Tenille does not even know." Interesting statement. He is my analyst, but I can still keep secrets from him. In fact, I do.

"Trust is the key to longevity. Breach of it can lead to an abrupt ending. The subject is off limits with Captain Snook." A giggle returned breaks the tension. I will leave a discussion on the use of Gadlins for another day. "What about memories?" This may explain my experience with Mashrin's biochip attack. Ouch.

"As far as we can tell, the original memories slowly get replaced by the new ones. It's almost like a complete reprogram. The original person is, to all intents and purposes, dead. I can't get my head around that. They're just gone." They must go somewhere. Oh oh. Thoughts of otherwordly explanations are creeping in, and those would be my dear brother's superstitions. *Belief is the source of vision, Elize.*

Well, I see quite fine with my eyes. No distractions.

"The flashpack is full. Can you hand me a clean one from that cabinet over there, Eli?" As I turn to reach for the new one, she snaps the old one out and quickly shoves it into a box in a locked cabinet. If I can just catch a glimpse of the label on the cover. Double-gasp! Witness Relocation Program. Oh oh. She saw me peek.

"You weren't supposed to see that." And technically not the ex-Gadlin on the table, either. I wish I could hear her thoughts because her eyes are piercing me. She sighs. "It's my job. You've been here long enough." She checks the clock on the wall. "Shite! Here's a map, take this exit. You need to get out fast. No. Left. See you tomorrow."

Oh oh. Sothese! Forget the proprieties. This calls for a mega pica ziga whateva sheiss! Where to now? Check the map. Another exit. Good. Surge like flood. Run run run. Look back. Phew. Turn the corner. Keep running. Turn the next corner. There it is. Look back. I am soaked. And the door is … there. Wave it open. No. Passcode. Got it. Virtafloor, please. Good. Jump on. Up the shoot. Whoa! The URA is deeper than the Restricted Sector. I hope it opens … like now!

Phew. Where am I? What was that? Oh no! Outside the biowall and here comes the toxic fog. Oh I am in big … Another flash. And another. Surrounded! What do I do? A slidercab? Out here? Ok. Just take it.

"Thank you. I got lost." That is the best I can come up with right now? *Serenity, Elize. You are enough.*

"Of course you did. Where to?" No questions? I like him already.

"Schrödinger University."

"We'll take the eastern route around. It's safer."

"Safer? That goes right by the Restricted Sector."

"I'll give it a wide berth. A little further out into the ocean, but no storm right now. Just fog." I wonder what is to the west then. Deep breath in ... and exhale. If he says so. "As you may have guessed, our fleet is unofficial. That will also be one hundred credits." That will be a problem.

"Do you accept coin?" He whips his head around and grins. I take that as a yes. Time to comm Keeto. "The east perimeter gate then." Pick up, dear brother. Pick up. Here he is. Three fingers? Ok. Three it is. "No time for questions. Meet me at the east campus gate and bring three of those coins ... Right. Those ones ... ten minutes ... no questions I said! ... And stay back ... go now!"

"Thank you, Miss ...?" Think of a name. Wipe the sweat.

"Terry." Hold back the giggle. Good. The blowers are barely giving us any visibility for the speed we are moving. Smooth sliding though. "What was that?" I am not liking the sharp zigzag moves, and he is not answering. "Are we being attacked? Sir?" Did I just see a tentacle? Breathe. Everything is calm now. Just breathe.

"Apologies, Miss Terry. There was some turbulence below." Zigzag turbulence? "Strange happenings these days." He looks back with a tight-lipped smile. Agreed. No questions. But I want answers. *Observe with an open mind and the answers shall come, Elize.* If you say so. *I do. I do. I do.*

We are hovering now with blowers on full. Now how are we going to get through that biowall grid? Oh. That is a handy little beam. A yellow puff on campus will not hurt anyone. Here come the frequenflyers to fix the gap. Handy little hybrids. Hehehe. Frankenflyers! *Insults, Elize.* Hey. Watching my language all the time is hard work. *Granted, Elize.* There is Keeto on the comm: "Just dropping now." Turn to the driver. "Stay here. I have the coins." Grab them from Keeto ... Run back to the slidercab ... Highland wave ... and off he goes.

"Eli! Are you bent? I thought you were in your wisdom mode. I question that." He points to the big yellow smoke cloud coming in from the slidercab breach on his way out.

Shrug. "No time to talk. I have a student assembly to run before class. Time is ticking." Major hands on hips and I-am-going-to-tie-you-down-from-now-on look. Hug him. He needs it. "I will explain later, I promise. And thanks for the coins. Your pirating came in handy." Poke, smile, and now run.

It must be a short meeting. I can be terse. Besides, those entities out there concern me. We should not meet as a group anymore. It will be safer. Here already? That was fast. *Focus changes the perception of time, Elize.*

"Way, fearless overseer. We thought you got clamped." No. But nearly something else. "Luckily, Stitch has been entertaining us with his bioscalp." Giggles all around. And a poke and a smile from my chum.

"I was worried." He is standing tall on purpose. Poke and smile back.

"Apologies for my tardiness. Three-minute summary, Jacinta?"

"Juicy. All nine branches report three hundred percent increase in recruits."

"That means we went from three to nine. That is not even one floor."

"People are afraid of a sweep. We need some protection." Vlad is right. Zafarian nods and leaves. He will find a way. I know he will.

"We need more support or the march will fail." Lupe from the L branch pipes in. Should I mention the alien blood? The cover up? No. That would cause a panic.

"I was late from an attempt on me." Gasps. Is that enough? "That means we are onto something big. The Pramam has to concede." Murmurs. Eyes locking. Nods. Good.

"Crazed. But I'm in, all the way, Miss Elize." Yes! Diego from N branch. And the others? Good.

"Very well. We communicate via the secure channel from now on. Dismissed. Stay hydrated everyone. The heat is coming." In more ways than one. Now off I go to see Dr. Tenille. What a busy day!

Oh oh. There is the counselor finishing his morning orchard walk. I will let him enter O'Leary Hall first, then tiptoe to the cabin. Soft knock. Captain Snook pokes his head down the hallway, then hushes me in. In all honesty. The counselor must know that we meet every day. Best keep playing along though, just in case. Giggle.

"And how is me Belle, this morning?"

"Ship shape, Captain, and ready with an open mind." *Focus on his voice, Elize. Hear nothing but his voice. His voice reassures you that you are free.*

✂ ✂ ✂

ELIZE

"Pica delicious! Ta to Mme Beaudoin for letting me ride to Nukamigrad with you, bud."

"She's not paying for it. Wakanda is." Soft giggle. Stitch spray painted a masterpiece on the window with his food. "She's the funding patron. She wants to make sure they're taken care of."

"Flyer mud, Keet. She's buying a favor, yeah? Wakanda didn't build her credit by being generous. Always leading the greed. Always hunting for thieves."

"Like me." Keet is ashamed of himself. I know why. Some quiet time is what he needs right now. Best let him journal ... journal ... journal ... Ok. Long enough.

"Did Caroline find the Galleon's sails yet?" I hope she is still staying away from him, though. No love in that relationship.

"Neah, Eli. Sothese either doesn't have them or he brought them to Ministburg." What is with Stitch's teeth? They are moving like waves. I am creating my own reality here. I must be hallucinating. "In all fairness, she doesn't really know what they are. I just said they are museum artifacts and worth something."

"You lied to her?" Not just a thief. A little creative with the truth, perhaps? What is with those teeth of his?

"Well, not exactly. Mme Beaudoin and the curator would consider them historic and would be willing to reward the one who returns them."

"So in what dimension is this not considered lying, Keet? You created your own narrative." A good one, though.

"Perk. If you believe in infinite parallel universes then—"

"Eek!" Keet pulls back, and Rango is going crazy again ...

on Stitch's head. Keet is ripping and rolling now. Soft giggle. "Ok, Rango." Grab him and take him to the corner to whisper his deactivation code "Me Tarzan." Back to Stitch and his row of insect arms coming out of his teeth and picking the food bits out. "Where on the planet do you come up with these ideas?" Stitch is howling at his own craziness.

"Creative, ya fig? And you, chum? How did you program my Orangugong to do that?" Shrug.

"It just started acting that way all of sudden. You must not be as Tess as you think." Poke him. He pokes back, but his scalp is drawing shifty eyes. Hmmm. He thinks I am lying. "That is not *my* version of creativity, Mr. Zaf." Glance sideways at Keet. Soft giggle.

✄ ✄ ✄

Those screams. What is happening? Where am I? Who is calling me?

"Eli? Hide over here." Oh, I am still in Dr. Tenille's office. What is happening out there? I must go. "No. Stay here. Eli!" Run down the hallway. My arm. Oh oh.

"Miss Elize!" Not the counselor. "They are looking for you. You must stay here. Come to my office." Dr. Tenille pokes his head out, nods, then hides back in his office. Ok. I go with the counselor and if anything happens, Dr. Tenille is my witness, but I feel ra—

✄ ✄ ✄

E L I Z E

Strange. Rather Strange. Walk to the window. The sentinels are coming into the building and no one is screaming. A little pinch just to be sure. "Ouch!"

"I assume you don't remember anything?" Not a loving attitude from my dear brother. I suppose he is upset about the slidercab payoff.

"Welcome back, chum. Keet had some steam out the ears earlier. Care to share?"

How do I say this without sounding paranoid? "How much time do we have?"

"I don't know about Stitch and me, but I wager you don't have much time … unless you spill it!" I see. Quite upset.

"Sothese has the same DNA mutation as the miniverse freak. Creepy threes are everywhere and they are after me. Something huge is living in the waters off the Restricted Sector. I lost hours in Captain Snook's cabin, off somewhere I do not recall. Then the counselor kept me in his office, I think, while whatever caused the GMU sweep went away. And apparently, I had a blackout." Think. Anything else? Think. "Oh and a biochip transplant reconfigures your DNA." Jaws on the floor means I confessed to impress.

"Whoa!"

"Creeps!"

"I can give you details later. Now, your turn." Keeto beats Zafarian to the first confession.

"Stitch is making his Gadlin cloak." He elbows Keeto. "It's a bloody mess so far." I fail to see the humor in … Disturbing. That is a piece of the shirt he dabbed my bloody head with, the night we found Mashrin's body. "That's right. Your DNA is now a patch in his life's story. Grody, eh?"

"I would add 'twisted' to that statement; however, my higher self would say experiences carry no judgment with them; that is something humans do." An eye-roll from Keeto. Lean into the board. "Ooooooooo, did you just crack the bioHealth frequency?" A huge grin from Zafarian.

"I can control the messaging now. Swish! But it has all sorts of traces on it. I can get away with one broadcast then I'm busted, yeah? It has to be right on credit."

"Oh, and a crack for Mashrin's biochip code too. Genius boy, you did it!"

"Neah. I dripped questions into the maze ages ago and someone just figged it. Let's roll through her memory flashes." Keeto and I lean in and hold our breath. "And the last person she saw alive was …"

We gasp in unison: "Caroline!"

K E E T O

I expect the unexpected in Nukamigrad, so I think it prudent to do a partial journal entry while Stitch and Eli are finishing up their meal, and I flip a pass on the main course since my appetite is wanting these days. After Eli commed me this morning, hysterical about being shadowed by someone she cannot recall, followed by a lengthy list of deplorable names for Caroline, who I know is on the cargo sliders right now, I was bracing for a long trip filled with profanity.

Summoning healing energies through my aching heart is not having its intended effect since our beloved Eli is losing herself inside intensifying hallucinations. Gratefully, however, my temerarious twin did not curse her way into the back water garden of the museum where our craft had just been moored. Instead, she arrived with bonbons for all of us and hugs ad nauseum, a further sign that her personality shifts are becoming more extreme and outwardly noticeable.

This morning, when we were shopping at Tir-na-nog in preparation for our trip, Eli bounced from store to store buying and returning clothing as a result of her constant change of mind. Even Mr. G stayed clear of her each time she walked through his door, at least half a dozen times may I add, and for some reason, he was not very hospitable towards me either. So when she pounced onto the private transport's deck, with Rango sporting a spiky psychedelic hair-dye job, I could not help but wonder what outpouring of torturous love she had inflicted on poor Cyd back in her room.

At least the Central Core zombie invasion took some of the focus off Eli's eccentricities. As we were returning from our spending extravaganza, Stitch froze his hip jiggling, yanked us into the medi-clinic lobby, and urged us to put on our headbands. That move did nothing to assuage my GHU anxiety, especially considering that the bioHealth frequency was in high alert, pasting horror on the faces of everyone in the city: "Northern biowall towers breached by Gadlin terrorists. All residents proceed to the central corridor for immediate evacuation."

We had a split second to decide. Either stay hidden and hope for the best or join the masses being corralled by the Global Military Unit sweep.

While I surveyed the north for a wall of yellow death heading our way, Eli argued with herself, and Stitch acted like a pickpocket with a zigazillion hands. He somehow found a personal bioshield while our biochips waited for instructions. But nothing came. It was simply a drill, thank the little baby prophet. Nevertheless, the greatest honor belongs to our fair damsel in psychological distress, for she not only survived the hormonal charge that sheer panic ignites, she pulled some brilliance from the universe, with a soft giggle and a creative: "Well, that would be a lovely way to comm together a fun street daze."

The three-way eye-lock we shared sparked the fastest and most spirited chumbud salute we have ever slapped together. All we needed was the date, a flawless execution, and for me to stop shaking my hands and pacing back and forth in my mind, as I do whenever I am really anxious.

For starters, keeping geese from stalking me while I physically walk might help. I do not usually make an issue of them, but I am beginning to suspect a fowl conspiracy to the point of considering Stitch's suggestion for a Waka-flyer game, since he is no more fond of them than I am. He figs that Wakanda is likely the Pramam's secret breeder, even as he wages war against her while she conveniently remains unclamped. "Breeding for the Unified golden eggs," he scoffs. So far though, goose mud for orchard fertilization is all that the groundskeeper collects from the campus nesting house.

Speaking of Wakanda, I am top ripping and rolling here. Stitch just spewed all his food on the window. Knowing that she has offered up the credit for the trip to Nukamigrad is causing an esophageal protest. Hehehe. At least it is a temporary constriction, unlike the one I have felt closing in again on me. And the tightness is more than anxiety induced by the gurgling in the middle of the night. I am dreaming, but you know that these are not ordinary dreams, because I sense you in them, Mother, while at the same time I sense you in me, bleeding from a wound no one can see, no one bound by human sensory factors, that is.

Unearthly darkness clutches our eyes, for motives I can only imagine exist to anesthetize us through terror and to deafen us from the murmurs that surround us by focusing our attention on the thunder mushrooming upwards from each successive blood drop smashing the stone below. The black appears as three cloaks shrouding the faces behind the voices, but myrrh overpowers the space and betrays who I know to be there, watching, circling, clawing at my soul, at your soul, at our souls … and there is another, hiding inside me, waiting, fearful, yet resigned to its fate. These are not the dreams that foretell the answers that Eli and I seek. I refute them. They are false, are they not?

For the past week, my mornings have become nightmares that end with a supercharged heart rate coincident with the ultraviolet lighting effect that Eli has been seeing for quite a while now. Originally, I thought that her eyes had been damaged by the plasma arcs in Almedina, but I no longer believe that. So, as an experiment, I asked her to note the time her dawn corneal flash burns occur into the journal she had bought from Mr. G's shop. As I had suspected, the bursts immediately precede my daily jolts out of sleep. Somehow, we exist together in a dreamworld, or rather a visceral hell, that Eli immediately forgets upon waking, yet I do not.

I remember the agony, the scent, the echoes, the metallic saliva, and the endless void. If only I could also see them. If only I knew for sure. If only Eli could recall any detail. Maybe she recognizes them during that momentary flash that startles us both, drenching her in sweat and leaving me panting.

Blindly, I muddle through clues in my waking hours, provoked by an enigma, sullied by the blood of children. Could Eli and I have once been on that hick of a list she absolves herself of responsibility with? You know who I mean. I just cannot bring myself to join her name to the accusations I am making. There has to be a reason. There always is, right? But in this case, is that reason enough to justify the means?

Well, if it is good for the gander, then let me be the goose and peck a little hair off the seductress for Eli to sneak over to Director Shakti for analysis. If Nathruyu, my beautiful stranger, is indeed "a female Sothese" as Caroline says, then a quick snap into the URA magnigram for her DNA will reveal all. I control the alabaster pieces on your game board now, Mother.

Caroline, of course, is no innocent bystander herself. Stitch has confirmed that Mashrin's biochip is perfectly preserved, which means that the evidence supporting a charge of kidnapping and accomplice to murder is, at the very least, irrefutable. On top of that, the chumbud who cracked the code sent a sketch out into the maze, for some due favors, that uncovered and analyzed the stolen biochips for eight of the nine children, Teddy's being the one missing. I cautiously assume that he is alive and safe in Nukamigrad, the city where, according to Mme Beaudoin, the lost children are concealed from the GHU.

News of a trusted friend's involvement in the most heinous of crimes is demoralizing to be sure, but the Ministry, specifically Caroline's obsessive taboo, Sothese, is where the credit stops. Emerald green eyes floated in the recovered biochip flashes from the previous seven kids, as did three sets of bright haunting ones. This suggests, to me, that Mashrin's and Teddy's abductions were unique and quite possibly preempted. Well, at least that is what I want to believe, because it would justify my now questionable relationships with both Nathruyu and Caroline. Could my judgment be compromised?

According to other revelations over these past seven days,

discernment, at least partially, still rules my emotions. A strange incident relating to Dr. Yarkovksy, nine years before you supposedly killed her, has also surfaced through several dust-crusted high council packets. Her university studies and subsequent years as an accredited medic were nothing worth digging into further, but the scar at the base of my skull, the mark of the hunted, as Dr. Tenille nervously emphasizes, that has made phantoms out of the hairs that used to live there, shot pins into my spine when we swept a report describing an attempt on Dr. Yarkovsky's life.

The inexplicable specter of malice that I have detected from time to time, the knowing that someone with less than honorable intentions had been there before, is the imprint left on the night Dr. Yarkovsky was all but terminated at the age of eighteen in the northeast corner on the ninth floor of Van Billund Hall's J branch — Eli's room. Questions are still outstanding, but this we know so far. Whoever assaulted her was not after her biochip, because she had none.

If I am to be honest with myself, the pangs in my stomach have nothing to do with hunger. I wager that my recent distaste for flyer bakes, or anything that began as a sentient being before it ended up on a midi platter, is related to non-physical changes outside the confines of my own body. It sounds crazy, I know, but whispers tell me that a shift is on the horizon, and adaptation is our salvation. *They* are gathering, and we must be ready.

To quote from the twisted mind of my own petrifying harbinger of death: "The real question is not what, but why." Why were so many children taken? Why are mothers of twins a threat? Why are twins hunted? Why this, that, and the other thing. Most of all, why Eli?

For now, I take comfort in the notion that although my sister may not be the model of sanity, the line between genius and folly is merely penciled in. Her wisdom increases with each transition, regardless of the influence that overtakes her, be it destructive, creative, or neutral. Thus the bar moves, challenging Stitch and me to communicate on her level as if the broadcast station she uses is drifting out of the frequency range we operate on.

Despite all of that, the divide is in fact widening, and I dread the prospect that the twin I have known all my life could fall into the same chasm you did, and all transmissions would pass aimlessly into an eternal abyss. I need your reassurance, Mother. Would that you send some my way. Please, send me a sign that will lift my spirit.

Ohhhm gee! Eli just screeched me out of the dark spiral of guilt and regret I was drowning in. Stitch and his inventions. What a rip!

Well, this is a good place to center my emotions. Whether Teddy is the key to unlocking Eli's dreams or not remains to be seen. Whether Nathruyu is simply sending us on a wild goose chase while she maneuvers her way into power is still a possibility. Anyway, Nukamigrad is on the horizon and faith is our chaperone.

✄ ✄ ✄

I suppose I should have warned Eli about the main industry

Nukamigrad is famous for, but then again, her reaction was priceless. The city is the hybrid research and manufacturing capital of the entire planet. Our docking experience alone was worth the trip in behind-the-back chumbud salutes between Stitch and me as Eli battled the aging lobcarts for our luggage. Hehehe. I consider the convoy of six-legged porters, whipping her butt with their benign stingers while she raced to our hired slider, well-earned payback for the Eli Monster we have been enduring back in Eadonberg.

Unfortunately, the last rib was not to be mine. Not only are there genetic-mechanical crosses in combinations that question the sanity of their architects, the entire city is overrun by them. Travel between one sealed building and the next involves double-layered bioshields and spin stabilizers on all sliders, and for those who dare to walk on land? Well, no one dares. The terrain is a half-dazed hybrid infestation with enough momentum to knock a three-meter platymoa off its feet, even with a shipment on its back.

Our brief souvenir shopping attempt on the way to the Museum of Antiquities artifacts hub very nearly ended with our craft somersaulting to our destination. Apparently, laughing at an ill-formed cleft-beaked loading dock reject trying to outrun disembodied pincers turns you into the perfect swatting target, not to mention the failed pollibot swarms looking for field weaknesses and human nectar. In Nukamigrad, even the biowall is an experiment that keeps resident menaces from escaping as well as filtering the toxic fog.

We forewent the mobile trading posts in favor of the more conventional boutiques, plugged into the museum's perimeter garden. While Mme Beaudoin cleared our permission slips with the local curator, gawking at Stitch's animated thoughts of pollinator warfare on his scalp, Eli stood in awe of the dreamcatcher paradise we had just leapt into. Exquisite colors, textures, sizes, shapes, and more, all meticulously woven, twinkled in the scorching sunlight. A delicate medallion-sized one was the focal point that drew her to a stop with the vendor's words: "Sometimes dreams are best kept close to your heart."

I now realize that it was not artistic admiration that took Eli's breath away but a short-lived episode that claimed her consciousness. A soft hand on her shoulder and a reassuring smile were gratefully the only intervention required in this particular instance since the voices of a hundred children were following a group of Gadlin nitapoks, leading them on a cultural trip through the touring exhibits. Stitch bowed in respect for the Gadlin Order as I shared a squashed frog face with my disoriented twin. There were only thirty apprentices or so, but each created the presence of three. Mme Beaudoin's stern hush-face answered the question as it arose. These were the lost children.

My heart soared with the hope that Teddy was amongst them, but fate has decided otherwise. These young ones are different. They are like Eli. Mme Beaudoin was quick to distract us with a crystal vendor at a docking pod at the far end of the garden while the orphans completed their tour. The shame in Eli's voice as her eyes teared up at Stitch mirrored my own guilt over wavering trust. "I'm so sorry, Stitch," was the apology stolen from my mouth for accusations of theft. Many pendants on display were exact replicas of the stolen one that Nathruyu claims is Eli's not yours.

Once the hallway was clear, we followed my supervisor's hushed excitement into the artifacts room, prompting Stitch's thoughts to draw a hand scratching his scalp at her unusual bounce. A flick of a switch and the darkness became an ancestral treasure trove that would put the garden dreamcatcher vendor out of business. Now I understand the risk-reward calculation that has seduced honest custodians. The sacred riches contained real feathers, leathers, sinew, and twigs from extinct species, many adorned with precious gemstones woven into their wispy fringes. How they have remained so well preserved is a mystery, but their authenticity is indisputable.

While Mme Beaudoin kept Stitch and Eli busy untangling the silky threads, she enthralled me with a jewel encrusted box containing an ancient scroll and impressed me with her translation skills. An obscure tale flowed from her lips recounting a medical procedure intended to purify blood through blue viscous fluid, restructured bonds, crimson crystal dust, blinding lights, intense heat, and a body, at which point she clamped her jaw, rolled up the scroll, slammed the box shut, cursed under her breath, and reprimanded the local curator, as she purposefully positioned herself between Eli and the text. "This does not belong here. Lock it up with the others," she snapped.

An abrupt "We will reconvene tomorrow" ushered us out the door to our quarters, where I now wait, but not before Wakanda charged in for an impromptu catalog check. Her welcome quickly turned sour when she saw Eli besi—

Come to tower three. (new voice)

Annotate new voice. Izionnis.

✂ ✂ ✂

Is it safe to speak now?

Yes. But mind your thoughts. We want calm waters. (Izionnis)

How far are we from the city?

Far enough never to be found. (Izionnis)

This was a bad idea. I want to go back now.

Indecision has no place in your future, Keeto. We stop here. (Izionnis)

An island? This was not on the slipmap. So we dock and—

No! This is a gyre. There is no solid ground. (Izionnis)

You mean, this is a toxic waste pool? Creeps!

Wear this suit and hook in. I will pull you out in time. (Izionnis)

You want me to swim in this garbage?

Not swim. Dive. (Izionnis)

Are you bent? Why don't *you* fetch it and I pull *you* out … in time? Geez!

Sothese will know. (Izionnis)

Juicy! A secret recorder is attached. What was that?

Nothing of concern. Just focus, Keeto. (Izionnis)

Just focus? Right. Nothing of concern. I want to know what that splash was.

Worry not. Quickly, Keeto. We need that dagger. Remember what I taught you. Center yourself. No overthinking. (Izionnis)

It's getting clo—

NOW! (Izionnis)

(scream, splash)

You are taking a big risk, Izionnis. Anubrat will not be pleased. (new voice)

Waiting is a greater risk. (Izionnis)

They followed. (new voice)

I know. Stay alert. (Izionnis)

(gurgling)

What are you wear— Shut it off! We have to get that jour— (new voice)

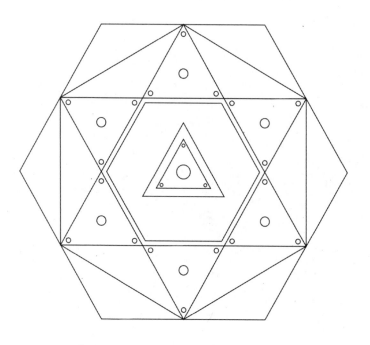

CHAPTER SEVEN

SOTHESE

Day 1068: morning

For millennia, water has been cleansing humans of their glorious sins, awash in the great rivers of ceremony, and now she is saturated with the hate of fallen civilizations. Her unquantifiable hydrogen-infused hands are thus groping for each other, in a desperate attempt to hold on to the joyful memories of what once was, before humanity injected its poisonous thoughts and deeds into the ethereal mist that connects all there is.

Flow died with the conveyor belt that shook the tincture of life from the oceans' depths to produce a stunted stagnant upwelling of toxicity, whereby the arms that had previously offered oxygen returned to the golden age where sulfur is king. Fortunately for Sothese, the Gadlins still control the great water well and the technology that operates the purification coils throughout the Unification; otherwise, the longevity-obsessed plaster messenger of Their divine teachings would have aborted, through his own ignorance, the protective bubble that he and his Unified congregation rely on.

Just to be clear, Gadlin survival is not necessary for Sothese's impending reign, but it does offload an enormous environmental burden that would otherwise be his to correct, lest he be forced to resign himself to cavorting with less palatable versions of humanity, weak with disease and scaly with thirst. As long as Wakanda understands who has the grip on power and submits to that power, as he so chooses, her kin will benefit from a friend in the Ministry. There are many favors owed he has yet to demand payment for.

▼ ▼ ▼

Personal chambers, infused with the scent of conquest, conjure images much too enticing for Sothese to ignore, as do their tenants, whose fervent fragrance he inhales with guiltless voracity. Invitations rooted in earthy deception are especially aromatic in their allure, and they just so happen to be one of the few reliable methods to ensure a temporary friendship that has the potential for mutual benefits. Wakanda earns the title of model disciple, in this regard, and all the trappings that this honor endows her with. Tonight, the endowment shall be replete with gifts that the advisor will gladly deliver, for requesting a private audience .with the Pramam is a grand service, deserving of the same.

A petition for entry is purposefully omitted as Sothese charges past the Gadlin escorts to interrupt a tasty indulgence. Wakanda sits at a table, unperturbed by the forceful intrusion, as she offers a sweet treat to her summoned guest. The arrogance evokes a suggestive discourse with Sothese controlling the pace until he notices the undoctored flashes of Nepharisse, catching his three officials operating on a steaming charred body in a secret subfloor of Eadonberg's university medical lab. This gatayok clearly has higher aspirations than her current mandate supports.

Impressed by her bold gambit, Sothese concedes to Wakanda's desire for a ministerial meeting but refuses the culinary tease with clarity on what, in particular, he prefers to eat. As the crabbots chase Nepharisse in the holographic evidence that would complicate his relationship with the Pramam were it to leak, the current scene plays ahead in Sothese's mind.

"You are inconsequential, do you not realize your lack of worth, Gatayok?"

"Yet you know you both need me."

"We are simply humoring you."

"Then this is a black comedy."

"More like a *tragédie*. Would you care to know how it ends?"

"With your black-pitted skin, hungering."

"How delightful. Someone has been spilling secrets."

"You need my help, Sothese. Only I have the ear of the twins."

"Then you know what they look like."

"And you do not? Interesting. An untrusted advisor."

Sothese walks through Nepharisse's likeness, aroused by her panting. "Tell me."

"One favor at a time, Sothese."

"Which I will demand when I feel the urge. Then tell me, Wakanda, do you still practice your training?"

A not so subtle penalty for promises denied should stress the point. What a range! Her ability to vocalize is simply stupendous. Sothese clamps down on her jaw and pinches her flaring nostrils shut. He licks the fluid oozing out the cracks, spits it back at her face, and laughs at her quaint provocation.

"You need a course in self-restraint."

"And *you* are the one to teach me, my darling?"

"I know what you want, and you are not going to get it owned by your lust."

"We shall see who owns whom. The Divine Messenger is all yours."

▲ ▲ ▲

Accounting may be a bore for the man of irresistible talents, but when it comes to compounding interest on scores unsettled, the field is lush with revenge. Wakanda's betrayal requires no evidence, nor does her recent and cleverly inspired disclosure zero the balance. In fact, she may not have enabled the Ministburg Lockdown escape, but she represents the only remaining ally of the three perpetrators, whose indiscretions Sothese was held responsible for and has yet to receive his joules of energy for. The clock shall stop with a tap, tap, tap between ticks, and the three traitors will subsist in agony, eternally trapped inside a custom prison of no return.

Fear, the great limbic motivator, lives at the edge of devolution, ready to attack reason as it recoils on itself in a desperate attempt at self-preservation. Over the course of merely a week, Sothese's inventory of associates has been dwindling. Caroline is distant, Wakanda and the Restricted Sector boss have disappeared, the Gayokcy is being challenged by the escaped Gadlins with suspicious connections, and the Entropist is less committed to controlled disruption than to planetary ataxia, a form of disarray beyond what humanity could ever imagine. Everything rides on the versal wave, and all must follow the laws that govern the ebb and flow of the physical plane. Sothese should, in fact, promote restraint, for hoarding the chosen ones leads to scarcity, and scarcity leads to destruction for all. A leader in deeds is the leader one heeds.

The bomb ticks as the hand clicks, short of a second, with a warning that his three officials are being hunted again. The herald flickers past, leaving a trail of steam across the Ministry House courtyard's watery veneer and into the glowing sajadum. The Pramam is summoning his advisor? Was his dawn regime a little too spicy for him today? Sothese meanders into the amethyst tetrahedron, hissing with self-indulgent laughter while Kainaten feeds off the advisor's cool air in order to anchor himself beyond the moment. Some housekeeping issues have arisen. How anticlimactic life has become ever since the Pramam's mother mysteriously departed.

Anabelle whispers Sothese's name under the fragrant canopy of the palace garden. Odwin's dismissal is proof enough of consent, in the absence of solicitation, and the self-professed agent of the source romances his emerald gemstone eyes into the heart of the Coalition.

No storm can cleave this particular prey from the power that funnels through his core since the child who would question these rapturous encounters is charged with a nine-year spiritual journey, orchestrated to entwine the future puppet's mother with a tightrope of lies, whimsically tossed across a Gadlin landscape with its end left purposefully loose.

The boy is to discover the self and to test his resolve against the ancient folklore that, in part, will restructure his faith. Via the icy-cold space between times, Sothese ensures the youth's success through guidance and otherworldly protection meant to slip his brilliant agenda into the gaps of an evolving ego. No one shall be left wanting under his watch.

▲ ▲ ▲

Murmurs, unenticing, replace the breathy swoons that sooth the rhythmic movements lying victorious in Sothese's mind. Affairs of state only become so when the Pramam and his vivacious valet are not fleshless apparitions. Nonetheless, this day may still give rise to surprises.

"A commendation is yours, Sothese. Dr. Shakti informs me that the biochip transplants are successful."

"With appreciation, my Pramam."

"I gather that you two have attained a workable power dynamic."

Sothese swallows thoughts of several playful exchanges. "Indeed. Shall I invite her to come?"

"Do as you please, on your own time. At present, your Ministry colleague is exploring the fortuitous side effects. Once previous memories can be transferred back to the recipient, future use by SIF agents shows promise."

"Gratitude is what has sparked this urgency, my Pramam?"

"You suspect a ruse. Your silence pains me, Sothese." Not as much as the forthcoming wrath. "Yet, your discernment impresses me, as always."

More flattery begets less cooperation. Sothese's discernment does not extend to his personal pleasures. "And what may Their Holy Trinity request?"

"Let it be known that Their request is for transparency. Your latest officials are a curious choice, Sothese." As is their apparent shirking of ministerial duties. The sajadum focal point is where he must stand for his beauty fix. "You are not invisible to the agents of the Divine Messenger. Through Their counsel, the Pramam sees all. Perfect are They … SILENCE is not an option in this instance."

"… They are One." But *they* who are gathering are many, and counting.

"Kainaten will ensure that your promise endures. Their law is your master, Sothese." Yet he who would dare to chastise perfection knows only of lies, not of laws. How soon They forget where the credit is due.

"Of course, my Pramam. I will investigate their credentials and any lack shall be rectified."

"I trust that you will, Sothese." And thrust he will, the pontificator's throne into the volcano that his Entropist-endorsed and supposedly qualified triad had emerged from, that is.

A curtsy and a flick of his lustrous red bangs follow the end of the official transmission. Sothese suspects that candor slithers down that Unified throat with his wriggling tonic, never to resurface except as excrement ejected into the water purification system servicing Ministburg's elite. His Holy impersonator is double-dipping at Sothese's buffet of stoolies on behalf of the Inner Council. Someone is pursing their lips at the wrong end of the carrot and expecting to gorge themselves with the boons of deceit of power.

Sniggers attempt to smother the fear smouldering inside, as homonyms for hominids make light of the darkness arrogance refuses to face. What-if scenarios nurture ambivalence, a weakness that stays the hand that fights it. Sothese defers this deficiency to the sapphire-eyed craving that he had bested in Eadonberg's ventilation shafts for the amethyst-eyed maverick. Yet the burn persists while Kainaten spins his pen-sized plasma sparker, counterclockwise, with his thumb and index finger.

"You must stop playing with time, Sothese. This morning went too far. I can no longer cover for you."

"The Pramam's world is dry and tasteless."

"If you say so. I would not know."

"Perhaps, one day you shall, Kainaten."

"Always promising and not delivering."

"And you? Keeping an eye on things? You should not have followed her to Albaraaton."

"Albaraaton?"

"Yes. The city of granite."

"Was that your touch, Sothese?"

"Unfortunately, not. Although how wistful it must have felt for you."

"Not all experiences are worthy of a homecoming."

"That would depend on your point of view. A scintillating voyage it would surely be."

There is always room for asserting one's position and stressing the other's place in the order of things. Sothese's obscure sarcasm, an element of his less suggestive personality, twists meaning into a subtle threat that invokes a toe-tapping smirk and an abrupt reversal of Kainaten's spinning stick.

"Perhaps *you* should follow *me*."

For the political fencewalker, history only exists in the consciousness that makes it pop in and out of form, as does the future, but for the aspiring star on the verge of self-imploding, all exists as part of a sensual continuum. Now, the conversation returns to its origins.

"Playing with time, you say?"

"Flashes do not lie when their holographer controls the timeline, Sothese."

Lightning strikes with the flip of a switch, sending Sothese crashing through a plasma echo, caught between the frames where movement weaves stories and barely shifting his focus in time to breach the sajadum walls. Fear turns to anger, which turns to rage, then back to fear, as visions of eternal frost and pitted purgatory collapse his life force into a bounded sheath. From root to crown, the pulsations that have spurred the stallion now submit to palpitations intent on castrating him.

With his hand-crafted leather shoes swelling below the surface of the rooftop pure-water garden, the proud and presumptuous gift to humanity finally glimpses his mortality, as the stone pool splashes his diluted blood onto the quartz tetrahedron from which the real power flows.

Darkness is the dagger which carves out hidden demons, my dear Sothese.

▼ ▼ ▼

This belligerent honking, every time that Sothese approaches the boy, suggests webbing in a form other than the one on its feet. The future Pramam needs only one guardian, yet the petulant toddler screeches whenever Anabelle's trustee attempts to corral the pestilent scout. A sudden and inexplicable death cannot compete with banishment as payback for desertion, so a forked tongue takes the spotlight, and a new goose, more cordial, and, most importantly, ignorant, becomes the blanket for juvenile anxieties.

▲ ▲ ▲

Condescension travels on wing tips as the honking fades westward, Sothese regains consciousness, and dread carves a window in the fog, exposing a pristine amethyst shine where the spots should be. His fingers resist the contours of his quivering lips, fearful of cracks or blisters, then survey his face for the same. The reflection in the still fluid that tempered his fall announces that the physical healing is complete. However, the emerald flint no longer shines in his arsenal of seduction. A cleaner has come and SIF agents, who are fiercely loyal to their benevolent Pramam, now have a name for the DNA. Sothese needs his highland hostage now.

A soft-spoken "Does the invitation still stand?" floats in

the mist that Sothese's rampage sprays and invigorates the channel that had constricted his joie de vivre a mere time lapse ago. The glint returns to his eyes and a new game begins.

"The Pramam aims to keep you partially informed, Director Corrient. The Witness Relocation Program is not what your discovery will enhance. He must not access my DNA imprint."

Tryst for trust would satisfy his reinvigorated sybaritic compulsions, but the moment belongs to self-preservation instead. Young Dr. Shakti redirects her coy smile to a sleuthing expedition in the URA territory that, by Their grace, through the words of the Pramam himself, is hers to command.

The network of holospies, on the other hand, belongs to her colleague, and they will deliver the girl twin.

✂ ✂ ✂

Sothese slices through the cold nothingness and charges the holoadvert, prancing around in the middle of the control center, to the jingle for the infamous ale. No material assault can torture the HSN-351, whose mandate is to locate Elize, into submission. Patience splicing cubes upon cubes of tagged footage is the only recourse, albeit with inconclusive results.

"Apologies, master. The 'insert-every-cursed-location-here' was experiencing EM interference at the time," is the splintered account of the past twenty days.

Flashpacks fly through the bearded mirage at volcanic speeds and shatter against the filing wall, for there is nothing else to redirect Sothese's explosion, until a familiar zap makes a randomized mosaic out of the HSN-351's appearance.

Begrudgingly, temperance has been served by Kainaten.

"The best leaders know when to follow, Sothese. Are you willing?" Sothese clenches his jaw at the very notion of subservience, yet he agrees just the same. "Your favorite redhead is misbehaving in Nukamigrad." And Anubrat-willing, so shall he.

✂ ✂ ✂

The frosty excursion is so much more enjoyable with a vintage Gadlin ceremonial coat to garner attention. Besides, one never knows what further gifts may come from those dextrous hands. Sothese leans against a leathery grey column, supporting the Nukamigrad Museum of Antiquities archway, and shoves the ear flap that guards its entrance. The hybrid swats back with force, only to inflict a bruise that immediately heals, sending the message that ornery elephant crosses are not in charge. The elepharc trumpets its displeasure and, coincidentally, Nepharisse's arrival.

These long curvy thighs are not the ones he had expected. Kainaten has outdone himself in playful subterfuge, an art Sothese is more than willing to share with an ally. Caroline can wait when Nepharisse is the bait, but an invasive reconciliation was not the purpose of the offering. The flirtatious swoop past his pelvis leaves him throbbing for more. She is goading him as his eyes follow the sapphire blue shoes clicking towards a different kind of pleasure.

Wakanda and Sothese's three ex-officials are colluding behind a uniportal, a gift from a recognizable emitter, sending its conversion frequency from around the adjoining building. Delights abound. To what does the illustrious advisor owe this cooperative change of heart? If he acts predictably brazen, will this be the trap that they had planned for the traitor … to deal with him later? Confront the greedy Gayok he shall, so that she can agonize over when, and how, she will be unpleasantly prompted to redeem herself. And of her blackmarket biochip connections? Their acumen as fugitives is to be tested.

The female double-crosser, of the three, surprised by the dissolving stone wall, narrows her gaze at Nepharisse, waving as she speeds by. Confusion ensues with Sothese gloating about his rekindled romance, with a quip about retribution due and dinner for two.

"No, Sothese. *You* watch what happens to those who betray *me*! I am sure you will find your used-to-be-Gadlin converts entertaining."

Commotion in the distance provides the opportunity for a conventional escape and a parting taunt from Wakanda that questions the motives inspiring his nubile Inner Council colleague's complicity. "By the way, Sothese, you should be careful who you share your secrets with."

The three hounds that Sothese had recently trained were fighting for their lives in the abandoned jungle of failed genetic experiments. A pack of three is no match for an apocalyptic crabseat armada and their lobcart cousins. Early models reflect the feeble intellect of their creators, and, as such, stingers are not necessarily neutralized. Neither is Sothese's.

Someone's sick joke doth attract his venerable sting.

ELIZE

Day 1068: afternoon

Another set of officials. I hope the Pramam is not visiting
Nukamigrad. He has no reason to unless … Paranoia is a
creative endeavor, Elize. But not fruitful. Enjoy the gorgeous
architecture instead.

"Hey lo, chum. Where have you been all morning?" Is it
after midi already? Nice sliderboards.

"I slept … I think. It was a war zone out here last night.
Hybrid antics. What about you two?" Jump up on this rock
and peak at Stitch's secret musings. Thumb twiddling and
puckered lips. A sign of guilt, no doubt. "Whoops! Hold still
while I jump off. My apologies." Soft giggle as the creature
oozes away. "Grody."

"My supervisor warned us to stay off the ground, Eli."
Keet pitches me a swirly, floral, and brightly colored plank.
Rango clings tightly as I hop on and start the gyroscope.

"What other creative gadgets did you find? Oh!" Did a
tentacle just pop out from his back? Swing this sliderboard
around and … "This is not a mammasack, Stitch."

"It's the tripest, chum!" Geez. Another hybrid! "A
geloctopack. It's for protection."

"From what?" Poke it. "It looks like a jelly bonbon and …
Surprise!" On my butt now. "Thanks for the hand up, Keet."

"It protects you from … ya fig." He sticks one on Rango's
back. Out come the mallets. Phew. Caught them in time. No

hybrid murders on Eli the Hugger's watch, little mammasack.

"No. I do not fig … and this one is dripping." Ink. Hmmm. I wonder if …

"Pica Picasso!" Stitch flicks a tentacle too.

"That's vandalism!"

"Oh laze, Keet. Graffiti is art. Look at what you can do with eight squirters. And eight more. Top juicy! Join in." Where is that crackling coming from? Oh oh. Now that is vandalism.

"See what you did? The ink is acidic. It's meant to disable an attack."

"And how is this safe? Stop jittering, Rango. Let me pull it off." Hand it back to Stitch. "Ta but no ta, chum. Jumpers!" That is the loudest horn I have ever heard. It came from the museum so we had better hurry. There must be an emergency somewhere. "Catch me if you can, boys." Slide on yonder and into the back garden. Keet's comm is buzzing.

"*Three* platymoas? Yes … I will, Mme Beaudoin."

"Perk. How many days are we here for, bud?" Keet looks overwhelmed. That is a lot of cataloging.

"Let's grab a sweet something in the snack room. Second floor." Great idea, Keet. Glucose feeds the creative mind. A non-crabseat by the window is fine, thank you. And a view of the city is …

This cannot be a coincidence. Caroline really is trying. Wave back. Is there a dust storm coming? An earthquake? Stitch and Keet feel it too. A crustacean armada? I think I need a snuggle just about now, Rango … and Keet … and Stitch. The poor dogs. How could they hurt those beautiful dogs? They are no ordinary canines, Elize. They shed no tears for you or anything they do. We gulp in unison. All that blood spray!

"I'll never look at a crabseat the same way again." Send Keet an I-told-you-so look. Soft giggle. A nip from the crabseat gave him a jumper. Rango hugs me tightly and checks behind him.

"Hide!" Keet is giving me that you-belong-in-a-jar look while Stitch's scalp draws a stick figure with a ponytail and drops it into a jar sketch. No soft giggle from me. "Did you not see them?" Head shakes. "They just ran past. They are popping up everywhere. Pop here. Pop there. Pop again. Pop pop pop. Creepy threes are taking over. The Pramam is up to something. We have to stop them. They are here to get the jewel." Lovingly place Keet's hand back to his side. "I am not ill. Your vision is failing. Look! Another three just showed up." A frown is all he can muster, but I am sweating just the same. Best change the subject.

"Now *that* you must have heard." And they did. Here comes Wakanda and out we go to hide in the artifacts room until the shipment arrives.

The piles are just as we left them last night, minus the scroll that Mme Beaudoin had the curator lock up, of course. I wonder why she hid it from me. It was obvious that she was disturbed by it. She read it to Keet, though. Perhaps it is a fascinating prophecy. Scooch up to Keet and whisper.

"Are there any more scrolls?"

"I can check the manifests. All traveling exhibits are inventoried. Why so interested?"

"It is quite the find. Wakanda must have spent good credit

on it. I imagine she would like to get her hands on Mother's book as well. We should keep avoiding her."

"Until you start feeling the love for her too? Like Caroline. Remember what you say about her in your rampages?" That is unfair.

"Of course, I remember. I remember everything, Keet. But I cannot control it."

"You're a mark for the GSU, yeah? And a Gadlin contract. Creeps!" Stitch is paranoid, I hope. Another reason to avoid Wakanda. Do not give that thought any energy, Elize. Yes. I remember. Thoughts are things. Yes, they are. Mind your thoughts, Elize.

"The symbols on the scrolls reminded me of one of the old languages in Mother's book."

"You mean the one I had lent Nathruyu? The Myths and Legends of Ancient Civilizations?"

"Exactly. Did you ever get it back?" The look of regret. "I think we should try to find that book." I get an eye-roll for that?

"Are we starting *that* again, Eli?" And a friendly squashed frog face. "Find the book, gotta find the book, find the bloody book."

"You look like an Orangugong." Soft giggle.

"Ok. I'll see if there's a slip version of it cataloged somewhere. Don't count your geese."

"Honk honk." Poke and a soft giggle. Where is my bopping chum? "Why so serious, Mr. Zaf?"

"Perk. Did you feel that?" Feel wha— "Clip out! Follow me." He has a slipmap, but we are already at the blue dot. A pop up! We are headed underground? The heat is unbearable … and the steam. Oh sweet little baby prophet, the canals are boiling away.

"Are you seeing this? Hey lo. Perk! Stitch!" No response. Focus on following him then. Keet is sticking close behind. Good. Oh no no no. I do not think so. "We are not going out there, Mr. Zaf. That is not love I see in those crabby eyes."

"They're rushing the biowall. The towers are blown. You're not the meal they're after, yeah?"

"Maybe not a meal, but a snack on the way, Stitch. Holy crap! Is that … lava? You're ribbing me. That's impossible. Volcanoes have been extinct for … well … for a long time." Keet is right.

"Slap this gelo back on, Eli, just in case." Good plan, Stitch. Creative. Innovative. Now where? A hole?

"Are you overdazed? We need to jump some lobcarts and get off this steamer!" What am I saying? These ones have poison stingers.

"Trust, Eli." His scalp is writing something. Soft giggle. Tess at work. Squeeze tight, Rango, into the hole we dive.

"Whoa! Ink blotch for you, lobcart. Cover your ears." That sounds so painful. Good aim, Keet.

"Hybrid warfare shows no mercy, bud." There goes the map. "Just a little red molten rock." A big grin. Stitch is actually enjoying this. "Get ready." Fumbling through a zigazillion pockets does not instill confidence. "Trip. Here it is. Lasso my chum. Lasso my bud. Lasso my butt. Ready and …"

"Eek! Mega pica ziga sheiss sh—" Too harsh, Elize. "With love, hugs, gratitude, love, love, love." Better? "Boiling up on us fast, Stitch!" And "Me Tarzan!" Sleep little mammasack. "We should stop now."

"Almost there. Keep your arms in, chumbuds. We need a smooth drop. Lean right when I tell you … Now!" And down another chute. Should I count? Should I breathe? Yes, breathing is good. Lovely. It smells fresh and … cool? And my stomach is in my feet. "Hang there while I add some slack." Gentle landing in the arms of insanity. Soft giggle. Keet is on the ground, annoyed. "Slap me, bud. The damsel in distress, yeah?" That was a slug. Preempt!

"Kiss and make up, boys. We are alive." Palm out. And the chumbuds are victorious once again, I think. "I hear voices. Do you hear voices?"

"It's all trip, yeah? They're coming from the nursery. This way."

Look at these beautiful planters, and flower beds, and green buds on shrubs. And the fragrance is exquisite. Whisper to Rango, "Me Jane." Sneaky hybrid. "No picking." Stitch is giving us the tour.

"And herbs!"

"Not your Father's garden I hope." A poke and a wink.

"For my migraines, ya fig?" Yes, the migraines. Stitch is simply amazing. I have heard that hum. Group hug! Keet is looking at them too. "This is the facility Mme Beaudoin told us about?" The children look happy. Stitch brings us to a nursery and introduces us to the caretaker. The lost children here are quiet and focused.

"They come here to heal their mind, Miss Elize and Mr. Keeto. The energy in the ancient soil keeps them grounded.

The experiments keep them connected, creative." Keet and I share a sigh. This is where Mother should have lived, not at the Almedina orphanage. Gratitude, Elize. Your life is entwined with hers. As is Keeto's.

Awww. Lo-flower hugs. Sniff. I miss Cyd. I hope he is drinking enough. Shudder the thought that Eadonberg could be exploding as well. Yes, Elize. Send love, not fear.

"How lovely. The lo-flowers are giggling."

"You mean pointing their leaves at you and laughing, don't you?"

"Not the way I see it, Keet." Through my love-colored glasses. Soft giggle. "But how can they grow down here? They need direct sunlight. Cyd is constantly facing the window, when he is not smiling at me, that is."

"They feed on photons from light. Any light works. Menaces remember, yeah?" Soft giggle.

"They are still smiling at me."

"Perk. Maybe you're not just juicy, you're shiny." A wink, but a scowl from Keet. "They also communicate with each other, so when one stares, they all stare. Trip, ya fig?" Keet rolls his eyes. "Everything has a soul, bud. It's like the twilight bark." And my brother is a squashed frog now. "You read ziga, bud. You've never heard of it? Ask Sparky." A secret poke starts the howling.

The lo-flowers are hiding their faces and jittering. Dare I think … snickering? Ouch. Hey! That was a butt slap. Hmmm. And they all conveniently face the sunshaft. I wonder how they acquire the hybrids in the first place.

"Eli." Did someone just whisper my name? "Eli. Go to the

river."

"Is everything alright, Miss Elize." Look greenish. "By the river, there is more oxygen. Take your time." Keet wants to follow. "She's safe here, Mr. Keeto." Stitch nods and off I go.

Follow my nose. This is just like the granite flats. Well, below the granite flats. Above there was quite the stench, but below … Deep breath in. Can you imagine living on an entire planet covered in beautiful water? Gasp. Heart, stop racing. Foot, tapping is not poise. Breathe in, breathe out, and smile … and say something … lovely. "What are you doing here, Shen?" Geez.

"A pleasure to see you here, Miss Elize." Here I go again. Just smile. "I am a hybrid architect and a Gadlin sympathizer, if you will. I sow the seeds. Open your hand." What a pretty color. Put it in my pocket.

"Thank you. So you are a hybrid architect." His turn to smile now. "That is why you do not show—- Ummm …" Still smiling.

"Have you been researching me?" Deep eerie giggle. Gasp. Check for my choker. Good. And what are *you* doing here? Time is shifting, Elize. This boy is too thirst quenching to miss. It's not your turn. You're budding in. Buds abound in the underground, Elize. Hahaha. You're so clever. Yes, I am. That is a compliment, and possi— No! It's not an invitation. Go away. It's so hot down here. The eruption must have started again. Shen takes my hand.

"Are you well?" Should I tell him? Yes, Elize. Let us see what this suitor is made of. How much he can take. Deep eerie giggle.

"I have a … condition. Voices. My mother." Hold it together, girl. I'm sweating now. He wipes my forehead, and my tears, and smiles. Look at those eyes! "What was that?"

"Just the river. You are wonderful, Eli. Do not let anyone make you feel otherwise. We all have had voices." Did you hear that, Elize? We are wonderful. Everybody loves us. Soft giggle. "Your medic is not labeling you, I hope. The GHU is a business." Yes, Elize. Captain Snook is a crook. Deep eerie giggle. No, he loves us, Elize. Everybody is looking out for us. *Life takes on many challenges, Elize. Breathe in your power.* Deep breath in … and out.

"He's a family friend."

"I meant no disrespect." He turns my palm upwards. Ohhhm gee. Is he really? "The trick is to focus." Oh! A friendship stone. Hehehe.

Eek! Ok. Breathe in my power, right? *Yes, Elize. Power flows through your breath.* Breathe, focus, breathe, focus, breathe, focus.

✂ ✂ ✂

Group hugs await, Elize. Lovely. Sure glad I left Rango in the nursery. Nothing can hurt me. Not even this gorgeous self-combusting molten rock. Ouch! Geez.

"You lost your focus. You need practice." Practice? Right, dweeb. Yank my hand away. Stop smiling. You're acting like Stitch. And speak of the— "I have to go back up. To gather the escapees." Creeps. Good idea. Hybrid rejects are a menace, but —

"Wait!" I wanted to introduce him, finally. Geez. Why the frown? Keet's running over too.

"Are you bent? Show me your hand." No. Take it back. Keet knows. "I'll ask the caretaker for the proper healing herb." The scalp of suspicion, again. Keet's staring at the river. "Let's meet back at the museum loading zone. The biowall is fixed now." Best keep quiet until we have some privacy.

"Try this mixture on her, Mr. Keeto. Three days and she'll be fine."

"Thanks." Keet takes me to a quiet corner, minus the lo-flower snoops, of course. We need to whisper. My hand is healed, already? And no scar! Gulp. "Maybe we're hybrids, Eli." Gasp.

"Oh, wouldn't that be top juicy!" Could that explain the aversion I have? Maybe I resonate with the part of them that wants to be human, but is angry because it can't. Keet's thinking the same thing. Hick. It's because they're wacks. That's all.

"Well, better top up your acting skills, Eli, so Stitch doesn't fig something, ya fig?" Giggle.

"You mean fake pain? Let's use a numbing rub, instead." He runs to get one. Ooo that's nice. "Are we really stuck here for three days? I need to get back. The clock keeps ticking. I feel time running out."

"You hear it during the day? How long? Why didn't you tell me?"

"If I told you everything I hear, you would be writing daily novels not journals."

"I wish I could record your thoughts." Well, that's very GHU of you, Keet.

"So you can find out how many times I really call you pup?" Hehehe. He's growling. "Well, maybe it's a good thing Shen dared me with the fire. Maybe I need more time away." Hey lo, squinty eyes. "You didn't see him? Shen. The boy who took me to the play, remember?"

"He followed you here?"

"No, fishy. Now who's paranoid. He's a hybrid architect. But he's sort of on the inside. He passes them to the underground. That's why he's so elusive. He's like us, hiding from authorities. Don't say anything."

"And he obviously has a fascination with fire." Eye-roll.

"It's all about focus. He has special training … like Stitch."

"I don't trust him."

"Geez. You don't trust anyone I get close to, Keet. Honestly! You're my brother, not the keeper of my virtue."

"Really. Only your hand then." He's blowing. But I'm right. Yes, you are, Elize. He is the one you cannot trust. Deep eerie giggle.

"Don't look at me that way. I'm not crazy! I'm not one of those lost children. I can take of myself!" Storm out of here.

"Eli. I never said that." He loves us, Elize. They all do. Let me back in, starting with a hug for our Keet. "Let's take the sunshaft topside. Grab your slipboard." Sniff. And Rango. There's Stitch waiting. Group hug. You too, little mammasack.

Surprise! Soft giggle giggle giggle. And pop out the chute. Start up the sliderboard. Slide into the cargo zone. Exhilarating! A flutterbot. Just what I need for this heat.

"Perk, Eli! Not that one." Slap. Ouch. At least it is not lethal. Soft giggle. The curator shoos it out the biodome and re-forms the grid. "Trip. Bring it back! The Gadlin Greed is in the house." Wag my finger at him. Mind your creed, Mr. Zaf. Poke and smile to laze him a bit.

"Awww, look. They are baby platymoas."

"What a relief! It's a small shipment." Who is that dark man with Wakanda?

Holy crap! What just happened?

"It's it's it's ..." Keet's frozen. He's dragging her by the hair! "F-f-fedora!" Ohhhm gee! "Eli! What are you doing?"

"You were supposed to leave the boy to *me*, Wakanda!" He's twisting her and dragging her on her face. That's horrible! Hang a sec, what *am* I doing? She tried to have Keet killed? Let her rot. Yes, Elize. Let her. No. Run faster, Elize. Help her. *This is not your way, Elize. You can save her. It is not her time.*

Into the shafts then. Where did they go? Dead end. Sheiss. Whoa! On my butt. It's a parallel ventilation system. The nook must be the bridge. Eek! Whack him, Rango. Ink blot. Again, again, again. Mega Pic— no time for cursing. RUN!

K E E T O

Where do I start? Underwater volcanoes, murderous hybrids, boiling waters, biowall tower explosions, lost children, thieves, spies, unannounced guests, and, gulp, the fedora freak? And then there's Eli, your beautiful daughter. I love her so much, Mother, this is so difficult for me to write. I wish … Why bother? Wishing will not change anything. You are gone, Father is a criminal for what he did to you, and good riddance, and then Eli. Sing to me, Mother. Sing me the lullaby … Please. My faith is timid. I need some hope, at least. Take me to the songstress in my mind.

There's a candle burning in my heart. There's a light glowing in the dark. Follow the light. The light is your guide. Always follow the light.

Yet it was Eli's blood-curdling screams in the pitch black of the ventilation shafts that were my only guide this afternoon. I could not see. Maybe Eli was right, my vision is failing, and my ability to protect her as well. Why did she feel compelled to protect someone that she, and Stitch, most emphatically, are convinced is coercing her way into the hollow in my soul that is aching for your motherly embrace?

I was fully prepared to let her rot in the black-pitted and scaly clutches of her destiny. I am not the one who had orchestrated the violation this time. It was not my responsibility to intervene, but, in her typical double-dealing ways, she managed to drag me in through Eli, just as my worse nightmare, second only to Eli's death, was dragging her across the rusted metal and broken glass from the shattered cooling generators below the city.

Tears poured down my face as I panted to no avail, and Eli ventured deeper and deeper into the dark. She was too fast. The screeching, the pounding, the horrifying cackle receded with my optimism until all I could hear were Eli's muffled shrieks and the deafening clicks of a lobcart infantry. I sank to the ground, in my most shameful moment, and cried, useless, a failure, no better than a defective hybrid. Actually, strike that, the hybrids have more courage. I had given up. Then I heard them. I heard voices tell me to ... *Find the nook. The nook is what you must find. The doorway is in the nook.*

My ears were definitely operating at a higher level of consciousness because there it was a hundred meters away, a crack in the duct walls where Eli had fallen through to the other side, an abandoned labyrinth of shafts, running parallel to the one I was withering in.

Eight tentacles deployed at once and only the high-pitched squeals rivaled the stench of melting exoskeletons. My second wind whisked me off my feet with superhuman speed, for I had already died from remorse and had nothing to lose. A desperate "Keet? Is that you?" became a duet with the song I kept repeating in my head. She was alive! There was still time.

Unbeknownst to me, while my world rumbled, Stitch had a lock on Eli's wristband. We can thank little Rango for risking his toes, scooping that from her privy shelf, the lovable thief. Our half-Gadlin boy genius was sliding along Eli's trajectory above ground and marking the access vents. When she stopped, so did he, and out came a laser cutter from … Well, I think you know where he stores his stuff by now. He dropped onto a massive lobcart and immediately sliced off the stinger with a "Give way, bud!" We did a triple attack with our geloctopacks and with twenty-four searing holes tunneling through the monster's body, it twitched, jerked, and squealed, ping-ponging its body against the metal walls towards an open hatch, which it never did quite reach. Grody!

Unfortunately, Eli was not entirely stable by the time the lobstrocities, as she calls them, were terminated. What am I saying? She was entirely incoherent, pacing back and forth arguing with herself and herself and herself. I counted three opponents in that verbal sparring match. In the end, the conclusion was, "This is not your way, Elize. You can save her. It is not her time." And then, as fast as she had bolted away from me outside the museum, she sprinted through the sweltering tubes hunting for her next adrenaline hit. My shattered sister is possessed! Crap! Strike that as well, just in case this quill has a hidden transmitter straight to the Global Spiritual Unit. Shudder the thought.

There was not much in Wakanda's possession, however, when we finally found her body, slumped in a cul-de-sac, glowing blue from an unexpectedly functional cooling generator. Her skin looked like a garden rake had been dragged across it, but she was still breathing through pinholes in her blood-encrusted nostrils. Her jaw was bolted shut with a stake made from a petrified willow branch. Geez. Wishing her head on the chopping block, like the mother of twins that she murdered, turns out to have been a happy demise compared to this desecration. In the end, Eli pulled the pegs out, ripped some fabric off her dress to plug the holes up with, commandeered our shirts, wrapped Wakanda up, flipped her onto her shoulders and carried her all the way back to the museum.

With gratitude gushing from my pours, my you-had-better-not-cross-her-in-a-dark-alley twin sister is now safely napping amidst her favorite plantrocities as I gather my thoughts in the cool, fresh company of Nukamigrad's underground aqueducts. Wakanda is also recovering well on a transport back to Albaraaton for a complete physical. Her injuries were, for the most part, superficial, but the message they were designed to convey read like a tribal skin branding. Mme Beaudoin has volunteered her translation skills once the wounds heal.

Regardless, our mission to find Teddy has turned out to be a real honker. When will I learn to trust the ones who earn it, like Stitch, and stop being a pawn to the ones who do not? When Wakanda regained consciousness and was fully hydrated, she confessed that she had intentionally misled her disgruntled business associate, which is what precipitated the attack. The client has a penchant for pendants, but not just any design, the one that causes trouble for us as well. In fact, the items are so critical that he is willing to kill for them.

Gulps all around ended that admission, although the crystals were not the underlying culprits. He had been stalking us, Eli in particular, and was looking to settle the score from the failed attempt on my own life, and Wakanda's part in it. And on top of that, the answers we came here for all point back to him, in a convoluted way.

Wakanda's lucrative crystal pendant trade, via vendors like the one we met yesterday, is tied to the lost children. The crystals belong to them until she graciously accepts them as payment for their care. "And the *GHU* is a business?" was Eli's reprimand before she highland curse-waved her goodbye. I wager that the biochips that she supplies Sothese with come from equally questionable contractual obligations.

I do not mean to discredit the Gadlin trading economy. Not all of the Gayokcy's dealings are self-serving, on the surface at least. Take, for example, the water trade, which really is not a trade at all. The Pramam simply invents all manner of conspiracies whenever the Gadlins have an influence. Without their water stewardship initiatives and hidden filtration testing facilities, like this one, the one under the granite flats, and the ingenious water purification coil technologies in every city, there would be no Unification, no Ministry, no Inner Council, and no Pramam.

Even the sound and scent of pristine rivers gushing past is food for the soul. I could sit here forever, with every cell in my body vibrating in tune with the purity that flows, her breezy nothingness blowing kisses through the mist. Sigh. Let my imagination carry my ears to the ocean shores that once were, to experience her story through the conch shells that are her lips. Her voice whispers to me: "I am here. Reach for me. Join with me."

We are here and we will reach for you, Siufflah. Creeps! Where did that come from? That name again. I must have relaxed too deeply and started writing nonsense. It does look like scribble. I was likely just fabricating a spooky end to Eli's geloctopack coming-of-age ceremony. Her lovely personality decided to "free the child of its inking slavery and cast him into the waters to go forth and flourish with abandon." Hehehe. The drama of it all.

At the very least, we all are holding the intention that any theatrical performance brings humor rather than heartache. Three days is an eternity when Miss Monster is pulling Eli's ponytail for attention and nagging her for an invitation to alienate just about everyone, six days early. Anyway, I should focus on more positive thoughts, so as not to birth a cycle of emotional dis-ease, and let their energy signature be swept up by the new current, ready to electrify humanity with pure potentiality.

Barely a minute after the Gayok's official transocean slider disappeared over the horizon, a small barge, carrying only its captain, snuck into the city through an opportune glitch in the biowall repair. Stitch had caught a glimpse of it first, and his scalp literally lit up with red hearts. We could hardly follow his sliderboard dodging the winged do-not-even-stop-to-ask hybrid rejects, racing to meet the craft. My teary eyes locked with Eli's when we realized who was womanning the craft, Sakari, the leader of the Odwin loyalists and loving mother to none other than our hip-jiggling, head-bopping, poke-happy, dweeby genius and fearless chumbud leader and best friend, Stitch.

The Gadlin movement is growing, and Sakari has come to pledge her support to the protest that Eli is organizing in Eadonberg. The plan is to expose the URA biochip transplant experiments, the illegal expropriation of Gadlin brains, fully intact in their live bodies, the manufactured Gadlin conspiracy and related terrorist sweeps for the sole purpose of using them as transplant guinea pigs. We would also expose the mutilation of orphaned children, those who are quite possibly the perpetrators in their parents' deaths, and the Pramam's active involvement and full support for these human rights violations.

For our part, we reciprocated with a summary of what we have learned about Wakanda's dealings and offered to report on her activities. Details of the crystal pendant trade caused Sakari's focus to drift towards the young nursery attendants then back towards her son, who had pulled her gift from a pocket and was holding it against his heart. Eli and I revisited the guilt tied to the piece as well.

Stitch is obviously his mother's son because she also had no compunction lambasting Wakanda's Gadlin Greed with respect to water and its place in her vision of a Gadlin Dominion. She stands in solidarity with Stitch when it comes to upholding the Gadlin Creed, and has made it her mission to ensure that everyone and every creature, has the right to their promising purification technologies. Water is absolutely not to be sold to the highest bidder.

Mention of the Gayok's murderous affinity to mothers of twins, however, had a more chilling effect. Sakari made us promise never to mention the incident or to write about it, probably in reference to my journaling habit. She knew who had recorded the secret Gadlin gathering, but oddly could not remember her face. So we chumbud swore, the four of us, and the mother and son reunion continued on in private.

Meanwhile, Eli and I took the opportunity to discuss a few secrets between ourselves, specifically Stitch's dawn ritual, which we have each separately witnessed but had kept secret from each other, as if that were a surprise in itself. Would that other undisclosed affairs be as honorably motivated. Dr. Tenille's self-cleaning flyer-bake-wrap decoys I can righteously justify, but my dithering sister's moods might lead to risky business with Shen, not that I am acting like a jealous match, of course. All my misdemeanors are for her protection.

As brilliant as Stitch's gadgetry portfolio is, his airborne virtacreature appears to sometimes sprout from the palm of his hands, and other times start off as a regular pop-up slip. We bounced several theories back and forth and ultimately settled on this brilliance. Stitch has obviously devised a microscopic virtual seed that he pulls, when no one is looking, from the pocket depot he calls clothing and sticks it to whatever surface he wants to use as its origins. At that, Eli yawned, hugged me, and left me to my writing, to snuggle with a particularly affectionate lo-flower.

I, on the other hand, was bouncing, which would explain my erratic start to tonight's diary. So I bundled up that energy and snuck into the museum's digital archives, looking for that cursed book, or blessed book. Time will tell either way, unless you do first. Sigh. Predictably, to cap a day that was anything but, the endless convoy of coincidences was on course to chronicle more adventures, starting with an old parchment tucked away inside yet another exquisite box, with text I could only understand in bits, describing something I was viscerally connected to, like the stories in my journals.

My gut feeling suddenly turned into torment for the tiny morsel of flyer bake that I had ventured to snack on earlier, when footsteps entered the artifacts room down the hallway. A quick visit into my esophagus and a labored swallow only just kept the sludge off the parchment as someone jumped me from behind. It was the Eli … the hugger. Phew. She too, could not sleep. Cyd, apparently, was talking too much. Hmmm. We shall revisit that one later.

Sometime during the course of our discussion about the strange parallels between the ancient writings and my nightly introspections, the treasure that I was enthralled by vanished. In truth, I wonder if it merely existed as a phantom in this whirlwind of a day, considering that hallucinations seem to have followed Eli to Nukamigrad. Maybe they are contagious, because fear certainly is.

Rummaging through the new batch of artifacts was a shadow of hurried hands. Anxiety fixed our eyes on the figure's head to check for a fedora, then having dripped a few beads of sweat, our attention turned to any reflection we could detect from the face or details off the coat. Narrowly avoiding a panic attack, we regrouped with our back against a stack of boxes. While I poked a recorder over the topmost transfer chest to document the dreamcatcher larceny in progress, Eli disappeared into the emotional abyss that her nightmares suck her into every night.

"Never let anybody steal your dreams," were your last words, all those years ago.

I tucked the incriminating flashes into my satchel, whispered into the main pouch: "Transcriptor on," and held my breath. Here are the results.

(rustling)

Crap! We need to get out of here.

We cannot let him get to her first. (new voice, click)

Who is that? Ok. The thief is gone. We need flashes of the goods. Hang a sec. Ok. Let's blister.

It sort of sounds like the Pramam. Most impressive, Keet. You bugged the Pramam? (Eli)

I'm not that stealthy ... yet. (laughter) Sothese must be with him.

We need to get back underground. Check the hall— Eek! (click)

Ease, bud! (Stitch, laughter)

Geez, Stitch.

The protest is gaining momentum. Someone has bypassed the bioHealth alerts. (new voice, click)

Annotate new voice. Pramam.

Swish! And pica sleuthing, bud. You bugged the Pramam? (Stitch, click)

Shhh. (Eli)

A further curfew would be ineffective. We must infiltrate the student population. (Pramam, click)

No Tess there, yeah? I can slap a bell on new registrations. (Stitch)

What if they have no biochips? Hick. Never mind. The scanners scream. (click, gasp)

Biochip transplants! (Eli)

We position it as a general sweep. If the Gayok's flash of her is real, then the distraction must be believable. (Pramam, click)

Traitor! Wakanda sold you for credit, chum. He must be on a comm. No one else is in range. (Stitch, click, gasp)

The counselor! It must be the counselor! And Nathruyu and Mr. G. They are all after me. (Eli)

Thirty days? Excellent. You know what to do. Anyone left standing, we take. I will prepare my SIF agents. (Pramam, click)

Perk! There's interference. The transcriptor is clicking. (Stitch, click)

He replicated them. Mr. G was angry. It must be bad. The counselor must be bad. He is saving me from Sothese to give me to the Pramam. I know it! (Eli)

What are you talking about?

Excellent. You know what to do. Perfect are They. (Pramam, click, snap, rustling, walking, muffles)

The counselor's protection is a scam to build trust. (Eli)

Transcriptor off.

And there you have the final horror of the day that started a leaf flapping panic in the underground nursery from Eli's meltdown. Sothese's coat is at Ministry Mansion but he could be anywhere, even here, and ready to strike! The Pramam is colluding with someone who can take Eli on campus at a moment's notice. And … This cannot be happening. I will not let it.

And neither will Sakari and the Odwin loyalists. Odwin helped us escape from Father. He was our first ally, Stitch was our second, and his mother will take care of us, like I wish you could.

Sakari laid out the plan, packed up her barge, and aimed for the falling moon with these parting words: "The SIF will act fast. We need to be faster. I'll start recruiting. Give me three weeks."

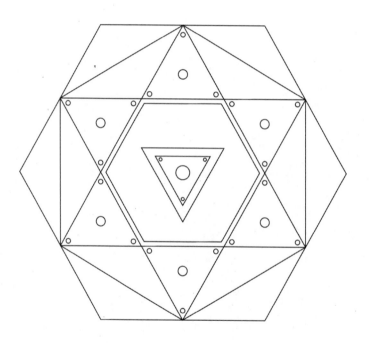

CHAPTER EIGHT

SOTHESE

Day 1090: wee hours

The evenings stretch into endless boredom even as desperate hopefuls vie for his guiding hand in their ministerial aspirations. Various abundantly qualified men, women, and those who avow to be neither or both, compete for the coveted positions of service, or rather, to service the Inner Council adjudicator, whose sidekicks, once again, have failed in their assignment by virtue of their untrusted cultural origins.

Yes, umpiring on a corrupt field, in the wee hours when desires arise, is where staffing decisions are ratified. Yet, despite the fleshly feast in and out of Sothese's grunting zone, vented frustrations drench his bedsheets, and infuse his Ministburg penthouse with regret. The ginger-auburn mirage that envelopes his opportunistic applicants does not heal the pangs resulting from the dagger of deceit. Fortuitously, the versal arts have taught him well, and the air clears when focused on the task, which, for Sothese, has always been to ride the ecstasy bursting from the turbulent swells. Fire is king and so is the sting.

Tonight, however, it is fear that grips the channel where pleasures grow. The gift strewn across his bed is not draped in silk, stained with his milk. It is small, tubular, and hard, with viscous blue contents marinating its passenger in the nectar that the Pramam cannot live without. Sothese's political insurance policy, and the very skin he worships, is now hostage to the whims of a contender, who knows the true worth of the elixir sealed inside this URA vial. The indispensable advisor is no longer so.

Sensations, habitually enjoyed through the facial contortions of Sothese's more barbaric distractions, become a firsthand experience as he flips through the faces of plausible rapscallions in his mind. But the potential damages are far greater than simple mischief can inflict. No, this is the meticulous scheming of someone, or something, with the power to seal him in a black pit of despair, bound to a world where the body no longer exists, where the soul screams for release, and where ice is the hell that burns.

An overzealous holographer could have been careless and have left certain flashes for prying eyes to find. Or perhaps he could have unwisely chosen to make good on a threat. Surely, Kainaten understands that promises will never be delivered if he proves complicit in eternal banishment. That assurance alone negates his support for the artificially preserved human leader, and thus dissolves any visions of betrayal attributable to the conciliator that Kainaten has become.

Whereas the physicality-challenged humanoid cleans up the mess that Sothese leaves when he tires of the Pramam's shrinking breeches, the cleaner actually does the opposite. Perhaps Corrient has done more than single out the three Gadlin shells that housed Sothese's latest officials. If honesty be one of his virtues, he would admit to a lack of due diligence with respect to Director Shakti's origins and affiliations. After all, the appointment to URA leadership was in retaliation for shaming the Divine Messenger's supposed benevolence with Nathruyu's avant-garde interrogation sessions. Thoroughness is so under-appreciated in this administration, is it not?

A further possible gift bearer could be Wakanda, if not for the recent branding, which Sothese regrettably had no active role in, spotlighting her frailty as a rusty old warrior. On the other hand, her business arrangement with the three ex-convicts, who had dared to undermine the lucrative biochip acquisition trade through which Sothese supplied URA experiments, may include access to the same weaponry that Sothese had employed to suck the light out of Nathruyu. Although the recoil would certainly kill her. If he only knew who was responsible for their escape, the trail of favors owed would unmask the miscreant, for it is the versal law that overrules, and, in that realm, Sothese carries the staff.

And of Gibayze's replicant? That is a relationship worth exploring. The Gayok's dispassionate abandonment of her own kin for experimental procedures suggests no connection at all, at least none with the clans endorsing her self-appointment. The rift in the enlightened Gadlin civilization grows deeper with every underground ocean revitalization system coming online. Murmurs of dissent sink below the honorable facade cloaking the itinerant merchant breed, while their hydrogeologists unplug the toxic ocean bath and return millennia of fossil water to their source at the earth's core, thereby sparking the genesis of a new Earth through reawakened volcanic activity.

All this time spent flipping between sizzling suspicions

and Sothese had overlooked the disclosure of guilt sitting there in plain view, attached to a warning wrapped in beautifully penned words on a parchment: "I believe you were looking for this."

Sothese's energy collapses in phase with the weight that crushes his lungs. A flicker of bright light pinching the outside corner of his left eye momentarily exposes a silhouette fading into the night. The note had arrived with a presence he does not recognize. Has Sothese gone too far?

The terror wave that consumes his body chases the phantom out into the polished corridor and out to the end of a Juliette balcony overlooking one of the city's three water purification coils. He gasps at the northern horizon, glowing with the fires of deliverance. The planet is shifting at a much faster pace than the Gadlins are able to mitigate. That was never the intent. A chain reaction has begun whilst the Pramam foolishly obsesses over exterminating those who can either directly, or indirectly, determine the fate of every body's life-support system.

They are gathering in far greater numbers than originally anticipated. The Entropist cannot properly train a new triad from sheer overload, and Sothese is now paralyzed by empathy, a foreign emotional state that his supra-humanity regards as a shackle for artistic expression. A tiny smirk shrinks from his lips as sure as the ethical intrusion plucks at his vocal chords. Agony, in a plea to expel the guilt, screeches across the white caps, tipped with sludge, reflecting the torment that Sothese's marbled perfection currently suffers.

As expected, the pain is short-lived, yet the trauma remains. Whoever is vying for succession is trying to turn the Pramam and the entire Ministry against the Inner Council god. Irreproachable as Sothese believes himself to be, he can recognize when overconfidence becomes the ego's concubine, and that is not a match that the governor to the Global Spiritual Unit deems wise to sanctify. The next three days require a level head, keen vision, and a swift strike. A little birdie will come his way, lovely wings and all.

The warning floating in the blue goo has been heeded. Now an audience with the Pramam is needed. Sothese dons his vintage Gadlin coat, snatches the specimen vial, and shatters the seal of space-time, once again, on his way to his dawn entertainment.

✂ ✂ ✂

A quick basking session in the blue glow below the city center, and out he pops onto the hovertrain platform in time to snigger at the white horse and its black herd, which is the Pramam-mobile and its procession of parasites, waiting for its false prophet to embark on his daily publicity rounds.

A soft tap, tap, tap plays in the corner of the room, suggesting that there is a hidden recorder on hand as a gentle reminder for restraint. Sothese holds the image of Wakanda's scarred body in lieu of the ritual Holy Heimlich game. The Pramam sours his face as the slime passes the hyoid bone and the flashes of their conference enter the halls of history.

"The tonic has a peculiar flavor this morning, Sothese."

"I hear that they cure as they age, my Pramam."

"Is there a supply chain problem that you should advise

me of?"

"You would have to consult the Gadlin and her three fugitives for that."

"Kainaten informs me that she suffers from health challenges. Would you be privy to such news?"

"Privy indeed, yet not responsible … unfortunately. Have They, through Their counsel, suggested a fondness for Wakanda?"

"Your tone, as always, reveals much, Sothese. It is her fondness for *you* that They are most interested in."

Sothese acknowledges his irresistibility. Yes, Wakanda willingly falls prey to his seduction but also to his savagery.

"And what Ministerial business were you conducting in Nukamigrad?"

"My own fondness for a certain sapphire-eyed beauty drew me there."

"I prefer that you focus on Director Corrient and the URA biochip transplants, Sothese."

"With pleasure."

"I am sure. And consider it an act of faith. Can I trust you?" Kainaten flicks into view then vanishes.

"Of course, my Pramam. Dr. Shakti is a voracious learner. Together we shall solve the memory issue. Are there SIF agents you would like me to recruit for testing?"

"Yes. That is most brilliant. With gratitude, Sothese. I shall alert them of your arrival." And arrive Sothese shall, with a gift for the decoy withering in the detention level.

To travel on the edge of nothingness, considering the foreboding signposts along the journey, is a technique that

Sothese has abused once too often. Wakanda may have repaid his ex-officials for her part in the Almedina Square betrayal, via the etching hand of their joint fedora-loving Restricted Sector associate, but the advisor who had ordered their takedown is still an outstanding mark. They know where to find him and how to trap him, and now that the mysterious fedora man has developed a symbiotic kinship with the escaped triad as Sothese had, statistics do, in fact, rule the verse. The figures are reliable, and Sothese is outnumbered.

Despite the risk, or even to spite his foes' codependency, the transocean transport becomes the decoy for a jump in time.

✂ ✂ ✂

Urgency begets impatience and priorities shift. Finding Elize must come second to squelching the vendetta against him, but only just so. If the training that had fostered his formidable conquests are as legends claim, thoughts will deliver all manner of things, beginning with a royal welcome on the SIF headquarters rooftop, as scheduled.

A windstorm announces the midi heat, straining Eadonberg's latest cooling generator upgrades, as Sothese removes the Gadlin ceremonial jacket and hides it inside his sliderbag, on the way down to the agent reassignment wing where he will recruit a non-Gadlin voluntary volunteer for the gentle-hearted Corrient.

An adult-sized transparent incubator slides by with a quasi-mummified figure laying supine on its surface and with tubes draining red-tinted fluids from incision points. The waiting room attendant calls a name to the registration desk, with no response. A second attempt to summon the SIF agent slated for redeployment results in the same thick silence, but the refusal is not accepted, and the new GHU-issue crabseat models activate their scanning eyes.

Sothese leans back against the counter, bemused, as round black balls on pliable sticks telescope to the back of their passengers' heads and blink. The hybrid carrying the requested biochip number scooches towards the examination room, digging its claws into the soft flooring to offset the man's attempt to do the same with his heels. Laughter breaks the reluctant patient's concentration, and the crabseat topples onto its side, sending the man flying into a woman's lap. The room snaps and sniggers in unison, while the advisor slaps a release slip to the obvious volunteer's dossier, with jealous stares murmuring their displeasure of the courtship: "The Pramam has a special assignment for you, Mr. Shaplo."

While GMU guards escort the willing subject to the Pramam's strategic advisor, readying his private quarters at the camouflaged URA facility, the actual master strategist slips on the famous coat and coils down the staircase to cell block A for the real star behind his brilliant suggestion. The security flaw that Sothese had programed into the access grid during his facility inspections nearly nine weeks ago is still intact. He resets the recorders to yesterday's flashes and breaches the observation area.

A sliver of light fades from a razor-thin slit in the wall adjoining cell block B, where the hapless remnants of the last Gadlin sweep live in daily fear of being separated from their cohorts, and for good reason. Not surprisingly, their survival training brings about clever escape plans, but they fail to anticipate the horrifying death that would be the result of a successful escape into the neighboring section.

Sothese, touched by his newfound empathy, of course, is more than willing to grant the accused conspirators their freedom, so he throws the black-pitted figure a frequency laser from the shadows and watches the process unfold to its tantalizing climax. The first Gadlin entrusts his feet to the cajoling sweetness awaiting her first meal and collapses in the brown arms of his reaper. A concerned voice through the opening whispers a name that no longer exists in the world of the living, followed by "Is the way clear?"

A candy-red mane pokes into the light to whisper "yes", startling the naked imposter at first, then receiving a respectful nod. The ensuing pause, while the stolen clothing adjusts to its new owner, prompts a second string of encouraging words, and a woman's face crosses the threshold to a gentle tug. The darling "not-Nathruyu" shivers as she stands between the newcomer and her late mate, pursing her quivering brown lips for a kiss as "a token for your life?", which the Gadlin unwittingly donates while Sothese's new ally's skin regenerates.

With enough energy to flee to the shafts, Nathruyu's carbon copy, with the carbon eyes, becomes the mouse in the maze seeking blue cheese to fulfill her hunger. The remaining Gadlins file into view, shivering, while her unexpected liberator exits the cell, seals it, turns off the refrigeration to keep the tenants alive for future volunteerism, reenables the recorders and follows the body double to his anticipated catch.

Anubrat is the one Sothese hunts, for he is positive that Elize lives within his reach. If he could trick him into talking as his sister had done in the distant past, then with Keeto's splintered twin as currency, the wily negotiator can trade her liberty for his own, and potentially, for help in eliminating the quartet colluding to usurp his rightful claim.

However, the sporting ends as his day began, engulfed by a sphere of influence shrinking into oblivion, except that, in this instance, panic shakes the core where anger and excitement mate and releases the anarchy he was saving for later. The Nathruyu semblance has disappeared into the deep ventilation labyrinth beneath the Restricted Sector.

"This is no place to linger," warns a familiar voice from behind. Kainaten leads Sothese along a generator dotted path backwards through time to the Gadlins filing into cell block B at the SIF headquarters. The escape plays out without a chase. Sothese releases the occupants, falsely accused of terrorism, and crashes into the URA's biochip experimentation lab to send an unequivocal message to the illustrious ingrate.

No other child of Anubrat can deliver that which he seeks, not even Anubrat himself.

The Witness Relocation Program cabinet is where the ransacking begins. Vials explode from a plasma sparker's beam and flashpacks melt under the intense heat. Tap goes the toe, swish goes the stick, and click goes the thumb with each tick, tick, tick, as Dr. Shakti's off-grid research enters the great versal storehouse, where the ancient genius of Nikola Tesla and other unsanctioned scientific breakthroughs reside.

A silent alarm triggers the soundproof rooms's internal buzzer, which startles the latest transplant volunteer still recovering under a thermal blanket. Accidental witnesses are regrettable participants in such high-profile larceny, yet simple to rectify with a sudden twist and snap of the neck. Albeit lacking extensive pleasure, it is the advisor's cleanest and most efficient termination tactic. Propitiously, the next intrusion is surely flitting down the hallway by now in unwitting pursuit of an Inner Council loyalty probe.

The door opens to a jab and a twist and a flick of the wrist, and a young woman slips on the sludge oozing from her disembowelment, twitching in the crimson pool at Dr. Shakti's feet, frozen behind the corpse at the entrance. Sothese flattens the director to the ground in the hallway while the body explodes into a ball of plasma and vanishes. Her horror beats him off and gawks at him while he surveys his pristine hands, intently, then smiles. His reward is finally earned. Security converges on the director and her savior, who is boring his emerald green eyes into hers for an alibi.

"The medical isotopes unexpectedly fissioned. Quarantine the room immediately," was the URA director's official statement that rushed the blood to his lips for an airy kiss and a licentious smile. The two retreat to a secure storage room while the Global Radiation Unit seals the area and begins the decontamination. Sothese's ears swim in the melody of Corrient's voice as she retrieves a labeled vial and pitches it at him, in disgust.

"The man who hit his head in the Ministry House courtyard. His name is—"

"Immaterial."

"Like my assistant, Mme Jaimeson?" Sothese shrugs off the insolence. "He's a GMU guard."

"Is?"

"Was." Corrient shifts her guilty eyes to the floor. The hairs on her skin stiffen to Sothese's long, gentle stroke, tracing a curve from her right shoulder to the inside of her wrist.

"My darling Corrient. How I long to kiss you!"

"Well, you can't." She jerks her body backwards and snatches the vial. "I still have the evidence."

"Blackmail? Delicious."

"I know your way with people, and you will not have it with me."

"I would never harm you, Corrient. I do like you ... even though you exposed my last officials as Gadlins."

"I did *not* tell the Pramam. I knew them from Albaraaton. Wakanda did, as well. She didn't negotiate for their release. They would have turned on you eventually, anyway."

"I doubt that very much, Director. They were very well vetted."

"Director Shakti?" Sothese blows into the gasp infusing his accomplice with fright. "Are you all right? ... Corrient?"

The door swings open just as Elize spins about and locks eyes with the venomous gemstone glint while her frantic confidante shrieks: "I told you to stay in the Senescence Center!"

Elize

Day 1090: early afternoon

Mega pica ziga sheiss to the sheissest sheiss! Mind yo—
Quiet!

Not now, not now, not now. Back up against the wall. Hold
on to the mallets. Stop wriggling, Rango! Noooooooooo. Don't
push off. Smash. He has me. Has has me in his arms! Ohhhm
gee. Oh crap! Run! I can't move. Come on legs, run! Corrient,
help me. She's just standing there, behind him, horrified. Hang
a sec. She's pressing a button. It's a panic button, thank the
little baby prophet.

"And who do we have here?" No words. I can't speak.
Gag. No saliva either. Corrient, please don't tell him. Are they
coming yet?

"A student of mine. She has to get back to her studies,
Sothese. Let her go." You heard her. Let me go. He's smirking
at me.

"Someone new. Interesting. And what would her name
be?" Don't tell him. Please. Who's at the panic station? Why
aren't they here yet?

"Terry. Terry Tan." That's right. Terry. Tan works. That's
my name. Try to smile. Fewer teeth. Ummm. Say something.

"Miss Terry Tan. Lovely almond-shaped eyes you have,
Miss Terry Tan. All the better to seduce me with." Not funny,
you narcissist wack, laughing at your own ribs. "From your
mother, I imagine, Miss Terry Tan?" Gulp. Stop repeating that

name. Pull away. Walk backwards. He's dragging Corrient along. She's terrified. I can feel it. And me? I'm absolutely petrified. Did she not push a panic button? Where on the planet are they? "Tell me, Miss Terry Tan, did you make up that name or did my darling Corrient?" Gasp! He's clutching her. She's wincing.

He knows. Sothese knows everything. I should never have come back. I have enough already to get the Pramam clamped. Why did I come back? I shouldn't be here. I should be preparing. Let go of me. That's it, Rango. Smash him. Smash him again. Hands off my mammasack. He's laughing. Speak it. Shout it.

"Hands off my mammasack!" Oh oh. Bad idea. "Give him back!" Oh crap. Worse idea. He throws him in the corner, pushes me back while he yanks Corrient out behind him, and seals the door. Just breathe, girl. *Rango is fine, Elize. Just breathe.*

"I dislike insolence, Miss Elize!" Eeeeeeeeek! No. Rango's trying to bust the door down. Where's my pup charm? Don't have it. No. Where is security? *Breathe. Center yourself, Elize.* I'm trying. Breathe in. Breathe out. I can't. You can do it, Elize. I will cheer you on. Breathe in. Breathe out. You are doing great, Elize. Keep going. Breathe in, now. Breathe— Elize? I can't. He's invading me with those eyes. Pant. Pant. Pant. Keep panting, Elize. Shallow breathing is what he lives for. Deep eerie giggle. Pant. Pant. Pa—

✂ ✂ ✂

ELIZE

Bright lights. So bright. Where am I? I can't move my arms. Gasp! My wrists are shackled. Get off me! Turn my head. He's breathing on me. No. This is not happening. Turn my face the other way. And again. Go away! Again.

"GO AWAY!" I hear murmurs. Who's there? I can't see. The lights are too bright. I'm scared. What am I wearing? It feels like … no … it's a hospital gown. Mother, help me! "GET AWAY FROM ME!" He's at my ear. I can feel his breath.

"Where is that bold woman who sat on my bed?"

"What are you talking about?"

"No need to be coy, Elize. They cannot hear us." Don't lick me, you wack! Pant. Pant. Pant. That is good, Elize. Keep panting. Deep eerie giggle. Let him. Feel his energy. Ooooooooo. The chills. Are they not pleasant, Elize? All these foreign sensations are electrifying, are they not?

"Sothese, that is not appropriate!" It's Corrient. Traitor. She's in on this. How could she?

"I am not her doctor. Is that not correct, Dr. Tenille?" NO! Not my captain. Sniff. I can't wipe. These shackles. Why? This must be a nightmare. I need to wake up. It will all go away.

"Yes, but I am. And the patient is wearing a gown, on a slab, in a surgery cell, and as the Pramam is my witness, I am in charge." He clears his throat. "With all due respect." Aye, Captain. But no respect for the scallywag. Your Belle is terrified.

"Very well, Doctor." He's whispering again. "We shall continue our conversation later, Miss Elize." Here comes Dr. Tenille with a syringe? What? But I thought he was going to save me. Pant. Pant. Pant. I can't kick either. My ankles are shackled. Help me. I need help! I would love to help, Elize. No. Not you. I am hurt. You cannot want her, Elize? Yes, she can. You need me for this monster, Elize. *There is a moment for peace and there is a moment for war, Elize. Choose what will get you to the next moment.* They're looking for blood, so war is what they deserve. I have your permission then, Elize? Yes. Do it. Anything. Just do it. Deep eerie giggle.

Crack the whip. You call them shackles? Mere toys!

"Eli? What are you doing? It's too early. I'm here to help. This is too dangerous." Dangerous for you, Dr. Never-gonna-find-those-sails-again!

"Shut up, saucer eyes. Drop that jaw so I can plug it with Sothese's di— And you … you …Whore! I trusted you, Miss Sothese's-latest-cavortasack! You are no better than that constantly disheveled strumpet. Yeah, you know who I am talking about, oh master of buggery! And you! *You* find this amusing, you Ministry lickspittle, vomit-inducing sycophant?" Yes. Yes. Yes, Elize. Can I be your sycophant? This is exhilarating. Let me empower you. I believe it is time for a revolution, mistress. Shall we? With absolute pleasure, my friend. Oh my, Elize. You should stop this. *Let the storm move through you, Elize. It will find its center, as shall you.*

"We can't let her go like that … Fo-foderick. You created this, Sothese!"

Sothese's delight is obvious as I storm the halls and leave the snickering smirk fading in the distance. His overconfidence shall be his undoing, Elize. Deep eerie giggle.

These tunnels are ridiculous. As if no one could find the URA anyway. Sajadums with trap doors. Do they really think everyone is a hick? I wonder if they are all hooked up together, and people get sucked down to their death if their morning meditation does not convert them into brainless bots. Unibots! Deep eerie giggle. That is exactly what they are. All these Unified converts mumbling their mumbo jumbo "They are One" mantras. None of that for us. We are taking the short cut right through the land of the poppers.

Here they come. Pop pop pop. Creepy three here. Creepy three there. Creepy there everywhere. Deep eerie giggle. Summon the slidercab. No. Forget about it. The Restricted Sector has a breach. We can plane through the hills.

Sheiss it! We left the Orangattackasackatrocity at the URA with our booties in its gut. Hey! Sweat bag! Blast that thing at someone else. We have no patience for this. We have a protest to lead. And oh what a leader we will be today. Hmmm. What about throwing a rock at the biowall? Good. It went through. Now our turn. Argh. That does not feel good. Well, who do we have here? Where have you been for the past three weeks, hot boy? Look at those eyes. What a thirst quencher, and we just happen to be a little parched.

"Trouble with the grid, Eli?"

"No just looking for it, Mr. Sizzle-lips." You like that? Of course, you do. Who would not like a little heat? Deep eerie giggle. Choker check. Good. Send him a flirty Caroline hair twirl … and the leg lean. She had some talent, after all. He is amused. Or perhaps something else? Juicy!

"Let me assist, then." Where is he going? Collecting things, we see. Quick, the creepy ones are closing in. Try the hand up. It worked. They stopped. "Look." And Shen is back … with

Mini-Lizzies. So this is where they all run off to. Hybrids! All menaces. "There is a secret switch on them." Flying lizard alert. Duck!

Not at our face, you wack! Oh, they stick to the biowall? Look at them go. Hehehe. Synchronized scurriers. They just formed a big hexagon and zap. Shen lends a hand and cross the reptilian threshold, we shall.

"Help me catch them. And flick the tail like this." That deserves a coy smile. How about we flick your tail. Deep eerie giggle. Oh, that is salacious, Elize. Thank you.

"You were blistering. How did you gather so many, so fast?"

"The trick is to focus, Eli, remember?" Yes and oh, I am focusing alright ... right on you. Swoon. Swoon. Swoon. Your heat is intoxicating. Whoops! Thanks for the catch. "I believe you need some fluids." YES! I thought you would never ask. Roll your eyes and ok, a soft giggle ... for effect, nothing more. Is the hug monster quiet? Not to worry, Elize. I feel especially invigorated right now. Deep eerie giggle.

"Are you well today?"

"Except for that whor— horrid URA director and wannabe pirate, we are just juicy!" Best use the "I" term from now on. We know *We are One*. Hehehe. "I mean Keeto and I ... and Zafarian. The pup and the dweeb. You know, they just are not figging it. They say they care but ... then they avoid me like I am some sort of hick reject dysfunctional hybrid or something. They are the ones who are wacks. They call me the Eli Monster. They always ask me to shift to the regular one, or the wiser one, or that nauseating hugging hick, as if I could on a whim.

Who needs them?" But we do need to get to the Central Core, Elize. Shen wipes the sweat off my forehead and smiles.

"I am not trying to change you, Eli. I love all of you for who you are … or they are." Whoa! What a heat rush. Focus, Elize. Time is running out.

"Do you have the time, my darling?"

"I can make the time … just for you." He is getting playful too. This is enticing.

"Well, if you were in Eadonberg more often …"

"There was a lot of work left to do in Nukamigrad. I am here to collect some things to take back with me." You can add me to your collection any day, Mr. Sizzle-lips.

"For how long are you here?"

"That depends. Are you inviting me to stick around?" Yes. Invite him. This whole virtue thing is overrated, Elize. You know Keeto is the one doing the banging, not Rango. Deep eerie giggle. Your turn. No need to trust him with any secrets for that! But protest first, then we celebrate and pant pant pant. Deep eerie giggle.

"Sh— Shen, what time is it?" Hehehe. He and Stitch definitely have to meet. "Is that an antique? It is in fact quite stunning." Ok. One compliment allowed, Elize.

"Yes. I spliced a few different ones together." I smell a hybrid. "Here. You can keep it." Not a good idea. Stitch is already angry about not meeting Shen. Wearing a Tess of a token would send his scalp sketching my demise, and he would find a way to loop it. And Keeto? Sheiss. Who needs them, Elize, remember? "If receiving it as a gift is uncomfortable, then consider it a loan. I can collect it on my day off, in three days." Well, it would be useful. "So I make time for you, like you asked." He is sneaky. I like it but still ... "Will you introduce me?"

"To the pup and the dweeb? Alright. We have a deal. In three days at the Snack Shack? It will not burst into flames, will it?" Just his body on mine. Hehehe. Hot hot hot. He drops the antique timepiece in my open palm and eek! Jokester.

"I promise that it will remain stable." Something I cannot promise you, but you seem fine with that. Ooooooooo. A heat rush with a cheek kiss. "We have a date."

"Be sure to come back in time?"

"And you especially, Eli." Blow him a kiss and blister to make history. Bye-bye Pramam!

There they are. The pup is pacing. Brace ourselves for the mother hen.

"Where were you?"

"No time to explain." Sheiss. Hide the timepiece in a pocket. "Sothese knows what I look like. We need this to work. Stitch?" What are you looking at, dweeb? "Well?"

"I'm on it, chum. Tune in." There it is:

> Northern biowall towers breached. All residents
> proceed to the central corridor for immediate
> evacuation.

A predictable edit. The dweeb is still a genius. The bioHealth crack is working. Here they come. Ridiculous. What a bunch of ignorant saps. All of them. They just do what they are told. The central corridor is infected with their stupidity.

"Jacinta is waiting for your comm, Eli. They're in the

orchard." Juicy! My personal army.

"Show us what you have, Jacinta." Excellent! Pretty much the entire campus. We will deal with traitors later. Deep eerie giggle. Here they come, over the Victory Bridge and up come the Gadlins from the shafts. I rule them all. Pardon me, Elize. Yes. We rule them all. Welcome to the Conspirator Cosway. "Sheiss! Who are they? Stitch! Come back here right now!"

"Taween! I thought you were dead."

"Enough with the hugs. You can bang each other later."

"Eli!!!"

"You never told me that my mother's hair tresses were Gadlin?" Look at them all. Like some sort of cult. Except for the hick we-commed-each-other-this-morning bunch. Those are the ugliest outfits we have ever seen.

"You never told me you went to a play with Shen?"

"Sheiss!" Duck. "We can argue later."

"Trip." We see that scribble on your head, dweeb. The local peons are in a panic. Mindless. Can they not see that we are not the threat? They have to stop throwing things at us.

"Dweeb! Put it in your pants and play the transcriptors." Oh, are you offended, Tawhatever your name is?

"Perk. Bud. We have to do something about the Eli Monster. This is supposed to be a peaceful protest."

"I heard that! Just focus on the task." We will make sure it remains full of pieces. Deep eerie giggle. Finally. The imbeciles are listening. Yes. That is the Pramam speaking and he is duping all you brainless bi— "What now, pup?"

"Can you cut the profanities? Can you channel that anger somehow?" Snare at him. Yes, dear brother. We can channel it at Caroline over there. How dare she show up! Sheiss. The pup got to her first.

"So you decided to show up, after all." He invited her? I did, Elize. Hug and make up.

"Way, Keet. It wasn't safe to meet you. Sothese is having me followed, but with this protest … Good luck to him finding me in this crowd."

"Try not to kill another child, eh?"

"Are you overdazed?"

"Stitch cracked Mashrin's biochip. We saw your face."

"Keet. She was probably staring at me at the medi clinic. Way, dazy gi—"

"Where did you get that crystal?" Ouch. "Let go of me, pup. I am channeling like you asked. She stole my crystal. Can you not see that the ball is—" Well, hey lo, Mr. Sizzle-lips. Jacinta has the chant going. Demand away, dear revolutionaries. Everything is going according to plan so … Highland wave at him.

Strange. All the red central corridor circles are lit up but no hovertrains. People are confused. There must be a malfunc— Sheiss in the name of the sheiss maker! Run! Ouch. The smoke is too thick. It came from the shafts … through the circles. Gasp! Hydrogen sulfide. They knew. Somehow they knew. They are using the ventilation shafts as a crowd control weapon. Everyone is passing out.

✂ ✂ ✂

Breathe. No. Don't breathe. Stitch is down. Crap! My best

friend. This is horrible and it's all my fault. Indeed it is, Elize. Deep eerie giggle. No. It's *your* fault. You took me over. You were not supposed to. Oh no, Elize. *You* asked me to. I take it back. Too late, Elize. We'll see about that.

Deep breath in. Deep breath out. Focus. Focus. Focus. Hang a sec. Why am I still standing? Hold back the tears. Go to Stitch. He's unconscious. I'm sorry, chum. I'm so sorry. Hold back the tears. Focus. Breathe. Gasp! The red crafts are coming. They're taking those still standing. Fall down. Fake it. *Her eyes weep the tale of her anguish, and her flesh becomes stone in its path. As the storm's assault disperses, all that persists is the tarnished wreckage of ignorance and deceit.* Give your head a shake, girl. Peek.

Eek! It's the fedora man. Holy crap! He's coming towards me. Keet? Good. He's running. He saw him too. I'd rather be picked up by the GHU or the SIF and take my chances with the Pramam than be anywhere near this freak. Shen's waving from the Victory Bridge. Flip Stitch over my shoulder and clip out. "I know a good hiding spot. Follow me, Shen."

Run to Rubrique Court. The arcade. Lay him down here. Check his head. Ohhhm gee. This is just like when

✂ ✂ ✂

"Are you alone?" Huh? Oh, Keet.

"No, Shen is here with me at the arcade."

"The arcade? Are … Can I talk to him?"

"My apologies. He is reviving our Mr. Zaf."

"Dump your headband. They're looking for the leader."

Oh, ok. Hey!

"It seems to be missing. It must have fallen off in the attack."

"I'll be right there." Lovely! He is alive, a little groggy, but alive.

"I have to go. They cannot find me here."

"Shen? Be careful." He winks. Sigh. Things are starting to cool off now. And here are Stitch's beautiful eyes, at last.

"Ta, chum."

"You can thank Shen, later. He had to go. If he gets caught, then the whole Nukamigrad nursery is in trouble."

"Perk, Eli. I— "

"Shhh! Someone is coming."

K E E T O

I have not been able to formulate any coherent account of the student march two days ago. The best I have mustered is scribble that makes no sense, almost as if I have been suffering from post traumatic stress. Fortunately, tonight, gibberish and symbols are no long spitting from my quill. I do not even recall sitting down to write, yet I surely must have been the author of the incomprehensible notations because, peppered amidst the nonsensical symbols, there are phrases that I recognize as my own handwriting, staring at me like the headlines in ancient periodicals you would find cataloged in the archives: "Triads gather on the outskirts of Eadonberg", "Escaped hybrids reproduce without assistance", "Weak ultrasonic frequencies detected around the Museum of Antiquities".

That horrifying scene in the Central Core still haunts me, especially because the body count keeps rising, and the Ministry has decided to use the resulting gore as a way to demonstrate the transparency that was listed as one of the top student demands, with the fortuitous side effect of redirecting all anger at the Gadlins and their co-conspirators, the students themselves. It seems surreal that selective blindness is still the affliction scouring the eyes of those who were actually there.

It feels like it happened just, well, the day before yesterday, which it did, yet at the same time, it feels like it happened ages ago. Did nobody see? From where I was still standing, to my amazement, I witnessed the ravages of destruction that a split second can create.

There were bodies everywhere. On the scaffolds, at the hovertrain drops, on the bridges, on campus … Anywhere there was a cooling shaft that vented to the surface from beneath, Eadonberg residents fell. The GHU sent their entire red fleet into the Central Core where most of us were gathered and carved out their territory. One by one, they sorted through each knockdown victim by scanning them first, no doubt creating a black list for future GHU intrusions, and then by selectively sucking certain individuals into their crafts, through their dreaded red energy beams. No one ever returns in "perfect order" as they claim, just in perfect obedience.

Meanwhile, the GMU arrived in full sweep gear from their training facility in the hills to the north of the city to clean up the carnage. They systematically rolled each subdued protestor onto their side and jammed a tagging gun in the back of their skull. The city filled with a whistling concert of micro explosions, but this was no historic firecracker celebration. The three-day hangover lingers on, as does the memory loss that this particular biochip enhancement surely triggered. I imagine that those who are "under quarantine in the GHU for treatment due to the recent Gadlin viral warfare assault on the city" are not faring much better.

And that is not the end of the Pramam's scapegoating. The anti-three decree has obviously failed, the protest being the result of that, as well as the bioHealth enhancement that mysteriously deleted its own programming instructions immediately following the fake evacuation order. Although a half-Gadlin is indeed the genius behind this positive mischief, it really was the creative version of my highland twin who sparked the idea. In spite of that, the anti-Gadlin rhetoric continues and the lies keep festering.

Endless frustration with the Ministry's ability to twist reality into their own narrative is testing the patience of everyone who still remembers the truth. Now we have to re-educate the ones whose memories the GMU has tampered with, retribution that we had not anticipated and that will buy the Divine Messenger time for more liberty infractions, all meant for our own protection, with Their counsel, of course. Hick!

Also unexpected was the Eli Monster's premature possession ... Strike that; no need for GSU fearmongering here, in case they are watching ... her despotic leadership, especially since that morning she was skipping around campus, dishing out hugs to anyone within arm's reach, and then some. Something happened in her bonding experience with Sothese at the URA. Something about his touch sent her central nervous system into an abysmal vortex.

Could that be the not-exactly-human aspect penetrating the skin? Should Nathruyu not have had that same effect on me? Her DNA is like his. I had asked her for a token of her silky hair, as Eli's quip had goaded me into doing, and to my surprise, she had agreed. That brings the URA count of not-exactly-humans up to three, although I suspect that there are many more. Similarly, my DNA is like Eli's, so why do our reactions oppose each other?

Because of Director Shakti's open access to URA

equipment, we could have analyzed both of our DNA signatures, but trepidation tramples our curiosity. You know what we will discover, Mother, you and Father both, with his three extra alien, yet inactive, chromosome pairs. Anyway, we realize that our different genetic makeup is a boon for all sides of this contest, be there two, three, or who knows how many different factions looking to "find" us, and I do use that term loosely since "kill" is on at least one player's agenda, the Fanatical Fedora Freak! Shudder.

Hydrogen sulfide immunity is but a small hint of our peculiarities. There is the prompt and scarless healing that may be a manifestation of the same process, but that involves the skin instead. Would that it extend to the brain, for Eli's sake. In my case, bouts of superhuman strength, like the time I attacked the dark figure in the arcade carrying Mashrin in a bundled blanket, or that I slammed Stitch down on Wakanda's barge on our way back from Albaraaton, which I secretly enjoyed, or the show of force that almost killed me for the utter shock of it during the protest I cannot clear my mind of.

While Eli's human anomalies are more of a handicap, splintering her into the three personalities that highjack her, mine are more of an advantage, fusing my thoughts. As I gain clarity and focus, she falls further into confusion and disarray. And time keeps ticking.

Eli blames herself especially for the innocent children who are trapped against the underwater portions of the city's biowall. Their lighter bodies had fallen into the toxic canals from the blasts, unconscious, and they drowned as debris entwined in the long, sinewy vines feeding the resplendent pink, blue, white, and purple lotuses transforming sunlight on the calm lavender waters. The central canal holoposts have become a transparent gauntlet of death, showcasing the swollen cadavers, jammed against the invisible wall holding back Eadonberg's liquid foundation from spilling into the ocean at low tide, while "the GSU works tirelessly to release their trinity to unite with Their Trinity, in peace," as the broadcasts explain.

The guilt has been tearing apart the sister I love so dearly at the core. It has transcended all of her personalities, in their own interesting, and I do mean interesting, ways, but this one common emotion suggests that a piece of her kind heart is still intact. Dr. Tenille even believes that she is now blaming herself for your death, Mother. I know that sounds crazy, but she, in effect ... I just cannot bring myself to admit it.

Crap. I mourn the sanity that I, alone, enjoy. Ashamedly, I must come to terms with the facts. What the high council packets and secure SIF transmissions, which, of course, Stitch has his scalp-sketching genius figging, are saying is true: "The mastermind behind the protest is crazy, and she is dangerous." That fact remains, no matter how much I use the visualization techniques that Izionnis has been teaching me during our recent late versal arts training sessions at a location I am sworn to secrecy on, and that includes my personal memoirs.

The young academic was insistent on discretion as he has been about the artifact that comprised my second real archeological dig, which turned out to be a dive apparently unsanctioned by this Anubrat character, who keeps being referenced by my unwitting remote transcriptor stars. So all I can relay to that effect is the bugging session during the expedition, until my mentor requests its deletion. For that, of course, he would have to know that the transmission has already reached my journal. Hehehe.

Regardless, the treasure's new home is far away from the unnamed faction in the government that controls the contents of the museum. It turns out that Wakanda simply handles acquisitions for the entity that requests them, and undoubtedly collects a hefty profit for their intact delivery. I wonder if she also has been trafficking in people as well. Someone tipped off the Pramam about our Gadlin-assisted gathering, based on the way the GHU crafts were only picking off certain non-Gadlins, until they were essentially blown out of the sky, that is.

Stitch's mom Sakari had been spending the past three weeks, as promised, recruiting gatayoks and their clans for moral support. They came fully armed in the most ingenious way. The crystal hair tresses that Eli mouthed off at Stitch about were not Überesque fashion statements; they were in fact cleverly disguised EMP blasters.

As is their way, and in accordance with the Gadlin Creed, violence is the last resort. In Sakari's opinion, the Pramam has done his generals a disservice by misrepresenting the Gadlin values of gratitude, opulence, honor, unity, nurture, and trust as pacifism, while at the same time painting their herbal practices as biological terrorism.

The GHU and the GMU were prepared for an airborne defense of a different kind, one that requires gas masks, when what they really should have been paying attention to was the twirling crystal balls summoning a multicolored light show from the sky and disabling the electrical systems on the red crafts in order to send them crashing into the southern waters. I certainly have a deep appreciation for Stitch's heritage, although, as his best chum pointed out to me again today, I still have trust issues. But she is one to talk.

Today, it took the entire morning appealing to Eli the Wise to convince her that Dr. Tenille and Dr. Shakti were not colluding with Sothese. His needle contained saline only since they were inventing medical protocol on the fly to stall the advisor until the SIF agents, who are fiercely loyal to the Pramam, showed up to intervene. Eli is unfortunately part of an internal power struggle on the Inner Council, and Corrient is right in the middle of it. She and our favorite pirate are walking the plank for your daughter, as he had done for you.

Beyond the political sparring, another struggle reminds us that time is running out, and fast. Ever since we returned from Nukamigrad, we can reasonably expect a new dawn every three days unveiling a stable personality ready to hug, curse, or zen out its turn. The end to the delirium has been refreshing, but the ever divergent extremes have not. What is worse, since the Gadlin-induced aurora event, the psychological shell game reshuffles daily.

And just to top us up over the edge, we are all in agreement that Eli is starting to harm herself. My suffering impales me with the phantom of the dagger I hid, slicing my heart in three, one gash for each time that Eli appears to have burnt herself, only one of which I had the forethought to document. This mythical man, named Shen, is the source of all this pain. Stitch is no more jealous of a new relationship muscling in on his chum than I am justified in questioning her highland propriety with a boy she has yet to introduce us to. Even Mr. G has been prying into the invisible boyfriend.

When I arrived at his shop later this afternoon, looking for a copy of that book of yours about myths and legends, the one Eli is convinced we need to find, he was more interested in this Shen friend than making a sale. After some none-of-your-business looks, what he finally told me dropped a bucket of ice on my head, freezing every cell in my body at once. Given the planetary heat wave, an actual ice shower would have been refreshing, but this? I ran out of there wheezing for oxygen. The last copy of the book in existence is now in the hands of the most senior spiritual sage of the GSU.

Given that curing hallucinations falls under their area of expertise, you can well imagine why panic has replaced logic. This thing with Shen is a textbook case that will invite torturous implements, the thought of which turns Dr. Tenille into a catatonic disaster. I have never before mentioned to you our conclusion because I thought that if I wrote it down, then it would become true. I was so hopeful, but Stitch actually saw Eli in Nukamigrad, talking to herself, just before she grabbed a molten rock that burst into flames with the palm of her hand as fuel.

This obsession with fire goes back to Father's study and the fireplace that had no chimney. Combustion is, after all, illegal, which is why, he told us, he had installed a special Ministry-approved device that inhaled the smoke. We never saw him use the fireplace, yet there were always ashes. He must have been burning books or ancient documents while we were asleep. It also provided a convenient hiding place for his flashes. Who would think to sift through the dust of secrets past, except for Eli?

Perhaps she is trying to find her own history in the ashes of scorched memories, so that she can end the nightmares that bake her body while she sleeps. All she is doing is risking ending her physical existence instead, which I suppose is one way to make them stop. In all honesty, I too am having trouble differentiating between reality and fiction, at least when it comes to public versus private disclosures.

Geez. It sure is hot in here. The mere notion of burning flesh is turning my crypt into an inferno.

My feet sense a heat source emanating from the wardrobe just three meters away as I lie here on the bed watching my stone floor broil. A trick of the night is always a possibility, considering adrenaline fatigue is a state that I have been drifting in and out of these days. Every hair follicle is on high alert, wary of the boogeyman with a skin engraving fetish who infiltrated the released Gadlin prisoners as a camouflage to claim his prize writing tablet, standing as an unspoiled obelisk on the central walkway in the golden fog — me.

From the viewpoint of those who collapsed around me, my immunity to the fumes may have appeared prophetic, but I was not the lone man standing at the end of the showdown. Once the yellow dust had settled, there were many others acting as beacons for the final pass through the human rubble. The SIF agents in charge of cleaning up after an accident, the ones that collect the blood of the not-exactly-humans, were interested in living samples this time.

To their displeasure, I am sure, most of us were quick to

clip out. I could see Eli escaping through a veneer of steam with Stitch unconscious across her shoulder, Nathruyu speeding towards Ministry House, the fedora man charging straight at me, a dozen or so strangers scattering, and then Caroline looking overdazed. "Not this time" is the thought that powered the ensuing chase, that met with an abrupt end in the ventilation shafts below the Station hovertrain drop. The giggly friend, who always knew "what" Eli and I are, whipped around to face me and screamed "DON'T FOLLOW ME!"

Something about the fear in her voice convinced me to let her go, but I can still hear her words ringing through the tunnels in my mind, along with distant echoes of Wakanda's agonizing screeches, digging ruts of terror as open sewers in my brain, spilling my tainted blood onto the slab in Eli's nightmares. What am I?

Never mind the mist off the water surrounding my floating homestead talking to me louder than ever. Tonight, I feel a definite presence right across from me, unless I am also hallucinating as dehydration shrivels my capacity to think. I feel compelled to scrunch into a ball against my backboard to protect the suspicions I am penning. Relief finally arrives with a wisp of moist air seeping through the narrow slit above my niche.

You do not have control of your hounds, S—Who wrote that? Is somebody here? Brrr. The generator is overcompensating now.

Juicy! The transcriptor is picking something up. Now we see through hypocrisy.

(faint ticking)

You look lovely tonight, as always, my darling. Have you decided to surrender to me, then? (Sothese)

Shall I take that coy smile as a yes? (Sothese)

(rustling, footsteps, chair dragging) I must say that, after our last oral exchange, I am both delighted and surprised to see you sitting on my bed. (Sothese, laughter)

(rustling, slap, laughter, chair dragging, footsteps, liquid pouring, footsteps, chair dragging) A token for you. The air is hot tonight, do you not sense it? (Sothese)

(swallowing, exhale) Why the sudden silence? I prefer vibrant discourse, as you know. (Sothese)

(snap, rummaging) Another message? Please, read it for me while I admire your thighs. (Sothese, toothy inhale)

You are overly presumptuous, Sothese. (Elize)

Annotate text. No! It can't be! It should write: "(Corrient)". There must be a glitch.

I have been looking for you, and all this time, you were right under my nose. (laughter) A bold woman indeed, Miss Elize. (Sothese, laughter)

Annotate text. He's lying. No. Ohhhm gee. She's trying to hurt herself. He'll do things to her. He'll … No. I can't think that. He'll kill her … I'll KILL HIM! Where the sheiss are they? Stitch will know. Clip out. Not my Eli. Noooooooooo!

The show is over, Mr. Keeto (Sothese, laughter, ping, high pitch)

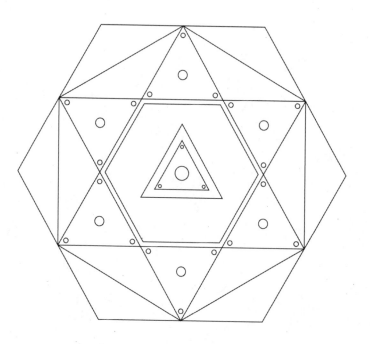

CHAPTER NINE

SOTHESE

Day 1092: evening

Out of the golden ashes emerges the king cobra in a sybaritic display of magnificence. *If only he were not propelled by his tail.*

Sothese flicks his tongue at the sensual turbulence created by the ginger-auburn goddess out of whose favor he has fallen. His response bewilders the sapphire-blue eyes surveying him from across the undulating dazers in the dance pit. Yet you would not have him any other way, Nepharisse.

The stone-faced retort skips along the heads bobbing to the triple-staccato beats of Trimorphic Rhythms, and pummels the chest in urgent need of deflation. *Your indiscretions diminish your worth. Your worth is under review. Deliberation will determine your worth.*

A hardened heart skips a beat, lost to the pause between fight and flight. The warning is clear, yet its intent paints the Restricted Sector club with the blood of past and future regrets. Now is the moment when opportunity brews. The aspiring monarch's burning rage is not the fire that threatens the return to serenity, but a mere spark in the verse of humanity. Sothese knows this, and, as such, understands his vulnerabilities.

One such weakness is swinging a scintillating blue-heeled

pendulum from her perch at the beverage counter. Her two familiar confederates look on eagerly, as their conspicuous coven crafts a fictitious world where all suffering vanishes. But it is not the reality that Sothese clearly recalls.

▼ ▼ ▼

A fate worse than death is the afterlife that unscrupulous religions use to coerce submission from their congregations. Unfortunately, truth is the filament that weaves through the nebulous sails captaining the ship of dreams. Indeed, there is a succession plan for humans, although a higher consciousness is the administrator responsible.

Of the sins that bring ecstasy to the flesh onto which these privileges are unjustly forbidden, Sothese is guilty. For the transgressions that relish the rapture unleashed through impious lordship claims, his crimes are punishable. Yet for a betrayal that can shatter the right order of things, destiny reserves an eternal prison on the plane of no end and no beginning.

Sothese has been there before, and blissful surrender is not what he has found. Being suspended in time as an absolutely frigid, sensory-deprived, cold slice of reality does not erase memories of sensations. On the contrary, it amplifies the longing for them. Such is the providence that rewards defiance and compliance alike since the power to ensnare or to liberate another is not a divine secret for those who wield it.

Through a well-executed wile, another's compassion unintentionally releases the prisoner to the brother he shall never be, so that the torment may live in the brother instead.

Until further notice, the favoritism that weighs down on the scale of impartiality belongs to Sothese, and his undeserved brush with empathy shall remain buried.

▲ ▲ ▲

Izionnis raises an eyebrow at the dare Nathruyu whispers through the crowd while Nepharisse stiffens her upper lip. The softly parted pucker that responds below the candy-red swoop signaling Sothese's intentions heads for his flirtatious redhead with the disheveled bun, shaking her hips to the music. The stealthy approach slowly raises the hair behind Caroline's neck, and her sudden gasp-induced step backwards draws a figure out from a curtained alcove.

Sothese's exploratory kiss knocks her knees towards the ground as he steadies her pelvis against his and leads the rhythmic grind. There are ways to leave a man wanting, but this little tease has crossed into a territorial dispute that downgrades her status to that of property. Her efforts to break free, as always, fail although her large round eyes, straining for help, manage to attract the assistance Sothese had suspected.

A cordial tap on the shoulder pulls Sothese's lips into a smirk and concludes the lubricious performance. The challenge explodes into emerald shards slicing the back of Sothese's brain: "I believe that this is *my* dance, Advisor." The Ministry official cedes the prize, with a disrespectful bow and a sideways glance at the harbingers of rejection near the bar. Some dynamics never change … Or do they? The three schemers squirm off their seats and promptly retreat to the back exit with their eyes fixed on Caroline's new playmate.

The annals of Sothese's human origins have no room for feelings of regret. Forgiveness and empathy already fill the tiny space reserved for bothersome emotions, those that promote destructive dithering. So he focuses on someone else with prospects of sinuous entwinement. And perhaps, if Caroline ever returns to her senses, she and her ex-dazing friend can partake in a guided reconciliation, with the master of subterfuge and seduction himself, as a hands-on instructor.

Fluid pressure builds a tower of debauchery with the images flashing through space as Sothese thunders into Ministry House's generator level from the connecting ventilation shafts. The abrupt end to his evening's entertainment requires an impromptu comm to room service. He winds his fleshly masterpiece up the palatial foyer's split staircase to his quarters to peruse the shift roster for a few servile interns, but the damsel sitting on his bed could conceivably handle his current predicament. At least, the desire for it raises his spirits.

Despite the scorching breeze whistling through the open balcony doors, Sothese reaches for the Gadlin ceremonial coat, taps the gifted button, and smirks out a "You look lovely tonight, as always, my darling. Have you decided to surrender to me, then?" followed by a pause and an additional "Shall I take that coy smile as a yes?"

A fresh performance begins. He files on the jacket and slides a chair over to the young woman with long, silky dark hair tied back in a pony tail and wearing a lovely pleated dress from the Stew Über Mariposa collection. Straddling the reversed chair across from her, he leans his arms presumptuously on the backrest. Their suggestive exchange records the exact words Sothese wants Keeto to hear as it has done since he was a little hard on Caroline's debut role as Gayok. She was quite impressive. Regardless, "The show is over, Mr. Keeto." saw the button yanked, dropped, and crushed under Sothese's red patent leather shoes.

Reverie turns Elize's nervous breath into a lustful melody to Sothese's ears. The many who come to him looking for strings to be pulled beat out the same tune day by day. But of this young minstrel? Something else has emboldened her, even as she knows through the closed-door and open-mic romantic encounters, that his love is not the kind that she surely seeks.

Fortuitously, her voluntary courtship arrives none too soon, stalling Anubrat's plan for another twenty years, at least, and, consequently killing all chances that the Pramam will be alive to infiltrate the tight circle for whom the boons are promised. There was an epoch when Sothese aimed to be amongst the coveted few, but those ties were severed with a jab and a twist and a flick of the wrist. He now prefers to thrust himself fully into more earthy endeavors.

To Sothese's repeated frustrations, however, a petition for his Mariposa-wearing guest to grace the air with her fluttering voice is denied as is entry beneath the folds of her skirt. Something stays his hand at her thighs that his impatient fingers cannot overpower, nor can he restrain an indomitable emotion that refuses its entombment. There is no message in the envelope that this nurturing Elize has retrieved from her evening purse, but a token that only Gibayze could have acquired from the treasure hunters, trading their questionable finds for coin in Albaraaton's Exchange Sector.

A small round object, wrapped in a thin, natural linen cloth, drops into Sothese's open left palm, and in that packet is a childhood treat, sticky with the sweetness he once adored. As he stares in shock for the feelings he believed he had cured himself of, Elize brushes his bangs back with her fingers, whispering "honey heals", then flits out of the room, just as the toe tapping begins.

Hot on her heels, Sothese chases her along the mezzanine, down the curved staircase, and into the foyer where GMU guards stand as sentries to visiting dignitaries. He senses a temporary shift that quickly dissipates, but he scans the faces of the unit on duty just in case. Commotion in the corridors surrounding the sajadum courtyard results in broken glass and a guard hanging by his ankles from the bannister. The distraction frees the main entrance, and Elize escapes into the night, to her brother's relief. Keeto pulls the upside down man back onto solid footing.

A new chase begins with the loyal twin as hunter until Sothese rushes to his quarters first and slams the door in his face, only to resurface to a fist that he easily deflects, sending Keeto head first into the backdrop for his spying sessions. The renewed toe tapping raises the stakes on the premature attack. The boy simply is not strong enough to challenge both of them.

Footsteps carrying the polished flesh of extinct mammals stop by Keeto's prone body and tap in concert with Sothese's flickering thoughts. Temptation rules over temperance, and he proceeds to demonstrate to the impulsive young man the nuances of loyal service while he elbows into Keeto's shoulder blades. The obedience lesson aborts when the mounter's leading knee squashes Elize's gooey gift and a glint of nostalgia overrules.

A chill follows a hand up from his uncharacteristically conflicted assailant and crystallizes the sweat off Keeto's brow. The shoving resumes capped with a bonus for the brother who would risk his life to avenge an assault that never took place. Sothese pitches the Gadlin ceremonial coat at Keeto as he flies backwards across the hallway and into the bulky drapery of the glassed-in rooftop courtyard. The piece represents the final intel Sothese cares to share with the second recipient of his unpleasurable restraint this late evening. "I am sure Gibayze can find you a new button. And send my ill-regards to Caroline. She is all yours."

Whistling lips call the guards to Keeto's aid. Sothese winks as they carry the Restricted Sector boss's new challenger out of the building, just seconds before the Pramam's personal slider lands by the rooftop sajadum.

Sothese curses the rain that strips the lustrous coif from the straw man mess that he grooms into perfection every morning. Considered a reasonable concession in order for the Pramam to demonstrate a sympathetic ear to the emphatically disgruntled populace, all coastal cities now follow a strict cloud seeding schedule to compensate for last year's full-time blower counterterrorism policy that scorched most greenery. The nonagonal crafts now hovering over the center of each city, in line with their nine biowall towers, not only act as propaganda for the pompous Pramam's responsiveness, but also serve as the power core for an acid filtration bioroof.

Furthermore, their ultimate replacement with central tower structures will provide new employment opportunities.

With most of the offending liquid fallout taking place at night, at least Sothese can still recharge in the light while he continues to keep the Pramam in the dark about his kinship with Nathruyu, especially since her double is no longer at SIF headquarters to dupe the ignoramus. As a matter of survival, suspicions must fall elsewhere and preferably onto the Restricted Sector contestant also vying for the throne, who has wooed Sothese's ex-officials to act as his supra human power source. The shafts are supporting a new tenant instead — the Pramam's increasingly anxious advisor.

The Pramam showcases his exquisite silk robe, with curiously familiar buttons on its cuffs, along the water garden's stone path. The two young valets, carrying a florapy, escort their apparent luminary into the building, plant the hybrid's double trunk into an urn outside the entrance and wait for his return. The Inner Council duo walk to the south wing in silence. Selective dialog is to be the appropriate conversational style going forward, yet geared to which audience is a question for this new age of falsehoods.

The formalities perk up Sothese's highfalutin ears for the pupil turned thankless master.

"Kainaten has informed me of your disregard for protocol, Sothese. You were not supposed to engage her. They must counsel the Pramam in these matters, and only the Pramam has the power to execute Their wishes." Self-consciousness overtakes the advisor's composure.

"Kainaten! Show yourself and defend these claims!"

The toes tap indecision. "You are nothing without me. I can take your life right now and take your place. I have done so before, my Pramam." Fear freezes in the cold air between the threatened and the accused while Kainaten flashes in.

"I would like to see you try that again, Sothese." Angst floats towards Sothese as Kainaten stands behind his earlier statement, taps his trusty recording device, then clears his time bending presence from the room.

"We all want the same result, Sothese, simply the means differ. However, differences can be fatal to Their goal. That will not do. You are not above death yourself, Advisor."

Sothese's secret strains to remain one, so he must be shrewd. "Is that a threat?"

"A warning. We are not your enemy, yet there are many who are. Our issues are simply that of non-compliance."

"Elize is disruptive and too unstable to be of any use to us. She masterminded the student uprising, my Pramam."

"The Gadlins are still behind her, and hence, once again, the deaths of innocent children. The official narrative is sound. We continue as planned and find a way to pacify the masses. Are we in agreement?"

"Perhaps she can stay with our complicit Gayok for a while. Out of sight, out of mind." Kainaten's interspatial words tease a smirk from Sothese as he parrots the idea as his own.

"Not without its irony, is it not? Then Wakanda closes the underground network, we start our campaign, and, of course, throw in some pleasantries to keep the populace distracted. Is this agreeable?"

"Excellent, Sothese. With Their counsel, we shall reframe

the girl twin's little uprising."

"We will need character witnesses, of course."

"Permission is granted onto you to find student volunteers for the SIF to retrain, Sothese."

"With pleasure, my Pramam. Perfect are They."

"That is my line, Advisor."

"Yes, of course. They are One." The overstep stirs some heat into the room as the Pramam leaves and Kainaten whispers a "Well done, my lord" in Sothese's ear.

▼ ▼ ▼

A life taken is a life awakened.

The king sits high with his retinue by his side, staring Sothese's failing body down as the emerald in his eyes sparks in response to the final blast that cracks the sheath that keeps him whole.

Spectators cheer as the monarch jeers at the last of the nine to relinquish their time. The green gemstone eyes dim, tearing as three blue lights bounce off the walls of the chamber, desperate to escape the open chest that is ready to encase them in an eternal darkness. One by one, they join their kin, for eternal life was their only sin.

They were one, but now, they are none.

▲ ▲ ▲

How soon most human cells lose their ability to remember. The ingrate whom Sothese reluctantly serves while he bides his time for revenge is the quintessential example of bipedal brainlessness. He is undeserving of the inferior chromosomes he currently disrespects, let alone the ones he aims to steal. A royal mandate he may have been given, but soon a dethroned Mr. Malik shall be the one splintered, never to return in all eternity, a fate worse than death.

▼ ▼ ▼

Energy moves in and out of form in the versal soup, yet there is one form that fears transition, that loathes change, that infects intelligent life with attachments to permanence when none exist, and so humanity was created as a mutation that fights to preserve itself in an evolving reality.

Yet Anabelle was different. Her love mended disputes and her wisdom united. However, with unity comes the change that is the enemy of those whose viral load anchors them to their physicality, a world of sensations that Sothese has become quite fond of. And so after nine years of slippery politics building powerful God-fearing alliances on the one hand and covert heretic mentorship in Malik's case, a new Unified religion was born. Consequently, Sothese's concubine and her contingent of moderates met with an abrupt transformation.

Nine years later, as Sothese welcomes the Pramam back from a second pilgrimage, a special *protégé* is in the making that will ensure the balance, just in case.

▲ ▲ ▲

Tonight, Sothese delivers on a promise. Insurance policies are not without their risk, but his waning strength and darkening skin foretell a horrific defeat that only unquestionable loyalty can save him from. And therein lies the greatest gamble of all.

✂ ✂ ✂

His thumb pauses at the latch, envisioning the desired outcome as Kainaten kneels between the sacrificial bodies, already enhanced for the gift they are about to receive.

The gold triangular box housing the other two ultraviolet lights that an ancient spiritual sage had shattered from its original donor opens. The orbs quickly find their new homes in the two figures that now rise to finally reunite with Kainaten, forming a triad of new officials, anchored as a unit to the physical world through Sothese's symbiotic presence.

"My mentors will never live up to us, Sothese."

"I expect no less from this leap of faith, Kainaten and company."

Kainaten admires his stable reflection in the mirror, and with a sparkle in his eyes, he tucks into position on the leader's right flank, flicks his plasma sparker, and the triad jumps through time to reconvene with Sothese for their first joint assignment.

✂ ✂ ✂

A cold chill grabs Dr. Tenille at the nape of the neck. This medic's personal journal could reveal so many private affairs.

However, the content of the partially woven Galleon's sails …
Now *that* is a tale to behold.

"Whose dreams would you be catching wind of, my good
Captain?"

The sound of delicate heels flitting, then pausing, then
stomping past in the hallway, followed by an urgent assault
on the counselor's door down the hall, is much more enticing
than the thud at Sothese's feet from his freshly malleable
informant's body.

As Elize's closest confidant attempts to drag himself
away from a sure death, Sothese expropriates the Galleon and
slips into the supply closet sharing a wall with the profanity
spewing from his delectably disturbed target. The poor girl
needs a vacation. Snigger.

E L I Z E

Day 1093: dawn

What a gorgeous morning! And a big smile to you as well, Cyd. I love waking up to your gentle caresses. Oh dear, did I cry again last night? I feel tired, but still fantastic. Catharsis. That is what all this sadness is about. I must send myself some gentle hugs for the nightmares that I can never remember. Yes, Elize. Fill yourself with love and it shall pour over the entire world through tears of joy instead. Do you approve of your decor diva, yours in earnest?

Perfect! You always make everything so perfect for me. I love you. I love you too, Elize. Now time to get up and spread your wings to the world. The clock is ticking, you know. What is this? Oh simply a gift from me ... to me. Soft giggle. I hope you enjoy it. It is our anniversary. Eighty-one days since you allowed all of us to finally come through to you. Although I was not your first choice, I still honor our birthdate. Your mother would be so proud that you made it this far, considering all the temptation. You know who I am talking about. Soft giggle giggle giggle.

This is delicious. Thank you. Honey heals, Elize. Rango! Well, I am sure it still tastes just as good as a saucer. Delicious. You never know what you'll get when you have a monkey in the kitchen. Soft giggle. Where is that antique timepiece hiding anyway? I hear it tick, tick, tick. It sounds muffled. The shag tentacles are swaying to the ticks. Nice moves, Shaggy. Thank you, Elize. That was flair, of course. And now pointing to the closet. Oh! What a lovely little bear holding Shen's timepiece. Pick it up. Is that another gift? Not from me, Elize. Hey. I recognize this toy. It belongs to … Gasp!

Teddy! How did this get … His eyes are glowing. Oh, he is a bearbot. I wonder if I sit him here … Wonderful! Now tell me your secrets, little fuzzy one. Tap the nose and here come the holograms. I hope I can remember the control gestures; otherwise, I might be watching these all day. Ok. Brace yourself, Elize. These could be his last moments alive. No. That fate is not in my heart. Deep breath in and let it all out. I am ready.

Here comes Teddy's smiling face. Bear hug. Now we are walking a little tilted but I can just tilt my head too. There. All these people are pointing and smiling at the lovely little bear. Speed up a bit … a bit more. Stop. Transport to Eadonberg now boarding. Gulp. Stop. Hold back the tears. This is the trip where his parents died. There is no need to become immersed in that. Just speed up the flashes. Stop! Who are those people? Or what are they?

We knew it! Stitch, Keet, and I had suspected it all along. There was no transport accident. But I never expected this! What the— go back a bit. Stop. Expand. Crap! Whoops, my apologies. The recorder is just a toy. There is not enough detail at that distance. There are three of them. I think I know who they are anyway. Sothese's creepy three. Shudder. His parents were taken! Wait. The bear is moving backwards. Someone is taking Teddy too! Twirling. Good. Let me see your face. Shoot! Better, Elize. Soft giggle. Inside a satchel now. I wish the bear could speak too. Hmmm. Check the mouth ... Oh well, it was worth a try.

At the orphanage now. Lots of children ... Master Chung ... some assistants ... nothing incriminating here. Speed up a bit. Does this bear ever sleep? I need to forward to the Snack Shack meeting. Deep breath in ... and release. Two more times. Ready now.

Nathruyu's face. Good. The bear turns around, and here comes Teddy's cheek. Bear kiss. Soft giggle. Maybe Nathruyu has a kind side to her. One can only hope, correct? Back to the show. Drippy flyer bake ... meteor storm ... tilted mayhem in the Central Core ... plopped on a table I imagine ... and here we are, Keet and I. Skip over the Keet-turning-to-mush section ... and ... sniff. I miss those hugs. He was such a sweetie. Stop that. He still is. I know he is ... somewhere. A few more breaths and bite my lip ... jump past when we left Teddy with Mme Beaudoin. Tilted walk to the Victory Bridge ... through the campus perimeter woods ... and there it is. The Gadlin barge ... and GASP! Wakanda!

Not the satchel again. Over. No more flashes. There must be more. Squeeze the bear. Smoosh him. Look for something hard. Yes! There is a hidden one. Someone wanted me to find this. I can feel it. Clip it into the back of his head. This looks more recent. I can tell by the trees. They are brown like they are now. Wonderful! Teddy is back on campus. No. He is on a barge again, floating up the western canal. Who is under that cloak? The counselor! They are heading to ... NO! Not the GHU. They took Mashrin there and she— Gasp. Sothese! There must be a timestamp on this. One, two, three .... Nine days ago. I have to sneak in there. I have to save him.

Be careful, Elize. Disguise Rango. The GHU and the GMU and, I am afraid, likely the GSU are still looking for the protest organizer. Best be incognito. Let me help. Come here, little mammasack, and hold still. It will be fun, I promise. Soft giggle. That looks good. What is this, Cyd? A lizzy tail ... and another and ... Show me your stash. So my Mini-Lizzy is still here somewhere and you two colluding hybrids are having some fun when I am out. Rango? I thought so. Ok. We paste them on and we now have a monsterpiece. That should keep spying eyes on my back and not my face.

Keet is on the comm.

"I need to talk to you, Miss Elize." Oh dear. He sounds very upset. Send him some love. He needs more than that, I wager. Send him some love again. There.

"Eli? Are you even listening?" Oh boy. He is steaming out the ears. Focus on the now.

"Yes, Keet. I am. I found Teddy. I am going to him. I have to run. Comm later. Love you. Big hugs."

Just one more loose end, and off to Teddy's rescue we go! Grab my comm and with a preemptive apology ...

"Not coming in. Stick a vial up your crotch, you whore!" Oh dear. I hope Corrient did not get offended, but I think it was effective. Who wants the Eli Monster in their lab? Double apologies, though. Accepted, Elize. There is an urgent matter to attend to. Quick thinking.

And quick running, too. Here already? I am not even winded. No eek-ing, Elize, or Rango will start banging. Mashrin was kept in this zone. Hey. I thought Keet said that

Caroline ran away. We can chat with her later. Flirty as always. Good. The guard is distracted. This room then. Tiptoe right in and shut the door softly. Deep breath in … and out. Ready for what may come.

These are the same probes and the same monitors and … should I check? Be strong, Elize. Peek under the thermal blanket. Gasp. His happy face socks are still on. Is this someone's idea of compassion? And a holographic mobile hanging above the slab? This is not kindness. This is the lollipop that kills. Bite my lip. Breathe in … and out. Oh dear, Teddy. He has the scar. They found him and are using his brain for experimentation. I have to get him out of here and take him to Nukamigrad. Unplug all this stuff and … Footsteps! Whispers.

"Kidnapping in progress. Here is a top down view. He wants her alive."

Gulp. Now what? Not a good time to chat, Caroline. Where did she go? Good. They are busy with a pretty redhead.

The boy is safe with me. Go where you need to be, but leave the boy. Leave the boy with me.

Snap decision, Elize. Believe in the good and run. Down, down, down into the generator level. Pull off the vents, crawl into the shaft, and drop. Phew. You can loosen the death grip now, Rango. We are safe down here, as long as … best not mention his name. Actually, I need to pick up my new dress in Tir-na-nog. Hopefully, this one is not defective.

Back topside and a quick jaunt to the shop. It should be ready now.

"Lovely today again, Miss Elize." Respectfully ignore the holoadvert. We are on a mission.

Here is the shop. Straight to the dressing room. Put it on. And the sandals. Lovely. Absolutely lovely.

"Thank you. It is perfect! Do you have an evening purse? Gorgeous." This is so exciting, Elize. We are going on a romantic date, but be careful. The holoadvert guy is too curious. Best take a different route. Good idea. Back in the orchard already? Time is just ticking today.

"Hey lo, Stitch." Highland wave and smile. Are those hearts on his scalp? Soft giggle. He is a nice boy too, Elize. Shhh. Mr. Zaf is just a chum.

"Trip! What a pica beautiful dress you have, chum!" Soft giggle. Cupids and arrows. This is awkward. I do love my chum, though. But not that way. "The back looks like butterfly wings. And those are ziga juicy sandals too." A poke and smile.

"Ta, chum. Socks in sandals, Stitch? The GFU will clamp you for that." Wink. He takes his socks off. Good. "Nice toes." They are actually nice. "Can you tap them? So talented." Soft giggle.

"Perk. I found the clicks." Huh? "The ones the Pramam transcript had. Your ninth birthday flashes have them too. I think it's recorder interference, yeah?"

"So you think the Pramam records his own conversations?"

"Maybe just the ones he wants to manipulate, ya fig?" Hmmm. "But no high council packets or shadow packets anywhere. I'm dunked on that one, chum."

"Do my father's flashes click too?"

"Only in one spot. The recorder was different, so it's not a defect. I need to modulate more." Squashed frog face. "To slow it down ... way down. Perk. Let me work on it." He pokes me again and smiles.

"I found Teddy." A jaw drop. "But I need to talk to the counselor right now. Time is running out."

"Ease, chum. The counselor is not your friend, remember, Miss little hug monster?"

"I have to know." The scalp of concern. "No worries. Can you comm Keet. He seems very angry with me for some reason." I saw that eye-roll. "We can meet back at the pond and make some sense of this. Hugs?" Ooooooooo. That was a nice squeeze.

"At the pond." Tick, tick, tick away to O'Leary Hall.

Feel the love, Elize. I am sure there is a perfectly valid explanation for the counselor's part in all this. Creek open the gate. Gulp. He saw me. He looks like his usual sour self in the window. Breathe in … and out … and into the building, down the hall—

Elize, stop! Do not go down that hallway. Be strong, Elize. Feel the love, remember? The counselor needs our love and understanding. He is good at heart. Everyone is. And they all love us. Do not listen to her, Elize. She is overdazed with Gadlin herbs. You know that pissy one. Twentieth century hippy, she is. The dweeb is her supplier. He is drugging her to get his way with you. He cannot be trusted. Read his scalp. None of them can. They all want a piece of you. Even the pup. Always hounding you to be chaste. He is just a dog. Wolf howl. Deep eerie giggle. Not to worry, Elize. I always make sure you are wearing yo— Just shut the sheiss up! Come with me, Elize. We have a fight to pick.

Stomp down the hall, bash his door in. Shove over. I caught

you in the act.

"What are you hiding? Hands off! You have no permission to touch me, you wack! Do you not think I know what you did? I saw your face. You did it. How much is the Pramam paying you? You think you can stop us? You have no idea who you are dealing with, you double wack! You triple wack. You—"

"Miss Elize! Please control yourself. I will call security." Move over. What are you hiding in that stand? A weapon. I know it.

"You are trying to kill me! Murderer. Let go of me." Hit him. Run to the door. Throw something. Destroy his books. Deep eerie giggle. That stand is next. Run for it.

"Elize! Leave my office NOW! Or I will have you expelled!" *Go do what has to be done.* Time is running out. Tick, tick, tick is all I hear.

"Go ahead. I need a vacation anyway. From all of you. Especially *you*." You triple-faced sheiss maker. Storm out of there. The nerve of him threatening me. Sheiss! It is so bloody hot here. Excellent show, Elize. You shut the sheiss up too. Yes, mistress. Deep eerie giggle.

I need to cool off before I hurt someone. Run to the south. The dweeb is sitting by the pond, waiting for me. Let him wait. Deep eerie giggle.

Whoa! Watch the edge there, Elize. The oceans are dropping. The Gadlins are stealing the water with their underground aqueducts. They know that you know. They sent the fedora man for you. You saw what he did to Wakanda. He wants the water for himself. He will torture you. You will die slowly and very painfully. Deep eerie giggle.

Not if I kill you first.

Yes! Do it! You know how to use the Mini-Lizzies. Look. I see three ... over there. That is all you need to make a gate. Let me help you. Now place them on the biowall. Flip the tail and all set. Excellent. Just give the order, mistress, and I will give you the nudge. Go closer. A little closer. Bite my lip. GMU ... GHU ... GSU ... and the fedora man, remember? All after you. You will die a twisted shell, just like your mother. No crying. Do you want that, Elize? No. Then ... DO IT!

NO! I need sultry not suicidal. Did you hear me? Yes, Elize. Loud and clear. Sultry it is. Deep eerie giggle. Now off to the Snack Shack. Shen is waiting.

Oh! Stitch.

"Perk, chum! I was at the pond." Hmmm. A little detour perhaps? "Are you even listening?" And there is the pup.

"You have been hanging around Mr. Keeto, I see. The whole Peter Pan thing." Deep eerie giggle.

"Yeah, we're bud buds, ya fig?" He is annoying now. Maybe I should just push him over the edge. Tick, tick, tick. Look at the time. We will be late. After all this effort getting prettied up? That will not do. "Where did you get that timepiece? Perk! You stole it from my room!"

"Are you wacked? I did *not* take it. How dare you, of all people, accuse *me*? It was a gift from Shen."

"Shen? The invisible boyfriend? Is that who this dress is for? Give it back!"

"No. It is Shen's not yours."

"And is this Shen going to burn you again? Where is that wind com— you were not going to—" Why is he tearing?

Dweeb. "Eli, please. I'm ziga worried about you. You're talking to yourself. You're hurting yourself, yeah? You're not well."

Sheiss! Now the pup. Just start walking. Ignore him following you.

"Eli! STOP!" Give him three minutes or hit him, Elize. Your choice.

"Three minutes, pup. Spill it."

"You have been feeding Sothese our every move, haven't you?"

"You call *me* paranoid? You are the delusional one. He is trying to kill me, like Mother. They are all trying to kill me. And now you are turning on me. Both of you. You want to send me to the GHU!"

"Your name came through my remote transcriptor. And I saw you there last night, running away. You were wearing that dress."

"You are psychotic. I got this dress a few hours ago. You both are trying to frame me." Shove him, Elize.

"Creeps! Bud, I got you."

"What the— You made a hole in the biowall? Eli, why?"

Why? Yes, Elize. The real question is not what, but why. Deep eerie giggle. "I am not going to the GHU! Get out of my way. I have a date."

Stitch is muttering under his breath, Elize. "Trip! We'll just follow you then, yeah?" Trip! we'll just follow you then, yeah? Good luck, dweeb.

Eat my dust, boys. Shen is supposed to be here. Breathe. Just Breathe. They are wrong. Where is he?

"Eli."

"You scared him off, PUP. Rot in the toxic soup!" Shove him in the canal. Finally, some peace.

Sheiss! It really is boiling. What are those things? Caroline! She is grabbing him.

Nothing is real. None of this is real. I need to run away. Run. Breathe. Run. Breathe. Run. Keep running. Tick, tick, tick.

✂ ✂ ✂

Home finally. Huh?

"How did you?" Slam. "Eek!" Bang. Bang. Bang.

"Me Tarzan!" NO! Rango's on the ground. "Rip its arms off." Squeal! Twang! Screech! Crunch!

"Murderers! Let go, you wacks! Shen! Help me." Too hot.

"Do you like your new room decor, Elize?"

"Monster! What did you do to Cyd?"

"He needed a trim! He slaps too much. My timepiece, please." Pitch it at him.

"You sheiss of a wack!" Kick the dagger hilt. Then him in the balls. How could that not hurt?

"Where is my sultry birthday girl?" Gasp. He knows? "With that attitude, this will not be very pleasurable!"

NO! Aaaaaaaaah! Water. I need water. "You're burning me. STOP!" Squeal! Aaaaaaaaah. "Shen, please!" Gag. Pant. Where's the dagger? NO! Aaaaaaaaah!

✂ ✂ ✂

ELIZE

Don't leave me, Keet. It's so cold.

✂ ✂ ✂

As it reaches for me
I slip away
To a dark dark
Moment in time
We're frozen in time
We're all out of time

K E E T O

Day 1093: near midnight

I am still shaken. Where do I start? Stitch and I are beyond concerned. We have been looking for her most of the evening and found nothing, except for a trail of gadgets that Stitch has been equipping us with for the past three years, and the Dr. Tenille issue choker, and the silver pup chain I gave her, and

…

I have to start a new page. I wet the last one. We found many of the items that she held dear, like the childhood treasures that you had given to her, the crystal hair tresses, the constellation charms, all the items she kept with her inside Rango, and even

…

Sorry. Another new page. I can barely see through my tears. Give me a moment.

I had to bring Sparky up here on the bed with me, because I just need so badly someone to hold. I wish you were here to make all this hurt, this worry, this fear disappear, Mother, so that I can attract Eli back to us with the right energy, the happy vortex, as opposed to this whirlpool of despair. We found her dreamcatcher. That is when I …

… Again. New Page.

That is when I heard her sing to me.

As they reach to take me
I drift away
To a dark dark

Place in my mind
We're frozen in time
We're all out of time

How did we not see this coming? Dr. Tenille had warned me, repeatedly, emphatically, and every other adverb that belabors the fact that her mental health was deteriorating beyond light speed. He could not guarantee her safety from the GHU anymore, as if they were really at the top of my list of closet demons. "S", both for Sothese and for Spiritual, is the middle letter fueling my panic. Izionnis has given me several graphic accounts of the exorcisms. The "unfortunate casualties" metric does not bode well for the GSU success ratio.

In any case, it turns out that Eli is her own biggest threat, and now she is completely off grid. Luckily, as irony would have it, the city is so locked down since the protest that we can at least be certain that Eli is still within a nine kilometer circle, unless … No. I will not allow my imagination to throw her through a biowall breach. As foreboding a feeling as I have about her safety, somehow I know that she remains in the city, either above or below ground, even possibly in the Restricted Sector. On second thought, let me envision her anywhere but there. I …

I just had to flip pages again. This is ridiculous. Transcriptor on.

Much better. I can pace and shake my hands of the anxiety.

(gurgling, sniffing, growling, sniffing) Leave the door alone, Sparky. Those things are gone now. Creeps. When Eli threw me into the canal this morning, I thought that was the end for me. This is the third time I have survived an attack from whatever those hound-like moat monsters are. I don't remember because I blank out, but I have a feeling that I've been near death each time. It's the hallucinations. I always see Caroline and the next thing I know, someone is reviving me and I'm coughing up sludge. Grody. The Gadlin coat is still here. I know where Caroline went and ... Geez. She must be suicidal.

(crying, sniffling) No. I am projecting what I dread finding out about Eli. Something is wrong, something is so very wrong I can —

(knock, knock, knock)

Elize is in danger. Hurry, there is still time. (Izionnis)

Transcriptor off.

✂ ✂ ✂

She is reaching out to me now. I can feel her presence. I can smell her myrrh, as I have since the beginning, as if she were sitting inside my crypt, on my bed, holding and comforting me, while her words keep my tears from erasing those that I am about to share with you.

Six hours ago, a knock at the door echoed the churning I was feeling inside, and I left with Izionnis, as terrified as he was frantic. I barely noticed the steam boiling off the western canal because all I could see as I blistered behind Izionnis, Nathruyu, and a third woman who, for the life of me, I cannot recall, was a chaotic room and a flash of a libidinous monster creeping into my mind, with Eli struggling to break its hold. I prefer to believe that the popular notion of constant repetition making things real is more of a lie than a law, but my belief is the actual lie.

I should have stood up to her, Miss Eli Monster, rather than avoided her. Instead, I allowed her the space to create a monster out of me, out of Stitch, and out of everyone who truly cares about her well-being.

Stitch was on the move as well. While the three not-exactly-humans put all their credit on my blind trust, the voice through the comm wavered and cracked out a breathless story. Our recently poke and smile devoid companion was clipping through the Van Billund Hall links, subduing any sentinel who so much as blinked an eye at him through their quartz melding stations in the ceilings and gunning straight for the same target I was — Eli's dorm, three towers away.

Stitch's mother had just sketched him in to a three-way secure channel alert with the Nukamigrad nursery caretaker, who had what remained of the Odwin loyalists from the GMU sweep at the Central Core protest, gathering for spiritual support. Rumors of prophetic proportions inspired an emergency nitapok meditation, once news of the lo-flowers slapping the walls, the soil, the air, the planters, and any human within their grasp reached the Gadlin Order. Smaller ones were shaking uncontrollably, as if in tears, while larger ones embraced them gently within their foliage. Even the hybrids nearest the underground channels were sending massive shockwaves in the water with their leaves.

If ever there were a time to believe in quantum communication making itself known through vibrations in the waters, this was it because, as we discovered a few minutes later, Cyd had been hacked to bits and was clinging to life.

The hurried conversation also panted out the past hour's findings from a distributed problem solving team that Stitch had patched together from chumbuds with the most Tess potential, a conglomeration of co-dweebs that I sadly do not qualify for yet. The clicks in Eli's obsessively favored birthday flashes, which we only took note of as a result of similar clicks on the Pramam's one-sided remote transcriptor plotting session, are not EM interferences from poorly shielded electronics in the recorder's vicinity. They are the instantaneous comings and goings of the mysterious watcher I had documented in last year's journal.

Here are my notes to that effect, for easy reference.

Crap! My journal is missing. I clearly remember locking it up with the rest of them in an antique chest I purchased from Mr. G's, or whatever-his-name's shop specifically for that purpose. My tunic theft our first year in Eadonberg was proof enough that Sparky valued his own life more than my musings, so all of my awe-inspiring wisdom is under physical lock and key now, except, apparently, the lost ones. I glorify myself in jest, by the way, desperately searching for a whimsical swirl amidst the tearful flood.

Do you see what I am doing again? Avoiding. Who cares about a hick of a book when my sister is still screaming, somewhere, for attention that is rightfully hers? I failed her, and I am still failing her while I continue to escape to my hovel in hell. How could this torment be anything but? That abomination has been stalking Eli ever since our ninth … our birthday ... or longer and ...

So sorry. I need a moment ... and a new page.

Now we have its inhumane face as proof.

Through the comm disclosure that will haunt me forever, I could almost hear the gears grinding on Stitch's scalp, as he blabbered on about some threshold frame rate below which our eyes cannot detect images, his conclusion loosely based on a theory using ancient moving picture films as an analogy. Extrapolating this thesis further leads to even more disturbing speculation. Is this cloaking capability simply an advanced, or even extraterrestrial, technology? Or could this quantum flickering be real? Gulp. What if there are more of them, watching us, always watching us.

Perhaps if we watched where we were headed ourselves, others would not be drawn to voyeurism. Signs of a large bruise on my shoulder may be gone, but the slice in my heart that followed the J-wing hallway collision is hemorrhaging. Stitch and I bashed into the horror together, while my three otherworldly guides readied technological weaponry that painted his head with incomprehensible equations. That there was enough brain power directed at the rest of the dweeby genius's body to stay upright, let alone engage in a vicious offensive, is stupefying.

In any case, three fewer peepers are skulking about, at least, we hope. Stitch was the first to charge in and at the stalker, who was straddling Eli as she lay unconscious, face up, and cooking in her own sweat. Cyd was toppled over, his leaves everywhere, and almost shredded, and Rango was ... I caught the tear in time, but ...

These ones I missed. Another new page.

Eli loved that hybrid, more than her normal self would admit, and I suspect that Stitch feels the same way towards her. He almost died to save her. When he jumped on the creep, who was wearing the shirt from which Stitch had cut a bloodstained section, spontaneous combustion set his clothing on fire and blasted him out the door, but not before he had ripped that shirt clean off. Fortunately, Nathruyu caught him and quickly snuffed out the flames, using nothing but her own body, a curious functionality due to her extra chromosomes, I assume.

Nothing appears to shock me anymore. I focused forward, ignoring what had just happened, and concentrated a massive internal power surge on the two accomplices attempting an ambush from their spectator vantage points flanking the entrance. The fury inside me kicked their surprised mugs right out the window.

The creepy duo of the three were more stunned by my explosiveness than I was by their steamy landing in the pond below, a feat worthy of many back pats under normal conditions, but, unfortunately, the prize we were after slipped right through all the commotion, flung over a fugitive's naked shoulder. Izionnis's non-interference is a philosophy I plan to debate with him extensively later today since he was clearly the one directing Nathruyu and the other woman. Regardless, delusions of invincibility kept my adrenaline stores at full capacity, and I beat Stitch to the sunshaft.

The lift ride down felt like it was fighting against gravity for the speed my thoughts were flying. In contrast, Mr. Zaf had lost his Tess and was revisiting his childhood, based on the leisurely preschool scribbles his scalp was coloring. Nevertheless, for what we were up against, his subconscious military training was all we needed. I sure hope he recovers soon. I need his genius going forward, more than ever.

Curiously, someone had blocked the kidnappers' beeline to the perimeter woods and had frozen them single-handedly as if the scene was a holographic cube projected onto the eastern clearing from a celestial viewer on pause, except that the ponytailed girl in the pleated dress was the only one moving. I was immobilized as well for a split second while my brain raced with conspiracy theories of an Eli imposter, but I was mostly consumed by a single question: "Where is Sothese in all of this?"

If I could have turned my head, I would have seen the Pramam's advisor sneaking up behind me, but I did not. Intervention, this time, came swiftly. With his new officials preparing Eli for a dreamless sleep, and me under his thumb, as he dug into the mark of the hunted at the base of my skull, whatever rewards he was planning to receive by owning the ever elusive twins were resting at the edge of a large brimmed hat.

I literally spat the tip of my sliced tongue out of my mouth when I saw the rising fedora-topped shadow on the ground and its cerated dagger. My limbs were not stuck in a phantasmagorical trick of the night at that point; they were anticipating rigor mortis, but my head was free to snap back onto the bridge of Sothese's nose, breaking it and the eerie silence that had mesmerized the three murderers.

To my utter theatrical relief, the ominous silhouette was

not the reaper of flesh that my imagination had conjured. It was Mr. G, and he had a score to settle with Sothese, thank the little baby prophet. If my sister were not on the verge of being stolen from me, I would have relished upchucking at the rightfully deserved goring about to take place, but I settled for Sothese's deathly howls, clawing at the night, as more than enough backdrop for the developments straight ahead, and as a little faith that justice does prevail in the end.

All that existed, however, was the glimmer of a fool's hope forming a tunnel towards Eli's limp body on the grass as the amethyst glow coming from Osler Hall reflected off her crystal pendant.

The stalker, on the other hand, treated the sudden appearance of the jewel as a cue to set himself and his two goons on fire. Needless to say, astonishment had to take a back seat to my legs as I sprinted to pull Eli from the flames, with Stitch right there beside me to smother stray cinders. I also needed my jaw attached to my head in order to administer CPR immediately.

In the throes of an emergency, details often get missed, and as much as I have experienced discreet episodes of extreme strength and clarity under duress, and as they relate to Eli's safety, a second stealth approach was pulling me away while a red beam sucked her up into the sky.

The GHU had taken her!

The dead stirred in their graves at the shrillness I bellowed. I could hear Eli's voice in my head "Don't leave me, Keet. It's so cold." The counselor, the holier-than-the-Pramam, who had apparently chosen non-interference with Sothese's assault on Mr. G and had remained conveniently in the shadows during the payback, could do nothing to appease, let alone control, the hatred I threw at him for tearing my sister and me apart. All of this was not "for the best" like he kept repeating, as if that would slap a robotic smile on my face with a shoulder shrug to parrot back, "It's for the best." And what about Stitch's inability to stand? In fact, he passed out on the lawn, shivering until his lips turned blue. Was that also "for the best"?

Well, at least the damage was enough to move Izionnis into action, although preempting the whole ordeal should have been his first choice, considering that he seemed to have no trouble subduing the creepy three in the archives, a couple of months ago. Sneaking my chum into Osler Hall for urgent medical treatment stinks of duplicity. And do not even get me started on Nathruyu. I saw how she handled herself that night in Almedina Square with Sothese's ex-officials. How so hypocritically good of her to cool the flames off Stitch when she let him catch fire in the first place. They all knew what we were dealing with.

None of this had to happen. I did not even get to say goodbye.

Izionnis could have stopped it, Nathruyu could have stopped it. Even that other woman, I wager, could have stopped it. Listen to me pointing fingers for my own failure. No, Mother. I am to blame for this. I really do deserve to rot in the toxic soup.

Two-faced Nathruyu made me promise that I would wait for her here because we apparently have to talk, but why bother? When did she ever care for that "stupid girl"? Nothing she can say will bring Eli back. The sun will rise soon, but not your daughter, not my sister, not Stitch's best chum, not the reason we came to Eadonberg, and not ... No more!

Come with me Sparky. (rustling)

(door opens, footsteps, gurgling, footsteps, door opens, footsteps, rustling)

Mme Beaudoin will take care of you. (whimpering, licking, sniffling, footsteps, door opens, footsteps, gurgling, running)

The answers you seek are in Elize's dreams. Right. (gurgling, running)

The book has the answers you seek. Right. (gurgling, running)

Riddles. Flyer mud. There are no answers. Eli took them with her. (crying, running, crunching, running)

All I need are some Mini-Lizzies. (scuttling, rustling) Got you, and you, and one more. Stick them on the biowall. Now flick the tails. (light puff) Don't look down. (crying)

We promised each other, Eli. You rushed into my room that night. You woke me up. That was three years ago, but it feels like last night in my heart. Remember? Remember what you said? This is it, Keet. Together. (crying, gurgling) Yes. You and I together forever, my twin heart. This is the only way now. (bubbling) I failed you, Eli. Please forgive me. Please forgive me, Mother. (splashing, sobbing)

Broken and torn shall she reveal herself to you in the darkest hour of her existence. And you shall come to her begging for forgiveness. And she should say to you there is nothing to forgive being that you and she are entangled in a dance for all eternity and shall become that which is right and virtuous through no misdeeds of your own. (Nathruyu, whispering)

You did not wait for me, Keeto. (Nathruyu, toothy inhale, gurgling)

This is her darkest hour? I came begging for her forgiveness. (sobbing)

And there is nothing to forgive. The SIF has her body. The GHU craft was a decoy. You must ensure that she is left intact. No post mortem. No organ donations. She must not be cremated. She must not unite with Their Trinity. (Nathruyu)

I can get us in there. (new voice)

Caroline? (sniffling)

No. My name is Nepharisse. In whom you trust answers come. In the answers you trust a hand appears. In the hand you choose, trust emerges. My hand for you. Travel with me. (new voice)

(unknown sound)

GLOSSARY

alias *n*
a nickname or user id inside the **maze**

all the wave *exp.*
popular, a fad that will eventually pass

assalam *v (anglicism from Arabic)*
to say goodbye, to leave

auto ... *n*
a sensing device performing a single task (e.g. autolock)

band *n*
see **secure band**

bang-o *n (Stitch slang)*
anglicism of Spanish word "baño", bathroom

bending *adj. (city slang)*
confusing

bent *adj. (highland slang)*
nuts, crazy

bioApp *n*
a program running on a **biochip**

biochip *n*
internal intelligent chip attached to a human brain

bioclothing *n*
clothing that is alive and often sentient

biodome *n*
a fully enclosed dome shaped **biowall**

bioRhythms *n*
a **bioApp** that transmits a music broadcast to the brain

bioroof *n*
a flat top on cities or structures using **biowall** technology

bioshield *n*
invisible shield surrounding a person to filter toxins

bioskin *n*
membrane to grow skin on wounds

biowall *n*
  invisible shield surrounding a city as a unidirectional filter
blister *v (highland slang)*
  to get things done fast, to move fast
blow *v (city slang)*
  make someone very angry or pissed
board *n*
  futuristic version of a computer screen
boogie *n*
  one-person barge for surfing the tides, extreme boogie board
bounce *v (city slang)*
  to feel unnaturally energetic, hyper
bumblebot *n*
  a hybrid automated bee programmed to pollinate plants
carebot *n*
  flying bear-looking vital sign stabilizing equipment for kids
chat something out *exp.*
  reach an agreement
chip down *v (slang)*
  to physically recover from a change in **biochip** program
chumbud *n (Stitch slang)*
  a friend, chum for opposite sex, bud for same sex
circle *n*
  circular neighborhood of homes protected by a **biodome**
clamp *v*
  to restrict someone to an area and track their whereabouts
cleanerbot *n*
  self-guided intelligent floor cleaner and garbage picker
clip *v (Stitch slang)*
  to hurry, to do something like yesterday
clip out *exp. (Stitch slang)*
  get out fast, head to the exit lightning fast
cloaked *adj. (Stitch slang)*
  encrypted, as it pertains to a communication device
comm *n* and *v*
  1 *n* personal communication device
  2 *v* to communicate using a **comm**

crabbot *n*
  self-guided intelligent crawling surveillance device
crabseat *n*
  genetic hybrid between a crab and a chair
crack *v (Stitch slang)*
  to panic
credit *n*
  the currency (there is no cash)
crazed *adj. (city slang)*
  nuts, crazy
crit *adj. (Stitch slang)*
  very important
creeps *n (highland slang)*
  a bummer, crap
cube *n*
  a freeze-frame of a holographic video (**flash**)
da ya *adv. (anglicism)*
  a double yes; once in Russian, once in German
daze *n and v (city slang)*
  1 *n* a party at an underground club
  2 *v* to party, to go to a **daze**
del *v*
  to delete
dizzy *adj. (city slang)*
  gross, disgusting to the point of an upchuck
drip questions into the maze *exp.*
  to broadcast a question for anyone to answer
drop *n*
  a stop on a **hovertrain** route
drop detector *n*
  detects when something draws power from the grid
dunked *adj. (Stitch slang)*
  to be totally lost, to not understand what is going on
(it's a) dunker *exp. (Stitch slang)*
  (it's a) wonder
dust *n*
  encryption to make images look like garbage to searches

dust filter *n*
 special type of **maze** sketch that can find **dust**ed images
emitter *n*
 device emitting frequencies to change properties of matter
ease *v (city slang)*
 to chill out, to calm down, to take it easy
eh *interj. (highland slang)*
 adopted from Canadian "eh?" at the end of a sentence
elepharc *n*
 hybrid between an elephant and an archway
explode *v*
 to zoom a **flash** or a **cube**
fig *v (Stitch slang)*
 to figure
fence formation *n*
 GMU tactic for securing a perimeter
fishy *n (highland slang)*
 turkey, silly, dumb-dumb
flagged *adj.*
 marked for Ministry investigation
flash *n* and *v*
 1 *n* holographic video, moving memories
 2 *v* to record a **flash** on a device
flashpack (flashes) *n*
 a pack of multiple **flash**es that plugs into a viewer
flatface *n (highland slang)*
 a stone faced, unfriendly, or vacant person
flip *interj. (highland slang)*
 bummer, crap
flip a pass *exp. (Stitch slang)*
 get out of something without permission (e.g. skip class)
floramug *n*
 waterproof leaves which fold into a drinking vessel
florapy *n*
 hybrid between leaves and a canopy
flutterbot *n*
 hybrid used to cool off, a flying fan with multiple wings

fly wild *exp. (Stitch slang)*
to let imagination control you, to go off on a tangent
flyer mud *n (Stitch slang)*
bullshit
frame *n*
freeze frame from a **flash**
frequenflyer *n*
hybrid between a flyer and a frequency repair device
Gayok *n*
the leader of all Gadlins, the chief
garbifact *n*
Elize's humorous way of referring to old junk
gatayok *n*
a Gadlin clan leader, a chieftain
geckohold *n*
hybrid for hands-free reading material such as **slip**s and **slippad**s
geloctopack *n*
hybrid between a gelatinous octopus and a backpack
ghostgrabber *n*
gadget to slice through **flash**es to see all the frames as stills from
infinite angles
GHU *acronym*
Global Health Unit
GMU *acronym*
Global Military Unit
GSU *acronym*
Global Spiritual Unit
good whip *exp. (highland slang)*
good comeback to a dig at someone
hanging low *adj. (Stitch slang)*
lacking energy, wiped out
hang for a sec *exp. (highland slang)*
Hold on for a minute, wait a moment
hey lo *exp. (highland slang)*
hi
hick *n (highland slang)*
"doh!" when used alone, dumb-dumb otherwise

hide between the packets *exp.*
to remove your id tag on a **packet** and thus be untraceable

holo ... *n*
interactive holographic objects (e.g. holopost)

hook *v*
fool someone with a white lie

hurts like a mangled scan *exp. (city slang)*
hurts like hell

hush *adj. (highland slang)*
to be quiet, to not make a sound, to be on **hush mode**

hush mode *exp.*
comm setting to emit close-range canceling frequencies

hovertrain *n*
inner city public transit hovering above walkways

imprint *v*
to transfer media to/from a **slip** by sticking it to a device

jabber one's way out *exp.*
talk oneself out of a situation

jam *adj. (city slang)*
used in expression "we're jam" to mean being in trouble

juicy *adj. (highland slang)*
cool, equiv. to **trip**

jump *v (slang)*
to scare someone, used in expression "you jumped me"

jumper *n (city slang)*
something that startles you

kittybot *n*
hybrid used to control vermin

knockout stick *n*
device that knocks people out

lie low *v (Stitch slang)*
to get some sleep

lifeshield *n*
a device that creates a field to protect from getting crushed

lift *n*
shaft with elevator platform that materializes when called

lo-flower *n*
lo moth (colorful North American moth) and flower hybrid
lobcart *n*
hybrid between a lobster and a luggage cart
loose *adj. (highland slang)*
relaxed
magnigram *n*
microscope to display something as a magnified hologram
magnoform *n*
magnetic field acting as a raised sleep surface
mammasack *n*
hybrid between a knapsack and a mammal with hands
match *n*
someone's spouse as matched by the Unified clergy
maze *n*
futuristic version of an internet-like network
messed *adj. (Stitch slang)*
appearing sick, horrible, pasty white
mick *n (anglicism)*
adapted from French slang "mec", meaning a dude
midi *n (highland slang)*
midday meal, lunch, adapted from French "midi"
miniverse *n*
social network based on the holographic principle
Mount *n*
the holy podium where only the **Pramam** speaks
MPD *acronym*
multiple personality disorder
naughtypad *n*
fake **slippad** that broadcasts written phrases to **biochip**s
neah *adv. (city slang)*
no
newb *n (slang)*
a newcomer
Nipok *n*
the leader of the Gadlin Order and head **nitapok**

nitapok *n*
Gadlin spiritual sage, part of the Gadlin Order

ohhhm gee *interj.*
equiv. to OMG, oh my god.

oh, the shards *exp. (city slang)*
you break my heart in a joking manner

one-way portal *n*
see **uniportal**

operative *n*
a stealthy and highly trained member of the **GMU**

Orangugong *n*
special adaptation to a **mammasack** created by Zafarian

out-of-bounds tag *n*
attached to an archive shelf when a document goes missing

overdazed *adj. (city slang)*
stoned, drugged up, out of it

packet *n*
a block of information existing in the **maze**

PAL (personal automated librarian) *acronym*
programmable flying book retriever, a type of **sniffer**

parked *adj. (slang)*
to be sitting waiting for someone

pass *n (Stitch slang)*
an out, an exit out of a tough situation

patch *n*
an update or fix to a malfunctioning **biochip**

Perfect are They *exp.*
ceremonial verse used as a lead in for **They are One**

perk *v (Stitch slang)*
to listen up, perk one's ears

permissions *n*
one or more access rights granted by the Unification

pica *adv. (Stitch slang)*
super, very

plane *v*
to **slide** just above ground with special shoes

plane like I'm on the slick *exp.*
  to hurry, derived from the sport of planing
platymoa *n*
  hybrid between a platypus and a moa, used as a forklift
poke a rib *exp. (Stitch slang)*
  to tease, to play a trick on
pollibot *n*
  self-guided intelligent pollinator
portablower *n*
  personal short-range device to blow fog away for visibility
privy ... *n*
  protective item container with teeth (e.g. privyshelf)
proximity reader n
  echolocation device used in the fog to detect obstacles
red craft *n*
  GHU ambulance
ride it *exp. (city slang)*
  go with the flow
ride *v (Stitch slang)*
  to not show up for work, just ride on by
rift *v*
  to change the properties of matter using frequency shifting
right on credit *exp.*
  right on the money, right on target
rip *v (highland slang)*
  to figuratively rip one's pants laughing, used like LOL
rip and roll *exp. (highland slang)*
  to laugh so hard you loose your balance, similar to LMFAO
ripping the leaf but never ... disappear *exp. (Stitch slang)*
  reference to Kirlian photography torn leaf experiment
roll *v (highland slang)*
  to laugh uncontrollably
rook *n (slang)*
  a rookie
rubber (narrow field rubber) *n*
  undetectable small frequency range canceling device

sajadum [sá-ha-doom] *n*
    small crystal building used for meditation; fits three people
sage master *n*
    an individual of highly cultivated wisdom through study
Savasana stance *n*
    standing version of Savasana yoga pose (the corpse pose)
scan *n* and *v*
    1 *n* result of reading a **biochip** for health/security purposes
    2 *v* to read someone's **biochip** using a frequency device
scan jam *exp.*
    jamming of the frequencies a device uses to read a **biochip**
scanning wall *n*
    a wall that continuously **scan**s **biochip**s within a meter of it
scrubber *n*
    program attached to a **packet** in the **maze** to wipe it clean
scuff *n (city slang)*
    a complication resulting in verbal or physical confrontation
secure band *n*
    a wristband with clearance level access past **sentinel** posts
sentinel *n*
    a hybrid species bred for security duty
señor *n (slang)*
    dude, adapted from Spanish
shakes *interj. (Stitch slang)*
    used as expression to mean "whoa"
shard *n*
    see **oh, the shards** for its use in city slang
sheiss *interj. (anglicism from German)*
    shit
shoe will stick to him something fierce *exp. (Stitch slang)*
    the boss will get on his case, give him a butt kick
SIF *acronym*
    Special Investigation Forces
sketch the maze *exp.*
    equiv. to web surfing but with sketching device
slack *v (slang)*
    to put something off, procrastinate

slam *n* and *v*

  1 *n (Stitch slang)* a scoring throw in a sports game

  2 *v* to lightly punch a friend when annoyed at them

slap me *exp. (Stitch slang)*

  I'm sorry

sleeper *n*

  portable sleeping surface

sleeve *n*

  an envelope style folder used to store loose documents

slick *n*

  futuristic sports rink based on hovering mechanism

slide *v*

  to arrive at a destination by way of a **slider**

slider *n*

  a personal vehicle that moves by sliding just above ground

sliderbag *n*

  a self-propelling piece of luggage with built-in **slider** capabilities

sliderboard *n*

  a futuristic skateboard based on **slider** technology

slidercab *n*

  a **slider** for hire, a futuristic version of a taxi cab

sliderpad *n*

  a place to store a **slider**, like a garage

sliderskid *n*

  platform which transports goods/people over short distances

slip *n*

  interactive membrane to store/display/manipulate media

slipbook n

  futuristic version of an e-book using the **slip** technology

slipclip n

  a clip to keep individual **slip**s together

slipmap *n*

  an interactive map imprinted on a **slip**

slippad *n*

  a stack of **slip**s temporarily bound to each other

slipwork *n*

  similar concept to paperwork except concerning **slip**s

snare *n*
facial expression, a cross between a stare and a sneer
sniff *v*
to use a **sniffer** to find something
sniffer *n*
device that finds things based on frequency detection
spongysuit *n*
self-cleaning body sock people use instead of showers/baths
sprinkle dust *v*
to encrypt an image or **packet** to render it unsearchable
stomp *v*
to go on a verbal rampage
stretch rodent *exp.*
sarcastic way of referring to a ferret-like animal
stroke *n*
one single line or gesture when sketching through the **maze**
sunshaft *n*
a lift shaft that captures and stores solar energy
sweep formation *n*
GMU tactic for fanning out and overtaking an area
sweep *n*
a complete search of an area using a **sweep formation**
swish *v (Stitch slang)*
got it, figured it out
ta *n (Stitch slang)*
thanks
tag *n*
location tracking and monitoring device or **biochip** flag
tagged *adj.*
biochip is altered and marked as a suspected criminal
Tess *adj. (Stitch slang)*
genius, derived from inventor Nikola Tesla
They *pron.*
The holy Trinity of Jesus, Mohammed, and Abraham
They are One *exp.*
ceremonial response to **Perfect are They**, equiv. to "Amen"

thrower (frequency thrower) *n*
a device that shoots frequencies at a specific point
top *adj.* and *v (highland slang)*
  1 *adj.* so much, as in "top juicy" meaning so cool, equiv. to **pica**
  2 *v* to ace, to pass with flying colors
topped up *adj. (highland slang)*
  stressed out
trace *v*
  to run a diagnostic on a **biochip** to find a defect
transcriptor *n*
  device to converting voice to text directly into a journal
transfer chest *n*
  a futuristic shipping crate used by the Gadlins
trip *adj. (city slang)*
  cool
trip out *exp. (city slang)*
  get lost, go cool off
trip with that *exp. (city slang)*
  I'm in, I'm cool with that, it's all good
uniportal *n*
  a thin membrane acting as a one-way viewing window
unit *n*
  a group of military personnel
URA *acronym*
  Unification Research Arm
valah *interj. (Stitch slang)*
  anglicism of French word "voilà"
versal arts *n*
  otherworldly form of mind, body, and spiritual practice
virta ... *n*
  a virtual object with solid properties (e.g. virtachair)
wack *n (highland slang)*
  creep, weirdo
way *exp. (city slang)*
  hi, equiv. to **hey lo**

weedel *n* and *v*

  1 *n* hose and weasel hybrid that vacuums up weeds

  2 *v* to concoct a story or to weasel out of something

wiggle hips over *exp.*

  happy to see, like wagging your tail for

wipe *n*

  a membrane typically used to wipe off sweat, like a hanky

whip *n (highland slang)*

  a comeback to a **rib**, as in "good whip!"

ya fig *exp. (Stitch slang)*

  you figure, equiv. to **eh**

yay with that *exp. (highland slang)*

  down with that, cool with it, all for it

yeah *adv. (city slang)*

  equiv. to **eh**

you-belong-in-a-jar look *exp. (highland slang)*

  you're nuts, you're a freak

yum it up *exp.*

  eat something voraciously

zap me back *exp.*

  I'll be, I'm surprised, will you look at that

zapped *adj. (slang)*

  touché, you got me, I fell into that one

zapper *n*

  a wearable alarm device that sends a mild shock

ziga *adv. (Stitch slang)*

  super super, even more than **pica**

zorro effect *exp. (Stitch slang)*

  when something masks the effect of something else, e.g. noise-canceling headphone

CHARACTER LIST

ANABELLE
The Pramam's mother and the leader of the previous world government — the Coalition.

ANUBRAT
A mysterious government outsider who has his hand in global affairs but is only known to a select few.

CAROLINE
A playful friend of the twins and Zafarian, who comes and goes into their lives. She has questionable romantic ties to Sothese.

(THE) COUNSELOR
The guidance counselor at Schrödinger University, who appears to have a special interest in the twins.

DR. CORRIENT SHAKTI
The director of the Unification Research Arm (URA), Strategic Advisor to the Pramam, and third member of the Inner Council. The Pramam favored her over Sothese as URA director.

DR. TENILLE (CAPTAIN SNOOK)
An eccentric pirate wannabe university professor, who mentors a crew of students, of which Elize is one. He was the last medic who had cared for the twins' deceased mother Monique.

ELIZE (ELI)
Keeto's twin sister and, together with her brother Keeto, the main protagonist in the series.

(THE) ENTROPIST
A high-ranking spiritual sage at the Global Spiritual Unit (GSU). He performs secret procedures that support Sothese's agenda.

(THE) FEDORA MAN
A mysterious black-eyed man, sporting a wide-brimmed fedora, who has strong influence in the Restricted Sector. His questionable dealings place him on several sides in the hunt for the twins.

IZIONNIS (THE ACADEMIC)

A young scholar, with a raised eyebrow at other people's business, who all but lives in the archives at the Museum of Antiquities.

KAINATEN

A loyal aid to the Pramam with a unique presence. He is a colleague of Sothese.

KEETO (KEET)

Elize's twin brother and, together with his sister Elize, the main protagonist in the series.

MME BEAUDOIN

Keeto's supervisor at the Museum of Antiquities. She and her boss, the curator, are secretly protective of Keeto.

MONIQUE

Keeto and Elize's mother. When the twins were nine years old, she died while under Dr. Tenille's care at the Global Health Unit (GHU) psychiatric wing.

MR. G

The owner of a shop in Tir-na-nog, Eadonberg's shopping district, that is popular with Keeto, Elize, and especially Zafarian.

NATHRUYU

The otherworldly co-narrator of Episode 1, *Nemecene: The Epoch of Redress*, who is involved in child abductions. She is one of Sothese's many foes.

NEPHARISSE

The otherworldly co-narrator of Episode 2, *Nemecene; The Gadlin Conspiracy*, acting as a messenger and facilitator for a larger purpose involving the twins. She is also one of Sothese's many foes.

ODWIN

The previous leader of the Gadlins from whom Wakanda has assumed power. His whereabouts are unknown and his presumed death is refuted by Gadlin clans who are loyal to him.

PRAMAM

The leader of the Unification and the Inner Council of the Ministry. He is both the political and religious world figurehead. The Unified religion is his divinely inspired creation.

SAKARI

Zafarian's mother, a Gadlin who is loyal to Odwin as the rightful Gayok, the Gadlin leader.

SHEN

A new friend of Elize's vying for her romantic attention.

SOTHESE

Personal advisor to the Pramam, member of the Inner Council, and governor of the Global Spiritual Unit (GSU), with hands in his own secret initiatives. His loyalties are to himself and his own agenda.

TEDDY

A boy whose fate is intertwined with the twins' search for answers.

(THE) THREE OFFICIALS (CREEPY THREE)

Sothese's unusual assistants who act as his gophers as well as his enforcers. They have a strange symbiotic relationship with Sothese.

VICTOR

Keeto and Elize's father. He is the previous director of the URA. His whereabouts are a mystery.

WAKANDA

The self-proclaimed Gayok — the Gadlin leader. Many Gadlins, including Zafarian and his mother Sakari, do not recognize her leadership. She also has a questionable relationship with Sothese.

ZAFARIAN (STITCH, ZAF)

The twin's best friend and half-Gadlin companion in all their adventures. He leads an underground society with his dweeby genius, special operations training, and penchant for creating mischief through custom gadgetry.

ABOUT THE AUTHOR

Kaz is not an author in the traditional sense. She creates fictional worlds using any media she can shape into a richly layered vision. Her strengths have always been imagination, design, and a natural ability to connect the dots, which she weaves into beautiful tapestries that engage the senses. Kaz uses the rhythms and nuances of words to successively reveal deeper meaning behind the narrative.

Nemecene: Through Fire And Ice is the third episode recounting the adventures in the greater Nemecene™ World — a place where you can engage in life-changing immersive experiences that inspire and empower you to think, feel, express, connect, and act in harmony with others, nature, and our life source, water.

Kaz has a bachelor in Applied Science (engineering) from Queen's University, a fashion degree from the Richard Robinson Fashion Design Academy, certifications in personal training and hypnosis, a US patent in user interface design, an IMBD credit as director, and has written extensively on environmental issues via WomanNotWaiting.com, LifeAsAHuman.com and her philanthropy mission at Aguacene.com.

When she is not scheming the perfect muahahaha moment, you can find her hanging around some four-legged friends. She speaks English, French, Spanish, and is currently learning Russian. She also strives to be a recovering chocoholic, with limited success, and to look more and more like her standard poodle every day.

ACKNOWLEDGMENTS

As the first trilogy of the Nemecene™ novels comes to a close, I am reminded of the ears that have listened and the voices that have shared their words of wisdom and encouragement along the way. There were hot days, and there were cold days, but through all the fire and ice I have personally experienced creating episode three, here are a few of many friends who were there to keep me focused forward.

Family gets first dibs, so hugs go out to Siobhan, Jeremy, and Lola (prancing canines rule). More hugs head over to parental and sibling humans: Art, Norma, Kylen, Laura, and Jenn. Massive high fives fly at Ena Sanguinetti, Jae Rang, Karusia Wroblewski, Rachel Oliver, Neil Oliver, Lisa Hawkyard, Alena Chapman, Amalia Kennedy, Bob Proctor, Sandy Gallagher and my PGI Matrixx friends, Amy Stoehr, Sylvia McConnell, Leslie Doyle, Mary Ellen Koroscil, Ariadni Athanassiadis, Amy Croll, Jennifer Beale, Ana Jorge, Kiara Jorge, everyone since the first novel, and many others.

A special thanks goes out to the ever-growing circles of esteemed ENVOYs, who join the weekly fun and expand my silly quiz-devising brain cells.

I also thank Les Petriw, Jason Brockwell, and the team at NBN (National Book Network, Inc.) as the ultimate distribu-nators, and the team at Marquis as the printe-nators..

They, who are currently nameless ;-), also make the future gratitude list for taking the first Nemecene™ trilogy to big and small immersive media experiences. Let's make it so.

THE MISSION

Do you love water? (say *yes*)

So do I.

We love water because we *are* water and pretty much everyone and everything we hold dear in our life is water.

What if every time you read a book, watched a movie, played a game, hung out, or nabbed some swag, in order to dream big with your friends inside a science fiction fantasy Nemecene™ World, you actually could define history for zigazillions of lives — human and non-human alike?

And you wouldn't have to become an activist, a kayaktivist, a slacktivist, or any other kind of -ivist … unless you wanted to juice it up a notch, of course. You can simply be a friend.

The Nemecene™ World immerses us in a future flooded by dead oceans and poisonous gases, but we don't have to manifest that. How we relate to water is the key.

We truly live in an epoch of water that is fast heading towards an epoch of redress. As founder of the Aguacene™ Fund at Tides Canada, my personal mission is to use all things Nemecene to fund water stewardship projects, starting with the Mackenzie River watershed and the Beaufort Sea.

Philanthropist through fun! And by purchasing this book, you now are one.

Thank you.

Kaz

GET EPISODE 4

NEMECENE

DREAMS FLOW IN STREAMS

What just happened? Episode 4 opens the second trilogy in this epic ten novel series with a whole new level of awareness. Are you ready to challenge your beliefs about reality? Sothese left you hungering for the physical plane, but now a new presence, Tuffurie, serves up a chilling platter on which worlds collide.

Stay connected with the Nemecene™ World for juicy teasers as the story unfolds.

www.NEMECENE.com/episode-4

Available Spring 2019!
For more information on where to buy
Nemecene™ episodes and products go to

www.GETNEMECENE.com